IMAGININGS OF A DARK MIND

BORGO PRESS BOOKS BY JAMES C. GLASS

Imaginings of a Dark Mind: Science Fiction Stories
Toth: A Science Fiction Novel
Visions: A Science Fiction Western

BOOKS FROM OTHER PUBLISHERS:

The Creators (2002)
Empress of Light (2001)
Matrix Dreams & Other Stories (2004)
Shanji (2001)
The Viper of Portello (2008)

IMAGININGS OF A DARK MIND

SCIENCE FICTION STORIES

by

JAMES C. GLASS

The Borgo Press
An Imprint of Wildside Press LLC

MMIX

CONTENTS

Introductions, by Steve Perry, M. J. Engh, John Dalmas 7
Foreword 9

Strings 13
Helen's Last Will 14
Bacon 'n' Eggs 31
Mildred's Garden 42
The Color of Pain 53
Reinventing Carl Hobbs 74
Deliverance Smith 87
Tikan's Choice 104
Mutiny on the *Phoebus* 119
A Special Child 142
Georgi 155
Axalay's Gifts 170
Bodyguard 185
Dark Peril 196
Beneath the Ice of Enceladus 211
Beware the Quantum Bunny 233

Acknowledgments 238
About the Author 239

DEDICATION

For Gary

And the good folks who worked
for you at Books in Motion

We had a good ride

INTRODUCTIONS

Jim Glass's new collection of short stories is a welcome addition to the list of novels he has written thus far, and the title, *Imaginings of a Dark Mind*, gives you an accurate preview of what is to come. From the opening short poem, "Strings," to the final story, "Beware the Quantum Bunny," Glass's tour-de-psyche covers a wide swath of fascinating speculative fiction.

There are bright spots and upbeat endings, but there are also dark threads that ensnare the reader, and the range includes everything from an AI version of a séance, to mysterious fatal illnesses, to aliens way more sentient than expected. Glass has a great handle on the science, and a deft touch with his characters. He tends to grab you with the first line and not let go until the last line, and it's an interesting ride all the way.

I do believe Glass has a winner here.

—Steve Perry

It's a rare writer who is equally at home in hard science fiction and occult horror. Add a probing interest in what humans (and others) can do to, with, and for each other, and you have James Glass.

—M. J. Engh

Imaginings of a Dark Mind is a baker's dozen of short stories, plus three others I wasn't able to classify, all by much-published science fiction author and professor of physics and astronomy, Dr. James C. Glass. They range from stories rooted in theoretical physics to stories bordering on the spiritual. What they have in common is a sweeping view of reality, an innate humanity, an incisive perceptiveness, and Dr. Glass's distinctive story-telling voice.

I myself believe the collection is misnamed. I would call it *Having Heart in the Real World*—something like that. Which may explain why I wasn't invited to the naming discussion.

This is good stuff. I commend it to you.

—John Dalmas

FOREWORD

I woke up one morning and suddenly realized I'd been publishing science fiction and fantasy for over twenty years. The story collection you hold in your hands is part of my celebration of those years.

I have never been a full-time writer, and have never considered trying to make a living at it. I never gave up my day job, and had a long career in physics that was very satisfying to me. I was lucky to be in industry during the 'golden age' of manned-space-exploration. I worked on ion and arcjet engines, did diagnostics on the F-1 engine and a mock-up of the first lunar excursion module. I returned to graduate school. After that came a thirty-plus year academic career teaching physics at all levels, making Ph.D. clones of myself, and doing research in molecular biophysics and superconductivity before moving into administration. And during all those years, my writing of science fiction and fantasy came in little bursts as the writing bug bit me again and again.

I wrote stories in high school. The first science fiction convention I attended was Westercon 3 in 1953. That makes me old. My best friend was an artist, and he sold a lot of his Chesley Bonestell-style art at the convention. We put out a fanzine together for over a year. One of our contributors, Joel Nydahl, published a story in *Galaxy* when he was a teenager. And I received my first rejection slip from *F&SF* with a handwritten note attached! But undergraduate school intervened, and I didn't write again until after graduation. I wrote a few stories, and was a dropout of 'The Famous Writers' School' after finishing over half the course. Raising a family and then graduate school had intervened again.

When a real desire to write is there, it does not go away, and sooner or later the call must be answered. The writing 'bug' gave me my terminal bite in the early eighties; I began writing regularly and sent in a few stories each year. The rejection slips I collected were the dues a writer pays to become an author. I continue paying those dues to this day.

My first published story was a mainstream piece in a literary publication called *The Best of Northlight* put out by Concordia College in 1988. The first story I was paid for was "Bodyguard," collected here, for which I was paid a fifty percent kill fee when the magazine I'd sold it to had to fold. These things happen to writers. "Axalay's Gifts' and "Mutiny on the *Phoebus*" suffered similar fates in later years, and are also printed here for the first time.

Things really started to happen around 1988, when I sold "Jet-Dancer" (anthologized elsewhere) to *Aboriginal Science Fiction*. I entered the Writers of the Future contest, but my story didn't even make the first cut. Shortly after that I took a shortened version of the Writers of the Future workshop, given by A. J. Budrys after a convention in Moscow, Idaho. And the first story I wrote after the workshop won the grand prize of Writers of the Future in 1990. That story, "Georgi," is again anthologized here with the kind permission of Galaxy Press, which does the annual WOTF anthology. The win opened many doors for me, and any writer wishing to be published is well advised to enter the contest. For their guidelines, go to www.writersofthefuture.com

That was the real beginning for me, but since then I've continued to be only a part-time writer. I got my active membership in Science Fiction & Fantasy Writers of America the hard way, with three stories sold to markets considered professional at the time. I sold short stories for years before even attempting a novel, and now have several books published. I've had no best sellers, except in audio editions. I've not made a lot of money, nor do I have a big name in the genre. But the creative satisfaction I've experienced, the professionals I've met in the business, the readers and fans at signings and conventions have enriched my life beyond imagination.

There have been several important people in my writing life. Algis Budrys was my first teacher and mentor. Rest in peace, A. J. I miss you. John Dalmas and M. J. Engh have been my teachers, first readers and friends for over a decade. Thanks for that. Thanks also to Steve Perry, Barb and J. C. Hendee, Patrick Swenson, Stan Schmidt, Ken Rand, and Catherine Asaro for readings, jacket blurbs, and editorial advice over the years. Wife Gail has patiently allowed me the quiet time to do the stuff I do. Thank you, dear. Special thanks go to John Goodwin and Galaxy Press for permission to include "Georgi" in this collection. And finally I give thanks to my editor Robert Reginald and publisher John Betancourt for their work on this volume and others.

It has been a blast, people, and I'm not finished yet.
Please visit my web site at:

www.sff.net/people/jglass/

—James C. Glass
Spokane, Washington
June 8, 2009

STRINGS

A flash of light within the void, two forms emerging, forever parted,
swirling separate ways, one free and fleeting,
one ponderous, entity of similitude, of perfect entropy.
A cosmic digit scribes, patterns forming,
webs of filaments where chaos beneath order reigns,
forever changing, seeking something grander, pleasing, permanent.
Force seeks beauty in symmetry, guiding strings till perfection finds,
perfection of a snowflake, fine fabric of mega parsec lace, busy
    graviton woven, each thread a billion atom stars, each electron
    spinning orb of elementals.
And from one electron in the cosmic snowflake, life gushes forth.

HELEN'S LAST WILL

The lobby of Advanced Technologies was steel struts and white polymer panels reaching towards a high vaulted ceiling of clear glass. The receptionist and an armed guard sat in a glass-enclosed booth on an otherwise vast but empty floor of black marble. Both looked up as Blanche approached the booth.

"May I help you, Madam?" asked the receptionist, a blond, pretty man in his twenties.

"I wish to see the body of my sister," said Blanche. "She was interred here last Thursday."

The young man smiled, fingers poised over a keyboard. "Name?"

"Helen Charlston Winslow. Age eighty-four. I believe the arrangements were made by Arthur Winslow, her son. It was all quite sudden, and I wasn't notified."

"Are you a relative?"

"Her sister, Blanche Charlston Packard." Blanche sniffed, and slid her national identity card under a partially opened window in the booth. The man looked at it, then at something on his computer screen.

"Helen Winslow, yes. She was brought here directly from her home. Arthur Winslow attended her admission to verify identity."

Blanche managed a sob. "I talked to her personal physician, and he didn't even know she'd been ill. I'm wondering why he wasn't called in or at least notified when she died."

The man gave her a sympathetic smile. "We have a staff of twenty physicians, Madam. Three attended your sister, and pronounced her dead at twenty forty five. Cause of death was a massive cerebral hemorrhage." He turned back to his computer screen, and studied it.

"Your sister had a long-term contract with us. Everything was done according to her specifications."

"Yes, of course. I knew she was an investor in your firm. When may I view her body?"

The young man's eyes wandered from hers. "Ah—that won't be possible. There are no viewings here. The clients are placed in sealed tanks. Decanting them for viewing would involve considerable expense. The tissue cannot be allowed to warm above liquid nitrogen temperature once it's quick-frozen."

Blanche's manner changed abruptly. "Save that for the believers, young man. I want to see my sister's remains, and I want to see them *now*."

The guard in the booth shifted his feet uneasily, and the receptionist forced a smile.

"I understand, Ms. Packard, I really do, but it isn't possible, and there are no exceptions. It's in the contract. The remains can be removed only for advanced medical treatment when there is a high probability for success, as determined by our physicians. There's so little to see, anyway. Your sister's contract allowed only her head to be preserved. The rest of her body has been designated for research purposes."

Blanche put a hand on the window, as if to ward off an evil spirit. "You decapitated my sister?" she asked softly.

"It's quite common, Ms. Packard. The expense for preserving the head is a fifth of that for the entire body. Over half our clients choose this option. The others have specific medical problems they wish to have solved when the technology is available in the future. It would seem your sister didn't have such a problem."

"Only a massive cerebral hemorrhage," said Blanche. "All right, I want to speak to one or more of the physicians who attended my sister, and find out what's going on here. This entire thing smells foul to me."

"If you leave your number, someone will call you and hopefully explain things better than I have."

Blanche gave him her card. "It had better be tonight, or we'll be talking about this in a court of law."

"I'll forward this card right away, and tell them your concerns," said the receptionist.

Blanche turned her back on him and marched away fuming, swinging her arms. She was dressed expensively in white pants suit and black tie, and looked important. She was a handsome woman, looking perhaps fifty, even forty, yet she had recently turned seventy-six. She pulled out her cell phone, and spoke a number. Waited, one foot tapping the floor.

"Arthur Winslow, please," she said, and waited again, then, "Arthur, this is Blanche. I'm here at Advanced Technologies, and I've just been told I can't see my sister because you've had her decapitated. Now what are you up to, you miserable little worm?"

She waited a moment, then punched the phone off in a fury.

Arthur had hung up on her.

* * * * * * *

"There's a conspiracy here, Randal, and I expect you to unravel it."

Randal Haug, Blanche's expensive attorney and longtime friend of her late husband Ralph, leaned over his expansive desk to study the document there, and thumped it with a finger.

"Nothing," he said. "Not one red cent. The last version I saw had you down for over two million in stocks and property alone. What happened between you and Helen?"

Blanche's fingers twisted together in her lap. "I don't know. We saw a lot of each other until a few years ago. I think it started when Fred died. Helen was a recluse for months after that, but Arthur was there to comfort her. Dear Arthur, her baby-boy. Fred didn't leave him a dime; it all went to Helen. Even then, she designated a portion of the estate for me; we'd talked about establishing a foundation to support local performing arts. I know Arthur opposed that. I heard him say so. The man is a financier, an accountant. He exists solely in his left brain."

"You think Arthur has manipulated his mother into changing her will?"

"I do."

"For what purpose? The bulk of the estate was left to him in the older version of the will, and he's an independently wealthy man without it. You don't need the money. Ralph left you, what, twenty five million? Fifty? I can't recall now."

Blanche's voice rose in pitch. "It's not the money, Randal. Not money for me, that is, but Helen and I had a foundation planned, and suddenly I'll have to do it alone while that son of hers puts all her money back into the company that has mutilated her for no reason. Cost, indeed! My sister would never have allowed her head to be removed and her body destroyed just to save a measly hundred thousand each year. They say it's in her contract, then tell me I can't see the thing to verify it. There's something sinister about this, Randal, and I want you to get to the bottom of it! I'm thinking of filing a

Wrongful Death suit against both the company and Arthur Winslow. Murder would be harder to prove."

"You're not serious," said Randal.

"I have inside sources. As of last Tuesday, Arthur owns twenty percent of Advanced Technologies. The buy he made Tuesday had to come from his inheritance; my sources can list the stocks he traded. We can link them to Helen's holdings. We have a motive, Randal. The method is harder to prove."

Randal seemed suddenly interested, and drummed the fingers of his right hand on the desktop, then pointed at Blanche and said, "I can write that in a way to force a Show Cause Hearing before a judge. But if I get one, will you accept the judgment? If it goes against you, will you drop all of this? Helen was also my friend, Blanche, and I think she'd be very unhappy with me for dragging her son into court. Arthur has always struck me as being smart and hard working. I don't think he'd do what you're suggesting here. He could just be making what he considers to be a wise investment with his inheritance. You have no physical evidence for anything else."

"You're not being supportive, Randal," said Blanche softly. "You've been my lawyer for years, but that can end right now."

Randal didn't even flinch. "It *will* end right now if you don't answer my question. Will you accept any judgment of a Show Cause Hearing? If not, then find yourself another lawyer."

Blanche glared at him. She did not like being pressured by hired help, but she needed the man. "If I'm convinced my sister wasn't murdered, I'll not press for anything beyond the judgment of a hearing," she said.

"Good," said Randal, then closed the file on his desk and gently hammered on it with a fist. "Let's go to court."

* * * * * * *

The call came late at night, when Blanche was preparing for bed. The kitchen help had left for the night, and Paula had retired to her basement bedroom after leaving a warm brandy and a cookie on the nightstand for her mistress. So when the telephone rang, Blanche picked it up quickly so Paula would not be awakened.

It was Arthur Winslow.

"I was served with a summons this afternoon. Wrongful Death? Have you totally lost your mind?"

"It's only a hearing, Arthur," said Blanche. "There are questions to be answered before I proceed with further litigation."

"For what? This is all about mom's will, isn't it? All the money you have, and you're greedy for more. That's why mom cut you out of it in the first place. You don't *need* more!"

"It isn't about money," said Blanche. "My sister died under mysterious circumstances, and I want them explained."

"You're nuts! Paranoid! Do you know what this hearing can do to my business if it gets into the papers?"

"That's nonsense. I'm just trying to—"

"You've always been a greedy bitch. Mom told me so. You were always after her to finance your social butterfly events, even when dad was alive. He went along with it. Well, I don't. You badgered mom for money when she was alive, and now you're doing it when she's dead. Finance your own social status, and leave us alone!"

The cell phone clicked in Blanche's ear.

"That's not fair," she said, but Arthur was gone.

* * * * * * *

A Show Cause Hearing was held in the court of Judge James Maxwell on a Friday. A team of lawyers from the firm of Abercrombie, Nels and Faber represented both Advanced Technologies and Arthur Winslow. They requested a private hearing in judge's chambers. Randal Haug opposed the request, arguing that the public had a right to know about the operations of the company. Judge Maxwell compromised when Advanced Technologies rebutted by saying that in order to adequately defend themselves it might be necessary to reveal company proprietary information related to pending patents.

The hearing was held in court, but was closed to all but participants on that Friday. Arthur arrived in financier's uniform, his pudgy, soft body encased in a finely tailored woolen suit that made him indistinguishable from his lawyers. They sat behind one table, Blanche and Randal behind another, facing the bench. There was a bailiff, court reporter, and physicians who could be called as witnesses. They all arose when Judge Maxwell entered court in the matter of Packard vs. Winslow and Industrial Technologies re the Wrongful Death of Helen Winslow.

Maxwell was in his fifties, respected by his peers, and known as a no-nonsense judge who got right to the point without theatrics. "This is a hearing, not a trial," he told them. "I don't want to hear objections, or attempts to withhold evidence. I *do* want to hear reasons why this issue should, or should not, go to trial, and I am confidant we can accomplish all of this today. Mister Haug, it's your serve."

Randal smiled, and arose chuckling at the judge's reference to his devotion to tennis. His opposition sat glumly silent.

Haug outlined his case: the mysterious death, an unseen contract, the bizarre beheading and storage of a client with only a son's knowledge of what was happening, and that son a major investor in Advanced Technologies, Incorporated. He demanded proof that all had been done according to the wishes of Helen Charlston Winslow, that she had indeed been dead before decapitation, and that an autopsy be ordered to prove cerebral hemorrhage as the cause of death.

Arthur Winslow stared straight ahead, and never made direct eye contact with Blanche. The spokesman for the legal team at his table, a wiry, little man named Richard Camus, described Arthur as a loving son whose mother had died in his arms, a devoted son who made sure her every wish was carried out by rushing her to a laboratory for preservation and hopeful rejuvenation in the future. Helen Winslow herself had had a long-term interest in their work, contributing considerable funds for the development of new technologies in the freezing and rejuvenation processes.

"Your Honor, we doubt that a loving son would allow his mother's body to be mutilated if he wanted her to be rejuvenated in the future," said Randal Haug.

"The head was the relevant part of the body in question, and there was considerable cost savings in preservation," rebutted Camus for the defense.

Haug snorted rudely. "The woman had a cerebral hemorrhage, we're told. It seems the rest of her body was fine, and you have disposed of that part of her when she could easily afford the cost. I don't accept that, and neither will a jury."

"It was all in her contract," said Camus.

"Then let's see it," returned Haug.

There was a long silence. Camus whispered to his colleagues, and Arthur leaned over to listen, frowning.

"As written, contracts with our clients include company confidential information on procedures, and the medical conditions they're applied to. Patents pending approval can be put at risk by public exposure, but the client approves each step of the procedure, and company-sensitive information must be included in the contract."

Judge Maxwell smiled, and looked at Haug.

"Then let's go to trial so I can subpoena the contract and any other admissible documents I need for my case," said Haug. "Your

Honor, this is a possible felony case. I have the right to know if legal procedures were followed during and after the death of Helen Winslow, and if those procedures were indeed according to her will."

Judge Maxwell folded his hands in front of him, and looked down at Richard Camus. "The contract is admissible, counselor. Your patents are applied for, and protected under patent law. Why the resistance?"

"I've just explained that, Your Honor," said Camus.

"I see. Well, let me explain something to you. I'm a simple man who likes simple solutions to problems. I've studied the briefs you gentlemen have submitted on behalf of your clients. The mystery is clear enough to justify further investigation at the least, and it seems to me we could learn a lot by having a look at that contract. We can learn even more by ordering the autopsy requested by Counselor Haug in his brief. Now, if I see nothing to substantiate a claim of Wrongful Death, there's no reason to move forward with a long and expensive trial. We could all be home in time for lunch, so to speak. Showing us the contract makes a lot of sense, counselor. What do you think?"

"I don't want to set a new precedent, Your Honor," said Camus. Arthur was pulling at the man's sleeve, whispering something.

"No precedents to be set, counselor. This is a hearing. We're seeking evidence to justify a trial."

Haug and Blanche had been hastily conferring, and Blanche nodded her head.

"Your Honor," said Haug, "my client will not pursue a request for an autopsy and will drop her charges if she's satisfied with the contents of her sister's contract with Advanced Technologies."

Arthur and his attorneys conferred again, and there was obvious disagreement. Arthur slapped his hand on the table to emphasize a point. Finally, Camus cleared his throat and said, "We did not come prepared to show the contract, Your Honor, but we can have copies brought here if it's absolutely necessary. We feel it's in the interest of all parties to avoid the expense and publicity of a trial."

Judge Maxwell checked his watch. "It's nearly ten. We will resume at one. I expect Counselor Haug will have at least an hour to study the contract and formulate his questions. One way or another, I hope we're going to settle this today." He smiled down on them all. "Coffee time," he said, and banged his gavel lightly.

* * * * * * *

"No wonder they didn't want us to see it," said Blanche. "This is not only outrageous, but obscene. Helen would never have agreed to this."

"You agree that's her signature?"

"Yes, it looks like it. Signatures can be forged, Randal."

"I doubt it here, Blanche. I think you'll have to accept that Helen was involved as a subject for experimentation with Advanced Technologies before her death, and what's happening now is an extension of that work."

"*What* work?"

"Good question. Whatever it is has to be approved by Arthur Winslow, but otherwise, 'my body can be used in any form or for any purpose within the AINI project.' That's both vague and specific. We have to find out what AINI means. It's the only unknown. Otherwise, Helen has allowed them to do anything they want with her after her death."

"Then they brainwashed her to get her money. This AINI thing is probably part of it."

"We can still argue for an autopsy," said Randal, "but my bet is she died the way they said she did. And seeing the contract hasn't strengthened our case, Blanche; it's weakened it. They've documented Helen's total consent to the procedure. All we can do is try to show that consent was somehow forced out of her."

They were sitting on a bench outside the courtroom. Arthur came down the hall with his entourage behind him, and Blanche glared at him.

Arthur broke away from the group. Camus made a grab for his arm, but missed. Arthur headed straight for Blanche. Randal stood up, prepared to defend her, but Arthur stopped short. His round face was flushed, and he posed angrily, hands on hips. Blanche had a sudden urge to laugh at him.

"Well, I suppose you're *still* not satisfied," said Arthur.

"We might be, if you tell us what the AINI project is," said Randal.

"That's none of your business."

"It might be if it involves coercion and fraud. Let's see what the judge thinks."

"Monster," said Blanche, "you've been allowing experiments with the body of your own mother."

"You don't know *anything*," shouted Arthur. "Mother would be furious if she heard you say that!"

Camus arrived, and pulled Arthur back. "You won't accomplish anything by this. They don't have a case," he said.

"We'll see," said Randal.

Blanche smiled, pleased by Arthur's boyish rage. "You always got away with tantrums when you didn't get your way, dear. If you'd been mine, I wouldn't have allowed it."

"How fortunate you weren't able to have children," snarled Arthur.

"Arthur, *please*!" Camus pulled him away backwards by both arms.

"No! This has to stop here. I'm going to have my AINI unit brought in for testimony. It'll settle everything once and for all."

"The patents, Arthur. We can't—"

"The patents are filed, and the hearing is closed. If anything leaks to the press we'll sue her for everything she has. Let me go!" Arthur twisted in Camus' grip, and broke it.

"Wait for me here. I need to make a private call." Arthur turned to Blanche and pointed a shaking finger at her. "*Now* you're going to get it!"

Everyone was amazed as Arthur stormed away from them. For one instant, Randal Haug and Richard Camus were sympathetic colleagues. Randal shrugged his shoulders in dismay, and Camus said, "What can I do? The funding was his, and he has the authority. The board, of course, will blame me."

Randal shook his head sadly. Blanche was mystified by everything she's just heard.

Two hours later, she understood everything.

* * * * * * *

"What's all this?" asked Judge Maxwell, after he'd seated himself. He gestured at a large, black screen and computer console with projection system that had been set up along one wall of the courtroom. Two fisheye cameras mounted on the console pointed outwards into the room.

"My client wishes to perform a demonstration he feels will clear up this entire matter, Your Honor," said Camus.

"Any objections to this, Counselor Haug?"

"No, Your Honor. The only questions we have regarding the contract relate to details about the AINI project, and we're told the demonstration will answer those questions."

"Good. You may proceed, Counselor Camus."

"Ah, the demonstration will be given by Arthur Winslow. He's familiar with the technology, and has been using it on a regular basis since his mother's death."

Maxwell looked at Haug.

"No problem, Your Honor."

Arthur stood up, adjusted the knot on his tie and walked to the computer, turned, cleared his throat and folded his hands together over his stomach.

"The apparatus behind me houses what we call the AINI Model 10. By AINI we mean 'Artificially Intelligent-Neural Integration.' It is basically a combination of a brain that stores data and a learning center that can synthesize new data from old. In other words, it's an artificial intelligence system with a solid state brain made up of rare-earth-impregnated-carbon-nanotubes."

Arthur opened two doors at the base of the console, revealing what looked like a solid cube of silver metal. "This is the brain."

Everyone looked at him blankly, searching for understanding and relevance. "Rubbish," muttered Blanche, and Arthur heard her.

He glared straight at her, closed the console doors behind him and softly said, "It's my mother's brain, now, and if you'll listen I'll tell you how that happened."

Blanche gasped. Randal squeezed her arm, and hushed her.

Arthur blushed, and his voice quavered. "It all started with the Josephson Junction SQUID arrays to map magnetic storms in the brains of epileptics, but as resolution increased, our scientists began to see repeated neural current patterns related to specific thoughts, especially in memory recollection. We were soon down to the neuron level in resolution. Each memory, each thought, is a definite, three dimensional current pattern in real time. It's like scanning a picture, and this is what AINI does, building up a library of memories and thoughts than can be reassembled by an AI system to satisfy any scenario."

Arthur's voice cracked. He seemed to be struggling, and took out a handkerchief to wipe his forehead. His eyes were suddenly quite moist.

"It was my mother who came up with the idea of using AINI to store more than the body of someone you loved when they died."

Arthur choked, cleared his throat again, and blew his nose with the handkerchief. Blanche rolled her eyes, and sighed.

"She was interested in many things, and she'd had a series of small strokes, little blackouts that frightened her. We were so close. She heard about the freezing process at Advanced Technologies. If something bad happened, we wanted to have hope. Medicine is advancing fast, and then the people at Advanced Tech told us about AINI. They were looking for human subjects for testing. And Mother volunteered her time and her money."

Arthur took two steps towards Blanche, and pointed a finger at her. "While *you* were flitting around with your elite social functions, my mother was making major contributions to both science and technology. She funded the entire project, and spent nearly five years of nights and many days under the SQUID array cap, having the neural currents of her own brain mapped and deciphered. She was still doing it the day she—she—"

Arthur paused, and breathed deeply, wiped his eyes with the handkerchief.

"This is sick," mumbled Blanche, too loudly.

Arthur gave her a look that promised pain and suffering. "Why don't we just let Mother tell you about it herself," he said softly.

"Randal, how long do we have to hear this?" said Blanche.

"Your Honor," began Randal, "I would like to—"

"I was about to give a demonstration relevant to this hearing, and I have the court's permission to do it," said Arthur.

"Then do it," said Judge Maxwell. "I don't think we need more background information at this time."

"This is company proprietary information, Your Honor," said Camus, suddenly standing as Arthur walked back to the apparatus. "We must have a guarantee the details of the demonstration will not go in any form beyond this room."

"This hearing is closed, ladies and gentlemen. *Any* information given here, including this demonstration, stays here. Any information leak will prejudice all future litigation, and be cause for breach of privacy. Are we clear on this?"

Everyone nodded in agreement. "Yes, Your Honor," chorused Randal and Camus.

There was a sudden hum that quickly faded. Arthur sat at the keyboard, fingers playing over the keys. He looked like an organ player sitting there, but this organ had a monitor in front of him, and a wide, black screen stretched like a sail on top of it, between two fisheye cameras. A ball of light had begun to glow, not *on* the screen but in front of it. Before their eyes a three dimensional view of a room appeared. The walls of the room were white, the floor carpeted in crimson. There was a sofa and two chairs in red leather, a glass coffee table with a vase of red roses in the foreground. Three shaggy weavings in a rainbow of colors hung on the walls.

There was an open doorway in the back of the room. Someone walked past it. A man. Blanche felt her heart skip a beat. Only a glimpse, but the face had seemed familiar.

And then a woman appeared. She was tall, draped in a red silken robe, her gray hair stylishly coifed in swirls framing her face.

She could have been fifty, or thirty. She walked like a model, posture erect and defiant, went to the sofa, sat down, crossed her legs and smiled.

Blanche gasped. "Dear God, it's Helen, the way she looked years ago," she whispered to Randal.

The woman seemed to look right at her. "Well, they say you should pick an age you like and stick with it. Hello again, Blanche. From that frown on your face I'd say we're still fighting. Are we?"

The voice was deep and husky, a voice Blanche had been jealous of for over sixty years. Men had been attracted to it like bears to honey. Blanche's mouth moved, but nothing came out.

"No? Well that's not what I hear." The woman's eyes moved. "Hi, sweetie. I guess this is court, huh?"

"Yes, Mother," said Arthur.

Judge Maxwell was smiling, and seemed fascinated by the display. "Perhaps you should introduce us to your, ah, demonstration," he said.

Arthur blushed crimson, and seemed embarrassed by the request. "I'm not quite sure what I—"

"Never mind, dear. I'm quite capable of introducing myself," said the woman's floating image. "Officially I'm AINI, but some of the techs like to pervert it by calling me Annie. It's cute, but inaccurate. In every way, you see, I'm Helen Winslow, based on me the person, but synthesized and evolved into my present form by the AINI system. I'd prefer you call me Helen, because that's who I am, but I'll accept Annie if you like."

"But you are an artificial intelligence system," said Maxwell.

"Everyone in this courtroom functions like an AI, Your Honor. We store and retrieve memories, we think and learn, and synthesize new ideas from old. The only difference between you and me is our computers. Yours is organic, incredibly compact, but slow. Mine is larger, but very fast."

"Do you know why you've been brought to this courtroom?"

"I think so. Arthur was rather upset when he tried to explain it to me."

The woman's gaze shifted to Blanche, and made eye contact. "I'd be upset, too, if someone tried to charge me with murder."

"This is a hearing, and no formal charges have been filed against anyone, Ms.—ah—" Maxwell paused.

The apparition laughed, a deep-throated laugh that Blanche remembered well. It had turned men's heads at gatherings large and small for years, without promising anything but her presence. "*You* don't know what to *call* me," she said. "If you say Helen, you acknowledge my transfiguration and oh, my goodness, what a precedent that would set!"

She laughed again. Maxwell grinned.

"Call me Annie, then, but remember who I really am when you hear what I have to say. This whole mess is partly my fault, anyway, and I intend to clean it up."

"Very well—Annie," said Maxwell, and turned to look at several anxiously waiting people in the room. "We're open for questions, gentlemen. Counselor Haug, would you like to begin?"

"Randal, this is absurd," whispered Blanche, as Randal stood up.

"Are we to consider this—Annie as a viable witness, Your Honor?" asked Randal.

"You wanted to know about the AINI system," said Maxwell, eyes twinkling in amusement. "Well, here she is."

"I really don't think a machine can be—"

"This will go nowhere, Your Honor," said Annie. "I never could talk sense to lawyers, even you, Randal, and it won't be any different now. This is all between two sisters, anyway. It's all about the money, and everything else is smoke. Talk to me, Blanche. We can settle this in a few minutes, if you'll let it happen."

"I doubt that very much," said Arthur, and frowned at Blanche.

"Now Arthur," said Annie, "you promised me you'd go along with whatever I agreed to today. No pouting. Just do what mother says. Sit down with your lawyers, and let me handle this."

"I will not talk with this—this *thing*," said Blanche.

"Your Honor, this is a sham," said Randal Haug. "Mister Winslow has obviously programmed the machine for this performance, and I must—"

"May I *please* be allowed to do something useful here?" said Annie. As she said it, a man appeared in the doorway behind her and said something softly. He wore a white bathrobe, and had a toothbrush in one hand. Annie turned, and said quite audibly, "Later, hon. I'm just getting warmed up here." The man looked disappointed, and went away from view.

Blanche's face flushed hotly. The man was Fred, Helen's late husband, only he looked to be in his forties or early fifties. The shock of recognition must have shown on her face, for the apparition called Annie smiled at her.

"He's such a dear, but so impatient, and I have a lot of fleshing out to do on him. So many of my memories are from when he was sick. You remember how hard that was, don't you, Blanche?"

"Yes," said Blanche, and caught her self. "I mean—"

"I know, I know," said Annie. "It's all so real for me, but not for you. It seems like yesterday I was old, and my joints were hurting, and I kept having these little blackouts, and then I can remember Arthur bending over me, screaming hysterically, and then—well, then there was nothing. No tunnel of light, no angels for old Helen. I was just suddenly here, still old at first, but no pain, and everything I thought, everything I remembered and wanted from the past—it just happened, when I wanted it to. Of course I also remembered all the downloading; my God, I wore that brain-sucking cap of theirs to bed for over five years! But there was no way I could really predict what it would be like until I got here."

Annie's eyes glistened wetly. "It was lonely here at first. Believe it or not, Tickle, I missed you. I knew you were mad at me, and I didn't make it up to you before I left. I'm sorry."

Blanche felt something catch in her throat. She hadn't been called Tickle since the age of seven. It even softened her heart for one instant, and then she turned it into stone again. "You've been doing some research, Arthur," she said. "It's not going to work with me."

Arthur lunged from his chair, but Camus grabbed him around the chest and held him tightly.

"Stop it, Arthur! If you want to speak to me again, you'll sit right down and be quiet. Tantrums are not excusable for a man your age. Do you want me to be ashamed?"

Arthur sat down as if struck. A tear rolled down one cheek.

Annie glared at Blanche. "You always *were* good at goading people, but you were a coward when it came to standing up to me, so don't try it. Yes, I want to convince you I'm what's left of Helen; I'm most of her, in fact, if you take away the physical form. I could spend hours reciting things only you and I would know, like the time you bit me when I wouldn't let you play with my dolls. We didn't even tell Mother about that. And then there was the time I caught you and your weird friend Ellen doing some interesting things with the little Waltham boy in our garage. I bet the details of that would perk things up in this hearing."

"You wouldn't dare!" shouted Blanche, standing, and shaking a fist.

"I *would* dare, but I won't, so sit down, Blanche," said Annie. She stood up, stepped forward and leaned over, as if peering into a camera lens. "It would be fun to watch you squirm again. Without me around, I bet you've been running roughshod over everyone. Want to hear something funny? I'm enjoying myself right now. I've missed our fights; they're stimulating.

Blanche's eyes filled with tears. "I haven't missed them at all. I haven't missed *you* at all."

"Oh, that was supposed to hurt, but it didn't. You miss me plenty, Tickle. Sisters know. It's one of the reasons you're so angry. Wow, the memories are still coming. I bet I could synthesize a somewhat younger version of you, and we could fight all the time right in my living room. Fred wouldn't mind. He got used to it a long time—"

"Ladies, ladies, *please*!" said Judge Maxwell. "There are important questions to be answered here, and you're not answering them."

Maxwell wasn't smiling this time. Blanche wondered if he saw through the sham of what Arthur was doing with his machine, the way his creature was making her look like a vicious, old fool. Her hands were shaking. It was just like her fights with Helen over all those years. So real, so real....

"Question one," said Maxwell. "How did Helen Winslow die?"

"A blackout, like I said, only this one brought me here. I'm told there was massive bleeding in my brain," said Annie. She sat down on her couch again, and crossed her legs.

"All right. Question two: why was Helen's head preserved by freezing, and the rest of her body separated from it?"

Annie thought for a moment. "Well, I remember it said in the contract my body could be used in any way to help the AINI project. Only the head was important, really; there was some data downloaded right after I—I should say Helen—died. Helen's last image of Arthur was there. Oh, I'm sorry, sweetie. I have to be Annie to answer the questions, but you know who I am."

Arthur was crying, his face buried in a handkerchief.

"Separating Helen's body wasn't a cost-saving measure?"

"Well, it saved money, but the body was worthless, all used up, nothing left to revive. No matter, now. I'm here, and I have my Fred, my Arthur. We talk whenever we want to, don't we, hon?"

Tears were running down Arthur's cheeks. He nodded his head, smiled, and blew his nose loudly in the handkerchief.

"He keeps us right in his living room," added Annie. "It was worth the extra cost, but there's where I got into trouble with Blanche. I never thought she's miss a couple of million; she always had more than Fred and I. I just got over enthused about the project, I guess. I was wrong. I was wrong because I promised Blanche the money for her foundation. But then the blackouts started, and Arthur was so upset and alone, and we—we just wanted to be together, at least until he finds that special girl."

Arthur began blubbering again. Everyone in the room avoided eye contact with each other.

"Dear God," said Blanche.

Annie bristled. "Oh shut up, Blanche. I don't expect you to understand, but there is nothing stronger than the love of a mother for her only son. You never had children because you didn't want them. I did, so try to respect that."

Her voice had risen in pitch. Her male companion came into the room, walked up behind her and put his hands on her shoulders, squeezing gently. "The ice is melting. I miss you." He kissed the crown of her head.

Annie put her hands on his, and pointed directly at Blanche. "See anyone there you recognize?"

The man looked closely. There was no doubt in Blanche's mind that she was looking at an image of Fred Winslow from at least thirty years before he'd died.

"Is that Blanche? How did she get to be so old?"

Again that husky laugh. "I'll explain later, sweet. Pull the cork. I'll be there in a minute. Kiss, kiss."

He kissed Annie delicately on the mouth, and went away.

Annie gave Blanche a sultry look. "More upgrades coming, but he's already quite a man. I've kept him waiting long enough, so let's get to it, Blanche. I'm Helen whether you like it or not, but I'm also a damn good AI. The judge here isn't going to help us. There are too many precedents involved: legality of AI testimony, the AI as a legal substitute for a human, dead *or* alive, *et cetera, et cetera*. I don't think he cares to appear in the legal journals that many times. Is that an accurate statement, Your Honor?"

"That is a reasonable approximation of what I'm thinking," said Maxwell, looking vaguely amused.

"So it's you and me, Blanche. How much will it take for you to drop all this mess? Two million? Three? How about four? That's tops. Otherwise you're going to trial, and there isn't a jury around that's smart enough or imaginative enough to believe I am who I say I am. And you will get nothing."

Blanche looked at Arthur. "I'll write a check for whatever amount Mother says, and make it payable to your arts foundation in the names of my parents," he said.

Randal shrugged his shoulders, and wiggled an eyebrow at her. The rest of the lawyers at the other table looked away. There was a long silence, horrible for everyone who waited.

"Three million," said Blanche.

"Write the check, Arthur," said Annie, standing up and smoothing her robed hips with her hands. "I'll talk to you tonight. Right now I have a date with your dad. Blanche, do come over for tea sometime. We must stay in touch, and Arthur will set up the machine for you, won't you dear?"

Arthur nodded numbly, not obviously pleased with the request.

"We should talk more often, and I'd really like to see how your foundation plays out. It's good for me to keep up a variety of interests, now that I have so much time. Promise you'll come soon?"

Blanche moved her lips, but could not bring herself to answer.

"Bye, then," said Annie, and left the room. Arthur turned off the machine, and the white room with red furnishings was gone. Annie was gone—and so was Helen.

"Let the record show the parties settled this matter out of court," said Maxwell, looking pleased and relieved. "This hearing is ended."

Everyone filed out of the courtroom. Arthur waited for Blanche at the door. "You'll have the check in a day or two," he said, then, "You know, Mother was really serious about visiting with you. Just give me some warning when you want to come over. I don't have to be home. My secretary knows how to boot AINI for her."

Blanche looked away from him. "I really don't think I'll be doing that, Arthur," she said.

Later, she changed her mind.

BACON 'N' EGGS

There were rats in the soufflé again.

At least that's what we told our cook when black speckles appeared on the eggs he served up. Now John Redcloud is the best chef you'll find on any probe between here and Sol, and he knows it, but it still pissed him off when his scrambled eggs were criticized. "You don't like it, there's toast and oatmeal," he said, and everyone groaned. We'd been eatin' that stuff for four-hundred and fifty days on Roosevelt's run to Procyon C and its trio of steamy planets. Even the sight of freeze-dried eggs and bacon bits was heaven to most of the crew. Me, I don't eat breakfast. Anyway, the crew laughed, picked out the little black things hiding among the bacon bits and snarfed it all down, leaving little for John to put back in the oven for warming.

I'd been operations chief for ten years, and it was my second planet fall. A probe crew spends most of a lifetime just traveling, and two drops was already pretty good for a career. We were all grateful for that, and there were worse places to explore. We'd picked Emerald because the other two planets were just hot rock and old lava flows, and here we were surrounded by plant life so thick we'd had a hard time finding a place to put down. It was botanical heaven: ferns and gnarled trees like arthritic hands draped in thick mosses in yellows and emerald green, red and purple flowers big as a dinner plate all over the place. Harry Burns and his botany team were spending as much outside time as their refrigeration units would allow, collecting plants somehow thriving at a temperature of a hundred and fifty degrees Fahrenheit.

Our third day on Emerald I was just finishing morning coffee when the intercom squealed, "Carl Doser down there?"

Harry's voice. I jumped up and answered quick because he wasn't due back in for five hours. "Yeah, Harry, what's up?"

"Meet me in lock three, Chief. I've got a problem here."

"On my way," I said, and moved quick as I always do when I hear concern in a man's voice.

Lock three was aft; two flights up so it took a minute. When I got there two people were stripping E suits and the UV was on behind the port so someone was still decontaminating. The door snapped open and there was Harry, red-faced, bending over a suited figure huddled on the floor. The others were busy stripping so I rushed straight to him. "What's up?" I asked, out of breath from the short sprint in 1.2 gee. I wasn't getting any younger, either. But I am a survivor.

"It's Sally," he said, fumbling at the helmet of the huddled figure at his feet. "We were coming back with moss samples and she started groaning, and then she doubled up and went down like a rock. Cramps, she says, and it seems severe. Help me with this, Chief."

We got the helmet off and Sally Dieter looked awful, face pinched up in pain and her skin sweaty and grey. Scared us both right away. When we unzipped her suit she screamed and writhed around like a crazy person, and that really scared us. We carried Sally in her suit, groaning and in a fetal position, all the way to sick bay where Doc Joan hustled us outside before she even made an examination. We went back to the lock to talk to the rest of the botany team, but they only scratched their heads. One minute Sally was fine, the next she was down on the ground yelling about pain in her stomach.

Joan came up two hours later to ask a bunch of questions and tell us Sally was seriously ill and she was doing some blood work on her. Whatever was wrong, she said, it was rough stuff.

The following day, it started happening to other members of the crew.

* * * * * * *

It was just me, Harry and Doc Joan having coffee in the mess room the morning of day eight on Emerald. John Redcloud poured the thick, black stuff for us and munched down his usual breakfast of dry toast. "Anyone for eggs?" he asked hopefully.

"Sure," said Harry, and John served him up a plate.

"We've got to radio Roosevelt and get a pickup," said Joan, rubbing her eyes. "I've got them stacked up in there like cordwood and I need lab help. I don't even have a decent microscope, and nothing is visible on the plates."

"You're sure it's some kind of bug?" asked Harry, brushing mini-rat turds off his eggs before eating a forkful of them. John frowned at him.

"Has to be," said Joan. "Probably viral, the way they keep spiking fevers, and the penicillin isn't doing a thing."

"Sally went up to a hundred-five and was crazy with pain until I got her in the cold tub and then in a few minutes she was coherent again, asking about the others and wanting to know if her plant samples were stowed. Fifteen minutes out of the bath she was raving again and I had to restrain her. It doesn't make any sense. I can't keep shuttling six people to and from the cold bath. I haven't had any sleep in two days and I'm out of ideas."

"Even if we call now," I put in, "we can't get Roosevelt back for maybe a week. They've followed those inner planets half way around Procyon by now."

"Terrific," said Joan. "Another day of no sleep, making ice as fast as I can." And then she seemed to brighten. "Maybe if the sick bay were cooler they'd at least get some rest. Cold seems to help."

Harry swallowed the last of his eggs. "The four of us are okay and we've been in close proximity to the others. Whatever it is can't be airborne and if we brought it in with us the UV had no effect. There has to be a common denominator, and we're not seeing it."

"You, Sally, Hadley, Estevez and Ono have been outside," I said, "and the rest of us have been in here the whole time. It's either airborne or contact, and I've handled the suits, too."

"Whatever," said Joan, and she ran off to turn down the thermostat in sick bay while Harry, John and I sat drinking coffee and puzzling at the table.

An hour later, Sally sat up in bed, screamed once very loud—and died.

The next morning, Harry was sick and out of his head like the rest of Joan's patients.

* * * * * * *

We were too scared to go outside so we put Sally in the aft lock and purged it good with nitrogen. The first good thing to happen in days was when I got Roosevelt on the horn and told them our troubles. The bad news was it'd be six days before we got a pickup. Hang on, they said, and that's when I discovered pretty Doc Joan could swear for five minutes without repeating herself. After she'd calmed down she tried to encourage John and me. "The rest of them are doing better, but I've got sick bay down to fifty degrees. All we need now is pneumonia, but this bug doesn't seem to like low temperature. It's evolved with the hundred-fifty degrees outside. I still can't get a culture. Come on, guys, there's three of us left here. What's the common link in all this? Think!"

So I thought. Five had been outside and five had not, and Harry had taken sick days after the others. We'd all been breathing the same air, and John usually washed our dishes and utensils in cold water. When someone got a cold we all got it, but not this time. John and I sat there staring at each other while Joan went back to start her patients on some kind of antibiotic, but she was back in a flash. "Well? Any ideas?"

"Not a clue," I said, and Joan sighed, looked real tired, her eyes kind of puffy. John leaned back against the stove and folded his arms across his chest, the look on his face unreadable as usual.

"Eggs," said John Redcloud.

"What?" said Joan tiredly.

"They all been eatin' eggs—except us three. Harry had 'em just yesterday and now he's sick too."

Joan looked startled, and me I was thinking fast and he was right. The entire botany team had fueled up on eggs the morning after planet fall, cleaning out the whole pan so there was nothing left for anyone else, but John had been making enough for the whole crew and more since then. John's a vegetarian and Joan is like me; breakfast is coffee and maybe some toast. And at that instant, something clicked in my head.

"What are the black specks on the eggs, John? Pepper?"

"Don't use pepper, just a little salt. People're picky about eggs."

"You know what I mean. The crew's been kidding you about it. Rat turds? Look like little peppercorns, they do."

"Nothin' I put in," said John, looking offended. "Maybe some burn from the oven."

Now Doc Joan was suddenly interested. "You cook the eggs in the oven?"

"Naw. I got only one skillet, not enough for everyone. I scramble eggs in relay and warm 'em in the oven."

Now Joan seemed real interested. "Show me the oven, John."

"Right here," he said, and opened it. I took one look and decided it needed cleaning, but Joan pushed me aside and got down on her knees to look all around inside the thing. Those black specks were scattered around on the bottom of the oven, but it was when Joan looked up at where the heating coils were that she gasped. "Oh, my God. Carl, get me a bowl or a cup—and a spoon, quick. I think I've found our bugs."

I was quick about it and in a second she was holding a cup up inside the oven, scraping away with the spoon while John and I exchanged curious looks. She put the cup on the table and we looked inside.

Rat turds. Half a cup-full.

"They're thick on the oven ceiling, clusters following the shape of the coil, and they're growing there. One of them popped open while I was inside. Close the oven door, John!" It was more than curiosity in Joan's voice, now. It was fear, and I remember thinking that the stuff in that cup was nothing to be fooled with. I stepped back a little from the table.

"I've got to do it here. Sick bay's too cold," she said. "Get some towels to cover the table, but don't touch the cup or the spoon. I'll be right back." She rushed off towards the sick bay.

John and I laid out some towels at one end of the table, and didn't go near that cup, and when Doc Joan returned we backed clear up against a wall to watch her.

She had a mask on, and surgical gloves, and carried a stack of those little dishes I'd seen her use for growing bug colonies on Roosevelt. She sat down at the table, put everything on towels, then poured some black stuff on a cup saucer and started worrying it with the spoon. Little peppercorns, like I said, but kind of squishy. "Like skin," she said. "I bet it's protein of some kind." But then she hit a hard one and it popped open, and even from six feet away I could see something yellow ooze out. It made my stomach crawl.

"Here it is," she said. "We've found it!"

Well you can have it, I thought, but she sure was excited. She popped some more, then smeared a bunch of stuff on those little dishes, some with black, some with the yellow gunk. It was past lunchtime, but I didn't have any appetite at all. "Got to keep these things warm," she said. "They've evolved at high T. John, turn the oven on again, right where you warm the eggs."

"Ain't going near that thing," said John.

"Just set the temperature for me!" said Joan angrily. "I'll open it up."

John did as he was told and I stayed where I was, feeling a little wimpy, but then Joan had the mask on and I didn't, and my mama did not raise a fool. So Doc put the dishes, cup and spoon in the oven and closed the door, looking tired but pleased with herself. "If I get a culture, I've got a good chance of finding something that'll kill it quick. I've already eliminated penicillin and half a dozen antibiotics. Now we just have to wait."

That didn't mean sitting. I was a one-man maintenance crew now and the environmental system was overloaded from that air-conditioner blasting away in sick bay. I spent the next twenty four hours resetting relays, sending status reports to Roosevelt and scraping frost from coils, buckets of it. The ice machine stopped twice and we were pouring frost into the cold tub while Joan fought with two more members of the botany team out of their heads with fever again. And it was damn cold in that room. All the while Doc Joan was looking more and more haggard, big purple swellings of flesh now under her eyes, and Roosevelt was starting to talk quarantine to us. Couldn't blame them; the whole probe had become a bug farm. I remember how thick and rancid the air seemed, and wondering if we were all breathing in yellow guck. I remember noticing stuffiness in my nose, and little pains in my stomach. It didn't occur to me it was because I hadn't eaten anything for twenty-four hours.

The next morning we rushed to the mess room, Joan walking jerky and looking ashen-faced. She opened the oven and placed its contents on the towel-draped table, took one look and dropped hard into a chair. "Damn," she said. "Damn, damn," and put her head in her hands.

I looked carefully over her shoulder. The volume of black stuff in the cup had grown considerable. But there was nothing in those bug dishes. Nothing.

And then Doc Joan groaned, tilted her head back towards me. Her eyelids fluttered, her eyes rolled back up in her head and she fell forward hard onto the table.

* * * * * * *

There were two of us left standing. At first we'd thought Joan had the bug, too, but the symptoms weren't there and we decided it was plain old exhaustion. We laid her out on a cot in the mess room and she slept like a dead person for fifteen hours before she started tossing and turning and mumbling. John and I cat-napped and nibbled some toast and Roosevelt called to say pick up would be in four days with a med team joining us in quarantine.

Bad turned to worse when we lost our second crew member. Harry was thrashing around and yelling again and we had to do another cold dip on him, but when we went to get him we found his neighbor patient Ono lying peacefully dead and covered with a horrible black mass he'd vomited up. So we dipped Harry until he was quiet and put Ono in the lock with Sally. We went back to check on Joan and found her sitting up on the cot. We told her about Ono and she bit her lip so hard it bled a little. Frustrated. Angry. After a while, though, she was thinking again.

"Eggs," she said. John and I looked at each other.

"Don't you see? They grow in eggs. Protein eaters! I'm doing the wrong culture. Help me up."

She stood there wobbly while we told her about the last fifteen hours. "Okay, so this is beyond serious, now. The whole crew can be dead in four days if I don't do something right. Carl, put some gloves on and get a sputum sample from Ono. John, you help me to the botany lab. I still can't find my feet. Carl, you meet us there."

We did that. I found her in the botany lab working with the bug dishes. "Protein eaters," she said again. "They're eating our crew up from the inside. So I'm using albumin for the culture plates. John, set that oven to one hundred-fifty exactly. This is our last chance."

John fled. I watched while Joan smeared ground peppercorns, yellow guck and Ono's horrible spit on the bug dishes. I helped carry them to the oven. Her excitement was there again and a little color had returned to her face. Quite a lady. The bugs were cooking and Joan was thinking aloud; "Got to get it right the first time. Penicillin and standard antibiotics are no good. There's a different pathway in these things. Maybe combinations. God, I don't even know the pathology! Could be an inhibitor. Shut these suckers down. How much for a hundred kilo male?" She suddenly became aware of John and I staring at her blankly. "Okay, you watch after my patients a while. I'm going to do some inventory in the botany lab." And she left the room.

Just in time. Now Harry was sitting up, eyes open—babbling. When we touched him he screamed and clawed at my face. I gave him a bear hug, told him everything was okay. Everything was under control. Yeah. He calmed down, went back to sleep, his forehead hot in the terrible cold of that room. John checked the ice machine when we noticed the silence. It was down again, a handful of ice cubes left. I reset the relay, scraped off two buckets of frost and set them at the ready.

Joan was in the mess room, smearing more guck on more bug dishes, a jar of white powder in front of her. "They like eggs, I'll give 'em eggs," she said. "If they don't culture out in Albumin, we're done for."

"You have eggs in there?" I squinted at the dishes.

"Albumin. Like egg white. Thank God for the botany lab." She added four more dishes to the stuff already cooking in the oven. "How're my patients? You guys doing alright?"

John and I nodded, but were concerned. She was ashen-faced again. "Why don't you lie down a while longer?" I said. "Maybe eat something?" She took my hand, squeezed it. "Thanks, Chief. I'd like that."

We fed Joan some toast with honey on it, a glass of water, and eased her back onto the cot. "We'll take care of everything," I said. She smiled, eyes fluttering, and was out like a light in seconds.

Four hours later we nearly lost Harry, tackled him at the door of sick bay as he was staggering out. We used up the last of the ice and frost to cool him down. He opened his eyes, grabbed my shoulder. "Water," he said. "I'm burning up inside, Chief." I looked around again, but the ice was gone. What the hell, I thought, and dipped a cup of water out of the cold tub. Harry gulped it down and I got another. He drank three cups, and went to sleep like a baby.

I'm no doctor, but Harry going to sleep like that gave me an idea. We fed cold water to the others by the cupful. They seemed to crave it, and one cup of the stuff gave me a cramp. But they all slept peacefully the entire night. So much for modern medicine.

John and I even slept some, and in the morning we got to the mess room just as Doc Joan was shuffling towards the oven. She put her hand on the door handle and turned towards us, face grey. "This is it, guys," she said solemnly. "Hold your breath."

She opened the oven, took a close look, and screamed, "Yes!"

She took the little dishes out of the oven one-by-one and put them on the table. The dishes with pieces of peppercorns on them were blank, but the four others were streaked with narrow rows of lemon-yellow fuzz topped with bulbous swellings. I thought of mushrooms in the hydroponic tanks on Roosevelt. "Pretty small for killers, aren't they?" said Joan, and then she turned around and kissed me right on the mouth. Nice. When she turned to John, he backed away from her quick up against the stove. "We did it! We found them! Now let's see if we can kill 'em."

Very excited, she was, and I was still feeling that kiss. She sent John and me for more dishes while she rummaged in her pharmacy, pulling out vials of stuff, rushing back to the botany lab and staying in there the rest of the morning while John and I ate cereal, drank coffee, scraped frost and looked in on the rest of the crew. Some of them were getting restless again. Harry moaned, opened his eyes. He looked like a man near-starved to death. "We aren't going to make it, are we Chief? We're all going to die here." A little tear leaked from one eye.

"We found the bugs," I said, patting him on a bony shoulder. "Doc is testing now to see what'll kill them. Hang on just a little longer, Harry. We'll get 'em. Besides, you've got to fly this probe for us."

"They're eating me up inside," said Harry, and moaned again. I have never felt as helpless in my life as I did at that moment, and now the others were moaning, twisting and pulling against the straps we'd used to keep them on their cots. Things were heating up again, next to no ice in the machine and one bucket of frost to work with. I tested the tub water with a finger. In that terrible cold room it felt warm.

Joan appeared in the doorway. "We're cooking again. The rate that first batch grew we should know something by early tomorrow. How're you doing?"

"Fevers coming again and the dip is warm. The ice machine can't keep up with what we need, and I think we'll need plenty before tonight is over."

"Hold the fort," said Joan. "I've got one more plate to make with a protease inhibitor I found in the lab. When I do that I've tried everything I could find. Okay?"

We nodded grimly, and Joan disappeared.

All the action started an hour later.

Alonzo, our electrician, sat up on his cot with a shout and pulled at his restraints hard enough to bend the one inch tubing of the frame beneath him. Black stuff was oozing from his mouth and he was making bluh-bluh sounds while his body jerked and shook. I grabbed him from behind while John ran for the frost bucket and headed for the tub and I screamed, "No! Bring it over here! We'll never get the tub cooled down!"

John, bless him, did as he was told. "Now get me a spoon and crush up what ice we have left in the machine. All of it."

John ran as I relaxed my grip on Alonzo, getting in front of him to wipe that horrible spittle from his mouth. "I'm here, I'm here," I said, near panic myself when I looked into his fear-filled eyes. "Oh, oh, oh," he said, over and over again.

John came back with Joan right behind him, handed me the spoon and I started shoveling frost into Alonzo's mouth and he was swallowing it fast.

"What are you doing?" screamed Joan.

I told her about my ice-water treatment, how it had calmed everyone right down. "I think the bugs are in his belly, and they can't work in cold. Ice or cold water in the stomach shocks them. That's what I think. It works, Doc. I've seen it."

Joan had reached for the spoon, but now she stepped back and sighed. "What the hell, try it. We've run out of options anyway."

So I shoveled and Alonzo swallowed and, sure enough, in a few minutes he calmed down and licked his lips. "Better," he said. "Thanks, Chief." I eased him back on the cot and turned towards Joan, who was looking broodingly at me.

"Okay, we'll do it your way," she said.

And we did. Five more times that night.

* * * * * * *

It was two in the morning. Everyone was resting quietly, but there was no more ice or frost. Joan looked at me, eyes sunken and dark-rimmed with fatigue. "It's now or never, Carl. If we don't start a treatment soon we'll lose all of them and maybe even ourselves. Let's check those cultures."

I followed her to the mess room where John was making coffee. She went straight to the oven, took out the little dishes one by one and put them on the table, an expression of gloomy despair growing with each trip. She sat down at the table and rested her chin in her hands. "Well, I tried," she said softly. "I did the best I could."

I leaned over her shoulder. The dishes were covered with neat rows of yellow fuzz like ripe grain fields seen from a kilometer above. Healthy, they were, and growing. I put a hand on her shoulder. "Sorry," I said. "You just didn't have enough to work with on something new like this. I'd better call Roosevelt and let them know." I looked at John, but he shifted his gaze to the floor in front of him.

"If only I'd—," she said, then jerked upright so fast my hand dropped away from her shoulder. "Wait a minute!" She pointed a finger, counting dishes, and then squinting closely at them, reading the little labels telling her which drug she had tried. She counted again. "There's a dish missing here. I had—oh shit!" She jumped up from the table.

"What?"

"The culture with the actinylprotease, I left it in the botany lab when you had trouble with Alonzo last night. It's been at room temperature all this time." She rushed out of the room and I was right behind her all the way to the lab. The dish was where she'd left it, a swivel lamp still burning close over the working area. Joan practically leaped at it, eyes inches from the dish. "I think—yes, look!"

I looked. Same thing, like rows of wheat, only fainter, and something was wrong with two of those rows, like locusts had been at them, eating them to the ground. There were jagged, bare lines in a field of yellow fuzz. There was no life there.

"Killed them!" shouted Joan right into my ear. "There's no time for a better test, Carl. I have to go with it, and now." She was making calculations on a piece of paper. "There's no telling what else it'll kill in a human. As far as I know it's only been used on small animals before now. This is a monstrous chance I'm taking here. I want you to understand that before I ask you to help me. Do you?"

"They're going to die for sure if we don't do something," I said solemnly. "What can I do?"

"Oh, Carl," said Joan, and she kissed me again, only this time I kissed back and managed to hold it for half a second until she pulled away and smiled at me. "Syringes in that left drawer. Help me fill them." She mixed and measured, her face flushed again with excitement. I helped her fill five syringes with the stuff she brewed, and handed them to her in sick bay when she shot it into her five patients. She sat down, and sighed. "I can see my whole career going down the drain for this. I just might have murdered five people."

* * * * * * *

But it didn't work out that way.

Harry was the first to feel better, I guess because the bugs hadn't been in him quite as long as for the others. Joan shot them up four times a day until Roosevelt arrived and it was another fourteen days before we were out of quarantine. The stuff in those syringes looked like swamp water, but in five days everyone was screaming for food and Joan started them on a liquid protein diet. None of us found it amusing when Harry asked for eggs.

We all felt bad about Sally and Ono. Another probe took them out for a deep space burial with a trajectory taking them into the furnace of Procyon C. It was a good way for a spacer to end it. There was relief when we discovered the bugs hadn't come in with anyone. There were clusters of peppercorns around the stove's vent to the outside, and the flue was full of them. That meant redesign before another probe landed on Emerald three years later.

When we climbed aboard Roosevelt, Joan and I were both sneezing from colds, giving each other sly looks and glad that nobody asked why we had the sniffles and the others didn't. We'd already decided we'd ship out together again if even the smallest opportunity arose.

And it did.

MILDRED'S GARDEN

The little children in the neighborhood called her the flower lady. Her real name was Mildred Hanson, and she lived alone in a white frame house surrounded by a short picket fence separating concrete from a world of beauty and sweet smells. It was a world of flowers.

Narrow dirt paths lined with creeping vines provided the only access to mounds of earth covered with roses, anchusas, purple delphiniums, iris, daffodils, daisies, and phlox. Mats of glowing pink petunias and scarlet zinnias were arranged in curving rows like toy soldiers keeping watch over the place. In a hollow at the center of the colorful jungle, and surrounded by tall bulb plants from Africa, a small shed was filled with tools and sacks of peat and exotic foods. There were no insecticides or other poisons there. Mildred Hanson did not believe in using them. Her garden was curiously free of insects.

The ladies of the neighborhood thought well of Mildred Hanson. A good woman, though somewhat eccentric, they said. Never a cross word for anyone, including that horrid little Davidson boy who periodically invaded her garden to damage plants and make noises that terrified the poor woman in the darkness.

The plants had become the focus of Mildred's life since Fred had died. She still missed her husband terribly. Her two children had left home long ago to raise families of their own, and they lived far away. Mildred rarely heard from them, and often wished they would visit so she could meet her grandchildren. That had not happened, so her plants had become her children, and she had something to love and care for again.

She arose early, when the eastern sky was colored orange with the promise of a new day. As the red disk of the sun appeared on the horizon she ate slowly at an oil-cloth-covered table by a window overlooking the garden. Each morning she watched her children awake sleepily, some of them opening up petal-lined faces to seek out the light and the warmth. She washed morning dishes in the kitchen sink, and dressed herself slowly and painfully with knuckle-swollen hands. The pain bothered her, but she didn't resent it; there was a purpose for everything, she thought. She stood before a mirror to put a fine net over thinning white hair, and then added a broad-brimmed hat to protect her sensitive skin from another long day in the sunlight. Straightening her hunched frame, after studying its image in the mirror, she shuffled to the door and stepped out into the morning cold.

"Good morning," she said aloud, listening for the faint rustling sounds from the garden.

It is a new day.

Mildred Hanson talked to her plants, imagined their responses in her mind. She knew it was foolish, knew the neighbors thought her eccentric because of it. But it caused no harm, and made her feel happy. She threaded her way slowly through the garden and out to the street, pausing to inspect the picket fence. It was intact.

There has been new mischief here.

"I know," said Mildred. "I heard a loud crash in the night."

No injuries this time

"I will tend to the problem when I find it." She walked back slowly along the narrow path until she came to the rose bed. The roses were her favorites, standing majestically in the morning light. She knelt painfully in front of them, reached out a hand to touch a petal.

"How are my darlings this morning?"

We are well, mother.

She ran stiff fingers through the rich soil, loosening it at the base of each plant, and picked off some dead petals. "Some of you have dirty faces today," she said, then cupped a withered rose in both hands.

I grow old.

"I know, dear. We all grow old; it is natural. Try to live each day as best you can, and think only about today." She carefully released the aging flower, watched it droop over on its long stem.

I will try.

"Good," she said, arose slowly and shuffled along the path to continue her morning rounds. She pulled a rare weed here and there, and an occasional flower that had withered and died after a full life. She stopped before a large snapdragon ensnarled by a neighboring vine, and bent over to touch it.

He will not leave me alone. His intrusion is constant.

"Naughty vine," said Mildred, and gently unraveled fragile vine from the flowering stalk.

I seek only space in which to grow properly.

"Then I will give it to you." She found an abandoned pole nearby, pushed it into the ground and carefully wound the vine around its base three times. "Now climb towards the sky," she said, *and away from me*, she imagined the snapdragon saying.

She reached the center of the garden and the tool shed, where plants towered above her head. Huge flowers like mutant daisies gone wild peered down at her from thick stalks thrust up from round trunks the size of a large man's waist. Other stalks drooped below the flowers, ending in closed pods, fist-like, covered with soft green fur resembling fine moss. Exotic plants, from Africa, the advertisement had said. Trifulus nunculadus. She had grown them with loving care from bulbs received by mail order from a company that had soon disappeared. She had nursed them through infancy, and agonized through times when it seemed they might die. But now they stood tall, proud and fresh looking, hovering around her protectively like giant sons. She loved them all, and their response to her left little to the imagination. When she touched these plants, they moved.

She stepped up to the largest plant, put an arm around its trunk and rubbed the velvet-like tissue with her hand. The plant shuddered; pods moved slightly, then relaxed. She spoke to it softly. "You're such a big boy, now. I wonder how much more you will grow, how much food you will need."

The blood meal has helped much, little mother. I'm doing well, now, as are my brothers and sisters.

She touched a pod, felt it recoil and relax again as she petted it. There was a buzzing sensation in her head, and the giant plant seemed to be humming to her. "You must be an adult by now. Are you hiding babies in these pods?"

There was no answer, and the plant continued to hum.

She stroked the pod, and suddenly noticed the tool shed door ajar. She hurried over to the shed, opened the door and found chaos. Tools had been pulled off the walls and lay in a tangled heap in one corner. Food sacks had been ripped open, contents thrown in every direction to mingle together on the floor, and two bottles of liquid food had shattered against one wall, staining it in red and green.

The boy was here again last night. Something must be done about him.

"Why does he *do* things like this?" she cried out. "I have *never* done anything to hurt him." She began to pick up the tools, hanging them on the wall again and wincing with pain from the bending and stretching. "I *don't* want to talk to his parents about this. They really don't care about anything he does."

He must be punished. The thought seemed to come from every direction in the garden, but for the moment she dismissed it as a vengeful thought of her own, and did what she could to repair the damage. By evening the shed was clean again. She ate a bowl of soup and some crackers for dinner, and fell into bed exhausted. Her sleep was deep, and in the night she did not hear the crash of a picket fence splintering, or the deep, sucking sounds. Peaceful in a subconscious state of quiet dreams, she did not hear the screams.

* * * * * * *

Mildred Hanson opened her eyes, startled by a shout in her mind. *Mother, come quickly. We're hurt!* "Angela?" she called out, and then she was awake. Silly woman, she thought. Angela was a thousand miles away with her own husband and children. A dream, perhaps, but something was wrong and she had overslept. The sun was high in the sky. She pulled on a robe and wandered towards the kitchen, worried by the jumble of thoughts exploding in her mind. *Outside, some of us are dying. Mother, please, help us.* She opened the kitchen door, looked outside, and saw the roses.

"Oh, dear God—NO!"

She stumbled down the porch steps and along the dirt path to the rose plot, dropping to her knees in front of it and holding her face in her hands as the tears came. The rose bushes lay on their sides, pulled cleanly from the ground, blossoms wilting rapidly in the heat. Beyond, a section of the picket fence lay flat on the ground, splintered into pieces. And Mildred cried over her garden.

He came in the night, and we stuck him with our thorns, but he reached below the thorns and pulled us from the ground, and now we are dying.

"NO!" cried Mildred. She stood up too quickly, pain knifing through her knees, and hurried towards the tool shed. If she worked fast the roses would not die; she stumbled crazily along the dirt path, almost running, trying to suppress the terrible thoughts and feelings that suddenly surged upwards to her consciousness. *The boy has gone too far. He must be dealt with severely.* Her breathing was rapid, and then she was gasping for air and there was a tight feeling in her chest. *We must make a plan to trap him, and punish him ourselves.* She felt her knees sagging as she lurched ahead, seeing the shed surrounded by tall, flowering sentries.

If the roses die—the boy should be killed.

"Oh," she cried. There was suddenly a terrible pain in her chest and arms. She dropped to both knees before the door of the shed, clutching at her chest and closing her eyes as she sucked in deep breaths of air. "Lord, don't let me think like this," she panted. "It's evil to have such thoughts. Take them away from me. Please!"

You are ill? Do not hurry so much. There is time.

She leaned up against the shed door, breathing deeply, and forced herself to relax. The pain subsided, was gone, leaving only a dull ache in her chest. The dreadful thoughts were also gone. She grasped the edge of the door and pulled herself up, found tape, strings, watering can and a small shovel. The walk back to the rose bed was slow and deliberate. She filled the watering can with cool water, got down on her knees and began to work. Several roots were damaged. She bound them up with tape and string, dug new holes and reset the plants with gentle hands. The task consumed her; she thought of nothing but the work. She picked up a Peace rose bush lying forlornly on its side, half-opened buds beginning to wilt in the heat of the day. *I'm hurt badly*, she thought. *I don't think I can make flowers again.* "But you live," said Mildred, setting the plant carefully into its new home, "and that's the important thing."

When she finished her work, it was dusk. After putting her tools away, she urged her aching body slowly to the house, heated a can of soup as the sun disappeared, and ate slowly by the window overlooking her garden, wondering about the reasons behind the brutal acts of the boy, and what she could do to stop him. That night she went to sleep without any answers to her questions.

* * * * * * *

Jerry Davidson waited impatiently for the lights to go out in the little white house across the street from the bushes he was hiding in. The old lady was staying up late tonight. Perhaps she was watching the garden, trying to set a trap for him. Probably not. She wouldn't be expecting anything tonight—not three nights in a row. He would have to stop for a while; it was getting too dangerous. The business with the roses had even enraged his mother, and she'd questioned him suspiciously about it. He'd denied any involvement, of course, but he was certain she didn't believe him. The ladies in the neighborhood wouldn't speak to her anymore. That's what *really* made her angry, he thought. And his father thought all the fuss about the old woman and her flowers was just plain silly. A crazy lady who talked to flowers, and walked around with a perpetual smile on her face belonged in a rest home, he said.

His parents were out again, so he could take his time getting home. But he wished the lights would go out soon so he could get it over with. The trick would not work once she was asleep. He pulled the tic-tac from his pocket: thread spool notched at the ends, wound with string and a large nail for the axle. When she was nearly asleep, he would press the spool on her bedroom window and pull the string hard. The racket would be terrifying in the dead of night. If he did it right, she would probably mess her pants.

The lights went out.

Jerry waited for a moment, heart pounding with excitement, then looked up and down the street before leaving his hiding place. Thin and fragile looking, he was quite small for an eleven-year-old boy, but more than made up for it with courage and fighting ability. The other boys at school had found that out the hard way. How many of them would have the guts to do what he was about to do? But now it was time to move. He poised for the attack, flexing slender muscles in his arms and legs, then slid out of the bushes, padded cat-like across the street and flattened himself in the tangled mass of flowering shrubs and vines near the tool shed. He lay there for a while, listening to his pounding heart, wondering if the old woman was watching from the darkened windows of the house. A light breeze was blowing, and he thought it strange here were no rustling sounds from the garden—no movement of the plants. He began to pull himself forward slowly on his stomach.

He had crawled only a few feet when he realized his choice of route had been a poor one. The place was a tangled mess of prickly shrubs and sticky vines that pulled and tore at his every move. Every place he put his hands seemed to be covered with sharp thorns that stuck his flesh and sent waves of pain up his arms. Some kind of nettle struck him, and he felt a numbing sensation move across a shoulder blade and up towards his neck. To turn around now would take too much time. He pressed his lips tightly together, and moved straight towards the shed, towards the giant plants silhouetted like sentries with flower-heads and skinny, outstretched arms ending in huge pod-fists. The vines were sticking to him, now, winding around his legs and chest and pulling at him. His breathing came hard, and he fought off sudden fear in the darkness as the garden seemed to move around him, without sound, encircling him with thorny vines and rope-like tendrils pulling him flat on his stomach.

He crashed down on his chin, vines crawling on him, pulling his arms to his sides. He kicked with both feet, and found his legs suddenly bound together. He reached to free them and the vines around his body tightened in a crushing embrace, and then he was thrashing around on the ground, worm-like, bound tightly from head to foot and suppressing an urge to scream. Looking up towards the shed, he saw vines snaking out towards him, searching for him, moving together as if part of a single organism, and then the giant plants by the shed were turning, flowered heads shaking, reaching out invitingly with big pod-fists. He knew that they wanted him, and he opened his mouth to scream.

It was a silent scream.

Something velvety soft, sour tasting and smelling sweetly was suddenly crammed into his mouth, filling it tightly and held in place by a vine looped several times around his face and neck. He felt large tendrils loop under his armpits, and then he was being dragged across the ground, screaming silently and thrashing against his bonds like a wounded snake until he lay beneath the monstrous plants by the shed, his eyes wide and staring up as thick stalks bent over flowered heads close to his face. Out of the corners of his eyes he saw plant arms moving pods towards his body, and they were opening up into yawning maws lined with rows of thorns like shark's teeth and a horrible, putrid odor filled his nostrils, and something thick and wet was dripping on him. The vines binding him suddenly twisted, flipping him over on his stomach. There was a mind shattering pain as the pods bit into him again and again, and a gag of flowers muffled the sound as he screamed—and screamed—and screamed.

* * * * * *

The two policemen in the patrol car saw Jerry Davidson leap out of Mildred Hanson's garden and lurch crazily across the street to his darkened house. A report of the incident was filed that night. The next morning a detective visited the Davidson home, informing the parents their son had been seen coming from the garden and that although Mildred Hanson had said nothing, there were several complaints from her neighbors and the boy would be arrested and his parents severely fined if there was any further vandalism. The boy was interviewed, looking pale and frightened, and admitted his guilt to the detective. The parents were furious, and Jerry's father slapped him on his bottom and sent him to his room for the entire day. The boy screamed in agony when his father hit him. Must be feeling really guilty, thought his father. I didn't hit him that hard.

In his room, Jerry pulled down his pants and used half a roll of toilet paper to stop new bleeding from several places on his bottom where chunks of flesh had been torn away.

Mildred Hanson was working in her garden when she saw the patrol car pull away from the Davidson house. Perhaps the boy has finally been caught for his mischief, she thought. I doubt he's really a bad boy, and the roses are alive. There's even a new bud since yesterday! She touched the tiny blossom, and then went to the shed for hammer and nails to repair the picket fence. The big African plants stood tall, holding their faces up towards the sun. She stroked the largest one, imagining its humming at her touch. "My big son looks very proud this morning," she said.

The plant made a strange sound.

Mildred stepped back in surprise. "Well, excuse *you*," she giggled.

The big plant belched again.

By late afternoon the garden was restored to Mildred's satisfaction, and she began to plant new borders of flock and short marigolds. The most difficult task had been unraveling a twisted mass of thorny vines and parasitic plants normally considered intruders in a garden. But they were living things, and she allowed them a place of their own far from the delicate flowers. Overnight they had become a tangled mess, and she moved slowly to avoid breaking a fragile tendril. Her old hands were brushed by many thorns that moved aside without scratching her. She had never been struck by a thorn.

The garden was curiously silent. Perhaps she was tired, and her imagination was sleeping, but the plants were not talking to her, and she felt a twinge of loneliness. But when she passed the big Trifulus nunculadus with the digestion problem, she patted its trunk and it hummed to her, and then she was happy again.

She had just finished a flock border around a bed of white iris, and was struggling to stand when she sensed someone watching her. She looked up and saw the Davidson boy standing by the picket fence. Dark eyes looked back, then away from her.

"Hello, Jerry," she said, and walked somewhat unsteadily towards him. He did not answer.

"Did you want to talk about something?"

No answer, then a quick look over his shoulder. In his house across the street, a window curtain moved. As she drew near, Mildred saw his tear stained face, lips pressed tightly together, and breath coming in near sobs. She suddenly felt sorry for him, and smiled, but he didn't look at her at first, and spoke to a point on the ground near her feet.

"Do you need any help with the gardening?"

"That would be nice," she said, and then suddenly frowned.

What are you doing? He is a murderer.

"Do you know how to work with plants?"

"I do the yard work at home," he said softly.

"I need to move some dirt for a new plot, and it's hard for me. You look strong." She opened the little gate in the fence and saw a smile flicker on his face.

The thorn of a vine crawling along the fence stuck him on one hand as he entered the garden.

Got you. You're not wanted here.

Jerry winced, and sucked blood from a punctured finger. "I *am* strong," he said, and fought back tears. Walking away from him, Mildred didn't notice his wound, and he quickly followed her.

There were rustling sounds in the garden. Mildred stopped—listening, and felt something creep into her mind.

He's not coming in here. This is too much to ask.

But he's sorry for what he did. He comes to help.

I'll stick him if I get the chance.

Bad thought. Go away—please.

I'm getting hungry again. Bring him to me.

Mildred stumbled, but regained her balance.

Be careful, mother. We love you, but let us deal properly with the boy.

STOP IT!

Mildred stumbled again, backwards, one hand covering her face. Jerry rushed to catch her, held her upright, his heart pounding in his ears. He wanted desperately to run away, but Mildred leaned against him for support and her face was suddenly glistening with sweat. He moved her to a bench by a small forest of roses, and she sat down heavily, breathing deeply with her eyes closed. Jerry sat down with her, still holding on.

Now you've done it. Mother is hurt. Be quiet, all of you, or I'll uproot myself and pinch your blossoms off.

The garden was silent again.

"I'll be all right," said Mildred. "I just need to rest a while. There's a pile of black dirt back by the shed, and a wheelbarrow. The new plot is right behind us. Could you move the dirt there, and level it for me?"

"Sure," said Jerry. He got up quickly and moved along the narrow dirt path. He had never felt so guilty. His imagination was running wild: voices in his head, and out of the corner of his eye it seemed petal heads turned to watch him, sending out green, ropy vines to snare his feet.

Leave him alone.

He filled the wheelbarrow with dark earth, working steadily, and dumped it on the plot Mildred had shown him. He repeated the task seven more times, and then raked the mound of black earth until it was level and smooth. Mildred went into the house, and a little later Jerry saw her watching him from a window. She probably doesn't trust me, he thought. Why should she?

She's a nice person who cares about all living things.

The guilt was still there; he would work hard to make up for the damage he'd caused. He still didn't understand why he had done it, knew now that he had nothing against the woman *or* her garden. He *liked* flowers. They were pretty to look at. It was attention he wanted. His parents were always so busy with grownup friends, and his father was usually amused by his son's pranks. Not this time.

You are lonely?

Yes, I'm lonely, thought Jerry.

When the work was finished, Mildred called him into the house for milk and a plate heaped with cookies, which he ate greedily.

"It's nice to have someone here to eat my cookies," she said. "My grandchildren are so far away. I hardly ever see them."

"Why do you live alone?"

"I prefer it that way since my husband died, and I'm getting used to it. I have my house and books, and the garden. The plants are my company, and they give me something to care for. It's not a bad way to live, but sometimes I think the plants are talking to me. Isn't that silly?" She laughed.

Jerry didn't say anything. He didn't think it was silly.

"I talk talking to people," she said, "whenever I have visitors. Like you, now. But it isn't often, so I talk to my flowers, and it makes me feel good, like I have small children again."

"I hurt them," said Jerry, and he couldn't look at her.

"That's over and done with, now. You were a big help today, Jerry."

"I like doing it."

"Could you help me some more?"

"Sure."

"I could pay you a little something."

"Whatever," he said, and jumped a little when she put a hand on his shoulder.

"I start early in the morning," she said.

"I'll be here."

At breakfast the next morning, Mildred saw him waiting for her in the garden.

They worked together, digging and planting under a hot sun. For Jerry, the insanity in his mind came only when Mildred had gone in the house for rest from the heat.

Monster, why are you really here?

I told you to be quiet.

I'm hot and dry all over.

Jerry watered a bed of petunias.

First I'm thirsty, and now I'm drowning.

Quit complaining. He's learning.

Jerry walked past the largest Trifulus by the shed and jumped to one side when the big plant suddenly shuddered. He remembered the bud-fists opening up, descending on him, the horrible stench from the tooth-lined maw, and the pain.

No fear. She likes you, and we begin to understand. Come rub me, and I'll sing you an old song.

The thoughts continued throughout the day, becoming more pleasant towards dusk. Mildred sensed the changing tone. Perhaps she really had been angry with Jerry, and her mind was now purged of bad feelings. At dusk she asked if he would help her the rest of the summer, and he happily agreed to do that. He turned to leave, and she went into the house, then remembered a cake pan she had left in the shed, and went to retrieve it. Midway along the dirt path she suddenly stopped. Jerry was standing near the shed, rubbing his hand gently up and down the velvety trunk of a Trifulus, and smiling.

There was a loud humming sound in the garden.

THE COLOR OF PAIN

"I didn't request your presence on Alysia, Mister Skinner, and quite frankly I don't want you here. I don't need a diplomat. What I need from Portos is a good biochemist who can analyze the toxin the Worms are using against us, and develop countermeasures. Our people are *dying* out there, sir. We have a right to defend ourselves."

Commander Bern Plueger tossed the diplomatic pouch chip carelessly on his desk, and frowned. Cameron Skinner frowned right back at him, irritated by the man's attitude, the stifling heat, and the smell of rotting jungle vegetation that permeated the metal hut.

"You do not have the right to systematically destroy a sentient species for any reason, Commander. The law is clear, with precedents going back to cases on a dozen planets over three hundred years. If our presence is incompatible with the safety and survival of native, sentient species, then we must remove ourselves from the planet."

"Whoever told you the Worms are sentient is speculating," said Plueger. "It doesn't take a higher brain to build mud towers, but it seems that everywhere we can plant our crops the Worms have to build their structures. Without the crops, without the land, our people are back to the poverty they had on Portos, and I will not let that happen. If the Worms kill us, we will kill them until we are safe. It's that simple."

"Not until I establish a dialog with them, or become convinced they're not sentient."

"And in the meantime I'm responsible for your safety. I'd rather send you back to Portos on the next ship out."

"The Governor will respond by returning me more millions of miles with a detachment of troops to enforce the law, if that's what you want."

Plueger glared at him, tapped a stylus rapidly on the desk top, then, "I've seen people die from worm spray: men, women and children. You can't imagine the horror until you've seen it. I'm not letting you into the field without an environmental suit."

"Fair enough," said Cameron. "I'd like to get started in the morning."

"A volunteer will accompany you. She's waiting for you in your hut right now. Except for sleeping, you will never be out of her sight. Understood?"

"Yes, Commander."

"Good. I have other duties now, Mister Skinner. If you have to see me again, and I hope you will not, then make an appointment with my adjutant. A cart is waiting for you outside, and your baggage has been taken to your hut. You have only one week, sir. That's what your orders say. Not much time, unless you're only here to justify closing this settlement, but please try to stay alive."

Plueger waved a hand in dismissal, and turned back to his computer. "A linguist, of all things," he mumbled, and shook his head.

Cameron turned on his heel, puzzled, then left the stifling interior of the hut and squinted at orange sunlight outside. Sweat ran into his eyes, and his loose-fitting shirt was sopping in the armpits. The odor of the air was a combination of rotting garbage and sour body fluids.

The settlement consisted of three dozen polymer-sided huts shaped like half-cylinders cut lengthwise. They lined both sides of a soft dirt road running off in two directions into a jungle of tall, tubular-leafed conifers and an undergrowth of man-sized palm fronds and ferns. There were no bird or animal sounds from the jungle, only the grumble and whine of an electric generator surrounded by a short wall of cinder blocks topped with charging batteries.

An electric cart with an awning was waiting for him, driven by a twelve-year-old boy who called himself Dolan and complained about the recent absence of cooling rain.

The drive was short; at the edge of the settlement they stopped in front of a hut painted battleship grey. A woman stood in the doorway, expecting them. She had brown skin, black hair tied in a single long braid down her back, and she was dressed in white smock and pants. She extended a hand as Cameron approached the doorway, and he shook it.

She smiled nicely, showing snow white teeth. "I am Rabi Sen. Welcome to Alysia, Mister Skinner."

They went inside. There was a frame bed, table, chair, and a standing closet. The metal floor creaked when they walked on it. Sunlight came in through a single window, and a bare light tube hung from the ceiling.

"It's simple, but you'll only be sleeping here," said Rabi. "Most of your time will be spent in the field, or my laboratory, you see."

"Ah, you're a scientist."

"Yes. We've been studying the Worms for nearly a year, my colleague and I. I will introduce him to you. We've made progress, but I fear we're running out of time. The Worms have become dangerous. Many of our people will kill them on sight, if allowed to. You've been brought here to prevent that."

"The law is clear on the destruction of native, sentient species," said Cameron.

"Ah, but we don't know they are sentient, Mister Skinner. We have only the suspicion of it."

Cameron frowned. "The letter to the Governor's Office on Portos said specifically that the Worms are highly sentient, with a well developed social structure and communication skills, and they are responding to what they perceive as a threat against them. I'm here to open a dialog with them."

Rabi twisted her hands together, and looked straight into his eyes. "That will take time, Mister Skinner. Their social structure might be no greater than that of some insects, and we have only a few vague ideas about how they communicate. We'd hoped for a team of scientists to speed our work, but Portos has sent us a linguist instead."

Cameron's face flushed red. "I'm both a linguist and a diplomat, Ms. Sen, and I have served on ten planets. Believe me, I've communicated with species stranger than intelligent worms, and—"

"The letter to the Governor was mine," said Rabi, "and now you're here as a consequence of my distortion of the truth. I only wanted time to save the species from extinction, and move this settlement totally away from their habitat, but it seems they are everywhere, you see. Everywhere we must plant, The Worms must live."

"So the letter is a lie. Commander Plueger was correct. I'll contact Portos immediately, and have myself recalled before the shuttle leaves. I intend to press charges, Ms. Sen. You have wasted the time and resources of your government."

Rabi grasped his arm. "Please *listen* to me. Commander Plueger gave his approval of my letter. He shares our suspicions about the Worms. With you here as the Governor's representative, he can now openly enforce the law regarding sentient species. It is an unpopular law with the planters, and he's under terrible pressure to destroy all the Worms. He doesn't want to lose the settlement over an uprising. Surely you know the Governor feels our operation isn't cost effective. Portos would close us down over the slightest provocation.

Please! Your presence gives us time to prove sentience and find a communication channel. How much time have you been given here?"

"One week," said Cameron.

Rabi gasped, her suspicions about the regional Governor on Portos now confirmed.

* * * * * * *

The cart bounced hard in and out of a rut. Sitting in the back, Cameron hung on grimly to an awning strut. "How far out do we have to go?" he asked through clenched teeth.

Lael Dowd was driving, Rabi seated next to him. Chemist and Zoologist, the two of them had spent the morning showing him their laboratory, photographs of Worms, and a model of the structures he was about to see. The sun was high, the heat oppressive, but inside the refrigerated environmental suit Cameron felt comfortable so long as he remained seated. Walking was another matter. The suits were like a layer of extra flesh, but stiff at the joints. Sounds from outside were variably amplified, so controlled communication was by radio, and Lael spoke too loudly. He was a small man, short and wiry, and energetic. "Half a klick and we stop. It's another two hundred meters on foot to Wormtown, but the Worms can be anywhere, so keep your helmet locked and your gloves on. It would be bad form for us to lose you your first day out."

The road ended where they stopped. Lael activated the locator, sending out pulses at sixty kilocycles. "It's the law," he explained. "Security wants to know where every vehicle is, and why it's there. If we're not headed back in an hour, they'll come after us."

Even with micron-size filters, the jungle stench was palpable inside the suit. The trail was more a line of bent fronds and ferns overhung with cylindrical leaves the size of a man's body. At night the leaves unfurled like great sails to capture dew. The ground was soft with trampled vegetation, and made walking sluggish, so it seemed a long time before they climbed a shallow hillock and peered beneath a rotted, moss-covered log lying at the summit.

And Cameron beheld a city of the Worms.

At the base of the hill the jungle had been cleared away across a circular area a hundred meters in diameter. A shallow dome of glistening red earth rose several meters above level ground, and was topped with several chimneys large enough to swallow a man. The black maws of four tunnel entrances were visible, and Worms came and went, huge things the size of a large dog, bodies wrinkled and glistening in a flickering rainbow of primary colors that changed by the minute, now red, then green, yellow, blue. They moved more like caterpillars, though no legs were visible. Many were partially erect, holding vegetation in mouths shaped like parrot beaks as they went into the tunnels. A few moved over the dome more slowly, leaving behind a thick, glistening trail of transparent material.

"The vegetation is both food and building material for them," said Lael. "The structures are a composite of earth and a polymer they make in their bodies. They add a catalyst, that clear liquid you see going on now. Once set, it's hard as concrete and sealed against the weather. One hell of an insulator, too. I've run a lot of tests on the stuff."

"They're nearly finished," said Rabi, "and they only started this a few days ago. Worm towns go up fast, and can be abandoned overnight."

"So close to the settlement?" asked Cameron. "I thought they avoided humans."

"They did at first, but then there was a Worm attack on a little girl at an experimental farm. A group of planters retaliated and flamed a structure like the one you see here. Killed every Worm. Confrontations have escalated ever since, usually one person in tall grass or thick foliage. Commander Plueger has moved the settlement twice to avoid them, but now it seems like the Worms are following us. They started construction here only days after we arrived."

"And there are five other structures underway around our settlement. It sounds paranoid, but this time I think they're surrounding us," added Lael.

"You mean war?" asked Cameron.

"Any sentient species that is attacked and feels threatened will fight to survive, Mister Skinner," said Rabi.

"Perhaps, but look how slowly they move. If they're truly sentient, they'll get as far away from you as they can."

"If they let our settlement expand, the day might come when they can't get far away from us."

"Okay, then maybe they're building before you have a chance to plow up the ground for planting. They're establishing territorial rights."

Lael tapped him on the shoulder. "We can't live long in these suits. Filters clog fast, and we come out for air and food. All they have to do is move in close some night and fill the air with their neurotoxin. We'd all be dead in a minute, covered with our own mucus and vomit. I personally don't want to die that way."

Cameron watched the ponderous labor of the Worms, and was inclined to disbelieve what Lael and Rabi had said, but that inclination disappeared only half an hour later when they returned to their cart and found it covered with white powder, the locator still beeping merrily away.

"Oh, oh, look sharp," said Lael. He and Rabi crowded in on Cameron and pushed him away from the cart. "Don't touch anything. We've been sprayed."

Lael went to the cart, opened a panel, and took out a cylinder with an attached hose and nozzle. A spray from the nozzle turned to icy fog; he sprayed the entire cart, then his gloved hand. "Liquid air kills most of it. We'll wait a few minutes, and sunlight will do the rest."

Cameron's head swiveled as he looked for movement in the foliage, and sweat beaded his forehead.

"Don't worry, Mister Skinner," said Rabi. "This wasn't an attack, but a warning, and probably for your benefit. We've been coming out here since the Worms first started work. They know we're just watching them, but you're someone new."

"Are you trying to say they see us, and can distinguish between different humans? I didn't see any eyes on those things. Do you?"

"Oh they see all right. We just don't know how, yet," said Lael. "I have some ideas about it if you want to listen."

"Okay," said Cameron. "I'm listening."

They talked about it all the way back to the settlement.

Commander Plueger was waiting for them in front of Cameron's hut.

"Sorry, but you'll have to remain in quarters the next day or two. There's been another attack, northwest, Plot Eighteen. A young boy is dead. Planters flamed the Worm, and are looking for its nest. I've sent police, but it might be too late to stop them. Give me some answers, people, and quickly! Communicate, negotiate, whatever, but get me a ceasefire before the Worms are flamed to oblivion and the Governor of Portos uses it to close this one settlement where his poorer citizens can obtain free land for a new beginning in their miserable lives."

Plueger took the cart keys from Lael, and drove it away.

"He's angry, and scared," said Rabi.

And passionate, thought Cameron.

"Yeah, but he thinks we'll win in a war," said Lael.

Cameron thought it, too, but didn't say so.

* * * * * * *

"The colors are also important," said Lael. "There are two pits on the head, where eyes would give depth perception. I've found two kinds of cells layered on the sides and bottom of the pits. Neither respond to pure optical wavelengths, but I get output for the large ones in the near IR, and the teeny cells put out sharp pulses in the low UV range. My Squid measurements show axon conduction in the forward brain area between the pits."

"That's similar to our own sight, in some respects," added Rabi.

Cameron looked through the microscope, comparing cell samples on two slides. "So they do see us, then, and communicate through color patterns in their bodies. I could begin with a color generator to detect and return what they transmit. If they're as sentient as you believe, we should be able to build a vocabulary, and start communicating."

"I think it's not just the colors, but the patterns. You'll have to reproduce the patterns," said Rabi.

"Charge-coupled detectors will give us—"

"There's more to it, I think, maybe a lot more," interrupted Lael. "There's scent, and perhaps charge. That's your work, Rabi."

Rabi blushed. "Sorry, but it's so preliminary I wasn't going to mention it yet."

"Scientific caution is fine, but I need to hear *anything* that might help me communicate with these things," said Cameron.

Rabi looked at both of them, then brightened. "All right, but we don't have synthetic models for any of this yet. Just behind the sight pits there are porous regions with multilayered membranes that become conductive in varying degrees when exposed to things such as ketones and esters. I think they're scent detectors. Lael has isolated seven different proteins from the membranes so far."

"If I can find the right substrate," said Lael, "I can incorporate these proteins and synthesize an odor detector, but I've just started work on it. There are good models using carbon atoms in polymer layers. Carbon absorbs an odor molecule, swells, and changes membrane conductivity".

"They might even detect sound, or electric fields," said Rabi. "There are two different kinds of fine hairs on their backs, but we haven't been able to—"

"Look, this is all interesting, but preliminary. I can see why you wanted a team of biochemists, but you got me instead, and I have one week, and that's not even time enough to get approval for an extension. Do whatever experiments you want, but first get me a color communicator I can use while suited. If the Worms know we're trying to talk they might not be so hostile. We have to start there."

"I can cobble that together in a couple of days," said Lael. "Then what?"

"Then I walk up to the Worms, and say hello," said Cameron.

Lael and Rabi looked at him with wide eyes, surprised.

* * * * * * *

The whole thing weighed fifteen pounds, camera and screen strapped across his chest, the powerpac on his lower back. The halogen lamp was hand held, with a color filter wheel in red, green, yellow and blue.

Rabi and Lael smiled at him through their faceplates, amused by his appearance. "You look like a large copy of a child's space toy," said Lael.

"It doesn't have to be pretty if it works," said Cameron. "Watch my back. I'll have all I can do to see what's going on in front of me."

They were nearing the top of the hillock overlooking Wormtown, and all three were still shaken by the morning's confrontation.

They'd left Cameron's hut at dawn and found a group of sullen planters surrounding their cart. Some were armed with Shredders, the smooth-bore weapons that could clear a thousand cubic yards of underbrush with a single shot. The group had parted silently, allowing them to load their gear and climb in, but then a large, swarthy man, stinking of old sweat, had stepped in front of them, hands on hips, and scowled menacingly at them.

"You the ones studyin' the Worms?"

"Yes," said Cameron. "Portos has sent me to talk with them, and stop the trouble you've been having."

"You wanna stop the trouble, just help us kill 'em all," growled the big man.

"Can't do that, Earl," said Lael. "It's the law. You kill more Worms and we'll have Portos troops here. You want that?"

There was grumbling in the group, then curses as Earl said, "Didn't see troops here after the buggers killed my only son."

"What you gonna do? Send us back to Portos to beg in the streets?" asked another man.

For a moment Cameron had thought the planters might tip their cart over, but the rocking ceased when Plueger pulled up and got out of his vehicle with the biggest nightstick Cameron had ever seen. Plueger punched Earl hard in the gut with it, ordered the planters to disperse, and they did. Then Plueger turned to the three of them huddled in the cart, and said, "Now get out of here," and they did.

That was the start of the day. "Good luck," said Lael. He and Rabi sat down on the rotted log at the top of the hillock. Their helmets were closed up and locked. Below them, Wormtown was active and glistening with a new layer of weather sealant put down by its workers. Cameron counted twenty Worms out, moving slowly over the domed surface as if polishing it. He plunged down the hillock as slowly as he could, but kept slipping in the thick carpet of soft vegetation. Near the bottom he sat down hard on his rump. A nearby Worm jerked half its body upright, and seemed to look at him. It opened its mouth to display a circular array of small, sharply pointed teeth, and let out a soft hiss like an exhalation of breath. Its long body suddenly rippled in a color band pattern in red and green.

Cameron froze, then turned on the camera and played back the color pattern on his chest screen. There was no immediate reaction from the Worm, except to close its mouth. The other Worms paid no attention to Cameron, and went about their business, but this one closest to him kept its upper body erect for nearly a minute, flashing ripples of color, turning its head this way and that, perhaps looking for movement. Finally it went back to work, resuming its slow crawl across the red earth, and leaving a glistening trail behind it.

Cameron's heart thumped hard; he'd forgotten to take a breath. "Well, they know I'm here," he said softly, but there was no answer. He got down on all fours and crawled slowly out onto the dome of Wormtown, pressing down with his hands to test the surface ahead of him. "Hard as rock," he said. "When I press down, the whole surface springs back a bit, like I'm crawling on a thin slab."

"The dome might be hollow. We've never been inside," said Lael.

"Well, that tunnel entrance looks large enough to accommodate me. Let's see how far I can get." Cameron waited for a Worm to pass, and then crawled towards the dark opening twenty yards ahead in a bulge by one of the chimneys. Other Worms came near, but only one lifted its body, writhing a bit, then holding steady as Cameron played back its own color pattern. "When I show them their color pattern, they seem to accept me, but they're checking something else, too, and it might be motion."

Cameron waved an arm. The Worm ignored it, and went back to its work. "It could be checking scents, or electric fields. Whatever it is, the Worms don't seem concerned," said Lael.

Near the tunnel opening he leaned against a chimney base and listened. "Vibrations here, and a moan. There's air going in or out of the chimney, a lot of it. And I can see some grit blowing out of this tunnel up here. There's a positive pressure in this thing."

"I really don't think you should go in there," said Rabi.

Cameron kept crawling. Two Worms came out of the tunnel and stopped, raising their bodies like Cobras preparing to strike. One faced the tunnel, and its body was suddenly a shivering pattern in violet and red. The other faced Cameron, its body deep crimson. The camera recorded both patterns, and returned them to the Worms. Suddenly there was confusion, Worms moving past him at surprising speed and crowding up together by the tunnel entrance.

"Pull back!" cried Lael. "They're attacking you!"

Cameron looked around. Several Worms had drawn nearer, raising their bodies, but now held their positions. Five Worms were at the tunnel entrance, heads swiveling, clearly watching each others' color patterns, but seeming confused. Cameron slowed, then stopped. The patterns changed, the violet in them fading, then gone, but the red pulsing faster and faster.

"Back away; there's nothing behind you," said Lael.

"No. I'm waiting here until they commit to something. Will this suit hold if they all spray me at once at this range?"

"A good question. We should test it sometime, but not now."

Cameron kneeled, hands on legs, and the screen on his chest displayed a dancing pattern in red and some green. "I'd think they would have done it by now. It's like they're waiting for instructions. I'm staying here."

Lael groaned. "Too late anyway. More Worms just moved in behind you. If they start spraying, just get up and run."

"Right," said Cameron. It was getting warm in the suit, and he breathed deeply to still his heart. He heard a sound, like the snapping of small twigs. The Worm facing the tunnel entrance suddenly turned and flashed a pattern in green and red. Other Worms drew back from him, and those at the tunnel entrance went inside, their bodies pulsing green.

Cameron hesitated. "Worms still behind you. They just backed off a bit," said Lael.

"I think they want me to go inside." Cameron moved closer to the entrance, looked back. The Worms stayed where they were.

Rabi and Lael disagreed, and started to argue with him. Cameron crawled up to the tunnel entrance, looked inside. Wide enough to fit into, dimly lit, it forked into two smaller tunnels descending left and right. "I'm going in," he said. When Rabi and Lael yelled at him together, he tapped his helmet pad and shut off the radio. "Just doing my job, people," he said to himself.

Blessed silence. He crawled into the tunnel several feet, a kind of foyer four times his girth and a yard high, but the two branching tunnels were barely large enough for him to fit into. He peered into both of them, saw only blackness, lay still for a moment and listened.

The sudden sound of twigs snapping startled him. It came from his right. He turned on his side, looked down the tunnel there and saw a pulsing, green glow. The screen on his chest returned it. The glow changed to blue, then red, then lobes of primary colors strobing hypnotically.

Something rattled. The glows disappeared. The tunnel was dark again.

"Okay, my turn." Cameron held out his lamp, dialed a blue filter, turned it on a second, then off a second, then on. Repeated the sequence in green, then red. Waited long seconds.

A bright spot of green appeared below him: on for a second, then off, repeated three times, and there was a sound like sandpaper rubbed on soft wood.

Cameron could barely control his excitement, and his mind whirled. *What now? Anything to show I'm trying to communicate.*

He switched the filter to green, sent a long series of flashes of equal length, then two quick flashes. What came back to him were two quick flashes followed by a pulsing blue glow so bright it illuminated the tunnel. Cameron squinted, and saw something move down there as clicking sounds came back to him. There was a thick, musky odor in his suit, and he wondered if it was his own nervous sweat or from outside. He answered with two long pulses with the blue filter, frustration building.

"Okay, we know we're trying to communicate, but what are we saying?" The sound of his voice was flat in the suit. He reached up to the helmet pad to turn on the radio, and—

There was a loud explosion—from outside the tunnel. A sharp rattling noise came with darkness, and scratching on earth below him. The walls seemed to close in; he pushed himself backwards, and nearly dropped the hand lamp into the tunnel. Something rubbery and rough crawled across the back of his legs as he came out into daylight. Around him was chaos, Worms flattened out and crawled like snakes with amazing speed, their bodies flashing ribbons of red and violet.

Another explosion, very close. Cameron stood up; saw a man coming towards him across the glistening dome. He carried a Shredder, reloading the double breech with new shells. He stomped a booted foot on an already dying Worm. The animal flashed deep purple as dark fluid ejected from its mouth. It was the man who'd accosted Cameron back at the settlement. He snapped his weapon closed and shot another Worm at point blank range, splattering it and red earth for yards around.

"Stop it!" screamed Cameron, but knew his voice was totally muffled by the suit. He waved his arms and charged at the man, horrified to see the gun raised until he was looking down two large bores and the man was grinning crazily at him.

The world was suddenly white as snow, as if a sheet had been pulled over his head. He stumbled on something and fell flat. Worms slithered away from him in every direction, and a heavy form crashed to the ground only feet away. Arms flailed the air, heavy boots beating a tattoo on the earth. The man's face was purple, and his mouth foamed. In seconds he was dead, eyes bulging.

The white cloud dissipated rapidly. The Worms were gone, except for the smashed bodies of three. Two suited figures rushed up to him, grabbed him under the arms and hauled him to his feet. Lael slapped the side of his helmet hard.

"Why did you turn off your radio? WHY?"

They dragged him off of Wormtown and back to the cart, only to find that the battery had been ripped from it and thrown away. Lael called Plueger, and told him what had happened. A cart was sent for them, and four troopers left behind to patrol the road near Wormtown.

Word about what had happened got around fast. By the time they returned to the settlement, a crowd of angry planters was already milling around in front of Plueger's hut.

* * * * * * *

The four of them sat around a table in Plueger's office, sipping tea while waiting for their evening meal to arrive.

"I have to go back tonight. There's no more time. That mob out there can't be controlled forever."

"What can you do in one night? We need weeks, not hours," said Lael glumly.

"Why can't I get you to believe I'd established the basis for communication when that gunman showed up?"

"So the Worms are good mimics," said Plueger. "That isn't communication."

"I don't think it was a Worm. It was black and quick, made rattling and scratching sounds. It didn't just mimic what I did; it changed color and flash sequences. We had no vocabulary to work with, but I'm convinced the Worm, or whatever it was, knew I was trying to talk. I think I already understand some things: green is safe communication, maybe also blue, red is caution, violet is fear, and purple is the color of pain. I saw it all in the Worms today. I can use this, but it has to be tonight before the planters get a chance to attack Wormtown."

Cameron looked directly at Plueger, and said, "If you allow them to do that, I'll immediately recommend to the Governor that this settlement be closed and moved off Alysia."

"I'm not surprised to hear you say that," said Plueger.

"The planters are poor people," said Rabi. "They came here for land."

"They'll fight," said Lael.

"That's not my problem."

"No, it's *my* problem," said Plueger. "For a diplomat, Mister Skinner, you're a bit quick to use threats."

Cameron blushed. "Maybe that's because I came very close to being killed by one of your own people today."

"We're talking about three hundred and fifty good people here, not one man. I have twenty men on the road outside of Wormtown, another twenty patrolling the road and a dozen more here in town. The planters are not going anywhere I don't want them to. You'll have to find another excuse to close us down."

Cameron bristled. "Why do you keep saying that? I'm here to communicate with the Worms. If you have problems with the Governor, I haven't heard about them, but if he wanted this settlement closed down I *would* know it. So help me here. I have three days left. What's the problem with taking me back to Wormtown tonight?"

"If the planters see you leave, they'll want to follow you. Word is you'll defend the Worms even when they kill people, and I don't need a riot right now."

"They don't have to see us leave," said Cameron, and then he told them how it could be done.

* * * * * * *

Just after midnight, twenty troopers finished their tour on road patrol and went back to their barracks. Twenty replaced them, and left the settlement crammed into four carts a few minutes later. By that time most of the protesting planters had either become tired enough or drunk enough to go home to bed. The men and two women left in the road paid little attention to the rotating guard unit.

There would be a news update in a few minutes, and so they crowded in front of Commander Plueger's hut to hear it.

Cameron, Rabi and Lael were bundled up in military fatigues over body armor and sealed helmets. They traveled in separate carts. At the end of the road they changed into environmental suits and hooked Cameron up to his equipment. He carried two hand lamps, one with the color wheel to which he'd added violet and purple. A smaller wheel went on his helmet, Lael's newest toy, a circle of twenty chips of carbon impregnated polymer for sensing odorous molecules, and operated by microwave. Rabi added a microphone with its own transmitter. With screen and camera he was now carrying ten extra pounds. He used it as an excuse when a trooper offered him a hand weapon, and he turned it down.

When the helmets were sealed, Lael batted him lightly alongside the head. "If you turn off that radio again, I will personally come out there and turn it on for you."

"Keep the talk to a minimum, then. Sound is another variable I don't need when I'm trying to communicate with these things, and the microphone should pick up only the sounds *they* make."

Under the trees and heavy foliage it was pitch black, but the sky was filled with stars providing light enough to see movement and general shapes in the clearings. Cameron's lamp shot a diverging beam that softly illuminated the trail ahead. The two hundred yards to Wormtown seemed like two miles. Behind him the feet of Lael, Rabi and two troopers made squishing sounds in the decaying vegetation.

They went straight to the log on the hillock summit overlooking Wormtown. No movement was obvious. Cameron dared to use his lamp, casting a soft glow over the dome, the chimneys, and the black maws of tunnel entrances. Not a single Worm was out; there was no sign of life. The bodies of dead Worms had been removed.

A sudden sound broke the usual silence of the Alysian night. It was like sticks rattling together, and came from the jungle behind them. "Did you hear that?" asked Lael.

"Yes. Come down with me, and stay by the edge of the dome. I want them to see we're together."

They half walked, half slid down the embankment. Cameron turned on his color hand lamp, dialed it to green and began flashing pulses towards the tunnel entrance he'd penetrated that day. Scattered light dimly illuminated the dome in front of him. He walked out a few steps and knelt there. The green light strobed for several minutes, but no Worms appeared.

"They're afraid of us," ventured Lael, "but I'm still hearing clicking sounds from the trees, and not just in one place. It's getting louder."

"Hold still," said Cameron. Whatever had communicated with him inside the tunnel was now outside in the darkness, and he was pretty sure it was *not* a Worm. He risked a test of his color theory, and dialed his lamp to violet for several pulses, then back to green.

The response was immediate. Rattling sounds came from the tunnel entrance, and a soft, flickering glow in green. Two Worms came out of the tunnel and posted themselves on either side of the entrance, bodies erect, pulsing a wave pattern in red and green. The glow behind them was brighter, and a shadow moved, became a silhouette heaving up to the entrance.

"Cameron," said Lael softly, "something big just filled up that tunnel entrance, and there's movement in the trees behind us."

"Stay put, Lael. Now would be a good time to start checking for odors too. Rabi, turn up the gain for sound. All this clicking and rattling is important. I'm hearing it from every direction, now. Are you getting it?"

"Yes," said Rabi, quite calmly, "and the movement isn't just behind us. It's all around the edge of Wormtown."

Cameron crawled forward several yards, flashed a long series of violet pulses, and then went back to green. The response was more clicks in broken sequence, and two bright glows appeared like lamps in the tunnel entrance. Two Worms crawled down to him as he held his breath, coming within a yard, then turning, crawling, hesitating, as if beckoning him to follow. Cameron got up on his haunches and started to follow them.

"Cameron. All around us," said Lael. "I think we should pull back."

Trees moved around the edge of Wormtown as black shapes pressed forward, a circle of humped shapes waving thick appendages that clacked and rattled as they came. Cameron dialed his lamp to violet and kept it there, but continued to move forward, and remembered to take a breath.

A huge, black creature filled the tunnel entrance. Multifaceted eyes glowed brilliant green from a wedge-shaped face below a highly domed head. It squatted in the entrance, resting its face on thick appendages ending in claw-like hands with four fingers which even now rubbed lightly together to produce a soft clacking sound. The odor was sudden, penetrating Cameron's suit, thick, musky, and strangely comforting.

"Get this odor," whispered Cameron.

"Getting it," said Lael. "We can even smell it over here."

"Odor, sound, color, all used together. We'll never figure this out. Cameron, they've come out onto the dome and stopped there. They look like huge beetles, but their bodies are soft. They jiggle when they move," said Rabi. "Nearly a year on Alysia, and we've never seen these creatures."

Cameron didn't answer, switched his lamp to green and put it on the ground in front of him. He held out his arms, palms up, in what he hoped was a universal gesture of friendliness.

The creature in front of him did not move or make a sound.

Now what? Behind him there were scratching sounds, something hard scraping on polymer impregnated earth.

"They're moving up behind you, Cameron. There must be two dozen of them. No, now they've stopped again. For God's sake, put the guns down! One shot, and we're finished here."

Cameron had almost forgotten about the two troopers who had come with them. He reached down and dialed in a violet filter, then rapidly flashed the lamp while looking into the eyes of the creature in front of him.

There was a barrage of clicks and rattles, and the creature's eyes were alive with a pulsing pattern in green, violet and red, each facet acting like a huge pixel, it seemed. In soft, reflected light, Cameron suddenly realized the creature was not so much insect-like as it was amphibian. Beneath the eyes, two other orifices opened and closed, and there was a wide mouth with no lips. It raised one appendage and spread four long fingers apart.

"Worms coming from your left, a line of them coming out of another tunnel. They're carrying something," said Lael, then, "Here comes another black beast, Cameron, at the end of the line. God, it moves like a crab! It has something in its mouth, a white thing. Don't move! Rabi's getting all this on disk."

Cameron let out a long exhalation of breath, leaned over and dialed his hand lamp back to green. Trust was a risk he had to take. His body responded by oozing sweat from every pore.

A large Worm arrived, body erect, a glistening teardrop-shaped sack in its mouth. It laid the sack within Cameron's reach and moved away. The sack was white, but transparent. Something was inside it. When Cameron leaned over to look closely, it moved.

Cameron jerked upright in surprise. His host flashed red, and then green again, extended an appendage. A long finger nudged the sack closer to Cameron, and closer again. He dared to pick it up, and held his breath. Even through gloved hands he could feel new life move in the sack, and his face flushed again.

"It's a larva of some kind. Lael, it looks like a small Worm!"

"Oh, my," said Rabi. "This changes everything."

"So the Worms are their young," said Cameron, "but how—"

He put the sack back down on the ground. A Worm moved up beside it, only two feet from Cameron's face, raised its upper body and hissed softly. He leaned back just in time to see something large approaching from his right. He turned and stared into the face of another black creature coming towards him fast. It moved on four legs ending in long, four-toed feet, its appendages helping to support a heavy, glistening sack in its mouth. Its eyes glowed red, then green as it approached, laid the sack within his reach and nudged it forward with both appendages.

Cameron again dared to pick it up. It was heavy, perhaps twenty pounds. The thing inside it lay still, but was black, and he could see two large, multifaceted eyes.

"A cocoon, right?" said Rabi.

"Seems so. After metamorphosis they must be night creatures."

"Sunlight might be vital in the Worm stage," said Lael. "That's why we—"

"This is not solving our problem," said Cameron. "I have to somehow show them what our conflict is all about, and all I can use is—"

He had a sudden idea, put the sack down and again held out his arms, palms up. The beast in front of him responded with a faint rattle made with the fingers on its right appendage.

Cameron held up his lamp, flashing green, and slowly pointed to the larval sack, the cocoon, and the beast in front of him. But when he came to the Worm he pointed to it, then himself, and slowly dialed in first red, then violet, then purple into the beam of his lamp.

The only initial response was a soft glow in red, then violet, then purple from the eyes of his host. There was a pause of several seconds as its eyes slowly returned to green, and then it suddenly moved. Fingers rattled together on both appendages, and its eyes pulsed in a myriad of colors to form patterns from red to purple. The other black beast picked up the cocoon in its mouth and backed away. The Worms all left, including the two who had remained like sentries at the tunnel entrance.

"What happened?" asked Lael. "The Worms have all left, but the big creatures have moved up closer to you. There are a lot of color patterns being signaled back and forth."

"I was trying to show it we're afraid of the Worms, and they're dangerous to us. It seemed to—"

"Hold on. Another adult just came out of the ground to your right. I don't even see a tunnel entrance there! It has a small Worm with it. Coming right at you!"

The beast was only feet away when Cameron turned and saw it. The Worm with it was small, a three-footer, but held its upper body proudly erect. It slithered up to the creature filling the tunnel entrance, and was touched gently by a four-fingered hand. Its body glowed green, with a hint of red. The hand caressed it, reached out, touched Cameron's gloved hand, touched the Worm, and nudged it forward.

Oh God, it wants me to touch it! Cameron felt a flush of heat on his face. All his sweating was making the air foul in the suit. He reached out one hand slowly. The Worm didn't flinch, but opened its mouth to show a circle of sharp teeth. Long fingers nudged it forward again. Cameron touched it; it leaned down as if to sniff the glove, flashed a soft red glow and crawled over his palm. He closed his hand slightly, felt a cylinder of firm muscle there, and released it.

"I think we've just shaken hands."

"With a Worm?" said Lael.

"Through a Worm. It's as if—"

Something tapped the top of his helmet. He looked up. The beast's hand was right there, four long, hard fingers with eight knuckles. They tapped on his faceplate, reached down to the seal at his throat, tugged gently upwards.

"Uh, oh. It wants me to take off my helmet."

The Worm's body left his open hand, remained within close reach, glowing green.

"No," said Rabi. "That's moving too fast. Another time."

"One spray from that Worm, and you're dead, Cameron. We don't need that kind of trouble with the Governor's Office," added Lael.

"It's my choice. My job. I don't think there will be another chance if I don't do it now. Got that on record?"

"Yes," said Rabi softly.

"No more talk. I'm shutting off the radio until my helmet is back on. I don't want your voices frightening them." Cameron didn't wait for a reply, reached up and tapped the radio off on his helmet pad. The beast's hand was there, too, a finger of loosely connected bones rattling when he touched it.

The hand withdrew. Multifaceted eyes glowed green, though now there were touches of red, even violet in them. Cameron reached to his throat, then the back of his neck, and levered open the seal of the helmet. He felt a rush of cool air, the odor of musk and something sharper.

Even as he lifted the helmet from his head, he noticed that the Worm had begun flashing red, then violet in bright pulses. It cringed backwards from him.

The helmet was off, and he was assailed by odors, sharp and pungent. Rattling of finger bones was all around him, but it was the Worm that held his attention.

The Worm tried to back into the tunnel, but was blocked. A big hand curled gently around it, but would not let it escape. The Worm opened its mouth, and gasped for breath. It began to writhe, glowing violet, then purple. It struggled against the fingers holding it, and finally bit one of them, dark fluid oozing from the wound. A low moan escaped from the beast holding it.

Cameron was momentarily frozen by the rush of odors, sights and sounds. It was seconds before his higher brain kicked in, motivated by a single piece of logic.

The Worm is suffering. If I don't get my helmet back on, I will be sprayed, and I will die.

Cameron slammed his helmet back on, and scrabbled with his hands to lever the seal shut. The Worm glowed purple, writhing and prostrate the entire length of its body, but within seconds something remarkable happened. Its color changed to violet. The writhing ceased and it lay still for a minute or so, mouth opening and closing while a long finger stroked its body. Glowing eyes of the elder who comforted it matched the colors of the young one.

Cameron suddenly felt very badly—and he understood. With his hands he made a motion to remove his helmet, then pointed to the Worm, reached down and dialed a purple filter into his hand lamp. Made a motion of putting his helmet back on, and dialed green.

His host responded by repeating the colors with its eyes. There was a soft rattle of knucklebones. The Worm lifted its head, and hissed. Its body glowed red, and did not return to green while Cameron was there.

Cameron wondered what the color of sorrow was.

He needed a gesture, and could think of only one. He reached out with a gloved hand, palm up, and held it there. The eyes of his host remained green, but dimmed as it raised an appendage and spread its four fingers wide. When it closed its hand, the long fingers grasped Cameron's hand and half his forearm. Cameron squeezed gently, and was released. The creature rattled twice, turned and went back into the tunnel, showing him multi-jointed, muscular legs beneath a sloping back. The Worm followed, glowing red, and in a second the tunnel was black again.

Cameron turned around; saw Lael, Rabi and the two troopers sitting only feet away from him. A semicircle of dark shapes was behind them, with eyes glowing red. A few changed to green as he sat there with his strobing lamp, but then Lael pointed to the control patch on his helmet. Cameron understood, slapped at the control switches on his helmet.

"On again. Did you see all that?"

"Most of it," said Lael. "We were afraid to get much closer. You okay?"

"Fine. I'm alive, and so is the Worm."

"I don't understand why it didn't spray you if it was in real pain," said Rabi.

"My guess is it was ordered not to. I wonder if any human would put their child through such agony just to demonstrate a problem to an ignorant alien. It's some kind of allergic reaction to our odor, the chemicals in our skin, maybe even our breath."

"I can see a lifetime of work coming up on this," said Lael. "In the meantime we'll have to cover up, even in the fields. The planters aren't going to like that."

Cameron stood up. The semicircle of black creatures backed away, opening a lane for them to exit Wormtown. "It's a start. I'll try to get you some help from Portos. We certainly have proof of intelligent life here, and a species never seen before. I bet I can generate some commercial interest in this polymer that hardens the surface of their structures."

The troopers led them back up the hillock to the trail through the jungle. Cameron turned off his lamp at the edge of the earthen works. Suddenly, he was not in such a hurry to leave. His report would go out in the morning, and within two days there would be new orders for him. He would have good arguments for a long extension. As a diplomat, his mission was just beginning, and that was good. As a linguist, he had barely begun communication with this new species, and that was even better.

He wanted to explain to these new beings the fears of the planters, the deadly rage of a father who had lost a son, the rage of others who'd lost loved ones. He wanted to express the sorrow he felt at the agony experienced by another's child in order to solve a human problem.

He wondered if the soft-bodied, beetle-like creatures still watching him from below would understand if he pointed to his heart and flashed a purple beam of light at them with his lamp.

If purple is the color of pain and sorrow, perhaps green is the color of peace, he thought.

The others plunged ahead down the jungle trail. Cameron paused one moment to send a series of green pulses towards the rattling crowd below the hillock. His heart lifted with the chorus of green flashes they returned to him.

REINVENTING CARL HOBBS

The limo swerved left out of the traffic pattern at level four and descended rapidly. Melody didn't react to the sudden move, but Tom Lesko gasped and clutched at his stomach. Twenty hours on high alert was beginning to tell on him, she thought.

"You're not going to get sick on me, are you?" Melody uncrossed her long legs and pushed herself deeper into the cushioned seat, but in the confinement of armrests and a protruding wet bar their knees were almost touching.

"Not funny," said Tom. "I'm paid to take death-threats seriously, even if you don't."

"That's why I have Carl, and he can do the worrying without getting an ulcer over it. Relax, Tom; try to have some fun tonight."

"You have the fun. I'll watch The Property," said Tom, and frowned at something he was hearing from the tiny receiver in his ear.

Melody laughed. "That's me. The Property. Global couldn't survive a week without me."

"That's more true than you realize," said Tom. "Bring up your glamorous self, now. We're coming in. There's one aisle through the crowd. Take Carl's left arm, and my right. No autographs. We're going straight inside."

"Yes, sir," she said, giving a mock salute that drew the hint of a smile from him. "I hear and obey, sir."

"That'll be the day I relax," said Tom.

The limo swerved again, and slowed. Through tinted polymer, Melody could barely see the theater below, and the crowd of expectant fans packed at the entrance. Laser beams scribed pulsating patterns on the surrounding towers of steel and glass, and 'Ariel's Vision' was lit up in meter-high letters on the theater's marquee. All the opening-night ceremonies she'd attended, and it was still a thrill for her. For the moment it was easy for her to forget that among her countless fans out there, one did not wish her well tonight, or any other night. One wished only to share in the experience of her death.

They descended straight down, outside the traffic patterns of levels three and two. Laser beams found them and played over the descending car. A sea of faces looked up, sprouting a forest of waving arms.

"Ariel's theme kicks in the second you get out of the car. Try to look like you're in love," said Tom.

Ariel's theme, from the love scene with Ariel and Nathan, their flawless white bodies entwined on a beach of black sand. Melody had gone deeply into her artistic soul to find the love, the agonizing want and passion for the scene, the synaptic multiplexer in her skull behind her left ear processing the data for narrow band transmission to the recorder for later multiplexing with the music on the sound track. Low to high frequency, passion to fear, the subliminal modulations were received by the viewing audience, inducing in them the same feelings and emotions experienced by the artist during her performance.

Melody Lane was a strikingly beautiful woman, but it was not beauty that made her the number one Holostar of Global Studios. It was the depth and intensity of her soul.

The limo touched down with a bump. Even in her sealed compartment, Melody could hear the screams outside. She thought of her lover, a faceless man in dreams. She sighed, and reached for the door.

"Wait for Carl," said Tom. "Let him take your hand."

Melody started to pull back her hand, but then the limo door was opened from outside. The sudden noise was deafening, and she squinted in the light. A black-gloved hand reached for her; she took it gently, and exited the limo. Carl Hobbs stood tall beside her, his plastic face shining brightly in the lights, dark glasses masking the stare of his huge eyes. He smelled like warm polymer and cutting oil, and his arm was hard as stone when she grasped it.

Tom Lesko exited right behind her, and Melody hugged his arm, smiling serenely as the sound of Ariel's theme burst forth from speakers above the entrance to the theater.

People screamed, and wept. Bodies strained against thick ropes bordering the red carpet leading into the theater. Police stationed along the way pushed them back. Carl moved quickly, pulling Melody and Tom into a near trot. Misha and Andrus, her human bodyguards, were right behind them, were never more than a few feet away when Melody was in public. Dressed in tuxedos, they still looked like thugs.

Hands reached out to her. She smiled back, but couldn't see faces in the bright lights. Ahead of her there was a scuffle. Someone had broken through the rope barrier, a young man in baggy pants and a loose-fitting woolen shirt. A policeman grabbed for him, but missed. The man sprinted towards her, holding out something sparkling with colors in his hand. His eyes seemed glazed, and his mouth hung open in a crazy grin.

"Carl," said Melody Lane.

Carl's right hand shot out like a piston and hit the man in the throat. The man fell heavily at Melody's feet, gurgling. The thing in his hand bounced once and came to rest. It was an artist's paperweight, filled with swirling colors.

Misha and Andrus hauled him roughly to his feet. The man coughed hard, his face tinted blue. He looked at Melody with the saddest eyes she'd ever seen, and pointed at the colorful glass at her feet. "I just wanted to give you a gift," he croaked, "but they won't let anyone get near you."

Tom leaned over and picked up the paperweight as police pulled the man to one side. He caught the man's eye and gestured to show the gift was received.

Carl pulled them ahead again, but Tom pulled back.

"God *damn* it, Carl, slow down! Do you realize what a mess you've just made?"

"He was protecting me, Tom."

"By striking an over-zealous fan in the throat? You've violated a fundamental principle, Carl, and you're supposed to be better than that. I want you in my office for assessment tomorrow morning."

Carl was mute. They entered the theater: plush red carpet, a crystal chandelier hanging from a high dome ceiling, a wide staircase leading up to balcony level. People rushed towards them: producers, directors and a few of Melody's peers. Melody felt a shiver pass through Carl's arm. She looked up at him, saw his mouth opening and closing without sound. His entire body began to shake.

"Oh, no," said Melody.

Tom took one look, and rolled his eyes. "Shit," he said softly.

Melody went up the stairs to her balcony seat with Misha as her escort. Unlike Carl's, Misha's arm was warm, and though muscular, had the tell-tale elasticity of human flesh.

Tom stayed behind long enough to be sure Carl was loaded safely into a van for transport to Shutz Fabrik, where early the next morning he was cleared of a crippling logic loop and rebooted for further service.

* * * * * * *

"Why don't you stop defending him?" asked Tom.

"And why don't you stop trying to tell me what to do?" said Melody. "You're my manager. You manage my business, not my personal life."

"Sorry. I just don't understand your patience. You certainly don't have any with me."

"You're human. No excuses for you. Carl is limited by his program, and his logic isn't fuzzy enough. They've made him too rigid. A good AI learns from mistakes, and Carl seems to break down every time he makes one. It's like he's continually anxious, and every mistake pushes him over the edge."

"So now you're an expert on artificial intelligence."

"Why not? Being an actress doesn't make me stupid. I think I can help him."

"How? Why?"

"I like having my own AI, Tom. I feel safe with him, and he's not demanding or too familiar like Misha and Andrus. I can talk to him. Input, you know. Let him know it's okay to make a mistake. For a moment last night I was really scared, Tom, and that's what triggered him. The error he made could have been made by any human under the same circumstances."

"You have scripts to read and another shoot in three weeks. Let Shutz Fabrik do the work with Carl."

Melody glared at him. "You weren't listening to me a minute ago. I want Carl assigned to my suite. I've caught Misha and Andrus asleep three times now. If my stalker shows up, I want someone awake to defend me."

"We don't know you're being stalked. Someone's just sending you threatening letters."

"It's more than that. I can feel it. There are times I'm alone, and I know I'm being watched. I keep waiting for someone to jump out at me from any closed door. I know it sounds stupid, but the feeling is real."

"Sounds more dramatic than stupid," said Tom, and immediately regretted it.

Melody's eyes narrowed to slits. "You work for me, Tom. Either get Shutz to assign Carl for duty in my suite, or find yourself another job. I want him to carry out any voice command I give, and I want to be able to teach him. Is that dramatic enough for you?"

"Clear enough," said Tom. "I'll get on it."

"What are you smiling at?"

Tom grinned. "Oh, I just get a kick out of dealing with strong-willed women. I'll have Shutz Fabrik call you by this evening and tell you when Carl will be ready."

"It had better be soon," said Melody.

And it was, for that evening she received another threatening letter.

* * * * * * *

Misha and Andrus were not happy with the new arrangement. "What happens if he freezes up again, or goes nuts? He could kill you with a single squeeze before we can react," said Misha.

"I'm willing to take that chance," said Melody.

"If he attacks you I'll blow his head off, and I won't wait for your permission to do it."

"Fair enough," said Melody, but shuddered at the look in Misha's eyes. She could not question his loyalty, only his competence.

Now, in the quiet of her suite, she felt safe again. The suite covered half of the twentieth floor of the Globus building, and looked out at the ocean. Up the beach, the Santa Monica shopping ring looped far out to sea. The walls and furniture were in beige, and lit by full spectrum tubes in ceiling panels to supplement the sunlight even in daytime. Melody snuggled in deep pillows on a sofa, a pile of scripts in her lap, a few placed to one side, many scattered on the floor after her rejection. Misha and Andrus patrolled the outside hallway while Carl made random rounds inside the suite. He moved silently, but always there was the odor of warm polymer and cutting oil in his presence. Melody looked up as he entered the room to check the sliding doors to the balcony.

"Talk to me, Carl. I'm tired of reading these things. Most of them are awful."

"One moment, Melody," said Carl, his voice a soothing and mellow baritone. He checked the balcony, the area above and below it, then closed the doors and sat down stiffly in a plush chair facing her. "What do you want to talk about today?" he asked. His mouth moved out of synch with his words, and without his dark glasses on, his large fisheye lenses made him look even more artificial.

"You," said Melody.

"Will you teach me today?"

"Maybe. Are you happy here, Carl?"

"Happy? I am fulfilled by my tasks."

"And how are you rewarded for that?" Melody put down the script she'd been reading, and cupped her chin in one hand.

"My reward is the completion of a task. There is a reset pulse, and it modulates my powerpac. I am energized."

"Clever." said Melody. "With humans it's biochemicals that affect parts of the brain to produce pleasurable sensations. Do you want to be more human, Carl?"

"That is one of my tasks. I learn by watching humans react to stimuli; I copy their average behavior for a given circumstance."

"There's a wide variety of human reactions. What happens when you choose the wrong one, when your reaction is not appropriate? I really want to know what happened to you at the theater the other night, when you hit that man who tried to give me a gift."

"That was an error in perception. My task was to protect you, Melody, but you were not in danger. I injured a human without reason. When I paused to correct the error there was no way to accomplish it and undo the injury I'd caused. I was caught in a logic loop for all processors simultaneously, and my task was not ended."

"You reacted hastily, perhaps, but you *did* protect me, Carl. That man was coming at me fast, and I was frightened. His behavior brought about his injury, not you. Your response was basically correct."

"Mister Lesko pointed out my error instantly. He was my human control at the time, and his opinion overrode my own."

"He was wrong, and now *I'm* your control. If you want to be more human you must be willing to tolerate mistakes you make, and learn from them. Rules are not cast in stone, Carl. If I'm threatened I want your response instantly. I do *not* want you worrying about hurting someone."

"You are frightened again. I can see it in your eyes, and the wrinkles in your brow."

"I'm an actress. I let my emotions show. If you can read my face you can learn my feelings the same way my audience does, by watching and listening to my performances. I want you to do that, a little each day. I'll sit with you."

"This is important to you," said Carl, a statement, not a question.

"Yes, it is," said Melody. "I want to make you better than you are. I want you to be more human."

* * * * * * *

Their routine was unbroken for two weeks, but then there was one frightening afternoon when Carl was picked up by a Shutz Fabrik van for upgrades ordered by Melody herself. The hard plastic of his face was to be replaced by soft polymer, and new lenses installed to get rid of his bug-eyed look. The work was routine, though expensive, and he was gone only five hours, but when he returned he found the hallway filled with police, and Melody was curled up in a little ball on her bed, crying softly. She reached out and held his hand when he stood by her bed, and she was suddenly calm.

"I was reading scripts, and something struck the door. I went to it, saw an envelope pushed beneath the door, a shadow moving. I called out, but nobody answered. It wasn't like the other letters, Carl. Those were full of sexual fantasies. This one describes how he wants to kill me, and soon. I was scared, then mad. I screamed until Misha and Andrus came. I'm afraid I called them some very bad names, and now I feel badly about it."

So yet another letter had been hand-delivered, slipped under her door in broad daylight. Talking to the police, Carl learned that whoever had delivered it had gained roof access to the elevator shaft and a service tunnel and dropped into the hall from an air return vent while Misha and Andrus were checking out the arrival of an empty elevator from ground floor. It had all happened in less than a minute.

Tom Lesko had been called, but had not yet arrived. Carl returned to Melody, and sat down on the edge of the bed when she ordered it. She clung to him like a little child.

"Whoever it was knew I was away," he said. "You should not send me away for any reason, Melody. The person must be watching you."

"He even knows what I wear to bed," sobbed Melody. "He says I should wear the purple teddy when he comes for me. He wants to have sex, and then watch my face while he slowly strangles me. Do you understand what I'm saying, Carl?"

"Yes." Carl stroked her hair with hard, stiff fingers. "He must be found by others. I will protect you. No human is as strong or quick as I. You'll feel better after you sleep, that thing you do when your eyes close at night. Sometimes your eyes move, and you say things. I have watched."

"I dream," said Melody. "It's a human way of reorganizing memories, analyzing things, sort of recreating myself each night. Tonight my dreams could be bad. If you're not in this room with me tonight I won't be able to sleep."

"I'll be here," said Carl.

Melody was more composed a few minutes later when Tom Lesko arrived, but felt even better after he held her hands and gushed over her. He even said something nice to Carl.

"What happened here was not your fault," he said.

"I know," said Carl. "The fault is in trusting humans to protect her."

Tom smiled. "How human of you, Carl. Arrogance is a human trait, but I think you'll have to share the responsibility for Melody's safety."

Tom turned to Melody. "You seem to be giving him a lot of freedom, dear."

"Maybe he needs even more. Misha and Andrus keep slipping up. That's four times, now. All it seems to take is a small distraction to make their attention wander."

"I understand your feeling, but I still want you to keep a leash on your personal bodyguard here. I don't want another person hurt without reason. I was lucky to keep the last incident out of the press."

"I see," said Melody. "It's okay, then, if I'm murdered in my bed."

Tom leaned close and softly said, "We don't really have to worry about that, do we. This is a terror campaign being waged by a demented fan. He could have broken in here, but didn't."

"He didn't have the time. Some night he will, and we'll be waiting for him. I'm tired of this conversation, Tom. I want to go to sleep. See Mister Lesko out, Carl, and come back here."

There was no arguing with her when she was like this. Tom gave up without a fight, allowed Carl to escort him out of the suite. Once outside he ordered Misha and Andrus to remain seated by the double doors to the suite, and talked to the police, who'd found nothing useful in their investigation. There was only the grate popped out of the hallway ceiling, and the letter under the door. Nothing else. The occupants of the suites across the hall from Melody's had not been home at the time. It bothered Tom that those suites had not been searched, but a police sergeant assured him they would be as soon as the owners returned and gave their permission. He was also bothered by the sloppy work of Misha and Andrus. Before leaving, he told both of them that one more letter would cost them their jobs. Neither man seemed to be bothered by his remarks, and he vowed to have them replaced within the week.

Back in her bedroom, Melody began to relax again. Carl stood in the doorway. In low light, his new eyes and face made him look almost human. "My protector," she said, and smiled.

"Yes," said Carl.

Melody yawned, and stretched. "I want to have nice dreams tonight, Carl. This has been a terrible day."

"I'll be right here until you sleep," he said.

Her eyes were already closed, and he felt her slip away, her brain still active, but going into a different state to reorganize and refresh. He'd watched her do this many times. She'd even given him a soundtrack made just for him, sweetly modulated sound allowing him to follow her into slumber. Once there, a part of her mind moved in random fashion, flitting here and there, while another part remained totally awake and ready for instant response to stimuli. Carl was amazed by the mix, but had been so far unable to duplicate it for himself. Melody's patient teaching had brought him to a point where, a few minutes each day, he would lie down and consciously shut out all visual and audio stimuli to review the events of the day, positives and negatives, and then build alternative scenarios to better fit his assigned tasks. The change had been gradual, but he felt it. It was as if, a few minutes each day, he was reinventing himself.

Melody's breathing was now slow and deep. Carl pondered the day's events, but remained alert. Something wasn't right. Something wasn't the way it seemed. He'd built several scenarios for the delivery of the threatening letter, and one of them disturbed him deeply. If true, it could mean that Melody was still in immediate danger.

Carl did not do his usual random checks of the suite that night. Instead, he stationed himself in a dark corner of the front room and near the double-door entrance.

He did not have to wait long for something to happen.

* * * * * * *

It was after dark when the police left.

Misha and Andrus remained at their station by the doors for about an hour, and then began wandering the halls again. Their attention spans seemed quite short, even by human standards. They spoke softly, but Carl's hearing was acute. Still, they were often far enough away to exceed his audio detection limit.

The elevator came and went several times, and he heard a door open and close twice, but otherwise there was only Misha and Andrus engaged in inane conversation, and not paying attention to their duties.

Well after midnight it was suddenly silent outside the suite, but only for a while. Minutes later, Carl could hear snoring; Melody's human guards were asleep again, and impotent. He resisted the temptation to go outside and awake them in a frightening way, not to injure them but to encourage their wakefulness. They were, after all, Melody's first line of defense.

Sometime later, in the darkness of his corner, Carl heard a faint thud, and felt a transient vibration in the floor. There was a sustained scuffing sound after that, and then the elevator arrived, a sharp note signaling the opening of the doors. The doors closed, and there was the whine of the motor running the elevator. Silence again, then a scraping, ripping sound, metal on metal. Carl left his corner, took several steps towards the doors and listened again.

More scuffing sounds, something hard dragging on the carpet outside. Something rattled metallically, and then there was a distant tone as if a great bell had been struck, a hollow sound with over-tones, fading quickly. Carl stepped up to one side of the doors, his audio sensitivity ramped to maximum.

At first there was nothing, though he continued to sense weak, transient vibrations in the floor. Suddenly there was a scratching sound from low on the doors, and then a soft moan. A human moan. Carl felt a single shock pass through the floor, and reached for the door latch, his left arm cocked and ready to deliver a lethal blow.

Nobody was there. The chairs by the doors were empty. The long hallway was empty. The doors to the elevator were open, but it was dark inside, and someone had ripped the air-return grate again from the ceiling and thrown it against a wall, damaging the wallpaper there.

Carl stepped outside, closed and locked the doors behind him. There was a red spot on the carpet by the doors, and two faint grooves in the fabric ran off towards the elevator. He followed them, nanoscale parallel processors busily building scenarios in his head as he noted his surroundings.

He even noticed that the door to the suite nearest the elevator was slightly ajar, but a sound ahead suddenly distracted him.

Three feet from the open elevator doors he realized the elevator wasn't there; he was looking into the open shaft at the black cables supporting the elevator somewhere below. He peered over the edge. The elevator cab was far below him, probably at ground level. There was a click behind him; he started to turn around.

Something heavy slammed into him, knocking him headlong into the elevator shaft. His arms and legs flailed wildly. In the six seconds of his fall, his brain reviewed nine different scenarios of what was happening now, and could happen soon. He chose one as his right hand caught a cable and squeezed. The only variable left was the identity of Melody's assailant. His hand crushed down on the cable, slowing him rapidly, but he crashed onto the top of the elevator car with considerable force.

A body was there, a human body, crushed and broken by a long fall. It was Andrus.

Carl dropped through the trapdoor in the ceiling of the elevator, found the controls smashed, and pried open the doors in one move with his hands. A few people waiting in the lobby jumped back in terror at the sight and sound of ripped and torn metal as he sprinted away towards the staircase.

* * * * * * *

Melody heard a sound, and was instantly awake. "Carl?" she asked, but there was no answer. It was cold when she got out of bed in her underclothes. She went to the closet, slipped into a silk robe and heard the front door open and close.

"I'm up, Carl. What's going on?"

Still no answer, but Carl often waited to reply when he was finishing a task. Melody pulled up her hair and tied it into a tail as she walked out into the front room. "I heard a noise," she said.

She was two steps into the room when someone grabbed her roughly from behind, a strong arm encircling her and a hand clamping down tightly over her mouth. The man's breath was hot in her ear.

"Your boyfriend is gone, and he ain't coming back. Time to party, bitch. Let's see if you're wearin' that purple thing I like so much."

Melody twisted, tried to drop out of Misha's grasp, but he pulled her up again, her feet leaving the floor and banging ineffectually against his massive legs. He grabbed her right wrist, twisted her around and tried to pull her right arm up behind her, but the arm wouldn't move for him. "Stronger than you look," he said. "This'll be more fun than I thought." He lifted her again, and began backing towards the bedroom.

Melody the actress moaned, and let herself go limp. As they reached the bedroom doorway, Misha's grip slackened for an instant as he began to change his hold on her. She suddenly kicked backwards off the door jamb and slammed him into a bedpost, twisted away and sprinted towards the front room. He caught up with her halfway to the doors, and grabbed her by the hair, jerking her back so hard her skullcap came loose and she was dangling from his hand by a thin sheet of polymer.

"What's this?" asked Misha. "What the fuck is *this*?"

The doors shattered into a thousand splinters as Carl came through them. And in the last second of his life, Misha seemed astonished by the sight of him. Carl caught him by the throat, swept him up in a high arc and slammed him head first into the floor.

Melody sobbed, and clutched at the back of her head. Carl stepped up to her, put one hand on her shoulder, the other touching the long tail of dangling hair at her back.

"I know, Melody. I know," he said. "I've always known."

* * * * * * *

"It looks like he was trying to set up Andrus as the killer," said Tom. "The drug ampoule we found was probably meant for Misha. We'd find him stoned out of his mind, and Carl with Andrus. He was willing to give up a profession to get at Melody. Guy was a deranged woman hater for sure. I don't think his story would have held up."

Carl sat close by Melody on the couch. "Do the police know about Melody, about her—?"

"No need for that, Carl. The guy's intent was murder. That makes it justifiable homicide. Melody and Nathan are Global Studios' best kept secrets, and we're not about to change that. If the press didn't know you're an AI I bet I could get *you* a part in Melody's next film." Tom smiled. "You two look like a couple, sitting there."

"Two peas in a pod," said Melody, and Carl looked at her.

"We're alike," she said. "You know, I would have taught you differently if I'd realized you knew about me."

"I had to tell him," said Tom. "Had to keep the pecking order straight, but it amazes me how quickly he picked up on your obstinacy."

"You love my obstinacy; it makes me more human, you said." Melody paused, then, "Tom, I want Carl to stay with me."

"I want that too," said Carl.

"Fine with me," said Tom. "I'm not even surprised. Let's see how far you can develop together, how human you can really become. Just remember to document everything; that's what pays the service bills for Carl, dear, and I'd like to keep it that way. Be good, now. I have to leave. Do whatever you do to rest. You'll be doing a lot of traveling soon. Showbiz. I love it."

He left them sitting on the sofa, exiting through newly installed but as yet unpainted doors. Melody held up a small, metallic ball with four fine wires hanging from it. "I have a new toy," she said.

"A toy? A thing to play with?"

She laughed. "It'll directly connect our synaptic multiplexers. You have one too, you know. I have a new disk to play, and I want to try out my imagination on you."

Melody took his hand, led him into the bedroom and put him down on his back on the bed.

"What are we doing?" he asked.

"We're being more human," she said, then turned on the disk player and lay down beside him. Sweet sound filled the room as she connected herself to him, and then draped an arm across his chest.

"Close your eyes," she said, and he did.

"Follow me where I go," she whispered. "We're going to reinvent you again."

And they slept.

DELIVERANCE SMITH

It was suddenly cold in the city, a brisk wind sweeping down into concrete and steel canyons like an angel of ice. Dressed for the summer heat, people were unprepared and fled to shops and cars.

Jack Herold fared better than the norm because his long trench coat, ragged as it was, served well as a windbreak, and its deep pockets allowed him to periodically warm his hands, one at a time. His free hand was necessary to hold up the eight-by-ten sign he had carefully block-lettered with laundry marker on cardboard. 'Homeless. Need food. God blesses the compassionate', it read.

Standing on his usual corner of the Fifth Street hill, right by the stoplight, Jack generally worked the commuters seven to nine and three to six. A good day was twenty dollars. It had been better when Nik was with him; the little mutt terrier had seemed to boil the generosity right up in people. But Nik was gone now. Disappeared within a day after Jeb Roth had arrived to dominate and terrorize Jack's back alley family. Jeb had probably slit Nik's throat and stuffed him in a sewer somewhere. He hated dogs and all other animals, including humans. Jeb Roth was a dark and dangerous person, and since he'd arrived there was no escaping him; he ruled them all with a six-inch blade, and took all the cash he could find on them.

Nowadays there was no cash to be found. A central cache was no longer kept by the family. They agreed on their needs ahead of time and each member was assigned a part of it to get with the day's take. What little was left over was individually squirreled away far from their back alley home, and away from Jeb Roth.

Jack's day had started well enough, but late afternoon was a wipeout, everyone hurrying to get out of the wind and the cold. By five he felt like the skin on his face was on fire. The marrow in his bones was frozen, and he had nine dollars to show for it. He bought day-old bread at a bakery on Dempsey, peanut butter and two bags of oatmeal at the neighborhood market where poor people were welcomed and not stared at. Two dollars went behind a loose brick in an alley near First and Fifth, and the coins went into his pocket as an offering to Jeb.

Harmony was returning from the recycler when Jack met her at First and Ninth. Stoned again, pupils huge, she shuffled along hanging onto Terry's arm as he pushed her nearly empty market basket for her. The basket had been heaped with aluminum cans that morning, and the bag of produce it now contained was the return on twenty hours of digging in trash bins. Once upon a time, Harmony Lucas had been a pretty woman. Now in her forties, she looked a hard seventy, courtesy of the chemicals she shot into herself. Nobody asked how she paid for the drugs. The money she made on cans always went for family food.

"Hi, Jack. How'd you do?" asked Terry. Tall and skinny, dressed in jeans and a ragged khaki shirt, the fifteen-year-old runaway smiled enough to show a gap in his teeth from his final encounter with a mean-drunk father.

"Not so good. Wind's so cold, people won't even roll down their windows tonight." Jack patted his bag of groceries. "Peanut butter, bread and oatmeal for the next few days."

"Got potatoes and a bag of beans here," said Terry. "Harmony did good; the price of aluminum has gone up four cents in a week."

Harmony smiled, patted the boy's arm and looked up at Jack with rheumy eyes. "You okay, Jack? You look frozen to the bone." Her speech was slurred, as if she was just coming out of a long sleep.

Jack put an arm around her, and squeezed. "Need a good woman to keep me warm," he said, and Harmony laughed loud, her teeth hanging from her gums like charred stumps of wood. Her breath smelled like fish oil.

Harmony walked slowly, and it was dusk when they reached the alley to their home, a winding passage between shops, a pizza restaurant, a dangerously vacant and flame scarred building where the street kids smoked their dope. Walls of black brick on both sides, a cobblestone street, dumpsters filled with reeking garbage, the stink was barely neutralized by the odor of dough baking. Two sharp turns away from the street and there was a small cul-de-sac ending at the loading dock of an empty warehouse. In front of the dock a barrel flamed wildly in the gusty wind, tended by a black man with white hair and beard. The fire cast flickering light on the three packing crates behind him which served as home for their family.

"Evenin', George," said Jack. "That fire sure is a welcome sight on a night like this."

"Be better if we'd somethin' to cook," said George. He pulled a blue, navy-issue blanket tighter around his shoulders, and leaned over to stare down at the flames.

"Right here," said Terry, and he smiled at Jack. "Baked potatoes slathered with peanut butter, and bread. I'll wrap 'em." The boy took the bag from Harmony's shopping cart, and went with her to the crate they shared in her imaginings of them as mother and son.

Jack stood with George a moment, the only sound that of fire crackling. The wind blew cold, and there were a few drops of rain, some shards of sleet that stung the cheeks.

"Jeb been by?" Jack finally asked.

George glared at him, the whites of his eyes flickering orange in firelight. "Took my last dollar, and emptied my bottle just to be mean. Said he'd be back. Why don't we just move, Jack? Either that or smack him with a board and stuff him down the sewer where he belongs."

Jack put a hand on the old man's shoulder. "That's not right, George. Besides, Jeb'll move on soon. He wants money, and we don't have it."

George's eyes flashed. "I don't like being bullied, Jack. When I was younger he wouldn't't've dared try that with me."

"I know," said Jack softly. "When we were younger, things were a lot different for all of us, I guess."

"Not for Terry," said George.

Jack smiled, thinking, *Wet brain or not, you are very aware of some things, my friend.*

The sleet was coming down harder by the time Terry came back with four potatoes wrapped in aluminum foil. Wind fanned the fire hot, and their wood was running low. They put the potatoes into the coals through a cutout in the base of the barrel, and added fuel sparingly. Harmony came out, wrapped in her navy blanket, and they all huddled silently by the fire for a while, the wind chilling backs and stinging faces. And then, quite suddenly, as if a cosmic switch had been pulled somewhere, it all stopped. The wind was gone, the rain and sleet was not striking their faces, and it was like a warm breath coming down the alley to caress them where they stood. From far away there came a sound, a high pitched thing, pure and clear, running up and down a scale, then a trill, like a voice of spring.

Terry looked at Jack. "Little late for a street musician."

"Sounds like a flute," said Jack. The sound had strangely increased his heartbeat, and there was a tingling in his chest. Another trill, and he felt like laughing. The music was louder, now, its source coming closer. Harmony suddenly giggled.

Out of the gloom came a man, and he was playing a cedar flute. He was a tall man, wearing a wide-brimmed hat and an ankle-length rain slicker, all in black. His eyebrows followed the beat of the music, and his head swayed back and forth as he played. He walked right up to them, made a final, high trill on his instrument, and then took it from his mouth.

"Good evening, fellow travelers," he said in a merry voice. "Might I find a morsel of food here for a tune or two? I've come a long way tonight, and my stomach's beginnin' to cramp." His eyes, dark as midnight, seemed to twinkle in the firelight.

"All we have are some potatoes and bread," said Jack.

"Whatever you can provide for me will be deeply appreciated, friend," said the man in black. He hunkered down by the fire-barrel and began playing a soft tune which instantly made Jack think of lost friends and family and opportunities. Jack was saddened, but then the tune changed to something brighter, and Jack's heart lifted again.

"You play very well," said Jack, then introduced himself and his companions.

"My real name is unimportant, though it is a familiar one," said the man who stirred their emotions with the sounds from a flute. "To my fellow travelers in the darkness I am known as Mister Smith. Those who know me well call me Deliverance, for that is my purpose in life, to ease the burdens of sorrow caused by sin."

"A preacher," said Terry, and smiled.

In flickering light, Smith's face seemed suddenly cadaverous, and his voice was deep. "Not really," he said. "I deal more in actions rather than words."

"Get the preacher a potato, Terry," said Harmony. "Maybe he can brighten the mood around here."

"We don't even know him," said George.

"Don't matter. I didn't know you either when you first showed up, or Terry, or Jack. We was all strangers once. And you can flop up there on the dock, Mister Smith."

"Thank you, madam, and please call me Deliverance."

George sulked in silence while the food cooked. Terry prepared a potato for Deliverance, and it was late when they ate together. They ate bread plain, but were generous with peanut butter on the hot potatoes, and Terry made camp coffee for all of them. They sat cross-legged near the coals at the base of the burn-barrel. Smith was last to eat, and he played soft, restful tunes that seemed in time with the flickering flames, tones penetrating bone to marrow and into the soul. Jack closed his eyes for a moment. When he opened them, he saw three rats, one the size of a small cat, huddled together at the edge of fire glow, only two arms distant yet apparently unafraid. But seconds after the music stopped, the little beasts had disappeared. Smith pulled his potato from the coals and ate it plain, holding it up after taking two bites, as if making an offering.

"To the generosity of my hosts," he said, "and to our fellowship in the darkness of this world. May goodness lighten the burdens of our lives." Smith's voice resonated deeply and echoed dully from the brick walls surrounding them.

George laughed. "Only burden I got is Jeb Roth. Maybe goodness'll drop him in a hole somewhere."

"Ah yes, Mister Roth," said Smith, smiling. "I was expecting to find him here tonight."

"You know him?" asked Jack, disappointed. "He's certainly no friend of ours; we'd be happiest if he never came back here again. If you're a friend of his, you'd better leave now. We don't need more trouble."

"Alas, I've never made the man's acquaintance," said Smith, fingering his cedar flute again, "but his reputation reaches far, and I am in search of him. He is a man crushed by the circumstances of life."

"He'll crush *your* life for a dollar, Mister Deliverance," said Harmony. "Have any money on you, best hide it before he comes back, if you want to stay here a while. The man's pure evil; nothing good to be said about him." She put an arm around Terry's waist, and leaned against him. Terry scowled.

"Indeed," said Smith, "I've also heard he is fond of young boys."

"Him and his knife," said Terry through clenched teeth.

"Then I've come to the right place," said Smith. "I will await the arrival of Mister Jeb Roth, and deliver him from the burdens of his sins."

Terry laughed, and Harmony shook her head sadly. "A fool," she mumbled.

"You preach to Jeb, he'll more'n likely stick his knife in you and hock that flute of yours," said Jack.

Smith seemed amused, smiling at some private thought. "Ah, murder, the ultimate sin. I will then play a requiem for the release of his soul."

The man is deranged, thought Jack, and then Smith looked at him with eyes black as coal. Jack felt a shiver at the base of his spine, as if someone had touched him softly there.

"I am that I am, friend," said Smith, "and when I'm placed upon a path I do not deviate from it. There are no choices for me. Those are gifted to mortals such as you. Listen."

Smith put the flute to his lips and began playing again, a mournful tune in low register, and suddenly Jack was thinking of a past life in another city, a wife, two children, a ranch-style home in an upscale suburb, all gone now. Tears came to his eyes and ran down his cheeks as Smith played on. Terry was crying, and Harmony hugged him. George's eyes glistened moistly in the firelight.

The tune faded to the hiss of soft breath, and was gone. Smith took the flute from his lips, and pointed the instrument at Jack. "Choices," he said softly. "Tomorrow we will speak of choices."

Without another word, Deliverance Smith left the fire, climbed up on the dock and snuggled up against the crate Jake and George would use that night. He pulled his slicker tightly around himself, settled his hat over his face, and was asleep in moments. Soon after that Harmony and Terry went to bed, then George, all of them still stunned by music heard and memories recalled that evening.

For nearly an hour, Jack was left alone by the fire. He could hear, at some distance, the moaning sound of wind rushing through the canyons of the city, yet the air around him remained still and warm. He thought about his past life, choices made, the choices he would make now if he could somehow be given another chance. But it was all in the past, he decided, and could not be undone. The thought depressed him. He wanted a drink, and George had forgotten his half-filled bottle of cheap red by the fire. Jack licked his lips. There were people depending on him, now. He took the bottle back to his crate, and put it by George's head before rolling himself up in his navy blanket and closing his eyes.

In the twilight of sleep, it seemed he heard the soothing tones of a cedar flute in his head.

* * * * * * *

The following morning, Jeb Roth returned to their camp.

"Out of the sack, rummies; I know you're in there." His voice was the rasp of a rough file on metal.

George mumbled a curse into his blanket as Jack called out, "You're wasting your time, Jeb. We spent all our money on food last night."

"Yeah, well I'll be the judge of that," said Jeb. "Now get out here before I set fire to them crates."

Jeb Roth did not make idle threats. They were all unrolled from their blankets and out of the crates in seconds, having slept in their clothing. Jeb was standing by the fire barrel, absently cleaning a fingernail with an eight-inch blade shaped like half a leaf, the one edge razor sharp, the other serrated like a saw for cutting wood. He was dressed in faded denim, with black boots and matching stocking cap. Deep-set brown eyes stared from a pock-marked, angular face. His right ear had been reshaped by a sharp knife, and was missing the lobe. "Okay, turn them pockets out, and let's see whatcha got."

They obeyed. Between the three of them, there was a little over a dollar in change, and Jeb took it. "Okay, where's the rest of it? Where do you keep your drinkin' stash, rummy?" He grabbed George by his collar and scraped the blade of his knife lightly on one cheek.

"Leave him alone, Jeb. You got all we have," said Jack.

Jeb let go of George and swung his blade towards Jack. "You want a piece of this, teacher? Maybe I can—"

"The sound of a commanding voice has awakened me! You, sir, must be Jeb Roth, a leader of men. It is a pleasure for me to meet you." Deliverance Smith jumped lightly off the dock and came forward with his hand outstretched.

Jeb ignored the hand. "Who the hell are you?"

"Smith, sir. You may call me Deliverance Smith, and I am at your service. Your reputation as a soldier of the street reaches far."

Now Jeb looked at Jack. "You know this psycho?"

Jack shook his head. "He just came in last night. Never seen him before."

"I've traveled far to meet you, sir," continued Smith. "Surely there's something I can do for you."

Jeb picked at a fingernail with his blade, and smiled nastily. "Okay. Got any money on you?"

"Money? Of course! Money is the underpinning of the empire. It is the fuel of leadership. It is also the target of vagabonds and thieves, so I'm careful not to carry it on my person when I travel."

Jeb's eyes narrowed; he pointed his blade at Smith's chest, but the man didn't seem to notice.

"I prefer to produce funds when the need arises—so," said Smith. He raised one hand. The black sleeve of his slicker fell slightly to reveal a slender wrist and forearm. Long fingers moved rapidly, manipulating an invisible something in the air. There was a flash, and a golden disk the size of a quarter appeared in Smith's hand. He handed it over to Jeb Roth as everyone gaped in surprise.

"My morning's offering to you, sir," Smith said humbly.

It was a plain metal disk, without inscriptions. Jeb turned it over in his hand, tested it with his teeth. "Soft," he said.

"It is pure gold, but there are coin establishments and banks which will exchange ordinary cash for it," said Smith. "When I work in other dimensions, only the pure elements are accessible to me."

"Right," said Jeb, biting the disk a second time hard, and bending it. "Well, I'll just check this out. If it's a phony you'd better be gone when I get back. And anywhere you go around here, I'll find you."

"I assure you it's genuine, sir. A man such as you deserves only pure gold." Smith bowed slightly. "And there's more when you desire it."

"I'll know soon enough," said Jeb, and he walked away from them.

Jack grabbed Smith's sleeve. "There's a hock shop and fence just down the street, and it deals in gold and silver. Jeb'll know about that metal in your disk in minutes."

"The disk is pure gold, Jack. Nothing to fear."

"He'll want more of it. He'll want your whole stash."

"There's no stash, Jack. The disk came to me from afar."

"Magic," said Terry. "Slight of hand. Show us the trick, Mister Smith."

"There was no trick, lad, and magic is only unexplained science. I don't pretend to understand it myself; my abilities are a gift."

"From God? Satan? Drop the con, Smith. What are you up to?" asked Jack.

"I'm here to deal with the burdens of Jeb Roth. In the short time I have, perhaps I can help you as well, all of you. I can see you're not a religious man, Jack, but there *are* powers beyond all of us."

"You mean God?" said Jack, thinking of a past life. "If he exists, he certainly doesn't help or interfere in everyday life, Mister Smith. What I believe in is the innate goodness and evil in people. And Jeb Roth is as evil as they get."

Smith shook his head. "There is one sin he lacks. He has not yet killed a man."

"You want to encourage it, just keep doing that trick of yours with the gold disk," said Jack.

Deliverance Smith just smiled.

* * * * * * *

The morning melody of the flute bored into Jack's soul, only this time there were no painful memories, only a soft, womb-like darkness gently holding him. They were all entranced, sitting by the fire barrel, and around them, only feet away, alley rats and two warehouse rats with humped backs circled warily, stopping when the melody was low-pitched, and standing on their haunches to sniff the air.

The rats suddenly scurried away, and there were footsteps. Jeb Roth came into their camp and went straight to Deliverance Smith, grabbing him by the collar and hauling him to his feet. The flute clattered to the cobblestones, and Jack quickly caught it up. Steel flashed in Jeb's right hand. He pressed the blade against Smith's neck. "Okay, where's the rest of it?" he growled.

"Coin was a fake," mumbled George. Harmony and Terry hurried back to their crate, leaving Jack frozen and feeling impotent by the barrel.

"Guy gave me a hundred thirty five dollars for that thing; said he'd take all I can get," said Jeb. "You must have a whole stash of 'em for that trick of yours. Hold still, now."

Jeb searched Smith all over, patting down his body and legs, going over the slicker, the hat, turning out pockets. All he found was a dirty handkerchief.

"You still don't believe me," said Smith. "The gold comes from a place far from here. You can't even reach the place in a material way. If you want more gold, just ask, and it'll be yours, my friend."

"I'm not your friend, but the gold I want," said Jeb, and thrust his knife at Smith's face.

Jack held Smith's flute tightly, and his hands were shaking. Around the camp the rats had returned and were watching. There were now five warehouse rats, and as Jack turned his head back towards Smith he saw a sixth arrive suddenly, out of nowhere.

"I'll give you all the gold you want if you honor one request I have to make of you," said Smith, unflinching, the point of Jeb's blade only an inch from his nose.

"You give me my weight in gold, I'll consider anything," said Jeb, grinning.

"Then your weight in gold it will be, if you promise never to come back here again, or bother these people in any way."

Jeb laughed. "Sure, I can do that. Now let's see the gold."

"If you break your promise, the consequences will be dire."

"That a threat?" Jeb's blade touched Smith's nose.

"It will not be by my hand directly, but by The One who governs all dimensions."

Jeb laughed again, unbelieving. "I promised, psycho. Now bring on the gold, a hundred seventy pounds of it."

Smith took a step backwards and held out his hands, cupped together. He mumbled something under his breath, an incantation or prayer, it seemed. Jeb grinned, and fingered his knife. The others watched expectantly. If Smith messed up now the least he could expect was a slashed face. At worst, he'd be dead.

The mumblings grew louder, a strange language Jack had never heard before, both guttural and hissing at once. Smith's hands began to glow orange, the skin seeming translucent in the instant the fingers gushed forth light in a great ball around the hands, a blinding light making them all squint. "Jesus!" said Jeb, and he stepped back, stumbling against the fire barrel.

There was a clink of metal against stone, then a rush of sound. Beneath the ball of light around Smith's hands were golden flashes, quickening, and at his feet was a pile of golden disks growing rapidly under the rain from above. In moments the pile of gold was ankle deep and spreading out, the bright ball of light fading, fading, then gone as the last few gold disks seemed to fall directly out of Smith's cupped hands.

Deliverance Smith opened his eyes and lowered his hands to his sides. "There, you have your weight in gold. Take it, now, and go. These people have nothing for you."

Jeb seemed paralyzed, staring at the pile of treasure in front of him, then suddenly realized the treasure was his. He dropped to his knees, filled his stocking cap with gold, stuffed his pockets, wrapped up a considerable quantity of disks in his denim jacket, and still much was left on the cobblestones.

"Find boxes, cans, so Mister Roth can be on his way," said Smith.

They all searched the alley, found two useable boxes and a coffee can. It was enough. Jeb loaded it all up and made four trips to wherever he was exchanging the gold for cash. It had to be close; he was only gone for minutes at a time and was finished within an hour. In the meantime, at Jeb's orders, Jack and the others retired to their sleeping crates to wait. To even touch a single golden disk meant the risk of death.

They emerged when Jeb was hefting his final load, a coffee can weighing nearly twenty pounds. Sweat beaded his face, and his clothes were soaked through.

"You will not come back here," said Smith.

Jeb grinned, chuckled, and strode away with the coffee can held tightly to his chest.

Jack watched the man go, then turned to Deliverance Smith. "I don't think we're rid of him," he said. "I think he'll come back, and soon."

Smith smiled wanly. "Yes. Tomorrow, or the next day, he'll be back. The man's greed cannot be equaled. But I have only two days to complete my work, two days to prepare for the restoration of his soul. They will be hard days, Jack. It is necessary for me to shed this mortal body of mine to deliver Jeb Roth's soul to its rightful home."

"Who are you?" cried Jack. "Your talk is crazy, like you think you're Christ on the cross, here to save sinners, but you're a man, a man whose flute music brings out the rats from their hiding places, and makes me remember things I don't want to remember, and then you make gold flow out of your hands like a waterfall. You're a magician for sure, but what else? Do you want us to think you're a space traveler, or from another dimension?"

"I am those things, and more," intoned Deliverance Smith, and then he put a warm hand on Jack's shoulder. Jack's throat was suddenly constricted, and tears welled up in his eyes.

"You're a good man, Jack Herold. You were once a fine teacher, before the use of alcohol overwhelmed you, and you've accepted the responsibility for that. Now you live for others, and don't think only of yourself. You've become a loving person, Jack."

Jack sniffled. "Terry's just a kid; the streets would eat him alive if he was alone. George and Harmony are still using, and always will, I guess. Using has retarded them, and they need me."

"They needed you, Jack, but now they need something else," said Smith. "It's time for your paths to separate. I will talk to the others in another way, but with you I will be direct."

Smith took his hand from Jack's shoulder, reached into empty air in front of him and scrabbled at it with his fingers. There was a snap, and a small card appeared in his hand. He handed the card to Jack.

"Salvatore Serra, K through 12 Tutor, all subjects," read Jack. "I've heard of this guy. He has the street kids writing stories and poems, and they're putting a book together. Works out of the Cataldo Mission on Twelfth Street. So?"

"He has a serious illness he's not aware of yet," said Smith. "He will soon need a great deal of help. And you are a teacher."

"Not for over a decade," said Jack.

Smith sighed loudly. "I will not try to persuade you. The choice is yours to make, as it always has been. Keep the card a few days after I'm gone, then decide. At least promise me this."

"Sure," said Jack, "that's no problem." He pocketed the card. "And now let me give *you* some advice. Get out of here, before Jeb comes back. Take your flute, your magic tricks, and go."

Smith patted Jack's shoulder. "I will be gone within two days, but you will see me once again after that. Now you need to get to work. You've already lost a morning, and the cold wind is gone."

Indeed, the public was quite generous that day. Jack worked the bottom of the Fifth Street hill only four hours, and came home with twenty-three dollars hidden in the heel of one shoe.

* * * * * * *

When Jeb returned to the alley camp the following evening, a reception awaited him.

Flute music filled the air, a merry tune with trills and long scales. The fire barrel was lit and the magician was sitting next to it, the others up on the dock, legs dangling over the edge, listening. What he didn't notice at first was the furtive movements in the shadows and the gleam of firelight reflected from the many eyes there. "Well, did y'all miss me?" he said.

"You promised not to come back here again," said the magician darkly. The music had stopped abruptly and the man stood up, flute in hand. From somewhere in the shadows there was a chattering sound.

"Not exactly. You said not to bother the rummies again, but my business is with you. I know a guy who'll take all the gold you can get. Spot price, minus ten per ounce, no questions asked. I take twenty percent for making the contact. Sound like a deal?"

"Get out of here," said the magician, and brought the flute up to his lips.

"Hey, that's no way to treat a guy giving you a—"

The flute shrieked and trilled, high-pitched. Jeb jumped backwards, startled, and then frightened as he saw movement in the shadows.

Long tails and humpbacks, eyes red in firelight, the creatures came at him out of the darkness. He backed up and they followed, not in a rush, but stalking him. Another trill, and the lead animals hissed, stood up on their hind legs, baring horrible incisors.

Jeb fled the camp, cursing. By the time he reached the street his rage was murderous. Heart pounding, he thought of many ways to kill the man, then chose the simplest. Catch him asleep, without the flute, and one quick thrust. The downside was not knowing where the rest of the gold was. The upside was watching the man's face while he died.

Jeb went down the street to an all night diner, ordered the best steak on the menu and left a ten dollar tip for the pretty waitress there. He walked the streets for hours, going over the grisly scene in his mind again and again, savoring it. He'd never killed a man before. The thought of doing it thrilled him.

And Jeb Roth struck just before dawn.

* * * * * *

Jack tried to sleep, but couldn't, and clutched the flute to his chest. Deliverance Smith had given him the flute for safekeeping, saying, "He'll come in the night, and my time will be over. You'll know the moment. You must blow hard, all finger holes open, and touch your tongue to the instrument. The note will be high, and harsh; you must blow it until the host comes to aid me in my task."

Jack had nodded numbly, caught up by the man's intensity, but wondering what crazy delusion he was participating in, and then Smith had grabbed him in a bear hug, burying his face into Jack's shoulder.

"What I do is difficult, though I have done it before. The desire to remain mortal, of flesh and blood, is always strong. You are a comfort, Jack Herold, and a good man. Use the card I gave you, and remember me. The others I have talked to in their sleep. Follow the new courses in your lives, and you will be blessed."

Paranoid delusion, or at best a Messiah complex, Jack decided, but then why did a part of him believe the man? The cold, black eyes, the magic, or the electric touch of unusually warm hands? And then, as he was stirring the coals of the fire barrel, preparing to retire, Terry had come up to him and stretched out a hand.

"It's been good knowin' you, Jack. I've decided to live with my aunt uptown. I called her this morning, and she wants me. I'll be able to go to a regular school."

Jack shook his hand. "Sounds great, Terry. What about your dad?"

The boy's upper lip curled up. "No matter. He's in some kind of trouble, and left town. I doubt I'll even see him again."

"You're a great kid, Terry. You deserve better. Good luck."

"You too, Jack, wherever you end up. You don't belong here."

Maybe, thought Jack. Later, he'd wondered how Harmony would hold up after Terry was gone. He went to bed. Smith had already rolled up in a blanket by the crate, and seemed sound asleep.

But George was awake, and as Jack was getting settled in the darkness, George said softly, "You know, it's not right I stay here all day while the rest of you provide. I can do sumpthin' too."

"Yeah?" said Jack, unsnarling a blanket by feel.

"Yeah. Mission needs kitchen help, and you gets extra meals, even a place to sleep. I can do that, Jack. Harmony too, if she can clean herself up."

"That's a big if, George."

"I know. But she can try. I can try, Jack."

"If you want to do it, George, then do it. Nobody can tell you not to."

A pause, then, "Okay," said George, and he was quiet after that.

But all that had been said rattled around in Jack's head, and he couldn't sleep. There was George's heavy breathing, faint street sounds and a snore that was probably Harmony. Usually the rats were out at night, and you could hear their claws scratching stone in a search for crumbs. Tonight they were silent, and it was strange. All that quiet, and no sleep would come. He was aware and alert for the slightest sound as the night wore on and on.

He did not hear death coming. No footsteps, no warning.

Something slammed hard into the crate, and there was a grunt from outside. "Hey!" yelled George, as Jack scrambled to get free of his blanket.

Fists thudded against clothing. "Uh—uh—ahhh," groaned Deliverance Smith, and then he laughed a crazy laugh, sending shivers up Jack's spine.

"You tell me where the gold is, I'll make it quick. Otherwise I skin you alive." Another thud, and Smith cried out in pain.

Jack kicked his blanket free. "You've got all the gold. Leave him alone!"

"Any of you set foot out here, I'll kill you. Come on, preacher, we're gonna have us a crucifixion."

Jack grabbed up the cedar flute in darkness, pushed aside the blanket covering the crate opening and rolled outside. Jeb was dragging Smith away by the collars of his slicker and shirt. By the embers of the fire barrel there was enough light for Jack to see Smith's eyes were open, and something black was gushing from his mouth.

"You come in here, I'll cut you!" screamed Harmony from her crate. It sounded like Terry was fighting to keep her inside.

Jeb dragged Smith around a trash bin and out of sight towards the end of the alley. A moment later there was the sound of metal rattling against metal, and then a horrible, shrill cry from the darkness.

Jack froze, not from the sound of pain, but from the explosion in his head. *Now. Do it now, before I die!* His head hurt front and back, like someone was squeezing it, and he instantly knew what he was supposed to do.

Jack put the cedar flute to his lips, all finger holes open, and blew very hard, flicking his tongue against the mouthpiece. The flute screeched, the scream of a bird, again, and again.

Shapes moved in the darkness, large and small, coming from the street, the buildings, the heaps of trash against brick walls. They came out of the warehouse behind the crates, claws scratching concrete and cobblestone, brushing past Jack's legs and leaping from the dock to join hundreds of other hump-backed vermin streaming towards the back of the alley. Their chattering was a din, and was soon joined by human screaming from nearby. Terrible shrieks of agony, the voice unidentifiable.

Jack leaped from the dock, rats scattering as he landed. Harmony was crawling out of her crate, Terry right behind her, and George's head peeked outside, eyes wide. "Stay here!" yelled Jack. "As long as I have the flute I'm safe."

Now where did I get that? thought Jack.

Vermin rushed past his feet, but didn't seem to notice him. Still, he stepped gingerly, squeezing the flute by one end as if it were a sword. The screams continued for long seconds, then reduced to moans as Jack rounded the trash bin. Ahead of him a streetlamp glowed from the next street over, but the alley was blocked by a chain link fence, and hanging on the fence, looking like a black cross, was a human being. Something was huddled at the base of the fence, and vermin swarmed over it. There was a coppery scent in the air.

Jack dared to step forward, and a path was somehow cleared for him.

Deliverance Smith hung from the fence, arms outstretched and wired to it. His head lolled to one side; he was unconscious, or dead. The moaning came from the huddled mass at his feet, writhing, struggling as huge rats tore at it with yellowed teeth. An arm flailed weakly, knocking two animals away, and then there was another agonized scream of pain.

Jeb Roth tried to sit up. Most of his clothing had been torn away, and he was covered with blood. Much of the skin on his face had been stripped away, and blood gushed from the stubs of two fingers on his left hand. A knife was in his right hand, the head of a wharf rat still clamped on his wrist as he waved the hand weakly to shake it off. And at that instant, the animals swarming him seemed to hesitate, sniffing the air, backing off and hunching down as if waiting for something. As Jack came closer, flute in hand, the animals backed off even further.

Jack knelt by Jeb's shivering, mutilated body and felt a rush of pity. The man's eyes were swollen shut, and he moaned again. Jack reached out to touch him, but there was suddenly a bright light above his head. He looked up. The body of Deliverance Smith was enveloped by a bright, blue glow. There was heat, and the pungent odor of seared metal. Jack shaded his eyes, then closed them against the brilliance. There was the odor of singed hair, and roasted flesh. The hoard of rats surrounding him suddenly chittered in unison, and scampered away.

Jack opened his eyes.

The chain link fence glowed cherry red. A figure stood there in silhouette, a man, cloaked and hooded. The man knelt, pulled Jeb Roth into a sitting position, and embraced him. Jeb writhed in agony, and moaned at the touch.

"With your final sin you are mine, and I will take you to The One who awaits," said the man, and it was the voice of Deliverance Smith.

"Smith?" said Jack. "I thought he'd killed you."

"All is forgiven. Your pain is over, your blood sacrifice complete. I will deliver you from the evil your life has been, now and forever." Long-fingered hands clasped the butchered chest of Jeb Roth, and the man began to cry. Smith's cloak seemed to expand, like the wings of a great bird. Within the dark hood, two eyes suddenly glowed a sky blue, and looked directly at Jack.

"You will return home by another way, friend. Keep my flute, and remember me by it. I will be watching."

Before Jack could answer, black wings enfolded Jeb Roth and muffled his sobs. There was a sharp, burning odor and Jack blinked hard. The figures in front of him seemed to fade, becoming transparent, the deep red of the still glowing fence showing through them. There was a pop, like two hands clapping, and only the fence was there, air rushing past Jack's head to fill the void.

Jack stared at the deepening glow of the fence, then gasped, for he'd been holding his breath. Behind him there was a footfall. He turned swiftly, holding out the flute as if to ward off some new evil. George, Harmony and Terry were all there, eyes glistening. Harmony came up to him, put a gnarled hand on his arm and softly said, "I prayed and prayed, and finally he been taken away."

* * * * * * *

Terry was gone early the next morning, and nobody heard him leave. For the rest of them there were no goodbyes to be said, for the new courses of their lives would often bring them together.

They walked down to Cataldo Mission together that first day. George and Harmony had never looked so clean. Jack carried the flute that would become his trademark with the kids, and over time he learned to play it well, his music soft and soothing to people whole lives were hard on the streets.

A magic flute, people said.

Jack agreed with them.

TIKAN'S CHOICE

The morning of the day his best friend was sacrificed to Tikan, Joseph Warmhand arose before dawn and took a long walk in the jungle.

Even the animals seemed to sense the solemn nature of this day. It was relatively quiet beneath the thick fronds of ferns and palms arching overhead. A few birds called out, and there was one distant scream of a *Jaguerre* returning from the hunt. Otherwise there was only the stench of rotting undergrowth crunching beneath his bare feet as he climbed to the summit of a hill where there was a view of the city.

The tops of trees formed a wavy sea of green to the horizon. Far out, the peaks of three pyramids broke the surface of the sea and glowed orange in morning sunlight. The image of the largest one was partially obscured by a brownish cloud. Even now, Tikan's fires were being prepared to consume the body of Joseph's friend.

The priests had come in the night to take Bernardo away, and Joseph had not been given the chance to say goodbye. They had grown up together, experienced the first signs of Tikan's gifts to them together. They were like brothers, family, and still the priests had not allowed them to say goodbye. Today he would watch from afar as Bernardo ascended the great pyramid to his death because his gifts were special, because he was best at what he did, because Tikan had chosen him.

It was not right. It did not make sense for the best to be taken away to appease an invisible god. And deep in his heart, as he watched the smoke drift from the distant pyramid, Joseph knew that the same thing could also happen to him, and he did not want to die.

There was a sound behind him. He turned, and saw Lazaro climbing up to join him. Lazaro was the only father Joseph had known since being orphaned by a terrible fire when he was three. The old Shaman was puffing hard, his breath a white mist, and his face glistened with sweat. His aura was cold blue, with dark filaments extending above his head. It was not good for an old man to be working so hard soon after sleep. Joseph went to him, took him by the arm and helped him climb the last few steps to the summit. He sat him down on a flat rock next to the stump on which he'd been perched to view the pyramids. "Why have you followed me?" he asked.

"You're grieving, and don't understand things," said Lazaro. "You only see the loss of a friend."

"I see a few priests manipulating our people into believing it's necessary to make human sacrifices to a mystical being who doesn't exist," said Joseph.

"Without Tikan you'd be common. All your gifts come from him."

"I don't believe that. My abilities come from my father, and his father before him. I come from a long line of healers. It's something in our blood. It has nothing to do with some god."

Lazaro Jumps In Water shook his head sadly. "You deceive yourself. It's true each family is known for certain abilities and skills. I speak only of the exceptional ones like Bernardo, perhaps even you. I knew your grandfather, Joseph. We were boyhood friends. He was skilled with medicines and ceremony, even more so than your father, but he didn't see the life-force as you do. He couldn't see into the human mind and heal it from the inside like Bernardo can. It's the exceptional people Tikan asks that we return to him. It's not a demand. We're not threatened with consequences if we don't comply."

"Then why do it? Bernardo is twenty; he has another sixty to eighty years to be a healer, and yet our people are willing to throw him away. That's insane, Lazaro."

"It's our tradition, and it only affects a few. Only the very best are returned to Tikan. Bernardo accepted it when the golden chain was hung around his neck. His family is honored, and will be richly compensated for their loss. And he will not disgrace them by showing fear or trying to run away. Would *you* do that, Joseph? You've also received the golden chain, but I notice you're not wearing it. Would you disgrace yourself, and me?" Lazaro's dark eyes glistened moistly, and the lines in his eighty-five-year-old face deepened.

"I will not disgrace myself or you, Lazaro, but I want to live. I want to live a long life with a wife, and children, and grandchildren. I will not give up my life for Tikan or any other god who asks for it."

"You will be the best of our healers, Joseph," said Lazaro.

"Then I must be certain I do not become the best," said Joseph.

Lazaro's eyes widened with surprise and horror at what he'd just heard.

* * * * * *

The great square in Tikanan was a field of flowers, people jammed together shoulder to shoulder with garlands in their hair, and wearing shirts or dresses in flowered prints. A hundred steps rose to the next level on which the pyramids stood. White-robed priests with feathered crowns stood on the steps, awaiting the arrival of Tikan's sacrifice. Behind them, a flower-covered cable car sat at the base of the central pyramid, steel rails running up a white granite ridge to the summit over a hundred meters above ground level. The summit was obscured by smoke that seemed to ooze from pores in the stone several meters below it.

The crowd was quiet, respectful and select. Only the best families of Florencia had been invited, ten thousand people out of a hundred thousand. Timing of this ceremony was tied conveniently to the positions of the moons Jacinta and Rita, now close together and nearing the zenith. Rita, glowing like a white pearl, would soon eclipse the larger Jacinta and its purplish, volcanic sands, for one moment giving the appearance of an eye in the sky. A special event, and in that moment a young man named Bernardo Tealsong would be given to Tikan.

The sacrifice came standing on a flower-covered platform carried on the shoulders of twenty men. He was shirtless, barefoot, and wore pants dyed in splotches of primary colors. His long, black hair had been braided, and decorated with tiny orchids, and he carried a basket of fruit which he would give to Tikan at the end of his journey. Behind him marched his family, parents and three sisters, and behind them the rest of those who wore the golden chains, and their families. A few people cheered, and threw flowers, but the sacrifice kept his eyes straight ahead.

Two priests met him at the steps. They held his arms lightly at his sides, led him to the cable car and entered it. The car moved upwards on shining rails and was soon lost in the brownish cloud hovering around the great pyramid's summit. A few minutes later the car came down again, but only the two priests got out of it.

The ground suddenly trembled, and there was a deep sound like a bell ringing. It seemed to come from the pyramid itself, and many people covered their ears with their hands. The brownish cloud moved, then swirled, disappearing as if sucked back into solid granite. The ground trembled again, and there was a roaring sound as if something were coming up from the bowels of the planet. People screamed in fear as a solid cylinder of flame, red, then orange, then blue, erupted from the summit of the pyramid and rushed hundreds of meters into the sky. Even at ground level the terrible heat could be felt, and the flame was blinding to behold. It lasted only seconds before winking out with an explosive pop that shook the ground again.

Everyone stood in stunned silence. Only two people wept. One was the mother of the sacrifice to Tikan. The other was his best friend, who also wore the golden chain of the chosen. He wept bitterly, so overcome by grief he would not speak to the priests when they came to comfort him.

* * * * * * *

Donata Skyblue patted his hand and gave him a gap-toothed smile, her breath smelling like old fish. "You are a good boy," she said.

At age ninety-three, Donata was old enough to say that. Her daughter, grandchildren and one great-grandchild also smiled, knowing that for the next few days at least, the matriarch of the family would have the use of her hands again. Joseph had taken her gnarled hands in his and let the heat come for twenty minutes. He did not know how this was done. He only thought it, and it was so. Lazaro mumbled a mantra while Joseph worked. It was a good show. Everyone was happy, and Lazaro accepted a dozen large chicken eggs as payment.

The four huts of the Skyblue compound were on the edge of the village, and it was a ten minute walk back to the dugout lodge with log beams, porch and thatched roof that served as their clinic. Lazaro put a hand on Joseph's shoulder and asked, "Anything else to be seen? You seemed concerned at one point."

"I was, but then not so much. She's had a small mass in her left breast for two years. It has grown, but only slightly. I will find a reason to check her again in a month."

"But you saw it without touching her," said Lazaro.

"The energy field of a living thing is sensitive to physical anomalies. Distortions are localized, and easy to see."

"Only for you, Joseph. Your gift is unique." Lazaro smiled, paused, then said, "You've been noticed by important people, you know. Wealthy merchants, not just the priests. They ask why you don't come with me to the city."

"You know why. I won't have anything to do with murderers or their religion. Why don't you tell them that?"

Lazaro smiled. "I don't think you want to attract such attention. You want to be invisible."

"I'm hardly invisible with this gold chain around my neck. It evokes trust by my patients, but the women my age see me as a celibate priest."

"Ah," said Lazaro.

"If I can't have a normal family life I can accept that, but I at least want to stay alive to do my work."

"I understand," said Lazaro, "but the fact remains you've been noticed. These are people who pay in gold, not eggs. Some will pay well if you only examine their life force. We need money for the clinic, Joseph. Eggs and chickens will not pay for our needs."

They walked in silence a while. Joseph had no argument against what Lazaro had said. Even a little money would allow them to do much more for the villagers. It was the poor who needed his services. The ambitious merchants who'd moved to the city had access to expensive surgery and standard medicine, and the white-skinned priests seemed immune to diseases of the jungle.

"I've taken the liberty of inviting someone to our clinic this afternoon. He's one of our people, Joseph; he's not a priest, but a dealer in textiles and the feathers of birds. He still believes in our ways."

"What's wrong with him?"

"He has a skin lesion that might be dangerous, and he doesn't want to be cut as his surgeons advise. All they know is the knife."

"Sometimes it's best, Lazaro. I've used it more than a few times in the clinic."

"With great skill," said Lazaro.

"We'll keep that between ourselves. The service is reserved for the poor."

"You're a healer, Joseph. Even the rich are human beings. When they need your services you should give them—well—for a price."

"You're only thinking of the money."

"Someone has to," said Lazaro, smiled, and pushed his shoulder against Joseph's.

"Very well, I'll see him, but I don't want the rich lining up at the clinic, and never, *ever* bring a priest to me."

"I understand," said Lazaro.

* * * * * * *

The man arrived on foot with an entourage of four people, two of them bearers, the other two armed with rifles. He was short and pudgy, dressed in a yellow robe of silk, and he extended a hand with ringed fingers. "I am Dionis Mendez. My family name is Redmoon."

Joseph shook his soft hand, took him inside the clinic while Lazaro remained outside with the others. Dionis sat on the edge of a table while Joseph examined the angry red, irregularly-shaped lesion on his forearm.

"This must be removed right away. It can spread to the rest of your body, and be fatal."

"I suspected that," said Dionis, "but I don't want to be cut. Friends of mine have died from infections after simple surgery."

"That's what happens when you live in the city with priests who carry foreign diseases," said Joseph. "I can remove this lesion without using a knife, but there will be pain."

Dionis' eyes widened. "I've heard your treatments are painless, that you use an energy coming through your hands."

"I can minimize pain, not eliminate it. Do you want me to proceed?"

"Of course. I want to be rid of this thing on my arm." He paused. "What are you doing?"

Joseph was moving his hands around the body and extremities of his patient without touching him. "I don't see any sign of metastasis, but your blood sugar is far too high. Eat more protein, and cut all sugars out of your diet. You're also far too heavy. Now hold out your arm."

Dionis scowled, but held out his arm. Joseph let him hold it there while he fetched a vial filled with thick, black goo. He rubbed the goo hard into the lesion, and Dionis winced. He put his hand over the lesion and squeezed hard. His hand grew warm, then hot. Dionis squirmed. "It's hurting," he complained.

"You have a low pain threshold," said Joseph. "It will only be a few minutes."

A few minutes later, Dionis was struggling to pull his arm away, and tears were running down his cheeks. "I think I'm going to faint," he moaned, and his eyes rolled wildly.

Joseph let go of the man's forearm, but grabbed his wrist and rubbed a yellowish liquid into the now mutilated area where the lesion had been. Dionis saw the horror, and cried out in fear and pain.

"Stop it. I'm nearly finished," said Joseph. "In a few seconds this enzyme will allow me to peel the skin off. Ah, there it is."

The skin around the lesion site had turned snow white, and was wrinkled like wadded paper. Joseph grabbed an edge of it with his fingertips, and ripped it off with a jerk.

"Ahhh!" screamed Dionis.

"See? No bleeding, and the lesion is gone. The scar should fade within a year. Do not bandage it, and keep it clean. The price is ten *donati*, in gold, please. You can pay Lazaro on your way out." Joseph turned away from him, placed his chemical vials back on a shelf.

Dionis was in a terrible hurry to leave. Outside, he hurled gold coins at an astonished Lazaro. "There's your money, you charlatan! The man is a primitive. He hurt me, and he's rude. I will never come back here again!"

Lazaro came back inside. "What did you do to him?"

Joseph described his treatment.

"That hasn't been used for over fifty years, and you know it," said Lazaro angrily. "I saw you treat a lesion on the little Hightree girl just two months ago. You used Blackbark sap and a red lamp, and she felt nothing! Joseph, you have deliberately hurt a patient in a vain attempt to make people believe you're not the best of our healers. It won't work, and if you ever do it again I'll have nothing more to do with you. You should be ashamed!"

Lazaro turned away, left the clinic, and slammed the door behind him.

And Joseph felt shame for what he had done.

* * * * * * *

Joseph was twenty-four when he was called by Tikan.

After the incident with the wealthy textile merchant he never again tried to make people believe he was incompetent or otherwise inferior as a healer or as a person. For four years he swallowed his fear of the priests, and what they might do to him for their god. He worked hard, and studied even harder. He performed surgeries without medications, going into the minds of his patients and blocking all sensations of pain. He stopped a heart by his mind alone, performing a delicate procedure, and then starting the organ pumping again. The herbs he used, the heat that came to his hands, performed miracles in the human body. The responsible enzymes were not found until many years after Joseph's death. Tumors shrank overnight. Wounds healed in hours or days. Old people regained their minds and strength in their bones.

Lazaro remained with him, singing the mantras and weaving his quieting spells over the sick, but it was Joseph the people looked to for their cures. He was a healer of the common people, and they felt ownership of him. He only occasionally took in patients from the city, if they had no other physician in their employ. He would not treat any priest, though a few came to him with minor complaints to test his resolve. Still they watched him, and heard inflated tales of his magic from Lazaro or other villagers, whom they bribed with gold.

Finally, one of the senior priests came to meet Joseph and try to neutralize the reasons behind his animosity towards them. He arrived with two other priests and two armed guards when Joseph was having a lunch of fruit with Lazaro on the front porch of the clinic. The senior priest stepped boldly onto the porch, bowed, and then extended his hand. "I am Cainan," he said.

Joseph shook his hand lightly, and quickly. "The clinic isn't open right now. We're having lunch."

"I'm not here for treatment," said Cainan. "I'm here to make peace with you if I can."

"I wasn't aware we were having a war," said Joseph, and laughed at his little joke.

"Can we talk privately?" asked Cainan.

Lazaro smiled. "I have things to do," he said, and left the porch before Joseph could stop him.

"Well, what is it? Has your god decided it's time for me to die?"

Cainan frowned. "I suspected it had something to do with that. You're not a believer."

"I don't believe in gods, only people, good or bad."

"Tikan is not a god. We don't worship him." Cainan looked up, and waved a hand at the sky. "He represents all that is: plants, animals, moons, the stars in the sky. He is a symbol."

"So you just make human sacrifices to him."

"On occasion, but only with the best of our kind. We give back to the universe what rightfully belongs to it."

"A free human being doesn't belong to anyone or anything," said Joseph, "so what gives you the right to take a human life in the name of the universe?"

"The people gave us that right when we came with them from the stars. We agreed to be all we could be, and to give away the best of us in return for our life here on Florencia. Each of the original families had the potential for certain abilities. When the abilities are realized the family line is honored through the sacrifice it makes."

"I know the mythology," said Joseph, "but I don't accept it as truth. Five years ago you took the life of my best friend. His family was honored, and now lives in a fine house with everything provided for them, but in five years his mother has not ceased grieving over the loss of her son, and neither have I."

Cainan closed his eyes. "I'm sorry. Now I understand. I don't know if it will help, but try to think of death as a change in form. Life continues, but in a way we can't imagine. We—"

"Save it for the believers, not me. Look, I know you're watching what I do. I'm not trying to hide anything. If you decide I'm to be a sacrifice to the stars and the people permit it then my life here is meaningless. If the people are willing to throw me away, they don't deserve the services I give to them. I've thought a lot about this, and I've stopped worrying over it."

"It's only a matter of time," said Cainan. "Your reputation is widespread, and the people expect your eventual sacrifice. We cannot play favorites, or set precedents regarding fundamental traditions."

"I understand," said Joseph, standing up. "Please leave, now. I have work to do, while I have time to do it. Maybe I can save a few lives before you take mine."

Cainan extended his hand, but Joseph refused it. "Someday soon you will understand," said the priest.

"Yes, I expect to have a long conversation with Tikan about it. Please leave."

Joseph went inside and closed the door behind him before the priest could say another word. He was bitter, angry and, quite suddenly, frightened again. Another feeling swelled in him at that instant. He was lonely. Except for Lazaro no person was really close to him, not since Bernardo had died. There had only been one woman, Reina, but now she was married, with two children. They had known each other since childhood, and she'd thought of him as a priest after he'd received the golden chain. But feelings remained between them. She'd asked him for his special blessing two days before her wedding. Her first child, Felipe, had been born in the first year of her marriage. The boy had huge eyes, and richly brown skin like honey. Joseph was reasonably certain that Felipe was his own child.

All that was past. There was only Lazaro, and he was quite old, would live at most a few more years. Work was Joseph's life, and he resolved to cram as much as he could into each day. At best, he would have only a few years left.

That was what he thought at that moment, but he was wrong.

He had only two weeks of life left to work with his people.

So Joseph Warmhand was only twenty four years old when the universe reclaimed him.

* * * * * * *

The beginning of the end came when there was a death at a farm near Joseph's village, and a young priest was sent to perform burial rites. The farm was near the edge of the jungle, and the priest felt safe traveling in the middle of the day by himself.

It was a foolish mistake. An old *Jaguerre* lay hidden at the edge of a pasture, awaiting the arrival of cattle slow enough for his ancient legs to outrun. His prey was in sight when suddenly a tall, white, sweet-smelling animal walked right by him.

He pounced on it. Nearly toothless, he ripped at the screaming animal's stomach with hind claws, but then herders of the cattle came with long knives and spears, and he ran away hungry again.

The herders pushed the priest's intestines back inside him and carried him back to the farmhouse while someone ran to fetch Santo Joseph the healer. One man held a slashed artery closed with his bare hand, and kept the man alive until help came.

By the time Joseph arrived, the priest had lost much blood. Joseph stitched the awful mess back together again and gave the young man a liter of blood from his universal donor stock. The priest did not respond; his blood pressure continued to drop, and his heart thumped feebly. Suddenly it stopped. Joseph massaged and hammered his heart, breathed into his mouth. No response.

This made Joseph angry. "He's a young man, but he's giving up. There's no reason for him to die."

Joseph put his hand on the priest's forehead, closed his own eyes—and went after him.

They met in a brightly lit place near the city of their ancestors. The priest, adorned in a gold robe and looking pious, was surprised to see Joseph there. He held up a hand in fear, and squinted against the brilliance of Joseph's image.

"What are you doing here? It's not time for you to die, and your injuries are repaired. Do not make a fool of me. Go back to your body right now!"

The priest obeyed, and all the watchers around him jumped back when he gasped and cried out, alive again.

Within one day everyone in the jungle knew what had happened to the young man. He was like a person reborn, and talked to everyone about it. Joseph had appeared as a Shaman priest, he said, holding a short spear in one hand, a snake in the other. His face and feathered head dress had glowed like the sun.

Within two days word reached the city and was brought to Cainan, who made his decision immediately and sent his people out to fetch Joseph. They took him in the middle of the night; he awoke with two priests and six soldiers standing around his bed. Lazaro hugged him long and hard, and promised to join him soon. The entire village turned out to see him off, smiling faces filled with pride, but tears streaking their cheeks.

They put him in a horse-drawn cart and took him to the city, straight to a top floor room in a building overlooking the square. A balcony was enclosed by iron grillwork. Servants came to bathe him in a monstrous tub of polished granite. They brought him clothing and food, and two remained with him at all times to see to his needs.

He asked for paper and stylus, and Cainan himself brought them to him. "Are you comfortable here?" asked the high priest.

"How comfortable should I be when I'm about to die?"

"You appear to be taking it calmly," said Cainan. "I'm not surprised, since it seems you've seen death and come back from it."

"My body wasn't being incinerated at the time," said Joseph nastily. "How long do I have to wait?"

"Five or six days. Some of our guests take that long to get here. I can tell you one thing, Joseph. There will be no pain, and since Lazaro is the only close person surviving you he'll be well cared for. I hear your bitterness. As you once suggested to me, you'll have to discuss it with Tikan."

"Of course," said Joseph the unbeliever. "In the meantime I'm going to write down every treatment I've done that hasn't been recorded yet, and all the questions I hoped to answer someday. Do what you want with it."

"That's a generous thing for you to do," said Cainan.

"It's only to keep my mind distracted," lied Joseph. Perhaps the questions alone would lead to important new discoveries in the future. At the moment it seemed to him a kind of vengeance, giving something back to people who were throwing him away out of religious ignorance. He did not want to be a martyr, though, but a person remembered respectfully for what he'd done.

For the next five days he slept little, ate little, and composed a substantial volume of pages in a style he hoped would be understood. On the evening of the fifth day he stood on the balcony and watched the crowd begin to assemble in the square, many spending the night there just to claim a good place to see the parade of the sacrifice. The great pyramid had not yet begun to spew smoke, but that night Joseph thought he saw points of light moving near its summit. He had a fine dinner, a long, hot bath and went to bed early.

He did not sleep deeply one minute that night, but dozed, awakened several times by the hammering of his heart. In the morning he felt drugged. He ate lightly, some cooked meal and fruit, and servants came to dress him in sandals, feathered crown, and shirt and pants from the pelts of *Jaguerren*. An herbal tea, laced with so much opiate he could taste it, was supposed to calm him, but didn't. His heart would be still one minute and pounding the next as the reality of his death day came and went.

They took him down stairs to the back of the building. He was put in a horse-drawn cart accompanied by ten soldiers and they went down back streets blocked off by more soldiers to a little square with a bubbling fountain where the procession was assembling. Twenty men already held aloft the platform on which he would be displayed. He stepped onto it directly from the cart and gazed out at the people who would follow him. Lazaro was there, Joseph's only family, and he was weeping. Otherwise there was not a single face Joseph recognized. He was a stranger to these people, even though several of them wore the golden chain of the chosen.

The remaining moments of his life seemed to rush by at an accelerating rate, and his breathing quickened. The crowd murmur was loud, then subdued, then gone as he approached. Ahead of him, the great pyramid had begun spewing smoke from its heights. The first flower landed on the platform. It was followed by a shower of color that continued along the entire route. People pressed in, many reaching out to touch the platform, thousands beyond them and not a sound to be heard. Men, women, children gazed up at him with an awe, a reverence that made him angry. They would honor him, then kill him as a part of a religious experience based on beliefs their victim didn't share.

Cainan met him on the steps leading to the base of the great pyramid, and took his hand in ceremony. Two other priests flanked them as they walked to the flower-covered railcar for the short trip to the pyramid's summit. Overhead, that summit was now obscured by a thick, brownish cloud.

They got into the car. A priest pressed a lever, and they moved upwards at a steep angle. Cainan still held Joseph's hand, and squeezed it. "Fine," he said softly. "You're doing fine. It will soon be over."

Suddenly they were in the brownish cloud, and there was a sharp odor in the car, but the cloud was quickly gone. The car stopped abruptly at the summit, and they exited onto a platform of metal grillwork scorched by great heat. Beneath the grillwork a shaft descended into blackness. Warm air came up from the shaft to swirl away the cloud at the summit. Cainan stood Joseph in the center of the grillwork, and put a hand on his shoulder. "You will be missed here. Now go with Tikan, and serve him as best you can."

Cainan got back into the car, and it descended out of sight into the cloud. Joseph clenched his fist, remembering the pillar of flame that had taken his friend, and understood he now awaited a quick death. Any second, now, the flame would come from beneath his feet, and he would be consumed.

The grillwork suddenly moved beneath his feet, and for an instant he felt he was floating. Dark walls rushed past him as he descended into the shaft. The odor of something like tree sap was sharp in his nostrils. He descended many meters, and the grillwork platform suddenly stopped with a clang. It was cold, and the light from above was a spot the size of half a hand held overhead. The odor was stifling; he wanted to sneeze, but the horrible pounding of his heart kept forcing it away.

A door opened three steps away from him, flooding the platform with light. A man stood there, strangely dressed in a single piece suit of rough, white cloth. "This way, please," he said, and motioned to Joseph.

Joseph hesitated. The man was tall, and white-skinned like Cainan and the other priests.

"Quickly, please. There won't be much air in here when the burners ignite." He held out a hand.

Joseph took it, stepped off the platform into a stairwell. The man closed and bolted the door, led Joseph down a flight of stone stairs to a brightly lit, metal-lined compartment where another man waited, also dressed in white. They stepped inside, and doors shut behind them. Joseph's stomach moved as the compartment began to descend. Seconds later there was a dull roar, and the walls vibrated.

"Fire in the sky," said one man.

The other man turned to Joseph and touched his arm, startling him. "Hey, relax. You're already dead," he said, and smiled.

The doors opened, and an older man was there. "I'm Marcus," he said, and took Joseph by the elbow. "I'm sure you're confused right now, and I'll explain a few things on the way to the terminal, but first you need a change of clothes."

Joseph was taken to a room where he changed into a white suit like the other men were wearing. "I'm not going to die here?" he asked hopefully.

"We haven't lost anyone yet," said Marcus. "When the priests serve up the end-product of their bioengineering, we're very careful with it. Last man we picked up here was five years ago."

Joseph's face flushed. "He's not dead?"

"Not likely. Last I saw Bernardo he was doing the psy-evaluation of my crew before we left Wolf System. That was three months ago. Do you know him?"

"He was my best friend," said Joseph, tearfully fumbling to button up his suit.

Marcus smiled. "Well, in three months you can take up where you left off. You'll be working together in the same clinic. I think you'll like Wolf, too. It's a new colony with a rich, virgin environment, and they need plenty of expertise in jungle medicine. From what I hear, you have that, and more. It's what you were engineered for. We depend a lot on genetic hives like Florencia for the special skills we need. The priests are a bit strange, but they do good work. On Wolf we've infiltrated an old culture with our study groups, and our mandate is to keep the culture intact. You have been raised in that culture right here on Florencia. We'll show you the bioengineering we want done, and the training you must do for the people involved. You'll be a priest on Wolf, a mentor to the newly gifted, giving back a service that was done for you here. I guess that's a shock. You just blushed."

"I have not been a friend to the priests here," said Joseph, and Marcus laughed.

"Ready? You have a twenty minute ride to the terminal. By this evening you'll be deep in space, looking at Jacinta close-up."

Joseph felt giddy. They went to a car resting on rails running into a long tunnel, and got in. The car lurched forward, and in seconds rock walls were rushing past them. Marcus smiled again. "Wow, you should see your eyes. Ask what you like, and I'll answer the best I can. In a way, you're starting your life all over again."

"Is there really a being named Tikan?" asked Joseph.

"You a believer?"

"No."

"That'll make it easier. I don't know who made up the word. It's derived from an ancient word meaning 'source of life'. Wherever life is, Tikan is there. Symbolism. The priests have formalized it to bring order to the disjointed societies of the hives. Tikan means life to them."

Now it was Joseph who smiled. "I thought I was going to die today, but instead I've been chosen for life."

"Nice way to look at it," said Marcus, and then spent the rest of the trip to the shuttle terminal telling Joseph all about the place where he would live it.

MUTINY ON THE *PHOEBUS*

Floyd Gibson was down to his last fifty credits pocket money when he landed the job on *Phoebus*, and for once it wasn't Jani who was the problem, but Floyd himself. *Phoebus* was a Class-Three tug, with little capacity for on-board cargo, but they would be hauling a year's supply of water and bottled gases for the biosphere on route to Korelco Station. There was work for one Webber, and Floyd was the only one who'd showed up in Merchant's Hall the day they signed on.

They'd snapped Jani right up, and of course Jani wouldn't go anywhere without Floyd, and said so. Jani Balodis was a scraper and painter, and *Phoebus* had just finished a two year ore haul through the belt. The hull was a peeling mess, down to bare metal in places, and Jani would be on EVA most of the trip just to get the scraping done.

So Floyd swallowed his pride, happy for Jani's sake, and when they left Merchant's Hall he'd reached up to put an arm around the big Latvian's shoulders. "Thanks for the job, Jani. I owe you one."

Jani blushed. "Aw, Floyd, I owe you more, and besides, we're buddies."

"You bet we are," said Floyd, and meant it, even though it was a most unlikely friendship. Floyd considered himself reasonably intelligent, a certified electrician and comp-tech before the market flooded with younger, cheaper men. Jani was—well, not exactly retarded—just slow. And likeable. A big, gentle guy who loved little animals, and little men who couldn't take care of themselves in bars. That's how they'd gotten together seven years before, in a bar on the Alco wheel off Luna, a drunk busily re-working Floyd's face until Jani had stepped in and crushed the man's fist with a single squeeze. They'd shipped out together ever since, and somewhere along the way had become like brothers.

"I'll buy you dinner," said Floyd, and they went to a fast food lounge aft of Alco Port II, where a huge screen gave them a good view of Mars, only five thousand klicks below them. The coin-operated dispensers served up what passed these days for meatloaf, potatoes, a greenish gruel reported to be spinach, and coffee. The lounge was nearly full, and they took the last table in a corner. Floyd wolfed down his meal, while Jani ate gingerly, savoring every bite, easy to please. In the midst of coffee, Floyd felt a hand on his shoulder.

"You shipping out on *Phoebus*? So am I, as number three. Roch Pendu. I'm the fitter, and com-tech." The man was Floyd's size, small but muscular, dark hair and eyes. Floyd nodded, introduced himself and Jani and they shook hands.

"I see some of the new crew here. Want to meet them?" said Roch.

"Sure," said Floyd, never keen on meeting new people, but he knew Jani would want to. Roch led them to a table in the center of the lounge, where five men, one of them distinguished looking and out of place compared to his companions, were hunched over in intense conversation. One man stood up, glaring at them. He was huge, heavier than Jani, square-jaw, predatory eyes. "This is a private conversation, Frenchy. Take a hike."

Floyd disliked the man immediately.

"Easy, Monk. Here's part of your new crew." Roch looked at Floyd. "This here's Monk Kyrillos, your Super and Bosun, and there's Jocko, Gurth, and Jabez, and—I don't know this man."

The distinguished looking man looked down at the table as if to hide his face from them.

"You don't need to know," growled Monk. "Like I said, this is private."

"This is Floyd Gibson, our new Webber, and—"

Jani was standing behind Floyd, hiding. Monk leaned to one side and smiled, showing gaps where two teeth should have been. "Who's the big guy?" he said.

"His name's Jani, and he's a scraper," said Floyd. Jani pulled on his jacket from behind. "Let's go, Floyd," he said softly. "They're busy."

"Yeah, we're busy. Very good. So I'll see you on board at four hours sharp. Don't be late, 'cause we can do without you. Goodbye, Frenchy."

Roch guided them away from the table, and out of the lounge. "Sorry," he said. "Walk soft around Monk, but do your job and he'll leave you alone. Don't do it, and bad things can happen, accidents, that sort of thing. I don't know why Captain Santos puts up with him, but he does. Word is that Monk has pull with execs in Alco, but

I don't see how. He's basically a port-side bully, but he's permanent crew, a Super, and acting Bosun, and I don't argue with him. Nobody argues with him. Look, I've got to go. Nice to meet you guys. I work com-panel. If you want to send a message home, just let me know, okay?"

"Sure," said Floyd. There would be no messages. Home was wherever he and Jani were together. "I call you Roch, or Frenchy?"

"Frenchy is fine," said the man, smiling. "See you tomorrow."

Jani tugged at his sleeve, looking worried. "That guy Monk, he don't like me, Floyd. I don't want to make trouble for you on board. Maybe I should—"

"We're a pair, Jani. You don't go, I don't go, and we need the money. I'll handle Monk. Don't worry about it."

Jani grinned, head cocked to one side like a bashful child. "Okay, Floyd. I'll do a good job, I promise. I always try to do a good job."

"You bet," said Floyd, patting him on the back as they headed to bunk bay for an early bed-time. The encounter in the lounge had disturbed him, for it was clear Monk had not been angry at meeting them, but by having a private conversation interrupted. He'd seen fear in the eyes of the others at that table. Fear of what? Being overheard?"

It was not until later that he learned part of what that conversation was all about. If he could have known sooner, he and Jani would gladly have risked losing their papers to avoid being shipped out on *Phoebus*. He couldn't have known it would be the last trip they would ever make together.

* * * * * * *

Loading began at four hours, and Floyd was still webbing shuttle-sized modules of water and liquid gases into place in forward bay when they pulled out of port at fourteen hours. *Phoebus* was an old tug, going back a hundred years, a two-hundred-mega kilo chunk of alloy shaped like a flat-iron with T-4 engine pontoons pulling a titanyl ball five times its size. The ball was a pleasure-sphere bound for the vicinity of Korelco Station and its crowds of miners and haulers in for a few days of escape from tumbling asteroids, cold, and black space. It would be several days before Floyd would see the marvels inside it. By the time he got to mess, everyone else had finished, but Jani was waiting for him and nursed a second cup of coffee while Floyd ate.

Jani seemed subdued, even thoughtful. "Floyd," he said, "how long're we gonna do this?"

"Nine or ten months, this time. We'll be half-way around the sun by the time we chase down Korelco."

"Then what, Floyd? We find another freighter?"

It was an old conversation. Jani was thinking about the desert again. "Maybe," he said, "if you want to. You thinking about Terra?"

"Yeah," said Jani, "and all the time I'll spend outside on this trip. It's so cold out there, Floyd, dark, and lonely. You get to stay inside all the time."

"Sunlight," said Floyd. "An adobe house in the Sonora desert, cool inside, but sunlight streaming in open windows, and fresh air, and quiet."

"And animals," said Jani.

"A cow, some sheep to tend—"

"Chickens and Geese, and a big vegetable garden like my ma had in the old country, Floyd. No more synthetic food, or cold."

"Yeah," said Floyd.

It was their dream.

"We got the money now, don't we, Floyd?"

"Not quite, Jani. That's the problem. We need at least twenty thousand credits to get started, and we're ten short of that. Merchant Guild mustering out pay will barely cover the shuttle back to Terra. I can show you our bank balance, Jani."

"That's okay. I believe you. How long?"

"Two trips, maybe, after this one. Three years, I guess."

Jani sighed. "That's a long time, but I can wait. You take care of our money, Floyd. If it weren't for you, I'd end up dying out here with a scraper in my hand. We're gonna have a real home someday."

Floyd smiled, reached over and squeezed Jani's huge, rough hand until the big guy grinned.

A shadow fell over their table. It was Monk, and he looked at Jani. "Your shift starts in an hour. Better suit up and get out there. You'll be working with Jocko, and he'll show you where to start. Get going. I want to talk with your friend here."

"Yes, sir," said Jani, getting up and leaving the room. Monk sat down opposite Floyd and sipped at a cup of coffee. "All battened down?"

"Finished an hour ago."

"Yeah, I saw. You know what you're doing."

Monk's face seemed softer, now, his former hostility gone. "Your papers say you're an electrician, too."

"Basic stuff," said Floyd. "Wiring for con-panels, motors, pumps, lighting, power supplies. Not much call for that, anymore."

"There is on this trip," said Monk. "You'll be spending most of your time in the biosphere we're towing, to do just that. We've only got seven months to get it operational. A smart guy like you should have it ready in three. I'll have a work order with timelines ready for you by tomorrow. Any problem with that?"

"No. Sounds interesting."

"Good," said Monk, standing, then leaning over the table, eyes glinting. "You guys do your jobs, and I take care of you. You do extra you get paid extra. You slough off, you get nothing, and I decide which way it goes. That clear?"

"You're the Super, Mister Kyrillos."

The big man put a hard paw on Floyd's shoulder. "Call me Monk. Like I say, I take care of my people. A smart guy like you can always use extra pay. You play ball with me, and I'll get it for you." He squeezed Floyd's shoulder, and left the room.

Floyd wondered afterwards how much of his conversation with Jani had been overheard by Monk.

* * * * * * *

The great biosphere called the Pleasure Dome was connected to *Phoebus* by a cylindrical tunnel one hundred meters long, with two fins at its end to tack in the weak plume eddies of the T-4's. The tunnel air was stale, mingled with odors of oil and fresh polymer as Floyd and Lyle Malone swung from hand hold to hand hold to the closed air-lock and eight-foot portal rigged with explosive bolts.

"Hang on," said Lyle. He showed Floyd the four-number sequence for the door, punched it in and the door swung inwards, a rushing wind raking their bodies and blowing them into horizontal positions as they held on with a hand. The wind ceased with the equalization of pressure in the tunnel. There was a sound like the whine of a turbine, and Floyd suddenly realized the circular portal was turning slowly counter-clockwise while ahead of him several bright working lights were moving in the opposite direction. He hesitated, momentarily disoriented, as Lyle drifted forward ahead of him and suddenly stopped. "Grab a strap tight, and get ready for point-three-gee." Lyle was now facing him, legs out of sight. Floyd pushed off, drifted up to Lyle and grabbed onto a webbed array of elastic polymer. Immediately his body rotated, head swirling until he felt a metal latticework touch his feet, but still he held on grimly.

Lyle laughed. "You can let go, now. The floor's right there. The sphere is rotating at point-two radians per second, and the outer shell compensates for the gyro-effect. Let go, Floyd." Lyle held on long enough to punch the lock closed, then dropped and was standing. "See, no hands."

Floyd dropped beside him, eyes adapting to the gloom. They had come out onto a latticed balcony, and below them were several levels lit by scattered work lights, curving out of sight to either side. The place was immense.

"There are five levels," said Lyle, leading him down stairs. "Top two are recreation: bars, restaurants, eco-lounges with holo-screens for your environment of choice. All the hydroponics are here. Level three is guest rooms, and the control area, levels four and five all the machinery, environmental control and recycling systems. Nothing will go to waste here. Alco must have spent five years profit outbidding three other corporations for this thing, but I bet they get it all back in two. Those miners have a lot of free money to spend, and once you get people in here it's basically a self-sustaining system. Clear profit."

They walked around the top level, past roll-down panels shutting off rooms from view, but now Floyd smelled odors he only remembered from Terra: plants, wet earth, and a sharper smell reminding him of manure. "You'll be doing all the lighting," said Lyle, "so you'll get to see everything room by room. Me, I'll be down in the bowels of this thing most of the time, getting the control boards in. Monk wants it all done in three months."

"Yeah, he told me that, too."

"Don't know why he's in such a rush. It'll be seven months before we reach Korelco. Must have been part of the deal to have it all ready to open when we get there."

"A long way to go," said Floyd.

"Not really. All the wiring has been pulled. Once the lighting panels are connected, you'll see how far along it is here. Hydroponics is already in, and stuff is growing. Lots to do yet, but extra shifts mean more pay, and if you're flexible on what you'll do, Monk will take care of you."

Level five was only closed rooms, level four bounded by glass which was the wall of a free-swimming fish tank running the circumference of the sphere and already filled with water and fine gravel on its bottom. "The first hatchlings are upstairs," said Lyle, "trout, bluegill, hybrid salmon. You see a few animals around, rabbits and chukkas, good breeders. That and hydroponics are the only fresh food; everything else is synth, and chemical storage is level four."

By mid-shift, Floyd had seen the entire sphere. Coming up the stairs to level four he looked up to see Monk waiting there with another man, older, smaller, a short, white beard. He was wearing slacks, and a black turtle-neck shirt.

"Well, what do you think?"

"A lot to do in three months," said Floyd.

"Not if you're willing to make a lot of extra pay," said Monk. "Floyd, I want you to meet Captain Santos. Captain, this is the new guy I was telling you about."

Santos stuck out a hand. His grip was dry, and hard. "Welcome aboard, Floyd. Monk tells me you do lots of things."

"Yes, sir, but I'm only certified for webbing and basic electrical."

Santos smiled. "The union doesn't matter here, Floyd. If you have the skills to do a job, plumbing, welding, whatever, that's all I care about. I run an open shop here. Monk knows what you've done before now; if he tells you to do something, you do it. Anything past first shift is time-and-a-half, anything past two is double-time. Sound good?"

Floyd watched Monk, the occasional nod of his head, eyes moving to and from the smaller, older man. Monk was a formidable presence among the crew, but it was now clear who was truly in charge. "I'll give you everything I've got, Captain," said Floyd, and Monk smiled.

Floyd would not encounter Captain Gregory Santos again for nearly three months, and by then the atmosphere would not be nearly as friendly as it was at that moment.

* * * * * * *

The weeks flew by, Floyd working double and occasional triple shifts from day one, pausing only to wolf down synth meals from the mess dispenser, and sleeping when he could. He saw little of Jani, who worked continuous double shifts on EVA, with a sleep break in between, and his friend was already complaining by the end of their fourth week. "I'm doing all the work, Floyd. Jocko isn't helping at all."

"He's out there, isn't he?"

"Yeah, but I'm doing all the scraping. He works at it a while, drags these boxes around and screws them in at places all over the hull, and then scrapes a little before we go inside. Most of what's done I've done, Floyd, and Jocko told me he's getting paid extra for the boxes. It isn't fair, Floyd. I'm working *hard*."

"Just keep your nose clean, Jani. Between the two of us the money is coming in good, and you know what that can mean."

"Yeah, I know, Floyd. It's just that I'm tired and cold all the time. I don't think I want to do this anymore, not after this trip. I want us to go home, Floyd. I want us to have our own place." Jani seemed despondent and exhausted, and there were at least five months of work ahead of him.

"Hang in there, buddy. Jocko's doing something extra for Monk that you probably can't do, is all. What are the boxes?"

"I don't know, and Jocko says he don't, either. They're about like this," and Jani vaguely outlined a shape with his hands, "and he screws them into little nipples all over the hull."

"Those are feed-throughs for sensory instruments," said Floyd. "Jocko's installing sensory devices of some kind, so he probably knows electronics, and you don't. Do your job, Jani, and let Jocko do his. With all the work we're getting, this could be our last trip."

That seemed to satisfy Jani, but even as Floyd reassured him he felt a crawling sensation in his stomach. That rough shape Jani had outlined with his hands; where had he seen it before?

The question would gnaw at him for two months before he would deem it necessary to find out exactly what those boxes were doing out there.

* * * * * * *

Floyd talked to Frenchy about it, but Frenchy didn't know any gossip about boxes. He was pondering a question of his own. "I'm getting a lot of incoming from Alco-T for Captain's ears only, and it seems a little strange. Our destination is Korelco Station, and Alco-T is clear out in orbit around Titan. They don't have anything to do with our cargo."

"Korelco, Alco, it's all the same company, right?"

"Yeah, but the stations have their own management, and different functions. I don't think they even talk to each other. Korelco's mining and refining, and Alco-T is a methane-based fuel refinery. They have nothing in common."

Floyd shrugged his shoulders, and went back to his shift, as did Frenchy. The question, though interesting, didn't seem important at the time.

The work in the biosphere went faster than he'd expected, and in another three weeks he'd finished all the lighting: bright white in interior halls of the mall-type structure, bluish hues in the growing rooms with their hydroponic stink, and soft reds in the eating and drinking lounges. He found one room lined with cages containing rabbits and chukka chicks, their food dispersed automatically, cage bottom trays withdrawn and cleaned regularly, all computer-controlled. The animals seemed lonely, rushing to the cage sides when he came up to talk to them, sniffing or pecking at his fingers. He could hardly wait to tell Jani about the animals, and when he did so Jani was desperate to see them. That would have to wait.

He spent another week helping Lyle finish up the control boards, each day fighting the nausea from starting at zero-gee, popping into point-three-gee, and back to zero again as he descended towards the center of the sphere. That, plus the usual zigzag walking pattern to keep from being thrown off balconies by Coriolis forces, continued to make his mid-shift meal a light affair.

Floyd kept his utility bag with him at all times: snack bars, tools, the old pistol he favored over knives traditionally carried by freighter crews. He'd faced down two dangerous men with it in twenty years of space-faring, and kept it oiled and loaded. Working with Lyle, he grew to know and like the man. A kid, really, with only five years space time, a wife and two little girls earth side, and another baby to be born about the time they reached Korelco Station. Listening to Lyle talk about them, Floyd thought of his own life as a spacer, all twenty years of it, with no family, no ties, only Jani. Perhaps, when he and Jani had their own place, it would be possible to think about a wife and family. But Floyd always lived in the present, and followed his own advice to Jani. 'Keep your head in the dream, and your feet in the present, and the dream will come true.' Financially, things were looking good, Monk seemed to like him, and he'd even been civil to Jani, who was working his heart out to please everyone.

But things began to deteriorate soon after that.

In-between shifts, Floyd routinely went to the forward bay to check on the containers he'd webbed there. Late in week nine, he made such an inspection, found a leak in the main valve of the large water container, and simply tightened the valve. It was a small leak, no liquid globules in the air, and he wiped container and valve clean with a cloth. It was hydroponic chemicals, not water. The big container was loaded with hydroponic chemicals! He was alone, his curiosity aroused. He used a poly-bottle to sample the other containers from bleeder valves, expecting a spurt of liquid gases, but brownish liquid bubbled from each of them. They were all the same, not liquid gases, but the raw carbohydrate and protein soup ingredients used in the synth dispensers. Extra supplies for the biosphere? If so, there was enough here for a lifetime of operation, once the recycling systems were underway. So why the lie about water and liquid gases?

It was the lie that bothered him, not the tank contents, and there was still that nagging feeling about the instruments Jocko had placed outside. Jani had quit complaining about it, because the job had been finished, and Jocko was back at the scraping again. But there was something clandestine about the way they'd been installed. Something about their shape, somehow familiar, and yet—

He kept these things to himself, until a few days later when Monk came to him and offered extra pay to help transfer the contents of all webbed tanks into the storage containers of the biosphere.

"We're not going to off-load these containers?" he asked.

"Korelco is short-handed, and agreed to pay a nice price if we load the sphere in-transit," said Monk. "Captain wants it done right away. You'll do the pumps while the transfer lines are run, and we'll need some webbing on the lines below level three in the Pleasure Dome. I'd say that's good for an extra thousand credits in your pocket."

"We'll need to leak-check the tanks in the sphere. We can lose a lot of vapor and gas in six months if there's even a small hole in a weld-seam."

Monk's eyes clouded for just a second, but enough for Floyd to see his momentary confusion. "Yeah—well, you'd better do that first. There's a helium-sniffer in the sphere, but hurry it up. Captain wants the transfer to be finished in two weeks. You want the job, or not?" Now the big man's eyes cleared, narrowing.

"I'm on it, starting with the leak checks," said Floyd.

Monk left, and Floyd was thinking, *he was confused when I said six months. That's the time to Korelco, but all our work-orders had three month time-lines, and now all the sphere needs to be operational will be on-board by then. What the hell is the big rush for, if we'll be drawing pay and sitting around idle for nearly five months at the rate we're going?*

He said nothing to Jani or Lyle, but confided in Frenchy over coffee after second shift, telling him about the container contents and their coming transfer. Frenchy wrinkled his brow. "Doesn't make sense to me, either. Monk is working the crew half to death, and all at extra pay. I got a message from Korelco Station a few hours ago, confirming intercept at eight-twenty and seven hours, and I passed it on to Captain Santos. That's nearly five and a half months from now, and we'll be ready for delivery in two *weeks*! But

I keep getting messages from Alco-T, for Santos only. Two a day, now."

"Are we on course?" asked Floyd.

"Yes. We coast all the way, and do one short burn about a week out from Korelco. Why?"

"I just wondered if the company had changed its mind, and wanted the sphere to go to Alco-T instead of Korelco," said Floyd.

"No way. That's another year out, and we'd have to do a major burn now to get on the right trajectory. We don't have enough fuel for that, and besides, Korelco is clearly expecting us. You look worried, Floyd."

"Yeah, I guess I am. Something's going on here, and we're not being told what it is. I think we're getting ready for delivery in three weeks, and that can't be to Korelco Station. I'd sure like to know what those instruments are that Jocko's installed on the hull. They might be signaling someone."

"You thinking piracy?"

"Maybe. It's happened for cargos a lot less valuable than the Pleasure Dome, and more than one Captain has turned over his ship for a fat retirement in hiding. It happens, Frenchy."

"Jesus! There could be some danger here. Monk, and the Captain—"

"And Jocko. I think he's in on it. Don't say anything to the crew. Right now this is wild speculation, but I'm going to find out what those hull instruments are doing. Keep your eyes and ears open, and let me know anything new you think is important."

Monk and two other crew members came in as Floyd and Frenchy were leaving the mess room. Monk looked at them, smiled, and his eyes were still on both of them as they left the room.

* * * * * * *

Floyd worked double shifts installing two pumps forward while transfer lines were run under decks to the tunnel leading to the biosphere and down into it. He webbed the lines to the superstructure below level three, and helped Lyle make the connections to the tanks there. It was ten days into the job when he finally got together with Jani for a talk in their sleeping cubicle. Jani was just getting up, slithering from the webbing of his vertical hammock, when Floyd came in from his shift.

"I want you to do something for me, Jani, and it might be dangerous," said Floyd.

"What's the matter? You got trouble?" said Jani.

"Maybe we all do, but I don't know yet, and the less you know the better it is for you. I need to know what those boxes are that Jocko installed outside, and I want you to get one for me to look at. Just a look, and then you put it right back."

Jani frowned. "Aw, Floyd, Jocko will see me do it, and I'll get in bad trouble for messing around with his stuff. He's out there all the time, and he doesn't like me much, anyway. He says I work too slow."

"You work side-by-side?"

"Not now. Jocko's on the other side, but he sort of checks up on me once in awhile, and I never know when. Always checking on me, like I was a little kid, but I don't say nothing. I don't make trouble, Floyd."

"Anyplace you can sort of hide yourself for a few minutes?"

"Only the big fins forward. I been working by them for a week, now. There's a box there, Floyd. I seen it. It's screwed in like the others."

"First thing when you're out there, this shift, wait 'til Jocko's out of sight, and right away remove the box. Put it in your utility pack. Bring it here. I'll look at it, then first thing next shift you put it back. Jocko will never know, and we haven't hurt anything. Okay?"

Jani twisted his fingers together. "I been good this trip, Floyd. Nobody is mad at me, or calling me names. I've been doing a good job, even if Jocko says I'm slow."

Floyd put an arm around him. "It's a risk, Jani, but it's important. It's very important for all of us."

Jani sighed. "All right, Floyd, I'll try."

Floyd felt lousy after Jani had left for his shift. He velcroed down the hall to the com room and told Frenchy what was going on. "Any way they might know if an instrument is disabled?"

"I don't know," said Frenchy. "Nothing's coming through here; maybe at the Captain station. Could be he doesn't know about those instruments; maybe it's Monk."

"I doubt that," said Floyd, thinking of excuses to make if Jani were caught. "Anything new?"

"Nothing. But Santos ordered me to stay here all the time, meals, sleep, anything. I think he's expecting more messages. And the crew is grumbling about all the shifts, and little sack time. Monk is pushing them hard."

"I'll check back when Jani returns. I'm supposed to be sleeping."

Floyd went back to his cubicle and webbed up, but all he could think about was Jani, scared to death, out there with Jocko in frozen vacuum, doing something dangerous because he'd been asked to do it by his only friend. He fell in and out of a doze, awakening each time to glance at the digital clock glowing in the darkness, and each time only a half hour or so had passed. His eyes began to burn, stomach rumbling as he floated in darkness, until finally the door slid open and he saw Jani there, grinning, and hauling his utility pack inside behind him. The door shut. "I got it, Floyd, and Jocko didn't see me."

Floyd reached out, flicked on the light, and struggled out of his hammock while Jani fumbled in his pack and pulled out a tan box the size of two boot boxes tied together. Unmarked, the box had an Ampex, threaded female adaptor on one side, and a short rod antenna on the other.

Floyd caught his breath as the nagging, foggy memory suddenly became clear. "Holy shit," he said. "We are in real trouble, for sure."

"What, Floyd?" said Jani

"It's a Wall-Banger, Jani, a box of plastic explosive that fires a shaped charge out the bottom. It must be ten years ago I had to re-pack a crate of these things on a freighter bound for Helios; miners use them to cut away well-defined slabs of rock in strip-mining operations. It's a bomb, Jani, electromagnetically activated. The right signal from inside or outside *Phoebus* can fire it off and blow a fist-sized hole through the hull of this ship. How many are out there?"

"Oh—lots," said Jani. "They're all over the hull, maybe ten or twenty of them. If they blow up, Floyd, that'll let the air out of the ship, won't it?"

"We could decompress in seconds. Jesus, whatever they're up to they don't intend to let the crew tag along. I've got to tell Frenchy. Wait here, and hide that thing. I'll be back in a few minutes."

The hall was dark and empty, but he could hear faint voices coming from the Captain's Station up stairs aft. Laughter. Monk. He drifted this time to the com shack, tapped with a finger, and Frenchy let him in. "Bad news," he said, and told Frenchy about what Jani had found.

"That's crazy, Floyd; you want him to *reinstall* the thing?"

"Twenty bombs, or nineteen, what's the difference? I don't want to warn Jocko we've found anything."

"It's piracy, then," said Frenchy. "I bet they're working with someone on Alco-T. They hire out a free-lancer, take the Pleasure Dome, and kill the crew. Sell the dome to another station outside the corporation. They're scattered all over the belt, and the rivalries are so bad they don't even talk to each other. Floyd, we've got to neutralize those bombs!"

"My bet is the radio-detonator for them is at the Captain's Station, or in Monk's room."

"Then we confront Santos, and put him in custody. The regs are clear on this, Floyd. Any merchant Captain who knowingly puts the lives of his crew in jeopardy can be relieved of command."

"Monk is number two," said Floyd.

"And I'm number three," said Frenchy. "I say we inform the crew, then confront Santos and Monk and take charge, at least until those bombs are neutralized. There are enough weapons on board to put up a good fight when the pirate ship arrives, and we'll be free to warn Korelco Station about what's happening."

"We could also grab Jocko, and have Jani remove the bombs before we confront Santos and Monk. I think that's safer."

Frenchy considered this. "Okay, I'll think about it until Jocko and Jani are back inside, but then we make a move. The more we wait, the more likely those bombs can go off even accidentally. We can't dick around with this. Be ready to move at the end of Jani's shift, and I'll come by your cubicle." He turned back to his panel. "Something's coming in. You'd better go."

Back in his cubicle, Floyd reconsidered one of Frenchy's concerns. He sawed off the stem of the Wall Banger's antenna connecting to *Phoebus'* interior, packed the cavity with toilet paper, then cut off the outside antenna and covered the scar with several layers of electrical tape while Jani watched quietly. "Not a hundred percent, but a lot safer than it was. Put it back first thing, Jani."

Jani nodded grimly. "Are we gonna die here, Floyd?"

"Not if I can help it, buddy." Floyd dug into his gear bag, pulled out the old revolver, and swung out the cylinder. Six cartridges had been there for ten years, and he couldn't even be sure the gun would go off if he had to use it. He carefully snicked the cylinder closed and stuffed the gun inside his waist belt, pulling his shirt down to hide it. "Look for me at the airlock after your shift. From now on, we're staying together. You understand?"

"Yes, Floyd." Jani put the bomb back in his utility pack, and then they crawled into their hammocks, knowing there would be no sleep. Floyd turned out the light, and moments later it was Jani who broke the silence.

"You take good care of us, Floyd. Thanks for being my friend."

"We take care of each other, Jani. That's the way it is. Try to sleep, now."

"Yes, Floyd."

But they didn't sleep, and what seemed like hours later they felt *Phoebus* suddenly shudder, then the distinctive hum of a superstructure under acceleration.

"Crap, we're doing a burn," said Floyd. It lasted for over a minute, a strong burn that momentarily pressed them firmly to the cubicle wall, and then they were weightless again. "I've got to see Frenchy about this." He struggled out of his hammock, but didn't even reach the door before there was a sharp rap on it. He gripped the revolver under his shirt, then opened the door.

It was Frenchy. He pulled himself inside quickly as the door shut.

"Another call came in earlier from Alco-T, and now we're changing course. Whatever's going on has started, Floyd, and we have to move quickly. Don't put that bomb back, Jani."

I've disabled it," said Floyd.

"Not good enough. Take it outside and give it a shove. And pull out as many of those things as you can."

"Jocko will find out," said Jani. "He'll try to stop me."

"Then you'll have to deal with him. Those bombs have to come out, or we're all going to die here. Jani, you're the only one who can do it for us."

"Aw, Floyd, this is real bad," moaned Jani.

"I know, but Frenchy's right. You can't possibly get all of them in one shift, but pull as many as you can. And if you see any explosions, keep your suit on and get back in here. I don't want you left outside if there's trouble here. Understand?"

Jani nodded, but he looked as scared as Floyd had ever seen him.

"I'm getting the crew together in forward bay in ten minutes," said Frenchy, "and we'll go to Santos together."

"Better give Jani some time," said Floyd.

Frenchy didn't agree. "We'll be safe as long as Monk and the Captain aren't suited up. No, we've got to move on the Captain's Station and neutralize what's going on there, at least force the ship back on course, and put in a call to Korelco."

"Then wait until Jani and Jocko are outside. If we meet now, Jocko might find out, go straight to Monk, and then they'll be waiting for us. That's just an hour, Frenchy. Wait one hour."

It took more talk, but Frenchy finally agreed to hold the meeting in forward bay right after Jani and Jocko had gone EVA. He left to return to the com shack, and in a muted way Floyd felt guilty about getting him to delay the meeting. It was his own motivation that bothered him, for it was selfish. A scenario of possible coming events had begun to develop in his mind. He was not thinking about Frenchy and the crew. He was only thinking about himself—and Jani.

* * * * * *

The meeting in the storage bay was brief, conducted in whispers. A fitter named Durth kept watch, chosen for the duty because he had the biggest knife in the group. All the crew showed knives, and said Monk was no exception, with a stiletto sheathed at his back. There would that to contend with, plus the pistol and automatic rifle the Captain kept at his station. Frenchy hoped for a peaceful confrontation: a demand for an explanation of the presence of Wall-Bangers on the hull, the accelerated work schedule, and a burn that was now taking them away from an intercept with Korelco Station.

Floyd said nothing about his pistol, hesitant to trust Gurth and Jabez, those crew members he'd seen with Jocko and Monk at the 'private' meeting back at port. Both men said the distinguished-looking man at that meeting was an Alco exec who'd promised big bonuses for extra shifts to have the Pleasure Dome ready in three months, and that's how the initial word had gotten out to the crew.

"Was he from Korelco?" Floyd had asked.

"No. He came up from the corporate office on Terra." Jabez had replied.

A long trip for a simple request. What *other* meetings had gone on while they were in port? Whatever was happening, it was now clear to Floyd that there was a tie-in with Alco's corporate office.

The crew was frightened by the presence of bombs on the hull, and they wanted to know *where* they were going. Frenchy argued for an immediate confrontation. Floyd argued for a delay until Jani was back inside and they could know for sure where Jocko was. He was voted down nine to two, only Lyle siding with him, and that because all Lyle could think of was what could happen to his wife and two-and-a-half kids if he got killed in a mutiny. And mutiny was what they were talking about.

Floyd thought Frenchy's plan was too quick and direct, with too many unknowns, but Frenchy was number three on *Phoebus* and twenty years in space had taught Floyd a simple truth. You don't argue with superiors; you just do what's necessary to protect your own ass.

"Jocko's obviously in on this with Monk and Santos, and for all we know he has the detonator on him for setting off the bombs. He's also out there with Jani. I want to wait at the lock, and neutralize Jocko when he comes in, and that could be anytime before the end of his shift. We don't need that weasel sneaking around behind us."

Frenchy agreed, and Floyd breathed a silent sigh of relief. He left before the others, while Frenchy was going over the demands with the others, and he hurried to the aft air-lock to wait for Jani and Jocko. He crouched anxiously by the hatch, checked his pistol, his watch, expecting a wait of hours when all hell could break loose in the ship at any minute.

Only a few minutes later, the red light over the hatch started flashing, and Floyd's heart skipped two beats, making him gasp. The outside hatch had opened; someone was entering the airlock from outside. He peeked through thick glass, saw a suited figure clamber inside, stabbing frantically at the wall panel to close the outside door and begin recycling. The hiss of compressed gas, and then the man inside was tearing the helmet from his head, his big face streaked with tears.

It was Jani.

The light over the hatch went from red to green, and Floyd cranked on the hatch wheel, swung it open as Jani recoiled in fright before seeing who it was there.

"Oh, Floyd, I done a bad thing, a bad, bad thing. He came at me, Floyd. He was all over me, hittin' and poundin' on my face plate, and I had this box loose, and I swung it up, and—and—aw, Floyd, it hit his face plate and broke it, and Jocko—Jocko—he just *exploded*! Blood come out his suit in big blobs, and I knew he was dead! I *killed* him, Floyd! I've made us a *lot* of trouble."

Jani was sobbing, and Floyd held him, inside the airlock, the interior hatch half-closed. "Easy, easy, it's over. How many bombs did you pull out, Jani? Tell me, quick!"

"I got four, and then the other I threw away. I just got the fourth out when Jocko found me. He was watching me, Floyd, just like I said!"

"Okay, quiet down. We've got a potential mutiny going on in here. Frenchy and the crew are on their way to the Captain, about the bombs and other things, and I'm going to hide you until things settle down. Take off your suit, and put it in front of the space hatch."

Jani got out of the suit extra fast, Floyd refastening the helmet and closing the face plate. They excited the airlock, closed and dogged the interior hatch, and Floyd slammed a fist on the big button opening the outer hatch. There was a roar, and Jani's suit sailed into space. "Maybe they'll think that's you out there. Where's Jocko?"

"Hanging at the end of his tether. Big blobs of blood all around him, and his eyes—"

"Stop it! He tried to kill you! I'm going to hide you in the big sphere, but we can't walk past Captain's Station. Follow me, and don't make a sound."

In the compartment adjacent to forward bay, Floyd removed a floor plate and they dropped into the crawl space beneath the Velcro-patched metal deck and catwalks, the broad tunnel through which they had run the lines to transfer chemicals into the biosphere. They would come out two compartments beyond Captain's Station, where even now it sounded like an argument was taking place. So Frenchy hadn't waited. Muffled voices, Frenchy's, Santos, then someone yelling, "Tell 'em they aren't going anywhere! They won't get past these stairs!"

Floyd led Jani in a crawl on all fours, one compartment over from the bunk cubicles and Captain's Station, but sound came through the grill-work like helium through a cracked weld.

The sound of the gunshot nearly ruptured their eardrums.

Floyd hugged the floor, heart pounding. There was a second shot. Men screamed, and something heavy slammed the grillwork only fifteen feet from where they sprawled on cold metal. Behind him, Jani groaned.

"Anyone else want to try that?" It was Monk's voice. "You okay, Captain?"

"Yes. Get this piece of shit out of here. It's bleeding all over the place."

There was the unmistakable sound of a body hitting metal. "This is what happens to mutineers, gentlemen. I ought to kill all of you where you stand, but I won't. I'm going to cool you off, instead, so turn around and march back to forward bay. Maybe some time in the dark will clear your heads. March!"

"It's the bombs that got us scared, Monk, nothing else. Why don't you pull them out, and we can get back to work."

"Shut up, Lyle," said Monk. "I don't deny things or make explanations to a mutinous crew. Now, MOVE!"

There were footsteps heading forward along the catwalk, Velcro crunching. Floyd and Jani drifted another few yards before stopping. A hatch clanged, and footsteps were again approaching them. Above, and to their left, Santos crunched down the stairs and they could see his boots. In front of him, a dark, sprawling shape blocked light coming down through the grillwork. It was the body of a man.

"All locked up?" said Santos.

"Safe and sound," said Monk.

"That's not everyone," said Santos. "Jocko and Jani are on EVA, and I didn't see the Webber just now. I'll call Jocko and have him do the big guy. You find the Webber."

"I'll take care of Mister Smarts personally. My bet is he and Frenchy were the ones who started this. I've seen 'em talking too much and too quiet lately."

"Do it, and start with his cubicle. In the meantime, I don't see a reason to wait any longer. The big tug is delayed, but it'll only be four weeks until it gets here. Everything is done. No use in paying a crew to sit idle. Jocko can handle any EV emergencies."

Monk chuckled. "Just hit keys eight and nine for forward bay, and this mutiny is over."

Floyd listened in horror, afraid to breathe. There were two clicking sounds, and the ship shuddered twice. "Bye, bye, bad boys," said Santos. "Now, find that Webber." Monk trotted off, and the Captain climbed the stairs up to his station.

I could have shot him from here. I could have saved them, if I'd known, and now they're dying. Floyd's fear turned to rage, then caution. *Later. I'll take care of Jani first.* He scrambled aft quickly, Jani right behind him. *Does Jani even know what just happened?* Two hatches away from Captain's Station, they came up out of the floor three meters from the tunnel to the biosphere. They scrambled the length of it, and ten minutes was spent coaxing Jani to make the short drop in point-three-gee. Floyd took Jani to one of the hydroponic rooms, ushered him in and pointed to a big tank of ferns in a corner. "Get behind there, and stay down. I've got a master key, but Monk and Santos probably have them, too. If and when the door opens again, don't get up unless you know it's me. Understand?"

"Yes, Floyd." Jani walked to the tank, then turned and looked at him like a child who had just watched his puppy crushed to death under the wheels of a car.

"Floyd?"

"What is it, Jani?"

"What Monk and the Captain did back there; I know the rest of the crew is dead, and there's only us two. Are we next, Floyd?"

So much for Jani being slow. "Not if me and this pistol of mine have anything to say about it. Get down, now, I'm locking the door."

Floyd saw tears in Jani's eyes as he closed the door on him.

Rage came back to Floyd, but this time it was a cool rush only serving to sharpen his mind and reflexes. He checked his pistol again, as if expecting the cartridges to have magically disappeared, and then went back to the tunnel entrance, and vaulted into the lock.

He drifted the tunnel length through one compartment with open hatches, into the second only meters from the Captain's Station. The hatch there was closed and dogged. Gun in hand, he put his ear to the hatch, and listened.

Voices were muffled at first, coming from upstairs at Captain's Station, then Monk's was clear. "He has to be in the dome. I've looked everywhere. You have to have that suit right *now*?"

There was a muffled reply.

"Well watch yourself. I'll be right back."

Footsteps descended stairs in two drops, growing fainter. Floyd waited, heart-beat loud in an ear pressed to the hatch. In minutes, the footsteps were there again, and then there were more muffled voices.

It was time to do it. Floyd swallowed hard, pulled on the hatch wheel and waited for a screech of metal-on-metal, but the hatch opened silently. It was three meters to the stairs and at their base lay two bodies floating just above the floor. He pushed off and drifted to the staircase, grabbed it, and looked down. One of the bodies was Frenchy, eyes open, a neat bullet hole in his forehead. The other dead man was Jabez.

"You sure Jocko's dead?" It was Monk's voice.

"Blood all around him," said Santos. "I'll cut him loose. The scraper is way out there, and in a couple of hours at most he's dead, too. That leaves one guy, Monk. Get him."

Floyd pulled himself silently up the stairs, raising his gun.

"I'm going to the dome right now," said Monk, and he was turning towards the stairwell when Floyd appeared, gun leveled.

"Don't bother, Monk, I'm right here." He cocked the weapon, and aimed it at Monk's face.

Monk drifted backwards until his back was against a wall, an automatic rifle held loosely in one hand. Santos sat at his console. He was suited up, helmet on, face-plate raised, and he smiled.

"Well, well, Mister Smart Guy has arrived."

"Let go of the rifle, Monk, and push it over here. The pistol on the console, too. Fingers only. Over here." Floyd's voice, and hand, was steady.

The weapons drifted over to him, and he pressed them against a wall. Monk lifted his hands; put them behind his head, eyes blazing.

"Now what?" said Santos. "You kill us, and navigate this ship back to port?"

Floyd smiled. "I couldn't navigate my way around a city block, Captain." His eyes never left Monk, but Santos was well within view.

"What, then? Make a deal? How about a three-way split; that's okay with you, isn't it, Monk?"

"Whatever you say, Captain," said Monk amiably. "Doesn't change anything for me."

"Or I could just kill you both for murdering the crew," said Floyd.

Santos looked shocked. "They mutinied, and we locked them in forward bay. They'll be okay." He smiled.

"I was right under your feet when you killed them, and I heard you say Jani and Jocko are dead, too."

Santos' smile disappeared. "We had nothing to do with the scraper. He and Jocko must have had a fight out there. Okay, the crew's gone, and there's just the three of us. You want a piece of this? It'll set you up for life."

"A piece of what? Piracy?"

"No, no. Fraud, maybe, but not piracy. There's no law against stealing from yourself, unless you let your insurance company pay for it. It's all company business we're doing here."

"Alco is stealing its own biosphere," said Floyd.

"Relocating is a better word. The company got in over its head in building the thing, and now they have a little cash-flow problem. We arrange an 'accident' in delivery to Korelco, and the insurance pays half the actual cost of the Pleasure Dome. It's a terrible loss for the company, but one hell of a tax break, and of course they still have the dome because we've moved it out to Alco-T. Two thousand isolated refinery workers there will pay everything they earn enjoying the thing. We'll give you Jocko's share, Floyd. That's just over a quarter of a million credits, plus free room and board for life at Alco-T. Sound good?"

Floyd. "If I thought I'd live to collect it. Or, I could kill you guys, and take the biosphere myself. I've always wanted my own place."

Now Santos laughed. "You, an electrician and Webber, are going to operate the ship and dome all by yourself."

"Yeah, I think so," said Floyd, and he saw their expressions change. "Like you said, I'm a smart guy."

Perhaps it was the look in Floyd's eyes, or what he'd just said, but it was at that instant Monk chose to make his move, and Floyd was ready for it. Monk's hand darted behind his neck, and reappeared with a shining dagger in one, short sweeping motion as Floyd fired a bullet straight into his forehead. The recoil, plus the knife striking him hilt-first on one shoulder spun him backwards into the stairwell. He struggled for two long seconds, hauling himself forward again as Santos locked his face-plate down and grabbed a keyed box off the console. It was a detonator. Santos grinned, and pressed a key as Floyd raised his gun, fully expecting his blood to boil in sudden vacuum in a matter of seconds.

Nothing happened.

"Bad luck, Captain. That must have been one of the bombs Jani removed."

Floyd fired twice.

* * * * * * *

The first four days had been a living nightmare, but now, seven weeks after their separation from *Phoebus*, things were beginning to settle down into a routine. There had been the emotional reunion with Jani, and then actions Monk and Santos could never have thought possible for an electrician and Webber. What they had minimized was twenty years of wiring and operations control checkout experience for every class of tug and freighter in the merchant fleet. The first day he'd set the engines for a burn taking them on a path twenty-five degrees up from and out of the plane of the ecliptic before firing up. He'd gone back to the sphere, and waited twenty minutes before firing the explosive bolts connecting them to *Phoebus*. The ship had pulled away from them, and it was forty-five minutes later when the twin stars made by the T-4's flickered out.

Floyd *was* a smart guy, he had to admit, and he knew how to learn. He *had* to learn, and fast. He was also a worrier, and it had nearly done him in the first few days: deployment of solar panels, booting up the operational programs, a hundred life-support systems review, and fast. The working manuals Lyle had left in the control room saved their lives more than once those first few days, and Floyd was haunted by his memory of the man, of the wife and little kids who would never see daddy again, and supported by a pension from the company that had murdered him.

One thing he *didn't* worry about was Alco coming after them. An intercept, even now, would require a continuous burn no freighter or tug was fueled for, and any major expedition would cost more than the biosphere itself. Alco would take its loss, as planned, and the refinery workers at Alco-T would have to find another form of recreation.

So here they were, climbing slowly up from the plane of the ecliptic along a straight line to nowhere, to gradually curve into an orbit far from the sun, but still well within the solar system. An unstable orbit, he was certain, but Jani and he would be long gone before they began the final spiral into that deep gravitational well.

The synth dispensers were doing their job, and Floyd was hungry. He went to level four for a bite to eat. Jani wasn't there, but he knew where to find him. After he'd finished eating, he went upstairs to the animal rooms, and found Jani by the cages, holding a black rabbit in one big hand.

"They're lonely, Floyd, and this one kept looking at me. We don't have to eat all of them, do we?"

"No, Jani, we don't. Not too many pets, though. These animals are going to be part of our food for a long time."

Jani grinned, stroked the rabbit, and said, "I guess this is *our* place now, ain't it?"

"It's the only home we've got, Jani."

Jani came over and put a big hand on his shoulder. "I always knew you'd get us our own place, Floyd."

For the moment, at least, that was all Floyd needed to hear.

A SPECIAL CHILD

Joanna Eaglestaff heard the screams the instant she closed the car door. It was a fifty yard sprint back to the playground, and the grocery bags in her arms made it seem forever. She deposited her load on a picnic table in the shelter and ran to where a crowd had gathered in a tight circle around the source of the noise. The children were all there, dark eyes looking at her expectantly, but without recognizable emotion. She pushed her way towards the center.

"Out of the way, please! Let me through, and stop this right now!"

They parted slowly, reluctantly, until she saw the boys pummeling each other and writing together on the ground. Four boys had their arms linked together, holding back the others and grinning at the action. Normals, all of them. She could see the evil glee in their eyes. She pushed against them when she saw that Robbi was one of the combatants, and not doing well, since his face was beet red. A trickle of blood was coming from his nose. He'd wrapped his arms around his assailant, and for the moment at least it was a thrashing stalemate. When the linked arms held her back, Joanna grabbed one and dug in with her fingernails, gratified by the yelp of pain and looks of sudden fear when they saw who she was.

The boy fighting with Robbi was the same bully she'd had trouble with before. He was a fat kid, with little snake-eyes and pudgy fingers, mean and strong and dull-normal. Blood boiling, she grabbed the ten-year-old's hair, pulled hard until he let go of Robbi and rolled off, screaming obscenities at her until she straddled him and put her face so close she was spitting on him.

"That's it! I've had enough of you!" she said. She put a long fingernail up against his jugular vein. "If you come back here again, I'll take your scalp!"

The white kid turned even whiter. He believed it.

She let him up and he fled with his friends, screaming all the way.

"RETARDS! RETARDS! RETARDS!"

Her children milled around confused, looking at Robbi who still sat on the ground crying and slamming his fists into the ground.

"Dunn, dunn, dunn, daaa, dunn, maaa...."

Joanna sat down beside him and put an arm around his shoulders. The other children pressed in close so that Robbi was with his family again, isolated from a so-called normal world that understood nothing about him, or cared to. He put his head against Joanna's shoulder and cried until he felt the wind and clung tightly to her to keep from falling off the great horse surging beneath them across the buffalo grass and bentonite clay that stretched from horizon to horizon. When she felt him relax, and the tears stopped, she projected the memory to him for another few minutes, and then pulled him to his feet.

"Are you okay, now?" she asked, hands on his shoulders.

Robbi nodded his head too quickly, she thought. His responses could be so quick, especially when he was excited, but when she probed him nothing came back to her, and even the more severely handicapped children came back with something: an emotion, a taste, even a glimpse of something good or bad that had happened to them. Not Robbi, he guarded himself well, even though he obviously enjoyed the journeys she took him on. Only during that time were they really together.

Joanna herded them all back to the shelter and got out the cookies and punch after she cleaned Robbi's face and settled him at a table. The children devoured the snack greedily, after all the excitement, and searched the grocery bags for more when it was all gone. The rest of the afternoon they played Two Little Blackbirds, and Creepy Bug, and Hold onto the Rope. Joanna projected a team of horses pulling a heavy wagon and Carolyn, the slowest in the group, led them around the little park two times, with Robbi bringing up the rear. By the time parents began arriving to pick up their children, everyone had forgotten the fight, and Robbi was grinning again. He came up to Joanna and wanted a hug, just as his grandmother arrived and walked towards them.

Ruth Tyson was a good, but bitter woman who had lost her husband, only child and daughter-in-law in the same accident, and now struggled to bring her retarded grandson to some kind of self-sufficiency before she died and left him alone. The slight of the slender woman with long, black hair now bending over to receive the outstretched arms of the little boy brought her to tears.

"Hey, save a hug for your grandma!"

"Maaaa!" cried the boy, and he gave her a huge hug, too.

"Hi, Joanna; how'd it go, today?"

"Not so good; there was another fight, and Robbi was in it."

Ruth's eyes narrowed. "That Lewiston brat again?"

"Yes, but I don't think he'll be back. I told him I'd take his hair if he ever came here again."

Ruth laughed, so that Robbi grinned at her. "I bet you would, too. Let's go, Robbi. Grandma's beat and she has a meal to cook yet. See you tomorrow, Jo."

As the car pulled away, Joanna felt something warm penetrate throughout her entire body. Her heart slowed, breath catching, as if her mind had suddenly fled to its secure beginnings in the womb of her mother. The feeling had come before, but it was more intense this time, and seemed to come from within her. The magnitude and spontaneity of the effect frightened her a little; she was used to controlling things.

Dinner that night was a chicken pot pie. She did a load of wash and cleaned up the tiny, one-bedroom apartment she lived in by herself only a block from the park. There were no men in her life, though they were attracted to her. For the moment, it was enough just to take care of herself.

Chores finished, she had just settled down to read when the telephone rang.

"Joanna? This is Ruth Tyson. Sorry to bother you, but I'll only take a minute."

"That's fine, Ruth. I was just relaxing."

"Well, I'll get right to the point. If anyone comes around asking about Robbi, you tell them to talk to me, and don't let him go with anyone, especially a tall, blond guy about thirty. He was just here, and scared both of us. He'll show you government credentials for a cloak and dagger outfit he works for, but they don't have any right to talk to Robbi, and they're just trying to cover up what they did to my son."

"Wow," said Joanna, unable to think of anything else.

"I know that sounds paranoid," said Ruth, "and maybe it is, but I have reason to believe it. My son worked for the government, too, but I'm not sure what all he did for them. One thing I know I should have told you before now. My son took part in a genetic engineering experiment, and Robbi was the result."

"Oh, God. Do you think they're worried about a lawsuit?"

"From who? My son died so conveniently for them. Besides, I'm just grandma, and lawyers are expensive. No, I think they want to see what's going on inside my grandson's big head. He's a very special child, Joanna."

"I agree."

"You don't know what I mean, but I think you will soon. I can't say this to anyone else, Joanna, and I'm taking a chance saying it to you, but there's a part of Robbi that's—well—different, in an exceptional way. If someone ever damages that part I know I'll do something really crazy. He trusts you, and you can help me keep him whole if—"

The voice on the telephone rambled on as Joanna's mind drifted from the conversation. There were differences, all right, and as a closet empathy she knew about being different. When people know you can feel their private emotions they don't hang around long, so you don't tell them you can do that. You clam up. Is that what Robbi's doing? Is that why he's always a blank, while I can get everything the other kids are feeling? And then there are times when I get feelings coming from every direction at once, and with such intensity that—

"—look after him if something happens to me? I still think the car crash was set up; I wouldn't put anything past them. Will you do that for me, Joanna?"

"Oh—well, sure, I can do that."

"I wouldn't blame you if you said no."

"I'd blame myself if I did that, Ruth. I'll look after Robbi; you can count on it."

"Thanks, Joanna. That makes this evening better."

That night, Joanna went to bed late, and slept poorly. Near dawn, she had an erotic dream about a tall, blond man.

The following day, she met him.

* * * * * * *

She felt fear, then curiosity. The fear was strong enough to make her heartbeat quicken. It was near the end of the day. Joanna was arranging snacks on little paper plates while the children played a non-competitive relay game nearby with Valerie, a high-school volunteer who assisted two days a week after school. Joanna looked up sharply to find the source of the fear washing over her, and saw a tall, blond man walking towards her from the street. He had sharp features, his hair cut short, and eyes so blue they just had to be behind contact lenses. A trench coat, yet. He walked straight up to her, and held out a little wallet containing an identity card.

"Miss Eaglestaff, I'd like to have a minute of your time if it's convenient now. I'm from the Department of Defense."

He started to withdraw the wallet, but Joanna grabbed it and peered closely at the card.

Michael Swontec, it said, Internal Security, United State Department of Defense.

"Internal Security?" She allowed him to withdraw his hand, and their fingers touched. Through his mind, she was suddenly conscious of the minute slant of her eyes, fullness of lips, and the proud way she held herself.

"We monitor all classified grants issued by the department," said Michael. "I believe you have a boy named Robbi Tyson in your class?"

"Yes."

"Could I see him for a moment, please?"

"No." Her reply was quick, and firm.

"I just want to ask him a few questions."

"Robbi does not talk to anyone. How can you expect to get answers from a child so handicapped he can't communicate? What can you possibly want from him?"

"Are you sure?"

"What?"

"Sure he's handicapped. Do you have any certification of that from a physician?"

"Well, I haven't actually seen such a document, but the school wouldn't have accepted him without it. I'm not going to answer any more of your questions. If you have a legitimate need to question Robbi, I'm sure you'll have no trouble getting a court order to do it. Now if you'll excuse me, please, we're going to have a snack."

Game over, the children came rushing back to the table and surrounded the new stranger, reaching out with pudgy fingers to pick at the many buckles on his coat while he looked uncomfortably at Joanna.

Joanna smiled. "You're interesting to them," she said sarcastically. "They've never seen a federal cop before." Privately, she was pleased to sense he felt no disgust or fear of the children, as did many so-called normals. For one instant, she'd worried about how he might react when they touched him.

Robbi came up to them, then, and looked directly at Michael without expression. It was not a vacant stare; as the boy tilted his head to one side, something cold brushed past Joanna, and Michael suddenly stiffened. She had a sensation of falling, faster and faster, towards blackness and cold, a tunnel from reality to dreams to oblivion, with no way back. She stumbled and sat down hard on a picnic table as warmth arrived, and Robbi leaned over to put his big head in her lap. Michael looked shaken, then angry, clenching and un-clenching his hands.

"When I come back, I'll have that court order," he said softly. "It's my job." He turned sharply, and stalked away towards the street.

Robbi hugged her tightly, something she ordinarily didn't encourage because of jealousy among the children, but right now she needed it for herself, and so she closed her eyes and took him to the muddy river, where they watched an eagle soar from a golden dome of sandstone.

After snacks was free time. Most of the children played on the swings and slides under Valerie's careful scrutiny, but Robbi stayed behind with three others, looking at picture books donated to the school. Always he went to the same book, and the same picture, putting the book in his lap and hunching over as if to memorize every detail of the colorful page. It was a picture of little children, holding hands and dancing in a circle. They had no shoes, and beneath their feet was tall grass and wildflowers. In the background were fir trees and snow-covered mountains reaching skyward. The children in the book were all laughing, delighted with their dance. Robbi stared at the picture, on and on.

Joanna sat down beside him and looked at the happy scene. "It looks like Switzerland," she said. "All those beautiful wildflowers and this little girl has them in her hair, too. See?" She pointed to the picture, and Robbi's eyes followed her finger.

"You can go there if you like, Robbi. Just think it. See yourself with the children in the picture, and you can be there. That's what's nice about picture books; they can let you go to other places and get away from here when you want to. Here, let's try it together."

Joanna focused on the picture, imagining herself and Robbi in the meadow. She could project only images, not having been to the place, but she knew the feelings of buffalo grass beneath her bare feet and cool, dry winds on the high plateaus, so she used those, too. She put a hand on Robbi's shoulder and closed her eyes; wind was in her hair, the sound of children's voices, faintly at first, then nearby. They were singing, but it was a strange language, like nothing she had ever heard. She felt Robbi take her hand as a gust of wind whipped hair and clothing, making her shiver. She opened her eyes, and found herself standing with Robbi in a meadow of tall grass and strange, colorful flowers on frantically waving stalks. The air was cold, coming down from mountains which soared into a violet sky. The mountains looked new: sharp, craggy protrusions above the plateau they were on, not yet sculptured by glaciers, wind or rain. Interesting, she thought, the abstractness of the scene, related to the picture in the book, but not the same at all.

She looked down, and saw Robbi standing serenely beside her, holding her hand and gazing before him. A group of children were dancing in a circle, but the dance ended when a little blond girl called, "Robbi!", and they rushed towards Joanna with smiling faces.

Robbi smiled.

The children surrounded them, talking excitedly in a language totally unfamiliar to Joanna, so that she frowned. Robbi squeezed her hand suddenly, and she glanced at him.

"You can understand, if you try," he said calmly.

Joanna looked at him incredulously.

"Oh, Robbi, you're back, and you brought your friend this time. Can you stay?" asked a little girl.

"Not now," said Robbi, "but very soon."

"You're just in time," said a boy. "We're going to build a cabin so we sleep away from the wind."

"Why don't you get rid of the wind?" asked Robbi.

"Oh, we can't do that. The wind moves the grass and the flowers, and cools us when we work or play hard, and besides, it's too much work to turn it on and off. That's why we voted to keep it at a constant level. Isn't that right, everyone?"

The children nodded their heads.

"We voted on it, Robbi."

"Oh, it's fine with me, but remember, I get to make the barn when it comes time. You won't do that while I'm gone."

"No, Robbi," said a blond girl, looking up at Joanna. "Your friend is pretty."

"But she's not one of us," said a boy.

"No," said Robbi, "but she's different, too, and she has been a very good friend."

"She can't stay, Robbi," said the blond girl.

"I know."

"She'll tell everyone about us," said another.

"No, she won't. Nobody would believe her, anyway. To them we're all freaks, and easy to forget."

"No matter," said a boy. "They can't touch us here."

Joanna cleared her throat, and the children looked at her expectantly with bright eyes. "Excuse me, but am I allowed to ask a question?"

"Of course," said Robbi, "you're my guest."

"Well, then, who *are* you people?"

Someone giggled.

"You might say we're brothers and sisters," said Robbi. "We all came about in the same way, and around the same time. Some of us have lost our parents, either by death or insanity, and all of us have suffered over trying to live in a world that won't be ready for us for hundreds of years."

"So we're making our own world," said another boy.

"But where is this place? Violet sky and I've never seen such strange flowers. This is all in my mind, and the things I feel are like when I take Robbi back to the places I loved when I was a little girl."

Robbi squeezed her hand affectionately. "I've enjoyed those journeys; you'd be much happier if you went back there."

Joanna frowned at him. "So serious—so adult. I'm imagining you talking to me, and this place is a dream."

"Oh, no," said someone.

"What you see here is real enough; we're going to live here, but you can't stay, even though you've been good to Robbi. This is our place, and we'll have our children here, and someday we'll die here," said the blond girl.

"It's difficult to explain," said Robbi. "We've never been asked to do it before now. But this isn't a dream; it's all quite real."

"It's about two nanoseconds ahead of your world," said a tall boy, punching with one finger on a small calculator in his hand.

"An alternate reality, if you like. It involves a quantized slip in time," said Robbi. "We go forward to create a new world, and backwards to change an old one. We can move in either direction, using a special free energy we have in us."

Joanna shook her head and laughed softly. "You're speaking to me, Robbi. I've never heard you speak before now. You have a nice voice; why do you hide it?"

The children looked suddenly grave, but Robbi smiled at them and said, "Here, we're what we choose to be. In your reality I have no voice; it's something we all have in common. The crude genetic engineering done to produce us required too large a volume for the energy matrix, so the speech center was eliminated. Depending on skull size, there were other problems as well."

"I'm confined to a wheelchair," said the blond girl, "and they feed me by hand."

"Better than me," said a boy. "I've never even gotten out of bed, and my head is so huge I can't lift it."

"What's happening here?" asked Joanna. "There's so much I don't understand."

Robbi looked thoughtful, and it was suddenly quiet. "Then maybe we should show you."

"Oh, Robbi, it will frighten her," said the blond girl.

"I don't think so, Susan, and it will only take a second. We'll use your room, Alex, and the rest of us will be around the foot of your bed, like we did when you were sick. Okay?"

The children nodded silently and formed a semi-circle, facing inwards, with Joanna at one end, the pretty little blond named Susan taking Joanna's hand and looking up at her with huge, blue eyes.

"Don't be afraid," she said softly.

"Projecting all together, now," said Robbi, "one...two... three...."

The mountains and grass dissolved, cold wind suddenly replaced by warm stagnant air and Joanna was standing in a white, sterile room staring at a child in a hospital bed, dark sunken eyes looking back at her from a head the size of a large watermelon. Two shriveled arms lay limp on starched sheets. The circle of children might have come from her class: vacant stares, drool oozing from an open mouth, slack posture, zombie-like, and a sudden hysterical giggle from a boy with a calculator in one hand.

Her hand was squeezed weakly. She looked down and saw attached to her the twisted arm leading to a baby stroller and in it a chromosome-damaged horror without chin or nose, and holes for ears, writing back and forth against a restraining harness, blowing foam. The only thing she recognized was the eyes. The startling, blue eyes.

Joanna sobbed, tears gushing.

Instantly the room dissolved, wind rushing through her hair and drying the tears.

"We're back, we're back!" shouted Susan, pulling at her. "Ooh, you're hurting my hand."

"Oh, I'm sorry. I'm so sorry," said Joanna, releasing her.

"That's okay," said Susan, flexing her fingers. "Look, Robbi, she cares. She really cares!"

"I knew she would," said Robbi.

Another little girl began to cry.

"Now, now, let's not think about it; our reality is right here, the way we want it, right?" said Robbi.

"Right!" they said in unison, smiles returning.

"We could go backwards," said the boy with the calculator, "and correct our physical problems, but we'd still be confined to your reality because there are too few of us to change things enough to make a big difference in people's attitudes. So we decided to go forward and start from scratch."

"We got together telepathically," said Robbi, "and it's only a few weeks since we've been coming here. We're still learning."

"We sort of duck in and out," said Susan, eyes sparkling mischievously.

"Hey, we came here to work on the cabin. I have to get back pretty quick before my mother comes in," said a boy. "What I've left there can't even respond to her, and she feels guilty enough as it is."

"I'm sorry," said Robbi. "I knew we had other plans, but I wanted my friend to see this place so she wouldn't feel bad later on when I'm here most of the time. Go ahead without me, and I'll be back in a wink."

The children moved away from them, talking excitedly, but Susan stayed behind, walked up to Joanna, and touched her hand. "Robbi has shared your thoughts with us; you're a nice person, and I'm sorry you can't stay, but you wouldn't be happy here."

"I know," said Joanna, "but I want it for you; happiness, I mean."

"We'll make it be here. Bye-bye." She turned to Robbi, and looked at him shyly. "Hurry back, Robbi, we need you with us."

The little girl skipped away to join the others.

Beyond the noisy group a structure had begun to appear, shimmering and undefined at first, then solid, then shimmering again as the children argued over design.

"This will take hours," said Robbi, "but by tomorrow the buildings will be ready, and then we'll bring over some animals. We've got to go back, now. Grandma will be waiting."

"Does she know about this place, Robbi?"

"Yes, but it was empty when I brought her here. She hasn't met the others. Someday, maybe. We'd better go, now."

"I'll miss hearing your voice."

"But you'll remember it, and you must never worry about me again. Promise?"

"Yes."

He took her hand, and the world around them dissolved to blackness. For an instant all feeling was gone, and she was disoriented, but then a cool breeze came again, and light, and she was sitting on a bench, next to a little boy hunched over a book, and Ruth Tyson was standing in front of them. Joanna sat up straight in surprise.

"About time you two came back; I've been standing here for a couple of minutes."

"Maaa," said Robbi, reaching out for a hug.

Ruth put her arms around the little boy, smiling. "You should see your face," she said to Joanna.

"How long have you known about Robbi, Ruth?"

"Only a few weeks and now you see why I call him a very special child."

"There are others, too. I just met them, and they're building a new world for themselves."

They both saw the image simultaneously: violet sky, craggy peaks, and a long, log cabin in a meadow filled with flowers.

"Did you see that?" asked Ruth.

"Yes. Those kids work fast."

Robbi grinned.

"Ruth, that blond-headed guy from the government was here today, and he threatened to get a court order to interrogate Robbi."

"I'm not surprised, and he'll get it, too. They started covering their tracks on this one a long time ago, but when they take him I think they'll find Robbi has left nothing they can use; there's only a little, severely retarded boy." Ruth tousled Robbi's hair and held his face in her hands. "Grandma loves Robbi, and she'll be satisfied with whatever part he leaves behind, especially if the other part will visit once in a while."

"Maaa," said Robbi, then held out a hand to Joanna and tensed his face in concentration. "Johh—Johh frenn," he said, and Joanna held his hand.

"I want to take him home, now," said Ruth. "It's probably the last night I'll have all of him. Do you mind if I spend the day with you tomorrow?"

"Of course not."

"Then I'll be here early—before *they* come."

Ruth took Robbi by the hand and led him to her car as other parents began to arrive to pick up their children, and Joanna busied herself, fighting back the tears.

* * * * * * *

They arrived quite early the following morning. Ruth had brought Robbi to the park a full hour before the other children were due to arrive, helping Joanna to unload two boxes of large, rubber balls and a sack full of food for snacks. Robbi went straight to a picnic table with his picture book, and sat there silently while they worked.

"How'd it go last night?" asked Joanna.

"Pretty nice. We made cookies, and I talked; mostly, I told him about his daddy as a little boy, and what kind of man he was. I know he understood everything. I could see it in his eyes, but he didn't try to say anything. Just listened." Her eyes were suddenly moist. "Oh, Joanna, Robbie's the last remaining piece of my son, and I'm scared."

"He'll be happy over there, and he can move back and forth whenever he wants. You'll know when he's here."

Ruth started to say something, then scowled as she looked over Joanna's shoulder. "Oh, they are *really* in a hurry."

A black van had pulled up in front of the park, and three men got out. One of them was Michael Swontec, and the instant he saw Joanna she felt fear and excitement simultaneously. Her body tingled as he came towards her, but he was near panic when he reached them and handed Ruth a packet of pages stapled together.

"The court has allowed us to examine Robbi for a period not to exceed thirty days, Missus Tyson. You can come along, if you like, and I promise we'll take good care of him."

Ruth shuffled the pages. "Sure got this fast. You people work together to cover up your mistakes, don't you?"

"I've heard you say that before, Missus Tyson, and I think I know what you mean, but you're wrong. There's nothing sinister going on here. The boy was involved in a project funded by our office, and this is a follow-up check, nothing more. He won't be harmed in any way, please believe that."

"I believe it," said Joanna, and Michael looked at her thankfully.

"All I'm here for is to pick up the boy and his grandmother if she wants to come with us, and go to the hospital," he said, looking directly at her.

I'm not a bad person, and I'm not working for bad people.

"Go with them, Ruth; I'll get Robbi." Joanna walked back to the table where Robbi was hunched over, staring at his picture book. She knelt before him, reached up to run a hand through his thick hair and brush away one tiny tear on his face.

"It's time to leave, Robbi," she whispered. "I'll miss you, and I hope you'll come back to visit when you can. Be happy in your new world—all of you."

The man will be back, and so will I.

Robbi closed his book, handed it to Joanna, and looked at her. What she saw was the vacant, sleepy stare of a severely handicapped child. She took him by the hand, and led him to the others.

"Robbi, you and grandma are going on a little trip," said Ruth brightly, but when she saw his eyes she looked at Joanna, who smiled weakly and shook her head.

"Look, we get to ride in that big car," said Ruth quickly, and then she led the boy away, flanked by two of the men. Michael held back for a moment, hands thrust deep in his coat pockets, looking embarrassed.

"He'll be okay; please don't worry about him. He should be back within a month. And—do you mind if I drop by to check up on him occasionally, just to see how he's doing?"

Joanna smiled, satisfied with herself when he blushed.

"That would be fine," she said.

After the big car pulled away, Joanna busied herself setting up easels for finger painting that morning. Shortly before the children arrived, she found Robbi's picture book where she had left it on a table, and decided to take it home to be sure it wasn't damaged or lost. When she picked it up, the book felt different: fresh, new, without scratches or other wear, though it was Robbi's favorite. She opened it to the picture of the dancing children, and let out her breath in a sob. The circle of smiling, happy faces was still there, but now they danced under a violet sky with virgin, sharp mountain peaks looming behind a farm with a cabin and huge, red barn with cattle and sheep scattered around on a meadow of tall grass and bright flowers on long stalks.

One of the dancing children was Robbi.

GEORGI

A North Dakota winter storm was charging in from the southwest. The sky was white as milk, and snow was already swirling in the back alleys of Fargo as Otis Boswick frantically searched for the basics of life: food, warm clothing or rags for feet, hands and head, a pot or utensil, and anything that would burn. Moms had made her rounds in the morning, had returned with a shopping basket piled high with old newspapers for the oil-can fire to keep them alive another night in the bitter cold. But now he was eight blocks from Moms, and Alf, and the others, eight blocks from the packing crate he called home beneath the second street bridge, and all he wanted was to be warm again. In a North Dakota blizzard, he could be dead in a walk of two blocks, and time was running out.

Otis scrabbled with stiff fingers in one of two dumpsters behind the Broadway Deli, pain stabbing through his arthritic, humped back as he leaned over beyond his limit. He found a broken box half-filled with stale crackers, and a brick of frozen jack cheese covered with frost and blue fuzz, passing up a piece of strange meat aged black. He packed the first treasures of the day in his knapsack, and moved to the second dumpster, which was tightly closed, but not locked. He pushed up hard on the lid, stood on tip toes to look inside, and got the shock of his life.

Inside the dumpster, in a pile of rancid garbage, a man was lying in a fetal position, groaning, clutching at his stomach with both hands.

"Hey, you can't stay in here! A storm's comin', and you'll freeze to death in all that wet! Here, you grab my hands, and come out of there!"

The man, his rugged face covered with fine, blond hair laced with ice crystals, turned over, opened his eyes to look at Otis, then pulled what looked like a garage door opener from beneath his body and pointed it at him. "Go away—or—I hurt."

Otis flinched, but still held out both hands. "Grab hold. I've got a warm place not far from here, unless you want to die. Make up your mind quick. Storm's comin' fast."

The man considered this silently for a moment, then lowered the garage-door-opener and stuffed it into a tattered rucksack at his side, groaning as he moved.

"You sick?"

The man answered in a deep voice, heavily accented. "Was hungry—ate something—bad for me—down here, Want—sleep." He rubbed his lower abdomen with one hand.

"Moms has a tea for that. It's only a few blocks, but we've got to hurry!" Otis grabbed the man's outstretched hands, cold as his own, grimacing as he hauled him upright. The man got out unaided, holding the rucksack tight to him, doubling over in pain as soon as his feet hit the pavement. Otis put an arm around him, and they half-stumbled the eight blocks back to the second street bridge in swirling snow and bitter wind-chill, people staring at them from passing cars. Two drunks ending another day early, their eyes said.

They climbed down the embankment under the bridge. A wrinkled, squat, black woman was warming her hands over an oil-can fire, body covered from head to foot in tattered sweaters and a long coat that made her look like a dirty snowball, leaving the fire's warmth to waddle towards them as they approached. "What you got there, Otis?" she shouted in a raspy voice. "You done found another victim o' society?"

"He's sick, Moms. Ate something bad."

"Well, you just bring him to Moms now, you hear? Po' thing."

Otis maneuvered the man to a broken piece of concrete by the fire, and sat him down on it, holding him steady. Moms ran fat, gentle fingers over his face, checked his eyes. When she put a hand lightly on his stomach, the man cried out sharply, and sagged unconscious into Otis's arms.

"Not good," said Moms. "Man's poisoned. Got to get that out of him *now*." She shuffled over to a wooden-planked hut stuffed with cardboard and rags backed up against one concrete buttress of the bridge, and crawled inside through a blanket-draped opening. "Otis, you quick heat some water over the fire! Man can't drink this cold!"

Otis put a screen over the top of the oil drum, and managed to heat some water in a shallow pan before Moms came back with a tin cup containing a yellow powder sprinkled with bits of blue and red. Otis's eyes widened as he recognized the potion, but Moms pushed the cup into his hands. "Got to get it out of him quick, Otis, and you know it."

They made the tea, forcing it down the partially conscious man who grimaced with each sip, Moms stroking his forehead. "Quick, man. We're tryin' to save your life here, and there's no hospitals for the likes of us. Drink it all up."

A few minutes later, the man's eyes snapped open, he lunged out of Otis's grasp to his hands and knees, and projectile-vomited the entire contents of his stomach onto the broken chunks of concrete beneath the bridge.

"I've got the room. He can stay with me," said Otis.

"Just so's I take care of him. You knows nothin' of the art." Moms smiled a toothless smile, looking satisfied with herself.

"Don't have to, Moms, not with you here. Where're the others?"

"Probably out killin' someone for a quarter, but Jason's inside, with Alf for protection. Jack was botherin' him again, skinny demon he is, but he sure is scared o' that dog."

Otis got the man on his feet, helped him over to the mammoth packing crate he lived in against the buttress opposite from Moms' hut. As he approached, there was a low, menacing growl from inside the crate.

"Alf, shut up! And get back, now! I got a friend here, and he's bad sick!" Otis pushed aside the blanket covering the small entrance, pulling the man in after him. The interior of the crate was a heap of sleeping bags and old blankets, dimly lit by a single candle. In one corner a frail boy sat upright in a sleeping bag, staring fearfully, arm around the neck of a mongrel mix of German Shepherd and Pit-Bull Terrier still growling low in its throat. "You hold onto him tight, Jason. I gotta get this man warm, and we got a blizzard comin!"

Otis got the man's rucksack off, and stuffed him fully clothed into a bag, piling on two blankets for good measure. Instantly, the man was asleep, and Alf stepped forward to cautiously sniff at him. "Friend, Alf. Friend," said Otis, scratching the massive head of the animal. Alf waggled a stump of a tail, and licked Otis's hand.

"You all right, boy?"

Jason Boggs, a fourteen-year-old runaway from Minneapolis, slouched in the sleeping bag, face grim. "Better now that you're back. That creep Jack grabbed me by the balls again this morning, and Alf bit him good. He said he'd kill Alf when he gets back. And then the cop was here again."

"Luis Penuel? He's a good man, Jason. Looks after us."

"Well, he's no friend of mine since he turned my name in. Says my stepfather has left home for good, and my mom is comin' to get me. He had no right turning me in like that!"

"Sure he did, Jason. You're only fourteen, with a whole life ahead of you. This ain't no way for you to live, on the run. Don't you want to be with your mom?"

"She's okay, I guess. It's my stepfather liked to beat up on me."

"Well, there you are. In the meantime you've got Moms and me and Alf for family. We'll take care of you. But consider it good, Jason. A boy needs a real home, not a packing crate."

"It's good enough for you and Moms."

"That's our choice, boy. It's our way of life, and we wouldn't have it any other way—except when it gets so damnable cold. What I wouldn't give for heat in winter, and then pack my friends in here. Wouldn't that be somethin'?"

Jason shook his head, and smiled. "You and Moms take care of everyone, Otis."

"What better way to live, boy? It's our callin'. Now you hunker down and get some sleep. I've got me a sick man to tend to, and it's gonna get terrible cold tonight."

Moms' call came from outside the crate, a cup of a new brew laced with sugar in her hands. Three times that night they awakened the man to feed him an energetic tea with numbed hands as the blizzard raged around them.

* * * * * * *

Otis awoke with a start, nostrils frozen shut, the interior of the crate filled with icy fog sparkling in a band of sunlight coming in where the blanket had been pulled aside from the entrance. The man he had found in the dumpster was sitting up in his sleeping bag, peering outside, holding the blanket aside with a bare hand. When Otis snorted to clear the ice from his nose, the man turned to look at him.

"Snow gone—light again."

"Yes, but now it'll get *really* cold, and we need more fuel for the fire. We used up all the newspapers while you were sleeping. Feel better now?"

"I have—hunger—here." The man rubbed his stomach carefully. "How long I—in this place?"

"Three nights and two days," said Otis. "You were bad poisoned, and for a day or so we thought you wouldn't make it. But Moms knows what she's doing; we've never lost a sick person."

"Now I eat," said the man matter-of-factly.

"Wish I could help you there, but all we've got left is some oatmeal, and we need to cook that. No fuel."

The man found his rucksack next to him, opened it, and reached inside. "You bring food—I cook—here." He withdrew a metal globe, silver, the size of a softball out of his sack, pushed aside some rags, and placed the globe carefully in his tea cup on the floor of the crate before rummaging in his pack again.

Otis held up a metal canteen and shook it soundlessly. "All our water's frozen. We need a lot of heat to thaw it."

"I do fast," said the man. "Get food." He pulled out a metal platform with sloped vanes and flat bottom, placed the globe in it, then screwed a wire coil with threaded shaft into a short, ceramic receptor on top of the globe.

"That some kind of hotplate?" said Otis.

"This cook—heat us good." He reached out a hand. "Give water."

Otis handed him the canteen, then searched in his own pack for a bag of oatmeal he had hoarded for months. Found it. Held it out to the man. "Here you go. Now that you're with us again, my name is Otis Boswick. What's yours?"

The man didn't answer, grasped a knurled knob at the side of the globe, twisted it, pulled out a shaft about an inch, twisted again. Immediately, the coil began to glow, first deep red, rapidly turning to bright red and orange. The interior of the crate was flooded with heat, while Otis stared in fascination. "Well, will you look at that! Say, if you don't want to give me a name, that's okay. It's only I'd like to have something to call you by."

"I am Georgi," said the man. He put the canteen on the glowing coil, and picked up the bag of oatmeal to look at it closely.

"Georgi. That's a Russian name. Thought I recognized the accent. You one of the new emigrants? This cold probably don't seem very different, then."

"No Russian," said Georgi.

"Oh," said Otis. *And no last name, either.* "No matter, I'm just curious, is all. Like to get to know people better, but don't mean to pry. People come through here are all runnin' from somethin', some of it pretty bad, but I don't pry. Live and let live, I say."

Georgi looked at him darkly. "You take care—me. I—thank."

"Nothing," said Otis. "Moms did it all, anyway."

Steam was squirting out from beneath the cap on the canteen, making a whistling sound. Jason stirred in his sleeping bag, Alf lying on top of him. "Where's the heat coming from?"

"Georgi here had a stove with him, Jason. We're cookin' up the oatmeal. Want some?"

"Sure," said the boy. "Those crackers didn't go very far with me yesterday." He sat up in his bag so that Alf was in his lap, and stroked the dog's head. "Alf must be hungry, too."

"We'll give him some oatmeal. Good for dogs."

Georgi poured half of the sack of oatmeal into a small pan, took some rags from the floor to lift off the scalding hot canteen and stirred water into the pan. Otis spooned the steaming cereal into cups, and they ate silently in the warm glow of the coil, heating themselves inside and out, a luxury Otis could not remember since several winters before when a guy had come through with a back-packer's stove, and they had all gotten a little drunk on hot wine. That was before Moms.

After he'd finished eating, Otis filled another cup with the last of the oatmeal. "This is for Moms," he explained. "Back in a min-ute." He crawled outside, and walked the few steps to Moms' hut, keeping a palm over the cup. "Moms! Rise and shine! We got food here. Hot oatmeal!"

A raspy shout greeted his offer. "Don't want none, Charlie! Now I told you to stay away from me, and here you are again! Go away!"

Oh, oh. Back inside herself again, the spells getting more fre-quent in the last year. "No, it's Otis, Moms. Here, I'll put the food by the doorway. Your patient cooked up breakfast this morning. You cured him, Moms, and his name is Georgi."

"Charlie, I'll sic the dog on you if you don't go away! I mean it!"

There was no arguing with her when she was like this, but at least she was in the hut. On the street, in this condition, she couldn't find her way home. But in a day it usually passed over, and Otis wondered if she was having little strokes, or maybe it was Alz-heimer's. He also wondered who Charlie was. He put the cup down by the hut's entrance, and turned as Georgi emerged from the crate, carrying a small, black box the size of a cigarette package in one hand. He barely glanced at Otis, walked straight up the embankment and out of sight. When he came down again a minute later, he was empty-handed. And the cup full of oatmeal had disappeared into the hut.

"We go out—get more food," said Georgi, and it was like a command. Otis was surprised by the sudden anger he felt surge in-side him.

"One nice thing about my life is I don't have to take orders from anyone, Georgi, not even you. Last time I did that was in the Korean war. Climb the cliff, the sergeant said, and take out that gun emplacement. Me, with a wife and two little babies back home. But it was an order in a combat zone, and I didn't want to get shot by my own people, so I climbed the damn thing. Halfway up, the cliff come loose and down I went. Broke my back bad, and all I got to show for it was a purple heart I hocked for food years ago. Lost the wife, and the babies, get lousy disability checks barely enough for me and my friends to live on, but I make do, and I *don't* take orders from *anyone* anymore. You got that?"

Georgi looked at him somberly. "You soldier—in battle?"

Otis looked away from those dark eyes. "A long time ago—when I was young."

Georgi put a big hand on Otis's shoulder, and squeezed gently. "I soldier, too. I do accident, too, in—ship. Georgi not hurt, but friend—my friend die, and he buried far to—home. No battle—we only look—friend dead. Now Georgi go home—friends find. Georgi stay alive—find food. I help Otis, who saves life. You show how?"

"Who are you?" asked Otis, wiping his eyes.

"I soldier—like Otis. We get food together. Come." He put an arm across Otis' humped back. "We go where you find me?"

"No—I have some money left, and it's too cold to stay out long. Fresh food is cheap, but it can't get frozen. How long will your stove run before the fuel is gone? We'll have to keep the crate warm inside."

"Run long time—to snow gone—fill with—water—run to snow come again. I show how."

"Never heard of such a stove. You bull-shittin' me?"

Georgi laughed, then, a big, deep-throated chuckle, and hugged Otis to him. "No—shittin," he said.

They walked ten blocks to a Seven-Eleven store that was accustomed to doing meager business with street people, the owner a friendly man who had known hard times himself, and occasionally paid them for odd jobs around the place. The owner wasn't there, and the clerk, a young girl around seventeen, eyed them apprehensively until Otis put his rumpled dollar bills onto the counter. A five-pound bag of potatoes and a box of oatmeal took everything he had, except for a nickel and three pennies.

Georgi scooped the coins up in a big hand. "I keep—remember Otis?"

"Sure, why not? Can't buy anything with it, anyway." He watched the coins disappear into Georgi's pocket.

They strolled back to the bridge, Otis pointing out the parking lot that had once been the Zephyr bar, a place to talk to friends, to belong, now gone. Across the street another bar, the Pink Pussycat, was being torn down along with an old hotel he had lived in for two years until it had been condemned. Slowly, but surely, the good folks of Fargo were forcing them out into the streets, back alleys, and under the bridges to freeze and die in the long winters. He had heard their favorite saying, of course: forty below keeps the riffraff out. Or kills them.

Sun-dogs were out in the icy air, two pillars of fire on either side of a sun low in the southern sky. They walked out onto the second street bridge to watch the Red River, a narrow channel of deep, black water winding through ice. Georgi carried the groceries in a paper bag, listening silently as Otis pointed out where he had found a body the summer before, half in and out of the river. "Old guy, just passing through. Some kids probably knifed him for fun. For the pure hell of it! Sure not my kind of people, none of them!"

Georgi shook his head sadly. "There is cruelty—with people—all place."

"Only for some of us," said Otis, and his head had turned sharply to the left to watch a police car pulling up below them, alongside the embankment. Two uniformed officers got out of the car, and picked their way carefully down the snowy slope. One of them was Luis Penuel. "Oh, oh, they're comin' for Jason. Get out of sight!" Otis pulled Georgi back from the edge of the bridge. "If he sees you, Penuel will want to know who you are, and where you come from. He's a friend, but he checks up on everyone who comes through here. Do you want that?"

"No," said Georgi firmly. "I here only little while, until—no trouble, Otis."

"Then don't let them see you. Wait up here until they're gone. I'll come back, but I've got to go down and see after Jason. He's only been here three weeks, but Penuel traced him, and his mom wants him back home."

"I wait here—you go," said Georgi.

Otis squeezed the big man's arm, then walked the length of the bridge, and fell down twice before reaching the bottom of the snowy embankment. Alf was barking angrily from inside the crate, and Moms was hugging Jason, the two officers pulling at his arms. Moms waved as the three walked towards Otis, and there were tears in her eyes. "You be good to your mom, you hear?" she cried.

Jason waved back to her, and he was smiling when he came up to Otis. Luis Penuel put an arm around him. "His mom is at the station cryin' her eyes out. She wants him back real bad, and it looks like a good situation for Jason, now, Otis. Thanks to you and Moms, he's going home in one piece."

Otis looked at the boy. "You want to go home, Jason?"

"Yeah. But I'll never forget you or Moms, and what you did for me. I'm gonna miss Alf, too. Mom says she'll get me a big dog when I get home, and I want one like Alf."

"Alf is special, all right. C'mere, boy." Otis held out his arms, and Jason was swallowed in his embrace while the officers found other things to look at.

"Do somethin' for street people someday, will you?"

"I promise, Otis. Take care of yourself—and Moms, too. She's still actin' kinda funny."

"You betcha," said Otis, releasing the boy, swallowing hard as one officer led him up the slope to the patrol car, and out of sight. Luis Penuel stayed behind a moment, an arm around Otis's hunched shoulders.

"He'll be fine, Otis. Just fine. And you watch out for yourself, too. Jack Cain is back in town. I saw him stumbling around by the tracks this morning, yelling at air. He gives you any more trouble you let me know, and I'll throw him right in the can. Got it?"

"Sure. I'll let you know. Anyway, Alf scares the hell out of him."

"Yeah, but Alf don't carry a knife or a gun. You watch out for that guy, He's pure, evil mean." Luis slapped Otis on the back, then climbed the embankment, and in an instant the patrol car, and Jason, were gone.

Moms was standing by the oil can, staring at the flames, when Otis trudged up the slope to find Georgi again. When he got to the top, he saw Georgi next to the span, balancing on snow, the little black box in his hand. He was wedging it into the rocky ground by the bridge, and carefully covering it with a tangle of frozen brush, looking up as Otis came close.

"Whatever that thing is, I sure as hell hope you ain't no Russian spy. I busted my back fightin' communists."

"I tell Otis. No Russian," said Georgi. "Jason gone, now?"

"Yeah, home to Minneapolis with his mom. No more freezing cold nights for him. A warm house, where boys oughta be. I'll miss him. Good kid."

Georgi picked up the grocery bag with one hand. "Otis feel better when eat. I cook—you show how."

Otis turned to start down the hill, taking a tentative first step, when suddenly, Georgi grabbed him from behind, sitting down with him, and sliding on his back all the way to the bottom, his excited shout echoing beneath the bridge.

"Both of you's crazy!" yelled Moms.

That night, with light snow falling, the three of them stayed in Otis's crate, warmed by the glowing stove, and feasted on boiled potatoes with one of Moms' special teas.

The following morning, Jack Cain returned to their camp.

* * * * * * *

The morning was clear, but breath-freezing cold, a foot of light, powder snow on the ground from the night before. Stomachs full, Otis and Georgi sipped hot tea in the warm crate, Moms still asleep, a shapeless mound in one corner. Alf watched them mournfully, curled up on Jason's sleeping bag, from which he had not moved since the boy had left. Georgi had shown Otis all the operating details of the stove, including where to fill it with ordinary water when the heating rate got low. He had tried to explain the source of the heat, talking about atoms sticking together, and the unbelievably hot gas somehow contained in a golf-ball-size volume within the globe. He drew diagrams, and strange chemical formulae, one Otis recognized as the one for water. The high school education he had not finished, before fleeing to break his back in a foreign war, was only a vague memory to him, now, and he found himself befuddled by most of Georgi's careful teaching. I should go to the library once in a while to read a newspaper, he thought, and catch up on what's going on in the world.

Georgi leaned against Otis, a sly grin on his face. "If Otis take heater, and what I draw here—take to great teacher—scientist—show this—can be rich—not live like this. Have much—money. Good for Otis."

Otis laughed. He thought little of money, because there was little of it to think about. Money was a transient thing, like most of his friends, like Georgi, and the stove. It appeared and disappeared from his life, without predictability. It was better to live a day at a time, and he had learned not to dwell on what could be, or what could have been. During his hard life, he had become a fatalist, coming to grips with the program laid out for him. His life was meant to be the struggle it was, for whatever reason, and he had accepted it. And so he dismissed Georgi's humorous fantasy with a laugh, knowing that a small part of him would think about it some more. What would it be like to have a lot of money? He could do all sorts of things that—

"—HEY, YOU BUMS! WHERE'RE YOU HIDIN'? I COME BACK TO KILL ME A DOG!"

Moms bolted upright in her sleeping bag. Alf's eyes narrowed, a growl rattling in his throat. "Jack Cain," whispered Moms. "Otis, he's back again. I thought we done rid o' that devil."

"Who?" said Georgi, suddenly tense.

"You stay in here, both of you. I'll go out, and talk to him."

"You're crazy," said Moms. "Man's drunk, and spoilin' for a fight. Leave 'im be."

"Come outta there! I hear you mumblin', and I can hear the dog, too. In one minute, he's dead!" A bottle crashed against the side of the crate, and Alf started barking hysterically. "That's it! Send Alf after me! One swipe of this knife, and his head's gone!"

"You come in here, Jack Cain, and I'll put the hex on you," yelled Moms. "You stick a head in, and I blow a powder on you make you blind, and suck your breath away, turn you blue, and put that knife in your own gut! You get out of here, now!"

Footsteps outside, then something hard and heavy hit the side of the crate. "Ain't afraid of you—crazy old bitch! I want that DOG!" The words were nearly drowned out by Alf's barking and snarling, froth spewing from his mouth, teeth bared. Moms grabbed the big dog, and hung on tightly.

"I have to go out," said Otis grimly.

Georgi grabbed his pack, fumbled inside it. "I come with Otis."

"NO! This is between Jack and me, and it's *my* dog he wants to cut up. You stay *put*!" Otis turned, crawling quickly outside before Georgi had a chance to answer, then stood up painfully, and faced Jack Cain a few feet away from the crate. The man's face was scarred and pock-marked, head bare, eyes puffed nearly shut from days of solid drinking. He was dying before Otis's eyes, a wasted skeleton of a man, army-surplus fatigues hanging tent-like from his thin frame, mouth twisted into a sinister grin that made him a specter of death itself. In one hand he held a large Bowie knife, waving it lazily at Otis's face.

"You still got that pretty little boy in there?"

"Jason's gone, and he ain't comin' back. You can't hurt him anymore, Jack."

"Shi-it, I kinda hoped for some fun after I carved up your dog—with this." Jack took a stumbling step forward, and now the knife was very close to Otis's face.

"I don't have any quarrel with you, Jack, and there's nothin' here for you anymore. Why don't you just leave?"

"Hey, you don't own this place, old man; now, you bring that dog out here so I can get it done quick, and *then* I'll leave." The cold blade of the big knife touched Otis's nose, then waved away again.

"I won't do that, Jack."

"Yeah! Well, then, I gotta do it another way." Jack made a short lunge, slicing a gash in Otis's cheek so that he cried out.

Alf was crazy, now, thrashing around inside the crate, Moms screaming. "I can't hold him, Otis!"

Otis felt warm blood running down his face. He circled to his left, away from the crate, stooping to grab up a chunk of broken concrete with one hand.

"Come on, Jack. You and me," he said, voice shaking with fear, hoping the others could somehow escape while Jack's back was turned.

"Hey, the old soldier. That's pretty good, Otis. Well, how about a little bayonet drill?" Jack lunged, Otis stumbling backwards, swinging the concrete chunk wildly, and missing the death's head by inches. Before he could recover, another lunge was coming, the knife sweeping past his face, and back again in an upward thrust. Otis swung weakly, punching Jack in one shoulder as he felt the knife burn into his left side. He staggered backwards, grabbing at his side, and dropping his only defense as Jack grinned wildly at him.

A loud voice boomed behind the man with the blood-stained knife.

"JACK CAIN!"

Jack jerked around in surprise, dropping into a crouch.

Georgi had emerged from the crate, the garage-door-looking thing in his hand, now pointing it at Jack.

Otis gasped for breath, pain flooding his left side. "It's my fight, Georgi," he said weakly.

"No. Now it Georgi fight," said the big man.

"You want some of this?" Jack lunged towards Georgi, the knife a spear before him.

The garage-door-thing flashed green, lighting up the entire underside of the bridge, and Jack Cain screamed. He dropped the knife, and fell writing to the ground, the heels of his boots digging grooves in frozen earth."

"You like pain? Here—Georgi give more." The weapon flashed again, and now Jack was shrieking, foam flying from his mouth. He flayed the ground with his arms for minutes, as Otis watched in horror, then curled up in a fetal position, and moaned.

Georgi picked up the knife, tossed it over to the entrance of the crate, then grasped Jack by the hair, and pulled him screaming to his knees. "Here, I show you something. I show you what happen you come back here again. You look at big rock—by where fire is." He grasped Jack by the hair again, and twisted his head in the direction of a two-hundred pound block of concrete by the oil can they used for a fire. Jack's eyes were nearly closed, his moaning pitiful even to the man he would eventually have killed.

"You look, now," said Georgi, and then he fiddled with the garage-door-opener. Pointed it. Fired.

The flash was bright red, concentrated in a narrow beam that struck the center of the rock. The concrete flashed yellow—and disappeared. Jack cried out, tears flowing down his cheeks as Georgi leaned over to look at him, their noses nearly touching. "You come back again—I do that to you. Now—you go."

Jack Cain stumbled to his feet, and fled from their camp— forever.

Georgi helped Otis back to the crate. The knife blade had gone in and out of his left side at a shallow angle near beltline, and the wound was bleeding profusely, but inside of an hour Moms had him bandaged up, and resting comfortable next to the stove, Georgi hovering over him. Moms left her patient for only a moment in order to conjure up a new poultice in her shack. While she was gone, Otis, drowsy with pain, looked up at Georgi, scanning his rugged features and dark eyes in the glow of the stove. "You sure ain't no Russian spy," he said softly. "You sure ain't nothin' from around here."

Georgi looked at him sadly. "I tell you—far to home."

And it was in the twilight of that very day when Georgi's friends came to take him away.

* * * * * * *

Moms had filled him with tea, and his bladder seemed ready to burst. Otis wiggled carefully out of the crate, and relieved himself against the bridge buttress. Georgi had started a fire in the oil can, and draped a towel across the top of it to dry. Moms was shuttling back and forth, moving her pharmacy into Otis's crate, mumbling to herself all the time about too many things to do. She was never happier than when she had a patient to take care of.

Otis zipped up his pants, and turned to say something to Georgi, freezing into silence at the look on the man's face. Georgi was looking past him; head tilted upwards, white teeth showing in a huge smile. He lifted both arms over his head and waved wildly, laughing. Otis spun around; saw two men descending the embankment, one of them carrying the little black box Georgi had hidden by the bridge. They waved back to Georgi, scrambled down the slope, and ran towards him. Both were dressed from head to toe in skintight, brown knitted suits, black belts around their waists hanging heavily with metal canisters of various sizes, reminding Otis of Rangers he had seen in the war.

Georgi ran to meet them, embracing each man with a huge hug, lifting them off the ground. Comrades. Otis's heart sank. Georgi's friends had found him, had come to take him away from them. But the look on the big man's face was pure joy. I must be happy for him, thought Otis. He has found his people again.

The three men talked in low tones, occasionally looking at Otis. *I'm being talked about.* His side was hurting again, and he sat down on a concrete chunk by the fire, feeling a sudden emptiness, a sense of loss. Friends were so temporary, friendships so fleeting in his life. Why must it be this way? But then he did have Moms, and Alf, and wasn't that enough? Not good to want too much, Otis. But, oh, how rapidly this big man from a place far away had become a friend of his.

Georgi broke away from the other two men, who remained where they were, and walked quickly to the crate. "I talk with Otis. Otis wait there." He ducked inside, and came out with the little weapon he had used against Jack Cain, but nothing else. The stove—the pack—both were still inside the crate. "Say nothing. I talk." He knelt before Otis, put a hand on his shoulder. "I tell—much lost—in river. Can't find. I leave things—you keep—for make Georgi live so friends find. I go home, now—remember Otis—my friend."

Moms came up behind Georgi, looked at Otis's face, and tears welled up in her eyes. "You's goin' home, is that it?"

"Yes. Friends find."

"Goin' home, goin' home, we's all goin' home one way or 'nother. You remember Moms now, too, you hear?"

Georgi reached out and took her hand in his, then squeezed Otis's shoulder with his other hand before standing up. Otis looked up at him, and smiled.

"You sure you ain't no Russian spy?"

Georgi laughed that deep-throated laugh again. "No, Otis. Russia—close. I go—far—far to home." He made a grand sweep with one arm. "Good—bye, bye." He turned suddenly, and walked back to the other men. They stood in a tight cluster, one of them fiddling with the little black box. And then suddenly it was as if a black sheet wrapped around them, appearing out of nowhere, blinking once—twice—then a flash of white light filling it, neutralizing it to nothingness, along with the men inside.

The bright flash left spots before Otis's eyes. He blinked—looked—blinked again. Georgi and the others were gone. Moms clapped her hands together. "Lord, I has seen the doorway to heaven! I has seen your angels come to take our friend to yo' holy person. I praise the power o' the Lord! Amen." Moms turned, wiped her eyes, and shuffled back towards the crate. "Someday, he'll come for us, Otis, but you git back inside, now. Tea's heatin', and you don't need getting' chilled out here."

Inside the crate, Otis turned the stove down until the coil glowed dull red, then snuggled in his sleeping bag, and sipped hot tea. For the first time in days, Alf left Jason's bag, and stepped gingerly past Moms to lie down by Otis, heavy head in his lap. Otis stroked Alf's head, and exchanged a smile with Moms when the dog sighed.

Georgi had left him the stove for a reason. To stay warm? Or to get rich? After what he's seen that day, Otis was sure there was no other stove like this one—anywhere—not on planet Earth. But to get rich meant dealing with people who weren't in his world, either, people who would find a way to steal the secrets in Georgi's diagrams for themselves, the same people who wouldn't part with a quarter for a street person, the ones who sneered at them through the windows of their passing cars.

His reverie was interrupted by a shout from outside.

"Hey, Otis! You in there?"

"That you, Two Feathers?" He hadn't seen the big Sioux for months.

"Yeah. Freezin' solid out here, Otis. Got an extra bag for the night? Gonna leave for Minneapolis tomorrow."

"When's the last time you ate?"

"Oh, two—maybe three days. Got a bag of raw beans with, but nothin' to cook 'em up. You got somethin'?"

Otis looked at Moms, and she nodded her okay.

"Well, you just get yourself in here, and bring the beans! We've got enough heat in here for everybody!"

AXALAY'S GIFTS

Balaban reached the knoll overlooking the last human farm when the first light of Ta was coloring the western horizon. As usual, he felt dismay at the sight of the little stone cabin with its woven roof of Rul limbs, a wisp of white smoke drifting from a metal chimney. With the fierce hot season near again he'd come to the knoll with increasing frequency, hoping to see the cabin abandoned, the man and his woman finally gone from the valley and back to the human city remaining on the coast beyond the mountains. He scanned the valley where once had been many such farms, the broken earth now covered with grass except in this one place, the human crops withered and dead. Only two humans were left, and he wanted them to be gone from the valley of the Tatun forever.

Grass crunched, and Balaban turned to see Axalay hunched over a walking stick as he climbed the last few steps to the knoll. His breathing was a wheeze, brow flaps grey in the morning light. Balaban rushed to hold him up. "Father, you should be in bed. What are you doing here?"

"To see what you find so interesting," grumbled the old Tatun. "I've spent enough time in the hut, and my blood is too thick. Would you have me die in darkness?" Axalay looked up at him with rheumy eyes, and his breath was sweet. It was not a good sign. "You can let go of my arm, now," he said. "Ah, I see the humans are still trying."

"Not for long. This season should finish them for good."

"You sound pleased about that," said Axalay. "I am not. They have been good neighbors. Ignorance is the cause of their misfortune, and they work hard. With seeds of Pash and Ofa, a supply of Ungstuntu and our advice on when to plant they could have a life here, if you would allow it."

"I will not allow it, father. I enforce the decision of The Council."

"Pfaa," said Axalay. He spat something horrible onto the ground. "The Council vote was two years ago, before I passed leadership to you. The valley was then filled with humans, and the animals were driven away by their numbers. Times change, and so do opinions. You resist new thinking by the Tatun who look to you for leadership. I did not teach you that." Almond-shaped eyes changed from brown to black, reflecting his mood. "I taught you compassion for all living things."

Balaban breathed deeply to control the anger at his father's rebuke. "It is not necessary that I always agree with you. You passed leadership to me, and that's the way it remains. Those in sympathy with your views are fewer than you imagine."

Axalay shook his head sadly. "You do not listen hard enough." He looked to the east, and pointed. "See, they return from the lake. They must have started out well before first light."

A well-worn trail ran eastward along the valley up gentle slopes to a small lake fed by mountain runoff and springs. Coming down the trail was a Pischela-drawn cart stacked with wooden barrels, the antlered animal pulling hard and led by the man while the woman shuffled along wearily behind, arms crossed over her swollen belly. On the slopes southward, and paralleling their course, something moved, a dark shape slinking through tall grass.

"A Rork follows them," said Balaban. "It is hungry for the Pischela, but the human sees it. He carries his weapon."

Axalay nodded. "It's good to see the big predators back again. It means the Pischela are growing in numbers."

"Not for long, perhaps. Look!"

The man had stopped the cart-load of water barrels and unslung his weapon. He pointed it up the hill; there was a flash, followed by a thundering report. The Rork fled.

"He missed," said Balaban. "Eventually he will kill all the animals, if he stays here."

"He meant only to frighten the Rork away. I've seen him bring down a Pischela at hundreds of paces, but only for food, nothing more. And if he saw the Rork, he certainly can see us up here. Believe me when I say he could kill us from where he stands if he considered us enemies. But he will not do that."

"How can you be so sure?" asked Balaban.

"Because I know he's a good neighbor. I think you will come to know it, too. Now, please help me back to the village. My legs are very tired."

Balaban grasped his father and took one last look. The human had reslung his weapon, and his face was dark in the first gleam of Ta. He was watching them.

The time of great heat was upon them, and the Tatun busied themselves indoors as much as possible during the day. Algst had appeared on schedule, beginning its slow walk across the sky while its brighter companion Ta appeared and disappeared one hundred and ninety times. There was no night with Algst there, bathing the world of Tatunstu in red light, and sleep was difficult, the air without moisture. The elderly were most endangered by the heat, and old Lilgh, who had nursed half of the Tatun of the home village when they were babies, died quietly in her sleep only a few days into the season.

The funeral and formal mourning was conducted on two nights, and on the second they burned her body to ash in an earthen oven and made Ungstuntu, mixing the ashes with earth, Rul-leaf mulch and the hairs of Ofa roots to form the rich, water absorbent fertilizer that nurtured their crops after the short rainy season. Lilgh had made no specific bequest, and so the fertilizer was divided equally among her four children. The ceremony was emotional, as usual, the ashen remains of the dead contributing to the future welfare of those they had left behind.

Axalay was quiet during the distribution of Ungstuntu, and there were tears on his face. Even his daughter-in-law Chiaspun could not seem to comfort him. Finally, she went to her husband and said, "Talk to your father, Balaban. He thinks only about death, and it's not good for him."

Balaban went to his father. "You seem troubled. What is it?"

"I think of the humans," said Axalay. "There are no relatives to make Ungstuntu for them. They are alone here."

"They're not Tatun, father, and they came here by choice to take our best land away from us. We had nothing to say about it, and now you feel sorry for *them*? Only our skill and knowledge has kept us alive since they came here."

Axalay sighed. "You exaggerate again. We only had to move, and our crops grow well on the plateau and high valleys. You simply don't want them to be here, two humans in the entire valley, and you haven't even met them. I have. Do you know they spoke our language when they arrived here? They didn't come to force us away from them. They came here to live *with* us."

"You've talked to them? The Council has said—"

"Pfaa on The Council and their outdated opinions. I live in the present, and you do not! I will speak to the humans when I please, and I invite you to join me."

"I forbid it, father."

"Words," said Axalay, and he turned away from Balaban to shuffle painfully back to his hut.

"I mean it, father," shouted Balaban. "It is the ruling of The Council that we make no contact with humans, or give them aid. It was *your* Council that made the ruling; it's my job to enforce it, and I *will*! Do you hear me?" It had become very quiet in the gathering of Tatun.

Axalay disappeared into his hut.

Chiaspun came up to grasp his arm. "What's wrong?"

"I will *never* make contact with the humans. Never!"

The following evening, he met them.

* * * * * * *

Twithst was discovered missing in the early morning. The toddler was forever wandering away, but was always found near the home village, usually in pursuit of a Whetsty, the furry hopper sometimes eaten by the Tatun and occasionally kept as pets for the children. This day, however, she was nowhere to be found, and the heat was stifling. Tatun scoured the area: plateau, high valleys, and the eastern valley clear to the lake. Not a trace. By late afternoon her parents were frantic, certain the child had been taken by a Rork or a pack of Mauders, the small predators with needle teeth which kept the Whetsty population in check. They wept as the Tatun gathered again within the circle of huts to begin an evening search of the high valleys.

"Ho!" called a foreign voice, and they all turned with a gasp, for striding boldly into the village were the two humans, and sitting on the shoulders of the male was little Twithst, chewing on a piece of dried meat and looking very pleased with herself. Everyone stood in their place, stunned, until the male lifted the child from his shoulders, placed her gently on her feet and she ran giggling into the hysterical embrace of her mother. "We had a visitor this morning," said the human. "She walked right into our cabin, sat down at the table and said she was hungry, so we fed her. I kept her inside because it was hot, and there's a Rork prowling in the valley. She kept us talking all day, and it was wonderful. I hope you weren't too worried about her." His command of the guttural Tatun language was excellent, spoken slowly and with confidence.

A horrible silence greeted him. Everyone stood transfixed, looking nervously at Balaban who was glaring sullenly at the visitor, his heart pounding with rage. The spell was broken by Axalay's shout as he emerged from his hut. "Ho, Armin and Laina! You've found our little wanderer, and returned her safely! Greetings of the Tatun!"

The old Tatun walked to the humans and embraced both of them while the others stood silently, their brow flaps rolled upwards in fright and dismay at such a sight. "Greetings to you, Axalay. We've missed you," said Armin, shaking him by the shoulders. Balaban took a step forward, but Chiaspun grabbed his arm in a firm grip and pulled him back.

"I cannot walk far in this heat," said Axalay. "Listen, all of you, these are our neighbors Armin and Laina Baisch. Come, and meet them. We owe them thanks for bringing Twithst home."

Silence. Nobody moved, all eyes on Balaban. Axalay's brow flaps nearly covered his eyes when he looked at his son. "Perhaps thanks will best come from our leader. It is his privilege and duty."

Chiaspun put a sharp elbow in his ribs and Balaban stepped forward, his anger barely controlled. "We thank you for returning the child," he mumbled. The human extended a hand, but Balaban ignored it, looking only at the long weapon strapped around the man's shoulders. Both humans frowned, sensing his mood, he noted. They knew the body language of the Tatun. "Your weapon will see you back safely. You may go now, if you wish."

"Not yet," said Axalay. "All of you meet our neighbors, even the little one that will soon be born." He put a hand on Laina's stomach, and she smiled.

Balaban felt paralyzed. Behind him, feet shuffled in the dirt, but nobody came forward, not even Twithst's parents. The humans frowned again.

"I don't think we're welcome here, Axalay," said Armin. His blue eyes focused on Balaban from a thin face burned brown by the heat.

"We have no contact with humans," said Balaban evenly. "We do not desire it now."

"That's not good news. I brought a bag of dried meat I'd hoped to trade for some Pash and Ofa, even some Rul root if you can spare it. Our crops have failed again, and the supplies we brought with us ran out weeks ago. Meat isn't enough, especially for Laina and the baby. She needs vegetables for the baby to be healthy."

"The human city is a five day walk. You can get food there," said Balaban, unblinking.

"We can't do that. We're on our own here."

"I don't understand. The others returned to the city."

"Only to leave Tatunstu and give up their farms to the heat. Our seeds won't grow here, and the rains are hard to predict. We have much to learn."

Jaquysht and Isakstu, members of The Council, came up to stand by Balaban and reassure him with their presence. "If your seeds don't grow, then why don't you leave?"

Armin's eyes narrowed to slits. "We have no money. The company took all our money just getting here. For us, it was a one-way trip. We stay here, and we die here, one way or the other."

Balaban understood the human word 'money', the little golden disks used as trading goods.

"Armin!" said Laina. There were tears in her eyes. "Let's go."

"Just a second. I want to make it clear we're here to stay. This is our home, now, as much as it is for the Tatun. We want to be friends, if you'll allow it, and we'll share what is ours. I'm not asking for a gift, I only want to trade some of our meat for Pash and Ofa so our baby can be healthy." The man's eyes glinted dangerously as the woman pulled at his arm.

"We do not deal with humans," said Balaban, nodding at his father. "It was Axalay's Council that made the ruling, and it is still the way of the Tatun. You must care for yourselves if you remain here."

Axalay's eyes peered from beneath brow folds nearly covering them. "Leave, my friends, and I will talk to them."

The man turned and stalked away, Laina clinging to his arm, stumbling to keep up with him.

"I demand to speak to The Council in my hut within the hour. As former leader, it is my privilege," Axalay said softly.

The meeting went on for an hour, and as The Council left Axalay's hut the entire village could hear him scream after them, "You are fools without compassion! The Tatun will live to regret their rudeness on this day!"

Balaban slept alone that night, for Chiaspun had suddenly decided to spend time with her mother four huts distant from their own. He didn't ask why, for he'd experienced her anger before, and it was always the same. But this time, it lasted for days.

* * * * * * *

Gentle Chiaspun he understood, but the reaction of the rest of the village was a surprise to Balaban. For days, the Tatun went out of their way to avoid him, making eye-contact only when he said something requiring an answer. When he asked Chiaspun about the strange silence, she only said, "What do you expect? You've refused food to an unborn child," and then she went about her business.

Only Jaquysht stood by him. "It's your father," he said. "He is persuasive, and many Tatun see nothing wrong with helping our human neighbors to survive here. The other members of The Council feel there should be a discussion and new vote on the ruling forbidding human contact."

"I will not call for such a vote," said Balaban, "and the rest of you must be unanimous to go against me."

"I stand with you, Balaban. If we help the humans, more are sure to come, as before."

Balaban found no cheer in Jaquysht's support, for it was clear the village felt otherwise, and for the first time in the two years since he'd been leader he felt threatened by the opinion of the Tatun. Suddenly he felt a burden of leadership, and late on an afternoon he walked the valley to a clump of Rul west of the lake to sit and probe the motives underlying his refusal to help the humans. The first humans had arrived when he was a child, claiming all of Tatunstu as *their* world, staking out the valley in little squares and posting a guard after herding the Tatun to the plateaus and high valleys. The settlers came, and their crops would not grow, and they were already beginning to leave when the humans Armin and Laina arrived. Why had they not known of the difficulty? Why wouldn't their own kind give them food? Why could they not...?"

In the heat of afternoon, Balaban fell asleep in tall grass beneath the leafy Ruls.

When he awoke, he was looking into the blue eyes and burned skin of Armin Baisch. The man was sitting right in front of him, the long weapon lying across his knees. Balaban pressed his back against the rough bark of the tree.

Armin did not smile. "Not a good idea to sleep here. A Rork has been spiraling in on these trees for an hour, so I came up to see what was so interesting."

"Where?" said Balaban, now wide awake.

"About a hundred paces out, but still there. He was a lot closer, but he knows what this can do." Armin patted the long weapon across his legs. "It can kill far."

"You could have killed *me*," said Balaban, relaxing a little.

"It's a thought, but I figure that blood all by itself makes lousy fertilizer. You want me to walk you back to the village?"

"No," said Balaban, looking away.

Armin spat on the ground. "What've you got against me? You don't like the way I talk or look?"

"You're a human."

"Right, and you're a Tatun. So what? We live right next to each other."

"On Tatun land."

Armin softened. "Yeah. Axalay told me about that, the whole story. The company robbed me, too, took everything I had just to get here and have my own place. They never told us the land was stolen.

They didn't say the heat was killing, or the soil rotten. I worked freighters for ten years to get here. Met Laina on one of them, and we had the same dream. So here we are, with a baby coming, dead crops, no supplies, and neighbors who hate us after we spent four years just learning their language and ways. Or is it just you?"

"I can't change the past," said Balaban.

"Neither can I. That still doesn't mean we can't live together, share the land. Damn ground and heat! I've got seed for potatoes, corn, wheat, things I know the Tatun would like to eat if I could just get a crop to *grow*! You know how, I've seen your fields. What am I doing *wrong*?"

Balaban remained silent.

"Pfaa," said Armin, in the way of the Tatun, and spat a huge, ceremonial glob on the ground as he got up. Balaban followed and took a step before the man stopped him. "Don't move," he said, raising his weapon. Only ten paces from them the grass moved, a long snout thrusting forth, a Rork moving forward on its belly. "You're getting too bold, old boy," said Armin, and he fired. A piece of the animal's right ear disappeared. It screamed, tumbled, and fled towards the lake, cutting a swath through the tall grass.

"You didn't kill it," said Balaban.

"Didn't mean to. It's only trying to survive like the rest of us." Armin turned, and stomped away towards his cabin.

Halfway back to the village Balaban could see the Rork still running near the lake. His afternoon to think out his problems had done no good. When he arrived at the village he was even more troubled than before.

Axalay was waiting for him.

"I have made a decision," he said, "and I've already informed The Council about it, so you needn't try to tell them otherwise."

"Now what is it?" said Balaban, still tired, and feeling irritable. They walked together towards Axalay's hut, father hanging on tightly to the son's arm. Tatun watched them silently from doorways.

"My death is near, Balaban. Something is broken in me, and there is blood in my bed each morning. Kartsku has been treating me with his various potions, but nothing works. I'm used up. So it is time to talk about the Ungstuntu that will be made from my body."

"Yes, father," said Balaban, uncomfortable with such talk.

"There is considerable surplus, enough for two seasons at least. As leader, you receive additional shares each year, and there's still only you and Chiaspun. She wants a child, you know."

"We've discussed it, yes. Perhaps this year; it is difficult to say. Her cycle is irregular by a few days, but we've been trying."

"Good," said Axalay. "I wish my bloodline to continue, even though my son is stubborn. You are honest and hard-working, Balaban, but there is wisdom in you that hasn't been used yet. Still, I'm proud of your good qualities, and I love you with all my heart. Do you believe that?"

"Of course, father. We argue, but—"

"What I'm asking will be a test of the wisdom and compassion that I know lies within you. It will not be easy, and I won't be here to persuade you. I trust you to honor the will of your father, and his memory. New life will rise from the ashes of my body on Tatunstu."

They had arrived at Axalay's hut. "Come inside," he said, "and sit with me a moment."

Balaban had a crawling feeling in his stomach. There was a horrible odor, sickly sweet, in the darkness of the hut. It was the smell of death. He sat down on the hard bed of woven Rul branches. Axalay sat down close beside him, put a hand on his knee, and patted it.

"It is my will that the Ungstuntu made from the ashes of my body be given entirely to the humans Armin and Laina. As heir, it is also your gift to them."

Balaban's heart was hammering, and Axalay squeezed his knee when he shuddered. "You leave me *nothing*?"

"I leave you with who you are, and can be. Everything else is already provided for you."

"But it will be *wasted*. The humans have no idea how or when to plant. They will scatter the Ungstuntu on the ground to be blown away by the wind."

"You will show them what to do, and provide them with seed from our reserves."

"Father!" said Balaban, his eyes suddenly moist in the dry air.

"And when the Whetsty leave their burrows to make nests under rocks and the perfume of cracked Rul-nut pods is in the air, you will warn the humans to plant quickly, for the rains arrive within a few days. You will do this so that my body will bring new life to Tatunstu."

"I—I cannot do this. The ruling is—"

"Change it. The human experiment has failed, and they live in their dirty cities to make profit on the rock they tear from the ground. There are only Tatun here, and in the valley. It will always be so."

"Pfaa. The real Tatun here will be outraged. I will no longer be leader," said Balaban bitterly, for he was caught now by conflicting laws: he must follow the death will of his father, but not give aid to the humans.

"You are mistaken. Caught up in your own opinion, you have not asked for theirs, but I think you know it. And you must follow it if you're a good leader." Axalay put an arm around his shoulders, hugged him. "Balaban, my son, my gift to the humans is also to you, a precious gift, and the right of your birth. Only a leader can give such a gift, don't you see?"

"I do not," said Balaban, rising so quickly his father nearly fell over trying to hold him still. "I see only that you have shamed me!" He stormed out of the hut in fury.

"Balaban!" called Axalay after him, but he kept going, straight to his hut, feeling the silent stares of those he had been chosen to lead. The tears of shame were on his face when Chiaspun embraced him, and he told her what had happened. She held him close, and said, "You are the one I have chosen to live my life with because you have qualities I could not find in another. But your vision of leadership is too narrow. Your responsibilities do not end with this single village, or those around it. They reach far beyond." And then she released him, and went to prepare their evening meal.

* * * * * * *

Algst disappeared in the east, and there was that first welcome day when Ta made a lonely path across the sky again. The first signs of rain came and went, the pods appearing on the Ruls, green, then brown, inside each the sweet nut the Tatun crushed and baked into flat cakes for special occasions. There had been two more deaths during the hot season, both in a village in the high valley: a grandmother, a still-born child. Balaban was reminded of the extent of his responsibilities to those living in the high places, and now he visited them more frequently, made Ungstuntu with them, pushed the wooden plows to break new ground. He was often gone for days at a time, away from confrontation with his father, away from the pressures he felt to call a meeting of The Council. Axalay was still alive, and as long as he was there was no issue for The Council to consider.

Balaban's days in the home village were well spent, for Chiaspun announced her pregnancy at his fourth return. Axalay was gladdened by the news. The old Tatun spent more and more time in his hut, but in Balaban's absence left the village in the evenings for long walks alone, refusing accompaniment despite the danger of the Rork still wandering the valley. But on the morning of Balaban's eighth return home, Axalay was discovered missing from his hut. Hearing this, Balaban went in search, first to the knoll overlooking the human cabin where he saw Armin breaking ground alone, and then east towards the lake. His heart lightened when he saw his father sitting beneath the trees he himself favored for quiet reflection, the place where he'd talked to Armin when the Rork was near. Axalay was sitting against a tree, looking at him as he approached.

"You are missed, father. Let me help you home."

Axalay was silent, still looking down the valley as Balaban stooped to help him up.

His body was rigid, and cold.

Axalay's being had flown away.

Balaban sat with him for a long time, closed his father's eyes, stroked his face, and watched him. Axalay's face was serene. If there had been pain, it did not show. After many long minutes, Balaban numbly hoisted the body over his shoulder and made the hot, slow walk back to the village, hearing the cries of grief even before arriving there, for the Tatun had seen him coming. His own grief showed itself later, when Chiaspun was holding him in the darkness of their hut.

They made Ungstuntu with the ashes of Balaban's father, and the bequest made by Axalay was announced. Jaquysht postured outrage. "This cannot be! Balaban has been put in an impossible situation by this!"

Balaban remained calm, aware that all were watching him. Inside, he was numb, both with grief for his father, and with dismay over what he must now do. "I honor my father and his memory before anything. I call a meeting of The Council this very evening to re-examine the issue of our contact with the humans."

There were murmurs of approval from those around him. Jaquysht rushed to his side. "I cast my vote with yours, Balaban," he whispered.

But when The Council met an hour later, and with little discussion, the vote was unanimously in favor of rescinding the old rule and allowing contact with and aid to any humans who dared to make a life on Tatun land. The village was enormously pleased with the decision, and Chiaspun cried with pride. Balaban sedately excused himself for meditation and took a long walk. He went back to the knoll at dusk and watched Armin still turning over dead crops by himself, pushing with all his might against the wooden plow, the female nowhere in sight. Balaban felt no pleasure in watching this, nor in his sudden increase in status, the obvious leap in respect the Tatun now showed him.

Inside himself, he felt sick from the thing he was now committed to do.

The morning after the Whetsty were first seen nesting in the rocks, Balaban pulled a cart laden with Ungstuntu and seed down into the valley. It was barely first light, and Armin was already in the fields, this time using his tamed Pischela to pull a device that smoothed the plowed ground. Balaban was vaguely amused by the wasted effort when only a digging tool and knowledge of planting was necessary in a valley which collected runoff from all the surrounding slopes. He rolled the cart up to where Armin stood waiting for him. "What is this?" said the man.

"The rains will come soon, and this is what you need to make your life here. It is a gift from my father."

"Axalay? How is he? I saw him two days ago, and he didn't look well."

Balaban told him about Axalay. Armin took off his hat and held it over his chest, looking grim, a simple gesture that strangely pleased Balaban. "I'm sorry," said Armin. "He was so good to us, to Laina and me. He was our only friend."

"This is his bequest to you, and you must begin immediately. I will show you what to do."

"You'll do that for us?" Armin seemed surprised.

"I do it for my father," said Balaban. "We have only a few days before the rains come. We should begin now. Can the woman help?"

"No," said Armin. "The baby will come any day now. I don't want to risk anything."

"Then it is our task. You'll need a planting digger, like this. Nothing else." He showed Armin his short, wooden trowel carved from Rul bark.

"I have something like it." Armin went back to the cabin, returned in minutes with a metal implement that would suffice. "I shouldn't have told Laina about Axalay. She was very upset when I left," he said, looking worried.

"Here is what you do," said Balaban, down on his knees. He showed Armin how to dig the funnel-shaped hole, the packing in of the Ungstuntu so it had room to swell with enough water to sustain a single plant after the short, hard rains, the seed encased in a hard ball of the same, a light covering of soil pressed hard to form a depression. "The ashes of the dead bring life to this field," he said ceremoniously, and his vision was clouded for just an instant.

"What?" said Armin, on his knees beside him.

"The ashes of my father are in the Ungstuntu that will feed your crop. He has given his body to you, and I help you to be certain it's not wasted."

"My God," said Armin. "Now I understand. And things between you and I are still the same."

"We must hurry," said Balaban.

They worked hard all day in silence. Evening fell, and Armin invited Balaban to share a meal with him, but Balaban declined and went back to the village. The next day was a repeat of the first, then another, and another, always in silence, each returning to his own home for a meal. On the fifth day they worked until well after dark, and it was suddenly humid, the first grey clouds of the season appearing in the east with the setting of Ta. "We can finish in the morning," said Armin. "Laina has prepared a meal from the things Axalay brought to us before he died. All the work you've done, it's only right we share it with you. Please?"

"He brought you food?"

"Yes, several bags of it, both Pash and Ofa, and a small bag of Rul nuts. He left instructions, but we need a Tatun opinion on the cooking. I'd like to share his gifts with you."

While I was out of the village. Who was most stubborn, father, you or I? Do you watch me even now?

"Then I accept your invitation," said Balaban, surprised at his own words.

They trudged back to the tiny cabin, light flickering from an open window. Laina was delighted to see him, though she looked exhausted and ready to burst with child at any moment, her face glistening in the candlelight. Still, she bustled around the tiny room: slat bed in one corner, a bench for eating, cooking hearth of stone, bare walls and another window looking into the Pischela's lean-to shelter. It was a humble dwelling, poorer than a Tatun hut, yet comfortable. Slabs of drying meat hung on poles over the hearth, and a woven box heaped with yellow Pash was on the earthen floor next to it. *My father carried that down here*, thought Balaban.

They ate in silence, Armin and Laina watching him, eating little themselves. The Pash was overcooked, the Ofa undercooked by a day and the Rul nuts had been used as seasoning instead of using grass tips. His stomach would regret this meal, but he was polite, eating everything. Finally, he looked up at Laina and said, "there are things you can do. I will bring Chiaspun to instruct you. I must go now. The rains might be here by morning, and half a day of work remains. Thank you—Laina—Armin."

Laina looked vaguely disappointed, and Armin walked with him outside, picking up his weapon by the doorway. "I'll go with you. The Rork, you know."

"I think not. It seeks shelter, now, so it is better you stay here. I will be very early tomorrow." He took a step, then turned with sudden impulse and said, "It is right that I help you, now. The rule about helping humans has been changed."

He left Armin with the man's mouth hanging open.

* * * * * * *

Chiaspun was delighted at the chance to help Laina, and made plans for it all night. There was little sleep for either of them, and before first light Balaban was fairly running to keep up with her. The grass was wet with dew and the air felt thick to breathe as they came into the valley and saw Armin on his knees in a corner of his field. Chiaspun went straight to the cabin.

"I'm trying a patch of potatoes to see if they'll grow the Tatun way," said Armin. The seeds were huge, and soft. Balaban sniffed at one, and the odor was pleasing. They finished the small patch of human food and worked hurriedly to do the rest of the field. It became light, but Ta was obscured in cloud cover and a wind came from the east, blowing gently at first, then hard. They were down to the last two bags of Ungstuntu when the first drops came. Balaban dug madly, rushing from place to place, looking up to see a grey veil rushing towards them, and somehow they were finished before it hit, a sheet of warm water that battered their eyes closed. Armin took off his hat and looked up at the sky, grinning.

Heads down, they ran towards the cabin in pouring rain. Someone was standing by the window. Laina. In her arms she held a thing wrapped in white. Armin screamed and ran like a panicked Rork while Balaban trotted on in blinding rain. Chiaspun met him at the doorway, led him dripping inside. "We did something more than cook today," she whispered.

Armin was embracing Laina by the window, and he was crying. This hard human, with gnarled hands and burned face, was shaking with emotion. He probed at the bundle in Laina's arms, pulled back a cloth to look carefully. The bundle let out an irritated squeak, and Laina said, "all the parts are there. He's fine, Armin. Perfect."

"He was born at mid-day," said Chiaspun. "It was as I've seen, and helped with, many times before."

Laina stepped over to Balaban, showed him the red-faced child now chewing toothlessly at one hand. "This is baby Lee," she said solemnly. Balaban looked at Laina, at Armin wiping away tears, then at a smiling Chiaspun, her own child, and his, now growing inside her body. At that instant, something gave way within him. The revelation came to him as if spoken by his father from a far distance. The pounding rain even now mixed with Axalay's ashes, and within days there would be the crackling sounds of plants thrusting from the ground. Tatun ground. And here, in this cabin, another life had arrived. Those here in this room were Balaban's responsibility as much as the many on the plateau and up in the high valleys.

There were no human strangers in this room.

There were only Tatun.

BODYGUARD

Marvin Polack checked three books out of the library and waited patiently while Susan stamped the due date in each volume. He watched her work, studied the finely chiseled features of her face and the auburn hair that framed it. His hands trembled a little as she handed the books to him, her fingers coming close to his, and he forced a slight smile. "Thank you," he said softly.

"Thank *you*, Mister Polack. You must have read every mystery novel in the library by now."

"Not quite," he said, and looked down at the books to avoid her eyes. "I'll be back for more in a few days."

"Well let me know if I can help you find anything."

"I will," said Marvin, still looking at the books, and then he turned away, seemingly lost in thought, and left the library and Susan Kensor behind. Susan watched him go, wondering what he found wrong with her, why she was unable to start up a meaningful conversation with him. The man intrigued her, a studious, soft-spoken person with startling blue eyes that made her skin tingle the few times he'd looked at her directly. He just didn't seem to notice her, and she wondered why.

When her work was finished for the day she walked the nine blocks back to her apartment along lonely side streets past yawning maws of dark alleys that always frightened her. She walked quickly, hands thrust into coat pockets, her face set in a mask of grim determination to reach home safely. If only she wasn't too cheap to take a cab, she thought. Eyes fixed straight ahead, she didn't notice Marvin Polack following a block behind her, or the slender man leafing through magazines and watching her through the dirty window of a bookstore across the street.

* * * * * * *

It was dark when Marvin stumbled up the wooden stairs to his apartment and opened the door. He was shaking so badly he needed both hands to guide his key into the lock, and then he was inside and it was very quiet. His mother hadn't come home from work, so she wouldn't have to ask him why he was trembling all over or why his face and forehead glistened with sweat. He went to his room, locked the door behind him and lay down on his bed in darkness, breathing deeply and forcing his mind back to reality. The murder of Susan Kensor had seemed so real, so horrible, yet a part of his mind fought to retain the image of her staring eyes. She had *not* died, he told himself. He had followed her home, as he'd been doing for several days now, watching her striding ahead of him in the growing darkness. In his imagination, he'd crept up behind her, clamped a hand over her mouth and dragged her backwards into an alley. When she saw who he was, she seemed to relax, and when he began to choke her she didn't struggle, only stared at him, eyes open wide with surprise. And he squeezed harder and harder . . .

But it hadn't happened that way. At the height of his fantasy, he'd watched her reach home safely, had seen the light go on in her room and he was standing outside in the street, shaking and sweating and feeling foolish. When he looked around the street was virtually empty, only a single pedestrian on the far side who glanced at him and walked on. He felt embarrassed, frightened, and then he had hurried home.

What frightened him was the way his fantasy had suddenly changed. Why would he want to hurt Susan? He liked her, a lot, even though she probably saw him as just one more bookworm who haunted the library. He usually imagined himself as her protector, a bodyguard, following his client in a neighborhood that had witnessed a rash of rapes and murders in recent months. He'd been protecting her—until tonight.

The images were still fresh in his mind, and he would have to get it all down on paper quickly. He got up from his bed, turned on the lamp over his desk in one corner of the bookshelf-lined room and rolled a sheet of paper into the typewriter. He thought for a moment, forming the scene more clearly in his mind, and then began to type rapidly. He was still pounding the keys of the machine when there was a soft knock on his door.

"Do you want something to eat, Marvin? It's seven o'clock."

"Just a second, mom. I'll be right there." He finished a paragraph, got up from his desk and turned on the room lights before he opened the door. His mother stood there smiling up at him, looking small and tired.

"TV dinners tonight," she said. "Do you mind?"

"No, that's fine, mom. You look beat. Why don't you let me do some of the cooking?" He walked back to the desk, his mother following closely behind, and sat down again before the typewriter.

"You have your writing to do. I'll handle the cooking. Did you have a good day?" She put a hand on his shoulder.

"Pretty good," he said, and studied the paper in the machine. "Ten pages written, and then I went to the library. But I got another story back in the mail. No comments, just the standard rejection slip. I wish I could figure out what I'm doing wrong."

"Keep at it," she said, and patted his shoulder. "Your father used to say a person had to write a lot of junk before anything worthwhile could be produced."

"I remember that," said Marvin, smiling, "but at least dad's newspaper job guaranteed him some kind of income. Maybe that's what I should be doing."

"Maybe," she said. "You'll have to decide that. But give it another year anyway. Your father always said you had a talent for it, could do better than he ever did. I just wish he was here to help you."

She squeezed his shoulder, and he put one hand on top of hers. "I'll keep working at it," he said softly.

They ate dinner in silence, and his mother went to bed early. Marvin read in bed until early in the morning, finishing one novel and beginning a collection of short stories. When his eyelids seemed heavy he turned off the light and stared into the darkness for a moment, thinking about the past day. And as he drifted into sleep, Susan was standing before him, reaching out a hand to touch his face.

* * * * * * *

Marvin Polack followed Susan for three more evenings before he realized someone else was also following her. At first he thought it was just his active imagination, something to enhance the bodyguard role he fantasized when he was near her. It was a role he expanded and glorified in pages of writing each evening. But as he strolled along behind her, locked in his dreams, he couldn't ignore the reality of the tall, slim man who walked in the lengthening shadows across the street, pausing occasionally to look in shop windows that showed nothing and twice moving quickly into a doorway when Susan turned to look across the street. It was certainly suspicious behavior, thought Marvin, yet there was nothing really sinister about the man. He was ordinary looking, clean cut, perhaps a student who lived in the neighborhood. He carried no briefcase or books, kept his hands in the pockets of a light jacket and moved with the springy steps of an athlete. But he always moved within shadows near the buildings, and he *was* watching Susan. When they reached her rooming house she went quickly inside as Marvin stepped into an alleyway a block away. The other man stood in a doorway across the street, looking up towards the window of Susan's room for a long time. The light went on. From time to time her thin figure was silhouetted in the window, and then the shade was suddenly pulled down. The man stepped out of the doorway, hurried down the street and disappeared from view around a corner. Marvin waited a few minutes as darkness came, and then left the alley and walked quickly back to his home. He was suddenly very frightened.

* * * * * * *

The next evening he followed Susan for a new reason and with a new sense of caution, staying nearly a block behind her the whole time and hovering close to the buildings and alleyways they passed. She walked quickly as usual, head down, not looking at the few people who passed her near the library. He knew she had to be afraid about walking home alone, especially with the recent attacks in the neighborhood. Why didn't she take a cab? Probably because she couldn't afford it. But her rooming house *did* look expensive from the outside. He'd thought about offering to walk home with her, but decided not to because he couldn't bear the thought of her turning him down. What would she want to do with a young writer who spent much of his time in a fantasy world, and who had no permanent employment? She could do better than that. But now he *was* walking home with her, protectively, but from a distance.

His heart jumped when he saw the man leave a bookstore across the street and begin to follow Susan as he had the evening before. There was no question about it, the man had been waiting for her. He paralleled her course again, keeping to the shadows and occasionally checking his watch. Marvin felt blood rush to his face and head. The man was timing her walk! And the times would be repeatable, since Susan left work at exactly the same time each evening and walked straight home without fail. Why did she have to follow such a regular schedule?

Marvin dropped far back, watching only the man now and wondering what he could do if Susan were attacked. The man looked wiry and strong. Marvin had no illusions about his own physical strength, but he could make a lot noise if he had to. The question was, would anyone respond to his shouts if Susan were in trouble? He doubted it. People in this neighborhood were not quick to become involved with the problems of others. They had enough problems of their own.

But nothing happened that evening. Susan reached the rooming house safely, and again the man watched the window of her room, until the shades were pulled down, and then walked quickly away. Marvin breathed an audible sigh of relief from his hiding place. He waited until after dark, staring at empty streets and thinking about what he should do. During the long walk back to his typewriter and books he decided that on the next evening he would arrive better prepared to deal with the situation.

He sat in front of the typewriter for three hours that night, but nothing would come. His fantasy world had been totally disrupted, his mind focused only on Susan and the man who followed her. It was nearly midnight when he gave up trying to write. He paced the floor for a while, and then went to his dresser. He pulled open a drawer and searched under neat stacks of socks and underwear until he found a heavy object wrapped in an old flannel shirt. He put the bundle on his bed, unwrapped it, and sat down next to the blue steel .357 magnum revolver exposed there. It was his father's gun. Marvin remembered the day he's learned how to shoot it. His father had been patient with a son who spent most of his time reading and writing and living in fantasy worlds that didn't exist. But shooting was something every boy should learn to do, his father had said. Marvin touched the blue steel of the big revolver, remembering what it was like when he pulled the trigger: the shock wave that went up and down his extended arm, the ear-shattering roar and the sheet of flame that flashed from the muzzle. The experience had terrified him, but with his father's patient coaxing he'd stuck with it until all his shots struck the paper target within an area the size of a dinner plate at a distance of twenty-five yards. Good enough, his father had said. But when that day was over, Marvin's entire body had been shaking. He'd been afraid of the gun since that time.

So now he sat on his bed, thinking about carrying the gun to protect Susan from a man who followed her home from work each evening. The whole idea seemed suddenly absurd. He was following her home himself, but meant her no harm. Or did he? The strong fantasy he'd had about her suddenly came back to him. But that had only been one time, his imagination running wild for a moment. After all, he *cared* about Susan Kensor.

Didn't he?

Marvin went to his desk and rummaged around in several drawers until he found a nearly empty box of cartridges for the gun. He loaded it carefully and pressed the cylinder back in alignment with the frame with a dull click before wiping it off with the flannel shirt. He placed the gun and cartridge box in a desk drawer and then undressed and went to bed, reading until he finished the last of the books he'd checked out of the library. Marvin slept poorly that night, awakening several times, and getting up once for a glass of water to get rid of the cardboard taste in his mouth. In the early morning he slept soundly, but under closed eye lids his eyes moved rapidly, following the action in several, intense dreams. He didn't remember the dreams.

* * * * * * *

The next day was hot and muggy. Marvin slept until late in the morning, and awoke drenched in sweat. After a coffee and toast breakfast he worked at the typewriter for three hours, but the writing came hard. His mind was a jumble of confused thoughts, and even with the windows open he found it difficult to breathe in his little room. He finished a story and read it over, scowling at the pages. The plot wandered, had no focus and the dialogue seemed dull and wooden. It was time to put it away and get out into the sun, he thought. He took the library books with him and wandered the streets for a while, watching the people he passed, describing them mentally to himself with words. He bought a hot dog from a street vendor and wandered some more until he suddenly found himself in front of the library. Force of habit, he thought. His travels always took him to where the books were.

When he turned in his books at the checkout desk Susan was sitting at a paper-heaped table, reading a book and eating a late lunch out of a brown paper bag. She wore a sleeveless, white blouse for the hot day and looked lovely, he thought. Engrossed in her reading she didn't see him standing there, and another girl took his books. He took a list from his wallet, and then went to the line of computer terminals along one side of the library and sat down in front of one of them to punch in titles and authors of the new books he wanted. The machine responded quickly. He wrote down the reference numbers and location codes on his list and began his search for the volumes along the hundreds of book shelves in the big room. He found three of them, but the fourth seemed to be missing, even though the computer had indicated it was not checked out. Perhaps it had been misplaced. He was scanning titles along the shelves when he suddenly smelled perfume.

"Can I help you with something?"

Susan Kensor stood behind him, replacing some books that had been checked in. She looked at him expectantly. Marvin looked down at his list, and swallowed hard.

"I'm looking for *Modern Guns of the World* by Ray Asmuth. It doesn't seem to be here, but it's not checked out." He fought to keep his voice from quivering.

She moved up close alongside him, and peered at his list. "Maybe it's a large-sized book—on the bottom shelf—here." She knelt down and quickly found the volume, grunting as she pulled it off the shelf and handed it up to him. "Heavy reading," she said. "Are you a shooter, or a collector?"

Marvin opened the book and looked at the table of contents. "I'm a writer," he said, "trying to find a proper gun for a mystery story I just finished."

"Really? I've never met a writer before. Do we have any of your books in the library?"

"No," he said, not wanting to tell her he hadn't published anything. "I write short stories for magazines."

"I read novels most of the time," she said quickly, "but I prefer mysteries and science fiction."

"So do I," he said, then looked at her and smiled. He was surprised at how easily the smile suddenly came. Susan smiled back, and for just an instant he thought he saw her blush.

"Well, let me know if you need more help. I have to get back to the desk now."

"Thanks, I will." His voice was steady.

Another smile, and then she was gone. Marvin followed her out into the reading room, found an empty table and sat down with his books, facing the circulation desk. For just a moment, something nice had passed between him and Susan. As he opened the first book, Marvin was feeling wonderful inside.

He read the rest of the afternoon, taking notes and gazing thoughtfully towards the circulation desk where he caught Susan glancing at him a few times. He studied pictures of guns, compared their ballistics, and found the gun his father had left to him. It was one of the most powerful guns listed in the book, and he decided to use it in his story. But exactly how was another problem he had to—

Susan chose that moment to glance at a clock on the wall, and check her watch. It was nearly five o'clock, and she would be going home soon.

The man would be waiting for her outside in the darkening streets.

Marvin pushed his chair back hard, grabbed the stack of books and hurried from the library. In his haste, he didn't see Susan wave to him shyly from the circulation desk.

When he reached home he was nearly running. He threw his books down on the bed, retrieved the gun in the desk drawer and shoved it into the front waistband of his pants. It felt heavy and made a huge bulge beneath the light shirt he was wearing. It would be just his luck to get picked up for carrying a concealed weapon without a permit. He put on a light jacket and studied himself in a mirror. Nothing obvious to see, but he was painfully aware of the big barrel pointing diagonally down along his left leg. He tried not to think of what would happen if he fell and the gun went off.

It was five o'clock as he hurried along the street, walking briskly and trotting across intersections. The air was heavy to breathe and he began to sweat in the light jacket, but people didn't seem to notice him. He might be hurrying along to catch a bus. A silent alarm was ringing in his head, urging him on. On hot days like this one the number of rapes and muggings in the city rose dramatically, and Susan was dressed lightly for heat, nothing provocative, but the sleeveless blouse was certainly enough to stimulate the imagination. Such a lovely target, he thought.

He felt relieved when he reached the library and saw her walking about a block ahead. He got in step with her, following far behind and closely watching the other side of the street. They passed buildings with little shops that had already closed for the day, and silent alleyways just beginning to fill with shadows. They passed the bookstore, and Marvin began to feel a little foolish.

The man wasn't there.

It puzzled him. The pattern had been so regular over the last three days; the man waited in the bookstore until Susan passed, and then he followed her. There could be no question about that. He had been watching only Susan, moving quickly out of sight when she looked around, timing her moves, watching the window of her room until the shades were pulled down. It wasn't just a product of the wild imagination Marvin poured out at his typewriter each day. He had *seen* it happening. So where was the man now and why was Marvin Polack walking along the street with a loaded cannon in his waistband?

The street was silent and empty now, except for Susan walking far ahead of him, and he could hear her footsteps faintly. He had felt drawn to her that day in the library, wondered why he felt so awkward when she tried to start up a conversation about his writing. She seemed interested; all he had to do was talk. So why was that difficult for him? And why had he once imagined himself grabbing Susan from behind and hurting her? The memory still haunted him, confused him, and he wondered about his motives in following her each evening. Why didn't he just ask her for a date and—

There was a scuffling sound ahead of him.

Marvin looked up towards the expected lone figure of Susan Kensor and saw two figures struggling there. A sharp cry, quickly muffled, and an overturned trash can clattered into the street. He tried to shout, but all that came out was a strangled gasp, and then it seemed like his body was on fire and he was running as fast as he could. Susan was dragged across the sidewalk, and then lifted off her feet. She lashed out with both legs, but struck only warm air and her arms were crushed tightly to her sides. The man pulled her backwards into a building as a second floor window suddenly opened on the other side of the street, and someone was shouting at them.

They disappeared from view, leaving the darkening street and the sounds of Marvin's feet pounding the sidewalk. Time seemed suspended, a distance of one block becoming an infinite space that he crawled slowly across. He slowed as he reached the place of the attack, looking for their exit from the street and seeing only the blank, stone wall of an old building.

"Hey!" someone shouted. Across the street, a man leaned out of a window, pointing near Marvin and clutching a crumpled newspaper in his other hand. "Some creep just grabbed a girl and dragged her in that door ahead of you!"

Marvin saw the door, stepped up to it, and pulled the gun from his waistband. His voice was hoarse and raspy as he fought for breath and shouted at the same time.

"Call the police right now! I'm going in."

The man's eyes widened when he saw the gun, but he nodded his head, slammed the window closed and moved quickly out of sight. Marvin put his ear to the door and heard nothing, opened it quickly and stepped inside and away from the doorway in one motion with the gun pointed ahead of him at stomach level. Darkness engulfed him, but there were sounds to follow: someone stumbling around on a wooden floor, bumping into walls and grunting, then a staccato thumping like a crazy tap dance. He moved slowly ahead towards the sounds, breathing rapidly. The gun felt slippery in his hand. He inched forward and stopped when a muffled scream that had to be from Susan came from directly ahead of him. He quickened his movement, and saw a small, dirty window and weak light from the street spilling into a room lined with folded cartons and metal drums, and on a pile of cardboard cartons two people were struggling furiously. Stepping lightly, he moved around the room, keeping out of the direct light, growing suddenly angry as he recognized Susan with a rag stuffed in her mouth and thrashing around under a man tearing frantically at her blouse. The man suddenly slapped her hard across the face, and Marvin's anger became a rage.

"Get off of her, mister!" he ordered from the darkness.

Things happened very fast after that.

The man jumped to his feet, breathing hard and startled by the intrusion. Marvin saw the knife coming up in a sweeping arc as the dark figure stumbled silently towards the sound of his voice. In the dim light Marvin could not aim the gun, but at essentially zero range pointing was good enough. He held the gun with both hands, and pulled the trigger.

The explosion was deafening in the darkened room. The man spun around and backwards, crashing into the wall just below the window. Marvin fired coldly, again and again, hammering his target into the wall both times. The man fell stiffly forward on his face and was still. Marvin went to Susan, who stared up at him with wide eyes. Her face was beginning to swell on one side. He touched it tenderly, and then pulled the rag from her mouth. She began to cry. Her arms had been bound to her sides by two turns of rough rope, and he was fumbling with a knot when Susan was suddenly bathed in bright light. He turned to see a large flashlight, and hear a rough voice in the darkness beyond.

"What 'n hell's going on here?"

* * * * * * *

The police questioned Marvin for over four hours that night. He didn't resent it; the circumstances of his involvement had to look strange to them. They were particularly concerned with citizens who carried concealed weapons and shot real or imagined criminals before bothering to call the police, and they wondered why he had been following Susan in the first place. He told them the truth: being a writer, walking through scenes in his stories, seeing the man following Susan, feeling the compulsion to protect her, and then details of the attack itself. In another room, Susan sat with an ice pack pressed to one side of her face and verified the important parts of his story.

The dead man had a history of sex offenses and was a principle suspect in the recent series of assaults on women in the neighborhood. There was no question that Marvin had saved Susan's life, but he had also broken the law. Apologetically, the police charged him with carrying a concealed weapon without a permit and confiscated his father's gun. The court, they said, would likely be lenient in view of the circumstances.

Marvin wasn't bothered by the charge against him. Susan was safe. But killing a man was not part of his nature, and he was inwardly shaken by it. A priest was called at his request. They talked until late in the morning about feelings of guilt, and suppressed desires, and the necessity of establishing clear boundaries between fantasy and reality. When he finally left the police station it was nearly dawn, and his true feelings about Susan had become very clear to him.

He waited patiently for two days until Susan returned to work, and then marched boldly to the circulation desk and asked her for a date. To his surprise, she accepted immediately, saying there was much for them to talk about.

They began to see a lot of each other after that day.

DARK PERIL

Two ships went out, but only one returned, and there was both fear and relief among colonists and crew when the survivors told their stories. The idea of being mangled, then maybe spit into another universe, was just too terrible.

Captain Halver took most of the public heat for the affair, but privately it was the scientists people blamed. For the thousand souls on board Cassandra I, the only mission was to get their great grandchildren safely to Eridani Blue, not to probe gravitational anomalies hidden within thick, molecular clouds. Three generations out from Aurigae and its crowds, Cassandra I led a flotilla of three worldships into the Orion arm of the galaxy, traveling nicely now at three-tenths c and scooping up enough reaction mass to last the remaining two generation lifetimes to Eridani. People weren't about to slow the ship for some harebrained mission dreamed up by a few.

The scientists, however, prevailed, arguing the mission would not slow the ship, and probe crew pickups could be arranged with Cassandra II or III following light days behind them. The research opportunity was unique, it seemed, and it was unlikely humanity would ever pass this way again.

Captain Halver agreed with them, and people muttered in dismay, for the probe ships were two of the eight shuttles designed to take them to the surface of Blue when they arrived.

Each probe had a crew of three. The crew members had all been up for five years since their latest twenty year cycle of frozen bliss. Pilots Anna and Yuri Pokorny left baby Katarina behind for the mission. Marines Lyn Kruger and Eric Brogan handled False Vacuum Communications and took a breather from what they thought was their secret romance. The scientists put Glade Adams and Sumio Tai on board for navigation and astronautics, but their real function was astrophysical modeling real time with what they observed. And in the end, it was Sumio who would make a place for himself in the history of Cassandra I.

Anna was first out of the docking bay, Yuri only minutes behind her, and they flew in close formation towards the spot where the big gravitational anomaly had been detected. It was only a few light days out, but the mission was far shorter. Whatever it was, the thing was complex, maybe six or seven objects close together, four of them oscillating in a quadrupole way that seemed to be in response to a strong gravitational wave. And that's what interested the scientists the most. Black holes they'd seen before; now they had a cluster of them, oscillating in response to something unseen. All of this buried in a thick, molecular cloud fragment, but surrounded by an expanding shell that was likely a supernova shock front sweeping gas and dust along with it.

Once they neared the shock front, they should be able to distinguish the separate objects behind it and perhaps locate the source of the gravitational waves. Or so the mission profile said.

Cassandra I faded behind them, looking like a bug with a peanut-shaped body; antennae twice its length were the twin coils of the Warberg generator, sucking up exotic matter from the false vacuum of space and slowing the accelerated expansion of the universe by an amount too small to imagine.

"I have program lock," said Anna, and gestured with her right hand, following the retinal display. Beside her in the narrow compartment Eric yawned, and Sumio frantically gestured to power up the array of telescopes and sensors newly installed on what had been built as a landing craft.

"Got it," answered Yuri. "On your tail, darlin'."

Eric laughed. "Too close, and hubby'll be fried." He turned to Sumio, and tapped his shoulder. "Hey, slow down. We've got two or three standard days before we get there. Slow and easy, man."

"Are you kidding?" said Sumio. "This is a flyby, and I'll have a few minutes to get everything at all wavelengths. Every sensor has to be a hundred percent. There won't be a second chance at this."

Eric shook his head. "Bunch of black holes. We won't see anything we haven't seen before."

"Maybe," said Anna, and smiled. "Check the ship link, Eric, and keep it open. We might have to talk fast anytime. Our burn ends in thirty four seconds."

Eric complied, and there was a shudder at engine shutdown. "Visual coming up", announced Sumio. "Visible band only. I'll have IR up next."

Anna gestured in the air, watching the real-time trajectory profile as the picture of the outside world came up beside it. Blackness, no stars showing, only two wisps of red where hot, blue stars nestled in the unusually small molecular cloud. They were in it, now, as if traveling through an extraordinarily thin mist.

"On the wire," said Yuri. "Not much to see, but Glade has started a gamma intensity scan. We'll post it when we have something."

"Check," said Anna. "Enjoy the ride."

Four boring hours later the x-ray telescopes finally came up, and there was something to see, a roughly circular patch of glow ahead of them marking the shock bubble they were to penetrate. Brighter patches within the bubble were still too close to be resolved.

They were startled by a sudden engine burn of two seconds, the ship responding to gravitometer feedback to the program governing their trajectory, a hyperbola in and out of the shock bubble. Yuri called Anna, sounding concerned.

"A bit early for that, isn't it? We're still well over two days out from the target."

"Two seconds is a very small correction," said Anna. They were traveling at three tenths c, and any change in velocity would be out a few decimal places at the least. She didn't say that such an early burn had also surprised her.

When normal space microwave travel time delays exceeded thirty minutes, Eric turned on the small Warberg coil to access False Vacuum and instantaneous communication via the exotic matter flow back to Cassandra I. There were more surprises during the next several hours, four more burns, two of them less than a second. Anna was concerned enough to call Cassandra I. Captain Halver was sympathetic, but obviously had scientists hovering around him when he replied. "As you come in closer you're probably starting to resolve those masses in the shock bubble. The distribution affects the trajectory, Anna. It's a fine correction."

"Yes, but I don't recall us taking a bunch of auxiliary burns into consideration when we calculated the fuel requirements for the trajectory. All these little burns can add up," she said.

There was a short pause, then, "It's not seen as a problem here, Anna. Don't worry about it. We're watching."

Eric chuckled. "Oh, that makes me feel so much better."

Anna glared at him.

"He's right about one thing," said Sumio. "Those individual masses are resolving nicely. I think we can start orbital calculations. I see seven masses now, Glade. Can you handle that work? I want to stick with our trajectory updates."

"I'm on it," said Glade. Six voices on one channel between the two ships, though Eric and Lyn were occasionally switching to another channel to murmur private nothings to each other.

The False Vacuum line to Cassandra I remained open, and Halver continued his reassurance whenever there was a new burn reminding them of a finite fuel supply. Glade came back with his orbital calculation display, and the first visual of what the scientists thought were gravitational waves. A cursor moved, pointing out features. "Seven masses, at first look, but this one is resolving into two, a black hole with a dwarf companion. That explains why it's the brightest of the bunch in the visible range. The other six are loners, and I estimate six to eight standard masses for each of them. This was probably a cluster of B-types formed together a few million years ago.

"They must have gone supernova with only short intervals between explosions. Seven closely spaced shock waves have literally blown a bubble inside this cloud, and even cleared out the supernova remnants we usually see."

"Is this new?" asked Anna.

"No. I've found records of similar results on systems of two or three black holes, but not from observations this close. Let me get this animation up, and I'll show you what's new."

They waited. "The motion is less than the resolution, to be honest, but the orbital modeling gives it consistently. Here it is," said Glade.

Seven objects, moving together on the retinal displays, a complex dance of colored balls in orbits about no obvious point, four of them oscillating back and forth from their orbital paths, in harmony. "The oscillations are highly exaggerated," said Glade. "They only show up on the Doppler spectra. The actual vibration amplitudes are probably only meters for these masses. But that's pretty large. They're interacting with a powerful gravitational wave, all right, and that's why we're here, to find the source of that wave."

Erik shook his head, and muttered something into his microphone. Sumio frowned. "How sure are you about these orbits?"

"Not so good. I've extrapolated from only a few hours of measurements. Another few hours should get the periods down within twenty percent," said Glade. "But the orbits are probably open."

"Maybe," said Sumio. "At first glance, I'd say they're all moving around something big, somewhere around here." A cursor moved on the display, sweeping out a line. "That's roughly on the plane of our own orbit as we sweep past the system."

"There's nothing there," said Anna.

"Closest approach is way out from those masses, Sumio," said Glade.

"But we've been getting a lot of burns our orbital model didn't predict. That's coming from gravimetric measurements. There's a mass we're not seeing here, Glade. A big one."

Now Anna frowned. Her display showed only a few patches of light ahead of them on their present course. "In a few hours we'll be inside the bubble, and should be able to see a lot more than we can now. But if your simulations show something dangerous, I want to know it instantly. Understood?"

"Yes, Ma'am," said Glade and Sumio together.

"On your mark," said Yuri, and Anna silently thanked her husband for acknowledging her role as senior pilot on the mission. He was a quiet man, more devoted to his books than to flying, and a wonderful father to little Katarina. For this, Anna loved him dearly.

Sumio and Glade continued updating their simulations, and Anna filed another report with Captain Halver, who seemed optimistic as ever. The scientists on board Cassandra I were following the calculations on the big machine there, and talking with Sumio and Glade on a separate line. They talked, even dozed a little, and sucked a meal from plastic bottles, and were cleaning up after the meal when they penetrated the wall of the great bubble surrounding the cluster of dark masses and found themselves again in clear space.

No surprises were immediately visible. Six of the seven masses appeared as whorls of glowing gas, faint in the visible region, brighter in ultraviolet and x-ray. The seventh was a binary system, a bright tendril of gas being sucked from a deep red companion into a vortex with a black dot of a center. Sumio did an overlay in ultraviolet and x-ray, then added the twelve hours of gamma ray data he'd accumulated. Now something new was there, a faint spot near the center of the cluster, a thin band radiating from it in opposite directions. "Ah," said Sumio.

"Pretty faint," said Glade. "Barely above noise. Could be high energy, though. The detectors are only good to a hundred MeV."

"I still believe it," said Sumio. "The gas density here must be close to intergalactic levels. The other masses are a good indicator of that, and their spectra peak in the UV. This new thing could peak in the high gamma range. That would make it pretty heavy."

There was a pause. Anna looked at Sumio anxiously. "Is that why we're getting all these extra burns?"

Sumio nodded. "Could be," then, "Hey, Glade, how are those orbital periods coming?"

Another pause. Anna stared at her display, the faint flashes there as a pattern grew, reminding her of a spiral galaxy seen edge-on. *Something big there.* Her stomach trembled.

"Coming up," said Glade, and then a picture of balls moving in their orbits appeared, a mesmerizing dance around a central point, but none of the orbits were closed, all of them precessing in the same direction.

"No closed orbits?" Sumio scowled.

"I know. It's a mess. I don't know what's going on," said Glade. "The data sample is so small we shouldn't see anything like precessions."

"So it's really more like a simulation. Well, then, let's simulate the simulation. You know the masses of the objects, right? Use the gamma picture to locate a central force source, and vary the mass of that until you get the orbital mess we're seeing here. It could at least give us an idea of how big the invisible mass is. Look here." Sumio superimposed the weak gamma display on the orbital simulation. "See, it's not centered on those orbits. The orbits are probably highly eccentric ellipses. Regardless of mass, even relativistic effects could give a precession."

"Okay, I'll try it," said Glade, "but remember that the data sample is still small. The simulation could be way off to begin with, and—"

They were interrupted by a shudder as the engine ignited, and there was a hard burn that lasted seconds.

Anna gritted her teeth. "Whatever you do, try to find out what that missing mass is! On this trajectory, we're using too much fuel trying to stay away from it!"

"Yes, Ma'am," replied Glade.

"Eric, give me Captain Halver. Sumio, tell him what we have so far. I don't want to get any closer to this system than I have to." There was a hard edge in Anna's voice. Suddenly, she was a command pilot.

Halver was on the line in seconds. Sumio gave his report. They waited while Halver conferred with his scientists. When he came back, Anna was less than pleased with his answer.

"Stay on course, is the word here. We estimate twenty percent fuel reserve at end of mission. There's a lot of interest in that gamma ray picture you're getting. We might even ask you to go in closer than we'd planned."

"Begging your pardon, Captain, but we don't really know what's out there, or how big it is," said Anna. "It must be quite large to generate gamma rays, sir. I would like to shorten the mission profile, concentrate on getting a good gamma picture, and get us out of here. That is a request, sir."

There was a long pause. Eric smiled again, and shook his head. Sumio was oblivious to it all, plugged into the big machine on Casandra I and doing research.

"We see no need here for a change in profile just yet," said Halver. "You're a good pilot, Anna; that's why you're there. If there's an emergency, we'll rely on your instincts, but there's no emergency at the present time. Just stay the course. We're watching your fuel consumptions rate closely, and you're in no danger we can see."

"That's the problem," mumbled Eric, but Anna put a finger to her lips in warning.

"Is there a problem with communications, corporal?" asked Halver.

"No, sir," said Eric. He grinned, then shrugged. "The line is clear here."

"Keep it that way, and everything will be fine," said Halver, and broke the connection.

Eric looked sheepishly at Anna. "Sorry, Ma'am."

"Understood," she said, and squinted at her display. "If it helps, I agree with you. Just remember what the Captain said about relying on my instincts in an emergency. That way you can testify in my behalf at the Court Martial."

"Not funny, Anna," said Yuri. "Not funny at all."

"I didn't mean it to be," she said softly.

* * * * * * *

"I get a best fit for a value of a thousand standard masses, but it could be a hundred or a million. The orbits are so eccentric I can't get reliable values for the periods yet," said Glade.

"A hundred is more like it if this was once a blue star cluster," said Sumio. "If the central mass was really huge, I don't see how the cluster could have been stable long enough for the stars to go supernova. But that thing sure is putting out gamma rays."

"Lousy picture," said Glade.

"Yeah, but that band is showing up better. I wonder if we're looking at a disk, edge-on. I don't see any jets going off perpendicular to the disk, either. Probably not enough local dust and gas to make jets."

Anna squinted hard. "I see the band, but no central point that's brighter."

"Even a large black hole wouldn't be visible from here with so little gas present. We're still a light-day out from it," said Sumio. Something strange crawled in his stomach as he said it.

The engine fired again, a two second burn.

"Sixty percent reserve," said Anna.

And an hour later, Captain Halver called to say the profile was being changed to conserve fuel. The new orbit would take them closer to their target by half a light-day.

Anna's face turned bright red. "Is that really necessary, sir? It seems risky to rely on a slingshot effect with all these large, perturbing masses around."

"The calculations show a two percent fuel savings, Anna," said Halver, "but there's another reason for the change. Your gravitometer is showing oscillations we think might be gravitational waves. The big mass you're seeing in the gamma camera might be the source. We want you to get in closer so we can get an estimate of power versus distance. This is central to your mission, Anna, and the risk is minimal. We're not hanging you out on this one. And it's still your decision to change the profile if something unforeseen goes wrong."

Anna clenched her teeth. "I'll hold you to that, Captain—sir," she said.

"As long as you have a darn good reason for making a change," said Halver softly.

Yeah, but who decides how good is darn good? thought Anna.

* * * * * * *

In visible light, they were in a black void, a few wisps of glowing, red gas in tiny vortices above and below them, one red star with a tendril of gas reaching out to another vortex, and ahead of them— nothing. They were hours from closest approach, and the gamma camera showed nothing new, only a clearer picture of what they'd seen before, what seemed like a thin band of high energy photons that might intercept their course. Sumio had begun monitoring the gravitometer reception forwarded from Cassandra I, and seemed concerned. The wave intensity was increasing; the source was ahead of them, also emitting gamma rays. A disk-shaped object? An accretion disk? Making gravitational waves? No, not the disk, but something at its center.

A black hole. A big one. Spinning.

Something was still wrong. He called Glade, told him his new idea.

"A Kerr hole could give measurable waves, I suppose, but it would have to be huge, and spinning very fast," said Glade.

"I was thinking that, too. That would sure spread out the accretion disk, but shouldn't we still see a whole spectrum of light and not just gammas? That band we see is entirely high energy. Something isn't fitting here."

There was a pause. "Yeah, I see what you mean. But if the hole is rapidly spinning, we could be looking at the innermost part of the accretion disk all spread out, and the rest is emitting too weakly to be seen."

It made sense, and for one moment Sumio felt he knew what was going on. "Okay, that's it, then. Another few hours, and we're out of here."

"Four hours to closest approach," said Glade. "Wave intensity is going up, but it sure doesn't look spherical. The source must be highly ellipsoidal."

"As expected, with a high spin. Take our pictures, and enjoy the ride," said Sumio, and believed it.

But that wasn't the way it happened.

Anna had listened to their conversation, less than assured they understood what they were heading for. She was a pilot, not an astrophysicist, and had instincts unrelated to equations, simulations, and neat mathematical models. Watching their trajectory, noting the increasing frequency of burns for the new mission profile, she felt something was missing in their environmental picture, a thing both hidden and sinister, a thing for which she must be ready. So her attention was rapt, even when Sumio and Glade had relaxed to do some personal research with the ship's vast computer. She even called Yuri.

"How far out do you want to be? I'd like to have you within fifty meters, please."

"Something wrong?" asked Yuri.

"No, just move in closer, so I can feel more motherly," she said, and Yuri complied, chuckling.

And an instinct told his wife they were safer than they had been a moment before.

She was only partially correct, for it was the private meanderings of Sumio in the ship's astronomical archives that would determine whether they lived or died during the next few hours.

* * * * * * *

An hour out from closest approach, they were all awake and alert when the ship suddenly vibrated violently with a low, resonating rumble. For one instant, the image of the black-hole-containing binary seemed to blur and drift, then was clear again as the vibration ceased as suddenly as it had begun.

"Yuri! We've just had a bad vibration here. Check our hull, please."

"We felt it, too," answered Yuri. "Checking—nothing to see. You're intact, Anna. It felt like our hull was rubbing up against something sticky. You okay?"

"Once I swallow my heart again," said Anna. She turned to Sumio, who was frowning in thought. Eric sat rigid, waiting for something more to happen. "A new phenomenon," she said, half joking. "What do you think, Sumio?"

"I don't know," he said, but his mind whirled, triggered by the vibration, putting together new pieces of what he'd been reading in the archives. "We're at least an hour out from closest approach, perhaps several light hours from the central mass, and the visibility is at best lousy. Even millions of standard masses would have an event horizon only tens of light seconds out, so we can't be anywhere near that."

"Uh—Sumio," said Glade. "We've taken the central mass to be off center from the orbits of the other masses. We haven't actually measured it."

"We have two position coordinates from the gamma camera, but the third coordinate is iffy," said Sumio.

"That's it. You know, that could be why we're having so much trouble with the orbital simulation."

"Break it down for me, gentlemen," said Anna. "What does this all mean for us?"

Sumio swallowed hard. "It means that the event horizon for this big, black hole is nearly invisible, and we could be right on top of it, Ma'am." As he said it, another thought crawled in his mind.

"Sounds like a good reason for a long burn to get out of here, Mister," said Anna. "You certain about this?"

"No, Ma'am," said Sumio. "I wish I was."

"Then we stick with it. Eric, get Halver on the line."

Anna reported to her Captain in a calm voice, giving him every detail of the incident and the conjectures of her navigators. Halver went to confer with his scientists, forcing her to wait for an answer, and they were now only minutes from closest approach. Outside the ship there was only a thin band of high energy radiation to be seen, yet Sumio knew a great mass was there, perhaps hours, even seconds away. How could something big be so invisible?

The answer came to him just as the vibrations began again, this time softer, but more sustained. Sumio looked at his display. The image of the black-hole binary was there again, only it wasn't one image, but several, and all were suddenly moving.

And Sumio knew. "We've got to get out of here, and fast!" he shouted. "That's not a black hole out there; it's a naked singularity, and we're skipping along the edge of its ergosphere!"

Anna's eyes got very large. "What?"

"A rapidly spinning black hole, spinning so fast it doesn't have an event horizon but an ergosphere, a region around it where space-time spins with it. We're right at the outer edge of it. If we drop inside, there's only one way to get out, and that's all theory, and anyway, naked singularities aren't even supposed to exist, and—"

"Stop it!" shouted Anna. "This is not telling me what do!"

"I recommend we get the hell out of here, Ma'am," said Eric.

"We're near maximum velocity at closest approach. It'll take a long burn now to change our orbit appreciably. A really long burn," growled Anna.

The vibrations were increasing. For an instant, Anna seemed frozen. Sumio was thinking furiously; the theory was unproven, and there was no time for calculations. They had minutes, at best, to make their move.

Halver was suddenly back to them. Anna's teeth were rattling as she screamed at him, "We're being shaken to pieces here. I have to abort the mission! Sumio, tell him what you think!"

Sumio told him, and there was disbelief. Naked singularities had been proven to be unstable, at best, years before, and probably did not exist. The concept of an ergosphere was thus nonsense. A twelve second burn would put them on a substantially safer trajectory and leave them with a two percent reserve.

That was the order given to Anna.

Two minutes later, she made the burn.

The vibrations did not cease, and the change in their trajectory was found to be negligible.

Ergosphere or not, they were now falling into an orbit around a great, unseen mass, with insufficient fuel to make an escape. Even Halver acknowledged that, and apologized for his assessment of the situation. "Sit tight," he said. "We'll work something out here." And then he left them.

Anna was strangely calm. She called Yuri, and they discussed who might care for little Katarina when they were gone. Eric mumbled quietly in his mike, undoubtedly to Lyn in her ship only meters away. Sumio made his calculations as fast as he could until Halver came back on line to tell them the scientists were still working on the problem.

The ship vibrations were continuous now. Likely they would slowly descend in a spiral orbit until they reached the singularity and oblivion, but here, near the top of the ergosphere, there was still a chance. When Halver switched off, and Anna was still chuckling at his stupidity, Sumio made his move.

"Ma'am? If you'll trust me, I can get us out of here."

Anna shook her head. "If you can do it with a fifteen second burn, I'll believe you. That's all we have left."

"If I'm right, Ma'am, we won't need all of it. The spin energy we pick up from this spinning singularity will be enough to kick us out hard. I just hope it doesn't tear us apart in the process. But we have to lose one of the ships.

"Oh, that's good news," growled Eric in disgust, and Anna raised an eyebrow. Sumio's faced flushed.

"Look, you have other options, just jump right in. My idea is based on an untested theory, all right, but the conditions are correct. For a brief instant we were spinning with the ergosphere, and you could see the relative motion of the neighboring black holes out there. From those motions, the ergosphere spin is opposite to our initial trajectory. In the archives, there's a theory by a guy named Penrose. You shoot a particle into an ergosphere, opposite to the spin direction. You fragment the particle; one piece is captured by the naked singularity nearby, the other piece is kicked out using a part of the singularity's spin energy. That's a lot of energy, it turns out. I've done a rough calculation. It won't put us back on our original trajectory, but it'll be close enough for us to be eventually picked up."

Eric laughed. "We're the particle. We blow up the ship, and part of it escapes. Come on, Sumio. Let's call someone to come in here and pick us up."

"Not enough time," said Anna. "What is the particle, Sumio? You said we'd have to lose a ship."

"We have to dock," said Sumio, "and all of us get into one ship. The main burn is against the flow of the ergosphere, but there's a shorter secondary burn for the empty ship, and then we blow the connector bolts for separation. The calculation is rough, Ma'am, but I'm sure it's good enough to get us out of here."

"This is crazy," said Eric.

"Yes, it is," said Anna, "but I do know a little physics. If that mass out there is as big as I think it is, we don't need to borrow much energy from it to get out of here. And we need to do something *now!*"

The ship suddenly lurched, as if in response to what she'd said. Anna called Yuri; they talked for only a minute, Yuri putting all in her hands. Anna said she'd be right back to him, then had Eric put in a connection to Captain Halver.

"Nothing new, Anna," said Halver. "We're working on it."

Anna grimaced her disgust. "No time anyway, Captain. We're going to try something here. If I'm not back to you within half an hour, then we're probably all dead."

"Don't do anything without our—" Halver began, and Anna cut him off. She turned to Eric. "No communications unless we survive this," she said coldly.

"Yes, Ma'am"," said Eric, and glared at Sumio. *This crazy idea of yours is going to get us killed,* he seemed to say.

But Anna was operating in action mode. She ordered Yuri to dock with her ship, a simple task in normal space, and they were only meters apart at the moment. But the entire operation took nearly half an hour; they were moving in and out of a spinning reference frame, and Yuri was fighting new Coriolis forces all the way. The only real progress was during the brief seconds when they were just above the edge of the ergosphere and again in normal space. Sumio held his breath a lot during docking, and kept his secret to himself; once they were completely buried in the ergosphere, there would be no docking possible, and they would all die.

He let out his breath in a whoosh when he heard the metallic clang of the docking ports locking together.

Yuri, Lyn and Glade came forward to the cockpit for brief, quietly emotional greetings before heading aft to strap themselves down in the yawning passenger bay designed for a hundred people. The way Lyn looked at Eric made Sumio envy the man for the first time. Anna and Yuri had merely touched foreheads, and closed their eyes.

Sumio loaded the new profile into the computer. It was a gimbaled burn, two seconds for a dip into the ergosphere, followed by five seconds against the flow, a two second burn by the empty ship just before locking bolts exploded for separation.

He was still surprised his idea had even been accepted by the others. But there were no other options. Only a slow spiral into a crushing depth. Outside, the phantom of an object said to be impossible glowed weakly in high energy gamma emission. If only he'd had detectors that could see far, far into the gamma range. A band, but not a band, really. A rapidly spinning core of quarks, strings, flattened out into a disk with a slight bulge at the center; this was the likely picture. How far out were they? Minutes? Nearly close enough to touch the very beginning of everything.

"Anything I need to do?" asked Anna, pulling hard on her shoulder harness.

"No, Ma'am, except hang on. My hope is we'll leave the ergosphere tangentially, but as we dip into it things could be rough. There will be a brief period of acceleration as we hit normal space. A short spike, real high, like a batted ball, I think. Strap in tight, Ma'am."

Anna gave everyone a few minutes to strap in tight, then turned to Sumio and sighed in a resigned sort of way that made Sumio's face flush again. "Okay," she said, "let's get this over with."

Sumio was strapped in so tight he had to stretch his index finger to move the cursor on his display. He started the countdown at twenty seconds, checking the status of both ships' engines. At ten seconds he punched in 'EXECUTE', then pressed his head back into his seat and closed his eyes.

The sudden bump, together with the sound of the engine burn was familiar, but the entire cockpit began to vibrate wildly around him. He felt a strange disorientation, then a thud, then it was as if he was slammed face first into a wall and held there in a suffocating stranglehold. He blacked out, but only for a moment. When he opened his eyes, his display showed a black void with the distant glow of hot, blue stars, and Halver was screaming into his ear.

"Anna! ANNA! What the hell is going on out there?"

* * * * * * *

They didn't get picked up for seven days.

The ergosphere had spit them out into a trajectory that nearly took them back to Cassandra I, but fell short, so they had to wait for Cassandra II two days. Their ship, fuel spent, was towed back by another shuttle and found to be intact, amazingly enough. There had been some interior damage from loose items flying around during acceleration, things like a writing stylus sticking into a steel wall. Tough instrument, and tougher people. Accelerometers on board went up to fifteen g's, and had gone off scale during the escape. Everyone had aches here and there, bruised shoulders and ribs, nothing serious, physically.

Mental problems hung on a while: a sense of detachment from the ship's busy world, short concentration spans, a kind of waking-dream-state that persisted even after a debriefing and then a formal reception with fine food and drink. People were thrilled by their adventure, and wanted to hear all about it. Anna and Yuri leaned warmly against each other, and said a few things. Eric and Lyn held hands, and said nothing. Anna graciously praised Sumio for solving the problem that had threatened their lives, but Sumio quietly left the room before she thought of proposing a toast to him.

Glade was sent to fetch him, found Sumio in the forward lounge, relaxed in a deep chair and staring up at the viewing screen for the outside panoramic camera. Glade pulled up a chair, put a bottle and two glasses down on the low table in front of them.

"I'm supposed to drag you back to the party," said Glade, and he filled the two glasses with bubbly wine. "Anna wants to toast your brilliance."

"It was both of us, Glade," said Sumio.

"Not really, but thanks anyway," said Glade. He offered a glass to Sumio, looked up at the screen. "From here, it looks really black, that little cloud. You'd never guess what's inside it. That cloud is doomed."

"We didn't even see it," said Sumio softly, "and we were so close it nearly killed us. A doorway to another universe, Glade, and we didn't see it."

"Pretty small door," said Glade. "A core a meter across, tops. We were not a good fit."

Sumio took a sip of wine. His eyes suddenly brightened. "If we come back with really big detectors that can go well into the TeV range, I bet we can see it."

Glade shook his head, grinned, and raised his glass. "To human curiosity," he said.

"I'd rather drink to Penrose," said Sumio, and laughed.

Their glasses clinked together.

BENEATH THE ICE OF ENCELADUS

Twelve hours out from Herschel Base, Anna Hegel finally vented when Phil made another crack about wasting space for 'bug' people on the mission. Her face flushed when she glared at him, and she tried hard to control the angry quaver in her voice.

"I really hope I'm not going to have a problem with you, Phil. We're going to be spending a lot of time together in close quarters, whether you like it or not."

Phil Yallowitz was seated in front of Anna, so she couldn't see his face.

"That's my point," said Phil. "This isn't a bug hunt for me, it's a test of a vessel I've worked on for seven years. I need an electronic tech, not a scientist."

Sitting next to Anna, the tech assigned to the submersible program seemed to take offense at that. "Hey, man, you've got *me*. I'm certified mechanical and electrical."

"I don't need to have any light tubes changed. How are you with spectrum analyzers?"

The tech chuckled and turned to Anna. "Don't feel bad, Doctor. He bad-mouths me, too."

Sitting at the shuttle control desk, Mission Commander Mike Goffin looked over his shoulder and raised an eyebrow at them. Above him, Enceladus was already huge on his view screen.

"Stop it, all of you."

"Yes sir!" said the tech, and grinned.

"Read the mission profile again, Phil. A mission specialist was a must. The only debate was whether it would be a geologist or an astrobiologist, and the bug people won. The only reason we're here is because the water is easy to get to. The Europa team is understandably furious about their budget being cut so we could get our one chance here. One shot, people, so you'd better be able to work together on this. It's a long way back to Earth for anyone who can't do it."

There was a long silence after Mike said that.

* * * * * * *

Herschel Base was fifty kilometers west and north of the South Pole, and the view screen showed a new yet strangely tortured surface there. Unlike the northern, lightly cratered hemisphere of Enceladus, the southern area, at long distance, appeared relatively smooth and thus geologically more recent, but close inspection had long ago revealed a jumbled surface of cracks and rills, valleys and depressions as if some great glacier had spread there. Saturn was a bright ball thirty degrees in diameter, rings edge-on and faintly visible. Icy Mimas was beginning a transit, and Titan was a large, fuzzy orb in a black sky as the shuttle began its vertical descent to the base. Looking at Titan, Anna thought of the research platform orbiting above its hazy atmosphere. It had been her home for the past three years.

At fifty kilometers altitude, four fractures were clearly visible, bounded on either side by ridges, features that had been known as 'tiger stripes' for well over a century. Closer, the fissures seemed choked with shining blocks and boulders—water ice with traces of ammonia, methane and other simple organics. Out on the horizon, a plume of vapor rose far above the descending shuttle.

Water vapor, thought to be coming from eruptions of liquid from a surface whose average temperature was only seventy-five degrees Kelvin.

Below the surface of Enceladus, liquid water had to exist.

And where there was water, there might be life.

Anna Hegel had arrived with the intention of finding it. This was an ambition she shared with three generations of women in her family. Time had run out for two of them, and was getting dangerously short for the third. Herschel Base appeared below them as a black, fifty-meter-diameter spot on a chaotic jumble of ice in the fissure, or sulcus, known as Damascus. The roof and access module bristled with instrument arrays and a microwave dish. There was a jolt beneath their feet when shuttle lock occurred. Anna felt a subtle gravity, one hundredth that of Earth, but she'd been living with ten times that on Titan Station for three years. Despite regular exercise her limbs were like sticks, and within a year or two she would have to decide whether to remain in space or abandon her life's work and return to Earth as her mother and grandmother had done.

For them, it had been too late.

The floor hatch screeched as Mike pulled it open. He gestured to Anna.

"Ladies first."

Anna looked down; saw hands waving to her from the end of a hollow cylinder a few meters long. She made a little hop, and dropped like a dust mote. Several seconds later, hands grasped her and pulled her to one side as the others came down.

A slender, blond woman reached out her hand.

"Welcome to Herschel."

"Wow, it's cold in here," said Anna, and shivered.

The woman smiled. "Nothing like outside. It'll be better down below."

Three men were with the woman, and reached up as first Phil and his tech came down the tube, then Mike after them. The woman shook Anna's hand. "I'm Helena. I'll be your lab tech, and introduce you to Commander Kassner."

The space they occupied ended in a shaft angled at thirty degrees from their vertical, and lined with hand rungs. Anna followed Helena through it with practiced ease, and they came out into a living space shaped like a ring. There were instrument panels and video monitors floor to ceiling. One monitor showed a tech guiding Mike into the shaft above them.

"It's smaller than I expected," said Anna.

"There are several levels," said Helena. "Bunks and mess are just below this one, but you'll be working out of the lower levels. The whole base is a tapered cylinder, and most of it is insulation and concentric vacuum layers. They literally pounded a cork into a volcanic vent when they made this place. And the two outer layers are spring-loaded composites that flex. The ice is constantly moving around us. You'll hear it soon enough."

Anna felt tightness in her throat, and Helena smiled.

"Don't worry. I've been here four months, and we haven't been crushed yet. This place really only has to last another two weeks if you people get your job done."

A joke, perhaps, but Anna wasn't amused by it.

Helena showed Anna around the ring. A central shaft with rungs on a pole took them down to the next level where there was the odor of coffee in the air and Mike was talking to a tall, square-jawed man in astronaut blues. The conversation stopped when Helena and Anna approached them, and Mike smiled.

"This is Doctor Anna Hegel, sir."

"Eric Kassner is our base commander," said Helena.

Kassner stuck out his hand, and his grip was bone hard. "It's a small universe. I knew your mother years ago. How is she these days?"

Anna blinked. "Sorry to say she's dead, sir, waited too long to return to Earth. Her heart couldn't take it."

"Sorry to hear that. She had everyone's respect on Europa. It has been a tough mission there."

"Too much ice, sir. I doubt if they'll ever get through it. I guess that's why I'm here."

"Plenty of ice here, too, but an ocean is right beneath us, and you people are going to tell us what's there."

"Yes, sir."

"So when do we see it?" asked Mike.

"Soon enough. The time is short, but we're not going to rush unnecessarily. The submersible has to be proven at depth, and we don't even know what we're diving into yet. This module is plugging what used to be a volcanic vent, and the shaft down has been changing ever since the water flow was restricted. We're floating in the thing, and sonar returns are garbled. There could be a sea, a lake or a puddle down there. First job is to find the end of the shaft and scan what's below it. There won't be much room for maneuvering."

"I'm sure Phil Yallowitz can handle it. The vessel is his baby," said Mike.

Kassner turned back to Anna. "Your mother was a patient person, and I hope you are too. The first dips will be with tech and pilot only."

"I understand, sir," said Anna, "as long as you remember we only have two weeks until our return window to Titan."

Kassner nodded. "I know that, doctor, but I also intend to send you home alive."

Anna suddenly felt a vibration, and the floor tilted beneath her feet, nearly tipping her over. She grabbed Mike's arm, as there was a terrible screech from the walls, like some metal talon was scraping there. Anna's heart hammered from the shock of it.

Kassner looked at her calmly. "Vapor bubble. You'll get used to them. Earthquakes are less frequent, but scarier. The water reservoir below us is under pressure, and is either very small, or there's a big heat source there. Please keep in mind this is an extraordinarily dynamic environment. Yes, we want to explore it as quickly as we can. We just don't want it to kill us."

The commander reached out and shook their hands again. "Welcome to Herschel Base. Helena will show you where to bunk, and there will be a general briefing for all of you in the mess in exactly two hours."

Helena touched Anna's elbow. "This way," she said, and took them away to their quarters.

* * * * * * *

Sleep was a challenge. Anna's satchel was inclined slightly from the vertical in a six cubic meter niche behind a poly-steel grill. It was not totally unlike the shuttle, but that had been quiet during what passed for night, and she'd floated around in her bag. On Herschel the floor and walls were forever heaving and shaking, and the constant groaning and screaming of hard ice and rock scraping metal kept her awake for most of her sleep shift. She fought off the effects with strong coffee until Helena gave her something that knocked her out cold, and life was good again.

Mike and Phil and two techs made the first dip two-work shifts after arrival. Anna went down to bottom level to watch their progress on a television monitor after they'd submerged. Phil's submersible was shaped like a shallow, inverted soup bowl with ports on the sides, bow steering and diving planes, and a nose bubble. Two retractable claws folded up along two sides, and there were three directional lights forward. Armor was sufficient for two thousand feet earth side, and was definitely overkill for what they were expecting, but in Phil's own words: "You never know."

There were no screws; three ports aft were all there was to see of a jet propulsion system fueled by hypergolic *Anistol*, as used for maneuvering by the shuttle. Water and hydrogen were the only emissions, and viewed as safe in any oxygen-free environment.

Anna watched as Mike, Phil and two techs opened the hatch on top of the submersible and climbed in. The yellow paint of the hull complimented the yellowish-green of the water it floated in, and there was a musty odor in the air. Commander Kassner manned the comm.-panel and Anna joined him there while a base tech closed and sealed the hatch.

"Diving," said Phil, and there was a roiling on the water surface where the submersible floated in its tank.

"Opening lock," said Kassner, and moved his hand. The submersible dropped into a lock below the tank, where pressure could be varied in transferring the vessel to the outside.

"Pressurizing," said Kassner, and Anna felt the floor move beneath her. The walls around them groaned. Kassner looked at her. "It's okay. We bob up and down a bit. In the low gravity, pressure changes are subtle. If there's an ocean below us I doubt if it's very deep." He looked up at a monitor. "Lights on. Opening outer door."

On the monitor, silvery doors slid aside and three bright beams of light disappeared into blackness, the beam edges tinged green.

"No particulates," said Anna.

"Pieces of ice once in a while, and those bubbles that come from some depth." Kassner smiled. "I'm sure you'd like to see something more interesting."

"That's why I'm here. Right now, I'll settle for water samples."

"Automatic, and real-time." Kassner pointed. "Follow that monitor. Readings are every four meters."

When Anna looked at the monitor, a simple spectrum was already building there: traces of ammonia, methane, sulfur and iron.

"The vent is widening," said Mike, and Anna looked at the other monitor again. Blackness ahead, the faint glow of ice from the sides. Suddenly, there was a faint reflection from something in front of the submersible.

"Slowing," said Phil. A shelf of ice came out of the blackness, oriented left to right and descending at a steep angle.

"The shaft turns here, and I see an edge to it. Cracks all over the place"

There was a faint, blue outline of something, and blackness beyond it.

"That's what has been scattering our sonar," said Kassner. "I'd put the first buoy right where it turns."

"Okay," said Mike, "but let's find the end first. I see it. We'll put the first buoy there."

"Don't go beyond that point. We'll check out the vessel at depth tomorrow. I want those relays in first."

"Right."

The monitor image faded, and then went to random noise and cosmic background. "What's happening?" asked Anna.

"They're around the corner. A relay buoy will go at the shaft opening, another at the turn by the shelf, and we should have data communication the rest of the way if there's really a large body of water there."

They waited nervously for half an hour, and suddenly the monitor showed a picture of ice close-up and a conical package anchored to it by a short chain.

"Are you getting sonar yet?" asked Mike, and his voice was extraordinarily loud and clear.

Kassner leaned to his left and looked at another monitor. "Got it. Multiplexing. The phones are even more exceptional. Sounds like you're with us here. So, let's see what we have down there."

They watched the multiplexed pattern of the pulsed sonar build for fifteen minutes before Kassner said, "It's a small sea or a lake, running parallel to the fissure. Depth goes to two or three hundred meters, and it's big, maybe ten klicks long, three wide. The vent comes out of the ceiling of the thing. The bottom reflections are coming up with rough areas, like there's some structure down there. And no, you can't take a quick look."

"Figured," said Mike. "Take 'er up, Phil."

The men returned to the base in a jubilant mood.

And Anna didn't sleep a wink that night.

* * * * * * *

It was three Earth-days until the next submersion. Erratic readings in the vessel's pilot deck were finally traced to a damaged optical cable, and a new one threaded through a wall to replace it. Only Mike and Phil would go down this time, and Anna tried hard to be patient.

"There's room for me, and all I want to do is look outside," she said.

"You'd do better to watch the spectrometer readouts here," said Mike. "This is a systems check, and we won't be going anywhere near the bottom."

"Watch the monitor," said Phil. "There's nothing to see until we go deep. You'll be bored."

Inside, she despised Phil's condescending tone of voice, but Anna kept her face expressionless.

"I can do that quietly, and not be in the way, Phil. And if you see anything at all interesting, I'm sure you'll be alert enough to include me in the discussion of it."

"Absolutely," said Mike, but Phil said nothing and looked away from her.

The submersible disappeared beneath the yellowish green surface with a gentle roil of bubbles. After a few minutes, Anna dismissed her irritation and carefully watched the spectrometer readings as the vessel reached the shelf at the bottom of the vent and sailed out into open water.

The water there was even more pristine than in the vent. The lines for ammonia and iron nearly disappeared. After a few minutes a small peak developed for sodium when the vessel was sailing near the ceiling of the mammoth cavern, and at one point there was a small spike in sulfur. Anna noted the exact time of each event; it was something to do. Commander Kassner's attention was focused on the sonar readings the entire time.

A few minutes later, things got more interesting when Phil began putting his machine through her paces, beginning with a test of the bow planes in turns and steep dives. The bottom was at three hundred meters at that point, and the dive went to one hundred. Anna stared hard at the monitor, but there were only three beams of light disappearing into darkness. Whatever was on the bottom was a poor reflector. But when she looked back at the spectrometer readings, a sharp line for sulfur was growing, and it suddenly stopped as Anna noted the time again.

"Local concentration of sulfur where you are," she said.

There was a pause. "Don't see anything," said Mike.

"The bottom is quite rough below you," said Kassner. "We're getting a lot of scattering."

"I'll want to go down there," said Anna, and then grabbed hard for a wall rung when the floor beneath her began shaking violently. She hung on grimly as the shaking went on for several seconds. It stopped as quickly as it had begun.

"That was no gas bubble," said Anna. Kassner turned to look at her, and she didn't like what she saw in his eyes.

"Quake," said Kassner. "There were a few of them when Herschel was first inserted into the vent, but this is the first big one since. Hope it didn't plug up the vent. Mike, are you there?"

"Loud and clear," said Mike. "We just had some turbulence here, and something dark dropped past us towards the bottom."

"We had a quake up here, pretty strong, a shaker. You'd better come up right away."

"Okay. We've gone through our list for now; the rest has to be done at depth. That must have been a rock that came past us. It went down like a chunk of iron. Good thing it didn't hit us."

"I'll feel better when you see the vent is clear," said Kassner.

"Blowing tanks," said Phil. "We'll be there in a minute or two."

Anna was worried, and Kassner saw it on her face. "Good communications, so the shaft can't be plugged."

As if in reply, Mike called in only seconds later, "We have a little problem here," and at that instant Anna felt the floor shake again beneath her feet.

"Some debris on the shelf here, and another rock just came down. Wouldn't take much to make a tight fit. We'll clean it off with the articulators. Stand by."

The news was worse a minute later.

"Now we have a *real* problem. The port articulator is frozen up, and the servo is showing an overload when I try to deploy it. Starboard claw is working fine, and we're cleaning off the shelf, but we need to have both articulators working at depth. This could be a major repair."

"We don't have the time," said Anna.

"We'll make the time," said Phil. "I'm not taking this thing down with a broken arm and then take the blame if we need it."

"Understood," said Kassner. "For now, let's play it by ear."

"And I'm going down on the next dive," added Anna.

Phil started to say something, but there was a click and his voice was cut off.

Ten minutes later the vessel surfaced in a roil of bubbles, and the hatch popped open. Phil climbed out and went straight to the port articulator folded tightly against yellow metal like an injured arm. "I need a speed wrench," he said, and a tech brought one to him.

Mike climbed out of the vessel, stepped over to the edge of the tank, and whispered to Kassner and Anna. "Let's get some coffee and let Phil work."

They went up one level and had coffee. "Dark down there, and clear," said Mike. "Any light color on the bottom would have shown up in our beams. There's rock peeking through ice on the walls, and especially on the ceiling. It was like a cave dive."

"Anything interesting will likely be on the bottom," said Anna. "The spectrometer showed some interesting sulfur spikes while you were down there."

"Oh," said Mike, "yes, there was one place where Phil thought he saw a couple of bubbles go by us."

Anna's heart leapt. "Did you record it?"

Mike shook his head. "Nope. It was just a few seconds after we came out of our dive."

"I'll backtrack it," said Anna. She turned to go back to lower level, and nearly ran into Phil as he came out of the central shaft connecting all levels. He looked both saddened and subdued.

"Well, I really screwed up."

"What?" Anna didn't know Phil was capable of admitting an error to anyone, let alone her.

"I should have inspected the articulators before we left Titan Base. A joint seal was split; God knows how long that bearing was exposed to hard vacuum. It looks like a porcupine."

Anna's mouth hung open in confusion.

"Epitaxial growth in hard vacuum has made hair crystals at the carbon boundaries, and welded the joint. I don't suppose we have a high-voltage unit here, something at say thirty kilovolts and a milli-amp?"

"Nothing like that," said Kassner.

Phil sighed, obviously upset with himself. Anna was strangely tempted to touch his arm in comfort.

"One quick check on Titan Station, and I would have found it. I can't burn it off, so I'll have to do it the hard way. I can snap the bearing out easy enough, but then I have to polish everything down to the original tolerances, and that's a trial-and-error hand job that could take days."

"We don't have days!" shouted Anna.

Phil winced, and Anna looked down at her feet.

"Sorry. We don't have time for blame, either. We only have ten Earth days at most. I'm willing to go down there with one articulator working."

"I don't think so," said Kassner, and Mike nodded in agreement.

"I need at least two dives to see what's down there," pleaded Anna. "In case you've forgotten, *that* is our primary mission."

"With help I can fix it in a day, two days tops," said Phil. "We'll work around the clock."

Everyone looked at Kassner, and he looked back at each of them in turn.

"I'm not hearing objections. Okay, recruit whoever you need, and do it."

"I'll help," said Anna.

Phil actually smiled at her. "No offense, but I'll use the techs. They know their way around a machine shop, and this is precision handwork we have to do. Thanks."

"I can use the time to go over the sonar scans and target some areas to look at. I'll have a plan ready for us in a day. Don't beat yourself up, Phil. We'll get this done," said Anna.

Phil couldn't look at her, simply mumbled something, turned, and climbed back down the central shaft to bottom level, where his work awaited him.

Mike put a hand on Anna's shoulder. "He's basically a good guy, you know. Right now his self-confidence is bruised, and we need to hope it heals fast."

"It has to," said Anna, but she worried about it. *This is my last chance*, she thought.

Her relief came a day and a half later, when Phil announced the articulator was now working, and Anna had to rush to finish her plan for the next dive.

* * * * * * *

There was another quake just before they submerged. Sonar showed no blockage in the vent below them, but a few small cracks had become big ones. The quakes were becoming more frequent. Kassner said it was a cyclic thing related to the positions of Titan and Mimas, and he expected the shaking to lessen soon.

Anna felt cramped in the submersible; she was seated on a shelf behind Mike and Phil where she could watch the instruments and look out both the portholes and nose bubble at the same time.

Phil blew tanks slowly to slow their decent in a low-gravity environment where pumps and water-jets were a substitute for buoyancy. Using the bow planes, Phil literally flew the vessel down the vent and out over the shelf into deep water. He made a few swoops and turns, deployed both articulators, tested each joint before turning his attention to a map of areas Anna had found interesting. Anna leaned over his shoulder and pointed at the map as Phil and Mike studied it.

"The rough areas on the bottom are most interesting. There's a lot of sonar scattering in these three regions, and lighter detail in some others. I'd like to hit these five if we can, and while we're at it we can look closer at the smoother regions."

"We'll have to get around enough to map the entire cavern, and that's one dive by itself," said Mike. "It's in the mission statement, Anna."

"We can extrapolate a lot if we stay close to the bottom in the thirty percent we've already scanned." Anna pointed. "Go here first. You were above this area when I got a nice sulfur spike on the spectrometer."

"Okay," said Phil. Map coordinates were relative to the pinging buoy in the vent below Herschel, and they were already close. Phil began a slow descent on a helical path towards the bottom.

Anna squinted, willing herself to see through the gloom. Her heartbeat quickened as Mike called off the distance to the bottom. At fifty meters they passed a bubble the size of a dinner plate. The view below was a dirty gray, and at twenty meters there was a dark splotch that moved across their view as Phil leveled out the dive and slowed.

At ten meters the bottom finally came into view, and at first Anna only felt disappointment. It looked like dark gray sand with occasional boulders protruding, nothing like what she'd expected from the sonar reflections.

But at three meters, Phil brought the vessel to a crawl, and the view outside was dramatically different. The boulders were now little towers of dark material like basalt, and the sand was a coarse gravel of dark rock and dirty ice. Even closer, the meter-high towers were made of dirty ice covered with an orange stain that reflected weakly in the bright lights. "We have to get a sample of that," said Anna.

Kassner had been watching everything from Herschel Base, and suddenly called in. "We're getting spikes for sulfur and sodium, and a trace of iron. The area you're in right now is *loaded* with methane, and it's over two-seven-seven Kelvin there. There was a sharp increase in temperature when you reached ten meters above bottom."

"Reminds me of Earthside smokers, but there's all kinds of complex life forms around those things," said Anna. "All I see here is some kind of stain. We're sampling it. Could be bacterial."

"Wishful thinking," said Phil. "Looks mineral to me."

Phil looked surprised when Anna said, "You're probably right, but let's get a good sample of it, and also the gravel and bottom ice. That has a different sheen to it."

"Bubbles," said Mike, pointing.

Anna looked, and saw a stream of small bubbles leaking from the base of a tower, rising slowly and coalescing to form a large bubble, which drifted lazily upwards. "Can we get a temperature reading on that tower's surface?"

"Should have it," said Phil. He'd been working an articulator to break off a small nubbin from the side of the tower, and was dropping it into the specimen basket beneath the nose bubble.

"Two-eight-three Kelvin," said Kassner

"The bottom must be porous," said Anna. "These towers could be crystallites of a rock-ice mix where heat channels are coming through. I bet we have a mix of rock and methane clathrate down here, but if there are any methane breathers I sure don't see them."

Phil steered the submersible at a crawl through a small forest of towers, and columns of small bubbles rose from a few of them, but there was no sign of a living thing or any remnants of life, and then the bottom was soon relatively smooth again. They stopped for samples several times, but spent most of the dive just in sight of the bottom. They mapped the extent of the cavern in all directions. It was not so much an underground sea as it was a lake, unstable at best with all the seismic activity, and unlikely to be large or stable enough for life to have evolved there. There were more forests of little, bubbling towers, and vast expanses of black rock mixed with methane in ice, and by the end of the dive they had explored all the prime interesting areas Anna had marked on the sonar maps. There was a secondary list of prospects where small echo dispersions had been observed, but both Mike and Phil felt they had "seen it all" when they returned to Herschel Base. They left Anna to analyze the specimens they'd brought up and to define targets for the next dive. They would also be mapping the cavern ceiling in a search for other vents, and that was scheduled to take much of the dive time.

Anna expected her specimen analysis to take days, and there would only be time for one more dive before she had to leave.

Kassner seemed to sense her dark mood, and shared a cup of coffee with her that first evening back from the depths.

"You're disappointed," he said.

"I guess, but I have to admit a moon this small probably hasn't been around long enough in a tidal environment to evolve any life forms. It was a long shot, and a negative result is still a result. That's science."

"Would have been nice for the family history," said Kassner.

"You have a *file* on me?"

"You bet I do. Your pedigree is what brought you here."

"You must mean my grandmother. Do you know the Martian bacteria she discovered are still controversial? Half the science community still thinks it was a contaminant. And mom had to return to Earth before they even got a fourth of the way through Europa's ice. New discoveries are wonderful, but circumstances and a lot of luck are involved. And I have one more dive to get some."

"Then let's drink to luck," said Kassner, and he raised his squeeze bottle

Their bottles touched as another small quake made the floor shudder beneath their feet.

* * * * * * *

Midway through the dive Anna felt herself relaxed but saddened, resigned to the fact the mission would be a scientifically interesting mapping of a subterranean lake beneath the surface of Enceladus. The geologists would be excited, but for Anna's colleagues in astrobiology there would be nothing to talk about. Her work on Titan had reached a dead end; the big moon had fascinating chemistry and geology, but no life. Perhaps she could return to Mars and build on what her grandmother had done. The gravity there was much higher, and she could then return to Earth in her later years and write up her lifetime of experiences in the outer regions of the solar system. It would also tie together the work of three generations of women in her family.

For Anna, it was a good plan, and an acceptable plan, though her dream of finding extraterrestrial life was fading fast.

But it was a plan that changed abruptly after the fourth hour of the dive.

Sample analysis had shown no life. There was silicate rock mixed with dense, rich methane clathrate, and the stain on the little towers was iron sulfide. The gas bubbles were likely hydrogen sulfide, though she'd not been able to sample them directly. Every test for bacteria, every test for chemical reactions used by known life forms, had been negative.

For nearly four hours they had cruised near the bottom, observing occasional clusters of crystalline towers, but mostly vast plains of pebbles and methane-rich water ice. Kassner had called in twice with news of renewed quake activity, and they had seen several large chunks of ice drifting downwards towards the bottom. Communication with Kassner had become garbled, cutting in and out after that. Mike was worried about it, and said so. "We might have to cut it short, Anna. With all these quakes, we don't want to be trapped down here."

Anna ignored his concerns. She had marked four places on the sonar maps where there were small depressions in the bottom that showed weak dispersions similar to what was seen with tower clusters. They were now nearing the first of them. Anna's attention had wandered a bit as she thought about returning to Mars, but something suddenly caught her eye.

"I see flashing lights," she said, and leaned forward to look ahead through the nose bubble. "Reflections?"

"No," said Phil. "I see it, too. Yellowish green—flickering, straight ahead."

"And beyond," said Mike. "One source is close, the other fainter."

In the darkness beneath the ice of Enceladus, the flashes of light suddenly ceased.

Phil had slowed to a crawl, but remained on course. The plain ahead was level, then rose a meter to form a hillock that curved away from them. And just beyond it was what Anna first thought was another tower, different this time, a feature glowing bronze in the bright lights of the submersible.

They came close, hovering over a crater-like depression two meters deep. The object it held reminded Anna of a dead tree with several bare branches. It was anchored in methane-clathrate and stood four meters high, and around it were several others only a meter tall. Branches swayed slowly in the turbulence created by the submersible's jets. Their surfaces were rough and mottled in bronze and dark brown, and from the dark areas streams of tiny bubbles pulsed in bursts that floated lazily upwards.

"Oh, my God, oh my God," gasped Anna, and she could scarcely breathe.

"It's soft," said Mike. "Hollow, maybe."

"Not rigid," whispered Anna. "Look at the tangle of tubules at its base, anchoring it to the ice. The bubbles have to be hydrogen. It's using methane. I think it's alive."

"A plant? Looks like a metal sculpture. Now it's not moving," said Mike.

"The jets are off. No more wake. The currents move it. That doesn't mean it's alive," said Phil, "but *something* was flashing lights at us until we got close."

"Not now."

"Turn off our lights."

"What? You want to be blind down here? I don't think so." Phil shook his head.

"Just the big headlights. We can still see close from the interior lights," said Anna.

"I can back off a bit." Phil frowned.

"No. I want to see if we can provoke a reaction."

"Why don't I just touch it with an articulator, then?"

"You might hurt it."

Mike reached over and turned off the exterior lights. "Enough," he said.

Outside, the strange tree-looking thing was dimly illuminated. They waited for long minutes, but nothing happened. "It's some kind of crystallized tower like the others, only a different shape," said Phil.

"We need to turn off the interior lights." Anna's heart was thumping hard in her excitement.

"How long?" asked Mike.

"A few minutes. It saw our lights and flashed at us, but stopped when we got close. I want to try something with this." Anna held up a small penlight she routinely carried with her on a ring with two keys and a flat, multiply bladed screwdriver.

Phil shook his head, but Mike put a hand on his shoulder. "Five minutes, and no longer. Turn the lights out, Phil, and start counting."

The lights went out, and they were sitting in pitch-blackness. "This is really dumb," said Phil.

They waited one minute, then two. There was a faint scraping sound from outside that came and went, and nothing to be seen. Finally, Anna moved her hand close to the nose bubble and began flashing her little penlight off and on. She continued for half a minute, and then stopped.

There was no response, but Phil suddenly shifted in his seat. "I see some faint flashes way off to the left of us. Maybe we should move."

Anna flashed her light several times, waited a few seconds, then did it again and held her breath.

From outside, green lights flickered dimly at first, like a dance of shy fireflies. The lights began near the edges of the nose bubble and moved inwards, getting brighter.

"Yes!" said Anna, and she flashed her little penlight again.

The response was immediate and bright; multiple points of flashing green illuminating the ends of branches. There was a scraping sound from the outer hull of the submersible, and suddenly a glowing tendril of green struck the center of the nose bubble and recoiled from it.

"Yikes!" gasped Phil, and with one hand hit the outside lights, while the other reached to start the engine pumps.

The thing outside had extended two branches to grasp the submersible just above the bow planes, and a third branch was now waving slowly back and forth in the bright lights. The jets went on with a whoosh and Phil backed up several meters to get out of its reach.

"Stop! Stop!" yelled Anna, but Phil had already done it. He smiled wanly at Mike, who was still staring at the thing. "Pretty fast for a rock," he said, and then turned to Anna. "I suppose you want samples, now. How do we do that? I could probably break something off with an articulator."

"Absolutely not," said Anna. "It could be a plant, a coral community or a single, intelligent entity. I will *not* take a chance on harming it before we have some idea what it is. The response could have been chemically or intelligently directed. If it's a plant there must be dead ones. Look for debris in the depression it's in."

Phil peered out the side of the nose bubble. "There's more than just this one. I see green lights flickering again from our left, maybe a few meters away."

The object of their attention had pulled its branches in tightly against the main trunk and was now motionless, an abstract statue mottled in bronze and dark brown.

They drew closer. Phil activated an articulator, extended a claw and poked gingerly at gravel and ice near the object's base. There was a short piece of something white and showing large pores that he placed in the sample box. Plant or animal, there were two small versions of the big one rooted there, but Anna insisted they not be touched. And even though they came within reach of it, the big one remained motionless the entire time the bright lights were on.

"Let's move," said Mike. "There's more to see left of us, but the lights have stopped flashing."

"Okay," said Anna. "Is it possible to dim our lights?"

"No. I'll come in slow this time, and turn off the lights when we get in close."

Phil backed off with a single jet pulse, and veered left in the direction of the other lights they'd seen. They saw another large chunk of ice come down and impact softly with the sea floor, stirring up a cloud of sand and pebbles.

It was twenty meters before they saw reflections from tall stalks rising from the bottom. Phil came in slowly this time. They saw several branched trunks standing close together, and from the end of one branch came a single flash of green. Two meters from the nearest branch, the submersible's lights went out. The interior lights illuminated the scene dimly, an abstract portrait of bronze figures on black.

"They're moving," whispered Anna.

Branches waved ever so gently in still water, the movement synchronous among several thick trunks. Even in dim light there were occasional flashes of green, which they could now see were coming from little nubbins on the ends of the branches. Mike looked off to the right.

"The one we just left is flashing again."

"They're talking about us," said Anna.

"Maybe, or just warning each other of danger. Whatever. You got what you came for, Anna. It's certainly a surprise to me," said Phil. "You sure you don't want a living sample of these things?"

"I can't do it. There's no precedent for any life form above bacterial level. It's a case for The Council of Nations. If it's allowed, someone else will have to do it, or maybe I'll get a chance to come back someday. We have our pictures and spectra, and all the water samples. That'll have to be enough for now."

Phil used the articulators to scoop up some samples near the bases of the trunks. The occupants of the little depression in gravel and methane clathrate seemed undisturbed by it. Bronze limbs waved gently and decorated themselves in flashes of green. Anna watched, mesmerized, burning the sight into her memory.

"We really have to finish our mapping and look for other vents," Mike finally said.

"Will we have time for another dive?" Anna felt an ache in her chest.

"Not this trip," said Mike. "You'll have to come back again, if you can."

"The base might get swallowed up, and the vents plugged. There might not be another chance."

"I know, but we have to finish the mission plan. Let's go, Phil."

Phil looked over his shoulder at Anna and frowned at the agony written on her face.

"Got to go, Anna. We'll call Kassner right now, and get your discovery on the record."

Anna nodded, and pressed her lips together as they backed away. Green flashes sent them on their way, light from living things anchored in ice at the bottom of a subterranean lake of a tiny, geologically active moon cold beyond belief, in the outer reaches of the solar system. It was a miracle, a thing to be studied for a lifetime, and she was being forced to leave it.

Mike called Kassner, but there was no response, not even static. "I don't like this. The signal was clear until a while ago."

"Could be scattering," said Phil. "There's a lot of rough topology near the bottom."

"So take us up a hundred feet or so."

Phil did it, and Mike tried again. "Herschel Base, can you hear us? Anna has a major discovery to report. Come in!"

Nothing.

"This is bad," said Mike. "With all those big cracks we saw in the vent, a piece of ice could have sheared off and taken out the transponder."

"Or plugged the vent," said Phil.

Anna's heart jumped. "How long can we stay down here?"

"Oh, another eight hours or so," Phil said calmly.

"I'm not abandoning the rest of this mission, people, but we'll have to hurry it up," said Mike. "Follow the profile, Phil, but double-time it. Finding another vent won't help us; we have no way to survive on the surface. We have to come up at Herschel Base. We have four hours left on the profile. Let's do it in two, and go home."

Mike said it with determination, but all three of them could hear the overtone of fear in his voice.

Getting back to base was suddenly not a matter of reporting an important discovery, but of survival.

Anna said little during the rest of the dive, and was on the edge of tears the entire time. For two hours they made sonar maps of the rest of the cavern, took several samples from the ceiling and walls, and saw what they thought was another vent, though it was too narrow for them to explore it. Mike kept on calling Kassner, but there was only dead silence in return. There was certainly no time for further exploration of the bottom. Anna distracted herself by pointing out several more areas on her sonar maps she was now certain harbored life. The little depressions were where the methane clathrate was exposed enough to serve as anchors for the life on Enceladus. But now there would be no time extensions for the mission. After two hours, worry had turned to fear, and they hurried back to the Herschel Base vent under full power.

What they found at the vent matched their worst fears.

A huge boulder of ice had calved from the vent wall, and was plugging it at a steep angle, its tip resting on the shelf that the transponder had been anchored to. As they came up to it, the ceiling above them shuddered and small pieces of ice clattered off the top of the submersible. Phil wiggled the controls, and they backed off to one side of the vent. "Pretty loose inside the vent," he said. "Let's see if my baby can unplug this thing in low gravity."

For nearly an hour Phil used the articulators to push against the icy plug in various directions, but even with the slightest movement there was an avalanche of debris from above that terrorized all of them. Mike was on the radio continuously, but getting nothing.

There was a sudden crash of boulders on the roof of the submersible. "See that?" said Phil. "It wobbled. The tip is wedged where the shelf comes out of the wall. The shelf is holding it up. Maybe if I can break off the tip—"

Phil moved in closer, used the articulators to pull back on the tip of the plug, and wiggled it back and forth. When Anna saw the movement her hope soared. They were making progress, the base only a hundred meters or so above them, and they had air left for hours.

And then, quite suddenly, they had minutes.

The plug wobbled, and there was a horrible impact on the roof of the submersible. The interior lights flickered, and Anna was momentarily deafened by a shriek of tortured metal from the hull walls.

The impact lifted her from her seat and slammed her sideways as she clapped her hands over her ears.

"No, no, NO!" gasped Phil. Mike hadn't strapped in, was on the floor and holding one hand to a bloody gash on his forehead.

"What's that hissing sound?" said Anna.

"We're losing our air and fuel! That last avalanche must have breached the outer hull. Mike, get up and strap in. Hang on, Anna. We've got to do this quick, or we're dead!"

Anna gulped, and grasped the arms of her chair, and the hissing sound was now loud in her ears. She smelled fuel, and her own sweat.

She had never thought about death, especially her own, but now it came to her.

Mike managed to get in his seat and strap in as Phil backed off a few meters from the vent shelf and the shower of debris coming down there.

"Sorry baby," said Phil, not talking to a person, "but we have to do this the hard way."

The submersible lurched forward and rushed towards the shelf at the bottom of the vent, crashing into it hard at a point just below the observation bubble.

"Phil!" screamed Anna, but Phil was backing off again, stopping, and the submersible lurched forward once more. The second crash seemed softer, ice resisting, crumbling, and allowing them a creep forward after contact. The craft jerked backwards in a blink, pitching Anna forward in her chair. Outside was chaos, a shattered shelf of ice falling away, the sharp tip of the plug sheared off at a steep angle with it. A huge fang of ice fell out of the vent, and disappeared from view.

The air in the cabin was musty, and Anna had a sudden headache. The submersible accelerated. Small pieces of ice clattered off the hull as they flew up the vent and through an open lock unprepared for them. They came out of the water in a roil of bubbles, and Anna had one glimpse of two shocked technicians jumping away from the pool.

* * * * * * *

For one moment, while Mike and Phil told their story, Anna was silent and just happy to be alive. But when the men turned it over to her and she described her discovery she was suddenly depressed again, and she came close to crying when Kassner and then Helena embraced and congratulated her.

It was at that moment when Phil climbed off the hull of his battered submersible and grinned at her. He had something wet and glistening in a gloved hand, and he handed it to Anna. "This should lighten your mood. Look what I found stuck between the base of the port articulator and the hull. When that thing grabbed us and I pulled away it must have snapped this off. No wonder the thing was thrashing around so much."

Anna's heart skipped a beat. In Phil's hand was a six-inch section from the end of a branch. The end nubbin was intact, the other end of the section shredded like a torn piece of Yucca stalk. The piece was still wet, but the mottled bronze and brown spots were fading before her eyes.

"Quick, get it in water!"

Mike grabbed a pan from a bench and filled it with water from the tank.

Anna giggled, grabbed Phil's arm and kissed him on the cheek. "Thank you! Oh, I've got to get some ice on this!"

Helena ran for ice. Anna grabbed the pan, and rushed away with her new treasure. Behind her, Phil said something that might have bothered her once, but didn't now in her moment of joy.

"Now *there's* a mood shift for you," said Phil.

* * * * * * *

One day out from Enceladus, Anna emerged from her cubicle and joined Mike and Phil on the control deck for a squeeze of tea.

"Ah, the scientist walks among us," said Mike. "Tea?"

"Thanks," said Anna, and accepted a squeeze bottle from him. "I've been writing up a summary of the examinations I made on Herschel. I can't do anything else until we get to Titan."

"Well, you'll have to tell us all about it," said Phil.

Anna took a suck of tea. "There isn't a lot I can say right now. The dead fragment you dug out of the gravel is almost as interesting as the fresh specimen. The closest thing I can think of on Earth is coral, but the structure is silicate, not carbonate. The bronze areas on the surface show iron sulfide. There could be bacteria producing that since there's both iron and sulfur in the dark gravel, and also in the ice, but on the whole I'm seeing a colony of tiny worm-like critters living in a labyrinth of tubules, and my bet is a methane metabolism with hydrogen output. I've frozen the sample in some water mixed with methane clathrate. We even have the little nubbin where the light is emitted. It seems to be silicate with trace sulfur. I radioed all of this ahead, and everyone at the lab is *so* excited.

Phil looked over his shoulder at her. "When you accept your Nobel Prize, we'll expect an invitation to the ceremony."

Anna smiled. "Well—that isn't going to happen."

"Why not?"

"Even if I got the award I wouldn't be there to accept it."

"I thought you were thinking about cycling back to Earth," said Mike.

"I was. I was thinking about it seriously until a few days ago."

"Ah," said Mike, and winked at Phil.

There was a pause while Anna took another suck of tea, and then said, "Commander Kassner said he and his crew are cycling out in two months. I'm coming back with the replacement crew. That will give me six months for dives to study the Ice Corals."

"That's what you're going to call them?" asked Mike.

"For now. I'll let some official give them a Latin name. I have a lifetime of work to do on this project, and I'm not going back to Earth to do it."

"Well, I guess we'll be seeing you around here, then," said Phil.

"You bet," said Anna, "just as long as the articulators work the first time."

"Ouch," said Phil.

BEWARE THE QUANTUM BUNNY

The Thursday seminars were always packed, and this one was no exception. Cavendish University faculty occupied the front rows, and the gallery was filled with students eager to hear how their teachers were pushing back the frontiers of science for their beloved Queen Victoria. Sir Ian Wintham had presented an update on his studies in atmospheric electricity. Professor Gilbert had shown examples of minerals he'd found which continued glowing in a variety of colors after exposure to natural sunlight. With twenty minutes of time remaining, the newest faculty member was introduced and asked to outline new research he might pursue in the physical sciences.

John Tallman had distinguished himself at Oxford for his studies of currents emitted by metals exposed to the light of arc lamps. He was a handsome young man, somewhat shy in demeanor, but when he went to the podium his voice was steady as he described what he might do. He placed a small box on the podium. It was rectangular, black, with an ellipsoidal nubbin on its top.

"I have invented a device that produces an electrical signal and light pulse at random," said John. "It consists of two rotating, toothed wheels, a metal plate and a piece of ore which emits ionizing radiations. I wish to use this device to investigate a concern I've developed in working with light-induced currents from metals. I think these currents are due to emissions of the recently discovered particle called the electron."

A few nodding heads in the audience encouraged John to continue.

"If a metal is built from countless atoms as we believe, then the electrons have a variety of states, or initial conditions, within the metal. By shortening light pulses to obtain brief current bursts I hope to obtain an approximation of those initial conditions over small intervals of time. My concern is that the experiment itself, with light impinging the metal surface, disturbs these conditions, leading me to false results. For things as small as electrons, the observation itself contributes to the experimental results. What we see is a kind of average, and is determined by the method of observation. If the electronic states are discrete rather than continuous, however, my work might show it in the form of sudden changes in current as the time duration of light pulses is shortened. Discrete states should be observable, regardless of their interaction with an observer, though the observer still determines the results of the experiment."

John placed a hand on the black box resting on the podium. "There is a macroscopic analog to this which I will now demonstrate. In this box I have placed a live rat just minutes ago. The bump you see on top of the box is my light pulse generator. In the past few minutes it has randomly fired once, activating a shield to assure only one light pulse is used in the experiment. One of two things has happened: the light gets past the two sets of rotating toothed wheels, or it doesn't. If it doesn't, nothing happens and if I open the box I will observe the rat is alive. If it does, a burst of cyanide gas has been activated which kills the rat instantly. These two states, if you will, alive and dead, are causally independent of my observation, but I must open the box to see which one exists."

John paused dramatically. "Any bets?" he said, and then lifted the cover from the box. His audience shifted uneasily in their seats when the box cover came off. John looked inside, and then tipped the box to show the twisted creature inside.

"Alas, this one was not so lucky. The pulse being random its survival rate was fifty percent. I have repeated this experiment one hundred times in the past several weeks; have found forty-seven rats alive and fifty-three dead. This is well within the uncertainties of random statistics. It convinces me that my photocurrent studies should indicate discrete electron states if they exist.

"This might well apply to larger systems as well, such as this rat in a box. We see two states, alive, or dead, half of one or the other. One might assign a number M to this system, M being the manifestation number. If we let M equal one half, then $2M+1$ is the number of possible states, which is two. This is only a statistical idea, of course. I attach no physical significance to it for large systems, but it might be useful in describing electron states in metals."

John closed the box. "Thank you for your attention."

There was some applause from the student gallery, but only amused looks and raised eyebrows among the faculty.

"Very entertaining, but certainly nothing one would dare report to The Royal Society," said Sir Wintham, and there was chuckling in the audience.

"It was only an educational demonstration, professor," said John.

"I sincerely hope so, but we do look forward to hearing the results of your photocurrent studies, and wish you welcome to our faculty. But please, no more experiments with rats."

John laughed with all of them, but left the podium with a disquieting feeling in the pit of his stomach. He walked to the back of the seminar room, opened the door and felt a hand grasp his elbow. A man with dark hair and beard and piercing eyes followed him out of the room.

The man shook John's hand. "I am Samuel Hunyadi, of the Magyar Institute of Physical Science. I have interest in your random light pulse machine. Can we talk for a moment?"

"Certainly. What do you want to know?"

"I wish to build one for myself. My institute can pay whatever you feel is proper."

"I have no interest in patents or compensation. I can give you detailed plans if you acknowledge my machine in your publications," said John.

"That is most generous, professor," said Samuel.

"Well, I do hope to be a professor someday, but I don't think I made a good impression on my colleagues in there today."

"They will soon forget the rat in the box. I find your idea interesting for an experiment of mine. I'll share credit with you for any discovery I make, of course."

"What are you working on?"

Samuel smiled. "For now it must be a secret. There are private interests involved. But your machine will be vital in doing the experiment properly. The results will be shared with you. I only need construction plans for your machine. All expenses will be mine."

"I'll give you a copy right now," said John. They went to his office and went over some details of the machine. Samuel shook his hand warmly and left with his prize. A moment later there was a knocking on the office door.

Sir Wintham was standing there. "I just saw Samuel Hunyadi leave your office. The man is an amateur, always trying to arrange joint research with our new faculty members."

John was immediately wary. "He said he was from the Magyar Institute of Physical Sciences. He was interested in my presentation."

"He's a financier, not a scientist," said Sir Wintham. "He's also a Romanian and a political activist. He's part of that bunch of Transylvanian protestors who sent the anti-Magyarization memorandum to Emperor Franz Joseph. Take my advice, and avoid him."

Sir Wintham walked away from him without waiting for an answer.

"Oh dear," thought John, "I've not done things at all well for my career today."

* * * * * *

Two years went by. John's research progressed well, and his colleagues were pleased with him. Senior professors were already favorable about his eventual promotion and tenure. But early on a Saturday morning a postal wagon pulled up in front of his residence and delivered fifty hat-box-sized parcels to him. An accompanying letter was from Samuel Hunyadi, posted in the city of Covasna, west of the Carpathian Mountains.

"Dear Professor Tallman," it said. "Again my thanks for allowing me to reproduce your light pulse machine. My experiment has been successfully completed, and rather than report results I have shipped you a duplicate experiment which you may complete yourself and publish under your own name if you wish. All you need do is open the boxes I've sent you, and record the results. There is some risk. You might want to have a barrier between you and the boxes when you open them. Do this privately. Your colleagues will find the results beyond their imagination. Your friend in Science, Samuel Hunyadi."

John took the delivered boxes quickly into the house and put them in his library. It was a cold day, and a warm fire was already crackling in the fireplace. He checked the boxes one by one; the light pulse generator on each had been fired. Samuel had likely run another version of John's experiment with the rats. The contents of the boxes would be some animal alive or dead. What could be the danger in opening the boxes? He threw caution to the wind and pulled off the cover of the first box.

A small rabbit with white coat and black ears lay curled on its side in the box, quite dead.

"Poor bunny," said John. "Why couldn't Samuel have used insects or something else quite different? There will be nothing new here."

Indeed when he opened the second box another bunny with white fur gazed up at him and wiggled its black ears. John put the animal near the fireplace to keep it warm. He retrieved a piece of paper on which he kept score: dead, alive, alive, dead, dead, dead, and so on. By the time he opened the forty-sixth box he had recorded twenty-two bunnies alive, and twenty-four dead.

"Random selection, two states. It's a doublet like the rats, and a manifestation M equal to one-half. There's no surprise here, just another animal. I'm disappointed in you, Samuel," said John out loud.

And then he opened the forty-seventh box.

Time seemed to move slowly. There was a stirring in the bottom of the box, and then something horrible leaped from it and straight towards John's face. Its eyes glowed ruby red and two terrible fangs protruded from it open mouth. It hissed, and then shrieked a terrible scream. John grabbed at it and found his hand clutching two black ears. The thing raked the sleeve of John's jacket with sharp claws and screamed again. Without thinking John twirled and threw the horror into the fireplace. It shrieked in the flames, and suddenly exploded in a cloud of putrid black ash that brought him close to gagging.

He sat there for several minutes, waiting for his heart to stop hammering. And then he used the back of a chair as a protective barrier when he opened the last three boxes. All told, the experiment yielded twenty-four live bunnies, twenty-five dead, and one beyond description.

John wrote to Samuel Hunyadi and told him what he'd discovered. But the man seemed to have disappeared, and John never heard from him again. The experiment itself was totally unpublishable and something John kept a secret during a long and successful academic career. But in later years his readings of Transylvanian history and folklore gave him clues as to what he had found.

John Tallman then had a quiet satisfaction in knowing he had shown and quantified in a scientific way a thing that had been declared in Transylvanian mythology for many years.

For unlike all other species of rabbits, the low energy state of the Transylvanian bunny is not a doublet, but a triplet, with a manifestation $M=1$.

(With apologies to Schrödinger's cat, and Monty Python)

ACKNOWLEDGMENTS

The stories in this anthology were originally sold to the following publications:

"Helen's Last Will" was first published in *Analog*, Mar. 2007.

"Bacon 'n' Eggs" was first published in *Moscon XV*, Sept. 1993.

"Mildred's Garden" was first published in *Talebones* #35, Summer 2007.

"The Color of Pain" was first published in *Analog*, Mar. 2004.

"Reinventing Carl Hobbs" was first published in *Analog*, Apr. 2005.

"Deliverance Smith" is published here for the first time.

"Tikan's Choice" is published here for the first time.

"Mutiny on the *Phoebus*" was first published in *Fantastic Worlds*, 1995.

"A Special Child" was first published in *Promises-Pro-Mss* #20, 1990.

"Georgi" was first published in *Writers of the Future VII*, Bridge Publications, 1990; used by permission of Galaxy Press.

"Axalay's Gifts" was first published in *Zero Gravity Freefall*, 1995.

"Bodyguard" was first published in *A Matter of Crime*, 1988.

"Dark Peril" was first published in *Analog*, Mar. 2005.

"Beneath the Ice of Enceladus" is published here for the first time.

"Beware the Quantum Bunny" is published here for the first time.

ABOUT THE AUTHOR

JAMES C. GLASS is a retired physics and astronomy professor and dean who now spends his time writing, painting, and traveling. He made his first story sale in 1988 and was the Grand Prize Winner of Writers of the Future in 1990. Since then he has sold six novels and a short story collection, and over forty short stories to magazines such as *Aboriginal S.F.*, *Analog*, and *Talebones*. Jim writes science fiction, fantasy, and dark fantasy. He now divides his time between Spokane, Washington and Desert Hot Springs, California with wife Gail, who is a costumer and healing dancer. There are five grown children and eleven grandchildren scattered around the country. Jim also paints mountain, desert, and red rock scenics in oils and pastels, and is often heard playing didgeridoo and Native American flute. For more details, please see his web site at:

www.sff.net/people/jglass/

www.ingramcontent.com/pod-product-compliance
Lightning Source LLC
Chambersburg PA
CBHW020805250626
47155CB00003B/1214